ODD MOM OUT

SANDY DAY

NANCY WICKSTROM
Relax, Read, Enjoy
Share or Return

ISBN ebook 978-1-9990735-7-2
ISBN paper book 978-1-9990735-8-9

Book Cover by Book Brush
Author Photo by Tony Hicks

·♥ · ♥ · ♥·♥·♥·

A delightful read! Very Bridget Jones-y.

Helen Pilz

A fun-filled, fast-paced romp with a very likeable heroine who, although full of self-doubts, is determined to overcome any and all obstacles.

Linda Simser

Funny and inspiring...A story which will leave you feeling good and hopeful for the future.

Lorraine Johnston

For Jada

ONE

Mother's television blares on like a fog horn. Across the hall, she's readying herself for a night of full-volume TV.

I turn up my radio to drown her out, and to try to catch the latest weather report. Here it comes now: "A rare spring storm moving across Southern Ontario is expected to bring another 10 centimeters of snow overnight. Ice and squalls are expected, creating hazardous road conditions. Exercise caution, and consider staying home this evening."

Not a chance.

I've already showered, slathered on deodorant, and blow-dried my hair. I just have to get dressed and make my way to the new Smokehouse for 6 o'clock.

I've been looking forward to this dinner with Jane all week, and not just for the food at the trendy new restaurant – which I *know* will be amazing – but because I need my best friend's support. I didn't want to move in here with Mother after Xavier left me, but Jane helped me realize, it was my only choice.

"It will be difficult, but not impossible," she'd said. "A means to an end."

After weighing my other options – none of which I could afford at the time – I decided I would try my best to survive living in this house with Mother, just until Xavier comes to his senses and we move back in together. But it's been three months now, and last week I found myself signing divorce papers. Being under Mother's constant scrutiny and criticism is starting to feel hopelessly permanent.

It's already past five o'clock and I've got to hurry. I don't want Jane to think I'm standing her up, again.

Mother's television goes silent and she calls, "Can you come in here and fix my TV?"

Grumbling under my breath, "Yes, your majesty," I trundle across the hall in my bra and undies.

"Oh, Trudy, cover up!" she scolds, peering at me from her oversized glasses. Her nose wrinkles, and she looks away, as though I wasn't birthed from her very body some fifty odd years ago.

She's on her bed, looking like a lazy fortune teller in one of the cheesy velour tracksuits she wears every day. A dark green turban with a giant pearl brooch from the Shopping Channel sits atop her head.

Once upon a time, I escaped Mother's non-stop running commentary on everything that's wrong with me and my life. For two decades as a married woman, I lived happily Mother-free but now, I'm back in her house due to some divorce-related financial mix-up, and she's taken up exactly where she left off, commenting on everything that pops into her tactless head. Just as she was doing when I landed a job, and moved out at age eighteen.

Trying to sound patient – if she senses I'm in a rush she'll get really ingenious with her delay tactics – I ask, "What's the matter with your TV?"

"It's the words again." She flaps her hands at the screen. "They're all over my show."

I'm clueless about techy stuff, but even I know how to use a remote. At least once a week we go through this song and dance: she switches on subtitles while watching some Scandinavian noir, and then doesn't remember how to turn them off again. She even applies subtitles to British shows – she's a monarchy fan. "Their accents are deplorable," she complains. "I can't understand a word they say."

I point the remote at the giant screen at the foot of her bed and adjust the settings.

At times like this, usually when it's most inconvenient for me, she acts like a big helpless baby. But I know she has successfully navigated alone for years, since my father died. And I don't let her fool me; at any moment she'll come roaring back as the meanest mean girl from the meanest mean girl show ever.

"Are you settled?" I ask.

She directs me away with an impatient hand. "You're blocking the screen."

Back in my room I dig around in my dresser drawers for something to wear. It doesn't need to be fancy, I'm just meeting Jane, but to get to the restaurant I need to trudge through knee-deep snow.

Tonight is the first time I've been out since the night Xavier dumped me, four months ago. I'd thought we were spending a romantic New Year's Eve at home in our condo, watching the hockey game in sweatpants, eating Chinese food, but he had other ideas.

"It's been a long time coming, Trudy," he told me, rubbing his nose with the palm of his hand, which he always did when he was making up excuses. "We have nothing in common anymore."

"I beg to differ!" I objected, and began enumerating. "We have our daughter, our life—"

"But you've changed," he continued, intently occupied with piling his suit-cases by the condo door. "We've drifted apart." He looked at me, his hand on the doorknob. "You used to be fun."

"I'm fun!" I yelled, leaping from the couch, trying to block him from opening the door.

Anyway…

I'm still unanchored, unmoored, and need desperately to discuss how I feel with Jane, my bestie since we were in hula hoops. She always knows what's good for me. But each time we've planned, since I finally stopped blubbering whenever I talked about Xavier, something has screwed up. Last time I inadvertently forgot, and left Jane twiddling her thumbs in The Pickle Barrel. She was mad. The time before that she came down with food poisoning from a bad tuna sandwich, and canceled. And way back in February, the weather put a stop to it; sheer ice, sleet, and a power outage. The storm tonight is a cakewalk in comparison. I am not missing this dinner with Jane.

I tug on warm socks, a pair of water-resistant cargo pants, and a clean sweat-shirt.

You wouldn't know it, but on the calendar, spring has sprung. And I too am determined to make a new start. I'll eat a yummy dinner at Lakeside's newest restaurant, and talk everything over with Jane. We'll come up with a plan on how I can win back my husband and move out of Mother's house as soon as possible. Living here is driving me bonkers.

The Smokehouse is nearby, just down to Maple Street, and then over a few blocks to the west. It'll be a bit of an adventure in this weather because my knees are bothering me, but I'm Canadian. What's a little snow in April?

I hurry from my room.

Half-way down the stairs, Mother calls again, "If you're going out – and leaving me all alone – can you at least fix me a plate?"

Argh! She's making me late.

"Yes, your Highness."

I rush down to the kitchen, rummage around in the freezer for one of the dinners she likes, slam it into the microwave, and punch at the buttons.

An accumulation of the day's dishes clutters the counter and just as I'm about to start tidying up, my eye is caught by a movement in the backyard. Snow is falling like flour through a sifter but on the wooden fence at the side of the garden, a tiny kitten is fighting its way through the blowing snow.

I step to the sliding glass door and peer outside.

The kitten skitters unsteadily, pausing, then stepping again along the fence toward the back of the garden, creeping like a mountain climber on Everest along the thin rail of the fence. A strong gust of wind blasts through the yard, scooting the kitten like a leaf off the top of the fence. It falls five feet into a drift of snow.

I stare hard, trying to determine the fate of the tiny thing that has disappeared into a drift beside the fence.

Nothing. It's gone.

Just more wind, more snow, and the hum of the microwave oven behind me.

Wrenching aside the sliding door to the deck I step out into the frigid cold in my socked feet. Immediately snow is up my pant legs, chilling the skin above my socks. At the edge of the deck, on the stairs, the snow reaches to my knees, but I wade through it across the patio toward the hole in the snow where I saw the kitten disappear.

Near the edge of the garden, I trip over a snow-buried flower pot and land hands first into a snow drift, eye to eye with a wet white kitten.

Startled and staring at me, it tries scrambling backwards through a wall of snow.

I scoop it up in my bare hands. "Don't worry, little fella. I've come to rescue you."

It's as light as a marshmallow but squirming in fear.

"Come on now, settle down, we'll go inside."

I struggle to my knees, then to my feet, which are now numb with cold, and make my way back to the deck, up the stairs in the foot-holes I made a minute ago, and into the warm kitchen.

The microwave is still humming; Mother's dinner sizzling inside.

The kitten wriggles in my hands. Tiny, skinny, ruffled, but feisty!

"Slow down, tiger," I tell it, wondering what I'm going to do with it. I open the door to the laundry room on the other side of the kitchen.

"This will do," I tell the kitten, holding it to my chest as I rummage for something to put it in. A cardboard box with a towel. I set the kitten inside the box on the floor. It mews pitifully.

"Oh, don't cry, little guy!" I stroke its head with a finger. "How about a saucer of milk?"

The bell on the microwave dings. "Wait here," I tell the kitten, "I'll be right back."

Quickly assembling Mother's dinner, I fill a tumbler with ice, crack open a can of cola, place it on a tray with the food. Before beginning the climb back upstairs to Mother's room I lean against the counter and peel off my wet socks, tossing them on the rug by the sliding doors.

I'm so late! Jane will be so pissed if I don't show up on time.

My knees complain as I struggle up the stairs. I was accustomed to condo living with an elevator in the building and all the rooms on the same floor. These stairs are horrendous, especially when I'm carrying something and can't use the banister to hang on to. With each step there's a twinging ping and grind. I should see the doctor but I keep putting it off, kidding myself that if I ignore it the trouble will go away.

"Don't tell me that's what you're wearing?" says Mother, the fashion icon, as I slide aside the dish of dried lavender on her bedside table to make room for the tray.

"Why? What's wrong with it?"

She smirks at me like I'm an idiot. "You're going out in public."

"I know! And there's a snowstorm."

"I still don't see why I can't come along." She picks up her fork and stirs the contents of her dinner around in the plastic dish. "I haven't been out for dinner in ages."

"Mother, it's a special dinner. Just me and Jane."

"But Jane likes me, we're great friends!"

I hate that she's right about this; Jane thinks my mother is a hoot.

"I know you are friends," I patronize her. "But tonight, it's just me and her. We'll have some dinner and then I'm coming home."

Mother purses her lips and looks at me. "If it's a special dinner, dear, why are you wearing those clown pants?"

My face heats up like I've got a sunburn.

The ancient clock radio on her bedside table ticks over another minute.

I stand in the doorway glaring at this querulous old woman, digesting yet another of her unwanted nuggets.

Gritting my teeth, I say, "I'll be home in a couple of hours. My cell phone will be on if you need me."

She dismisses me with a wave of her fork.

I don't know why I worry about her. She's lived alone for a decade. But it freaks me out how sloppy and inebriated she gets every night. Who knows how many bathtubs she could overflow? Or how much microwave popcorn she could scorch before burning down the whole house?

I rush into my room, grab a fresh pair of socks, perch on the side of my bed, and struggle to pull them on over my puffy damp feet.

Finally, when the socks are on straight, I rush down to the kitchen to pour a saucer of milk.

The kitten is not in the box where I left it.

Why did I think a cardboard box would hold a creature that can scale a 5-foot fence?

He's sitting on the rug in front of the dryer licking the fur on an outstretched leg. He stops when he notices me setting the saucer of milk down but makes a run for the open door.

"Oh no you don't," I say, blocking his escape with my foot, scooping him up and shutting us inside the laundry room. "Believe me, you don't want to meet my mother." I tickle his little head. "She's allergic to anything as soft, fuzzy, or adorable as you."

I set the kitten down in front of the saucer of milk. His tiny pink tongue begins lapping furiously, his eyes squinting in pleasure.

I always wanted a cat when I was little, but no matter how many times I begged and wheedled, Mother said no. "Who's going to pay for all the upholstery it will claw up?" she'd ask, filing her fingernails.

The poor little thing is so hungry. He must be lost. I sure hope he wasn't abandoned and left to face the rest of his life on his own.

Someone must be missing him like crazy.

I'll figure out what to do with him tomorrow but for tonight he's safe and warm, and right now I've got to go meet Jane.

I pull on snow boots with a deep tread on the soles and zip myself into my parka, hopefully for the last time this year. It's a ten-minute walk to the restaurant. If I don't slip and break my neck, I may just make it in time.

The snow is blowing around and any shoveling my neighbours did earlier has blown into drifts. I plow my way through like the Abominable Snowman.

Halfway down the street I realize I probably should have told Mother about the kitten.

Is it too late to go back?

I stop and watch the snow falling through the light of a streetlamp.

Yes, it's too late.

She won't even notice.

I pray nothing bad will come of tonight and forge on. The lights of Maple Street at the bottom of my road glow through the gusts of snow; streetcars, lit up inside, pass along in muffled silence. I hurry.

Two

The Smokehouse gleams like a beacon in the distance as I slog over the messy sidewalks in front of closed businesses. Twinkle lights and square velvet cushions welcome me from The Smokehouse's snow-blasted front window.

It's hard to conjure up a picture of Foxes & Jocks, the shabby sports bar that used to operate in this spot. Years ago, on birthdays and anniversaries, Xavier and I would bring Madison. She'd eat chicken fingers and drink ginger ale while we enjoyed suicide wings, jalapeño poppers, and draft beer. Those days seem far, far away now.

Stamping snow from my boots and banishing nostalgia from my mind, I pull open The Smokehouse door and am met with a blast of hickory smoke, boisterous voices, the clink of glassware and the clatter of cutlery against dishes.

Tipping back the hood of my parka, I scatter snow across a sopping grey carpet-mat and am startled by a chorus of greeting from the line-cooks in the open kitchen directly across. Feeling slightly flustered to be hailed so heartily, I send a grateful wiggle of my fingers back at them, then stuff my black parka in amongst all the other black coats on the packed coat rack.

The vibe of The Smokehouse is certainly different than the old Foxes & Jocks where customers had to find their own tables, usually still covered in the last party's dishes, and wait until they could flag down a harassed waitress. Thinking back, it was sort of awful, but Xavier loved the place and being surrounded by TV screens, all tuned to a different game.

A hostess in high-top runners, a black t-shirt with rolled sleeves, *The Smokehouse* emblazoned across her chest, approaches. "Here alone?"

"No," I answer, defensive at her instant assumption that I am a loser-loner. "I'm meeting my friend: Jane Summerfield."

She consults the tablet in her hands, a senseless scribble of words, numbers, and a diagram on the screen.

"Oh ya," she says. "Follow me."

She leads the way through the half-full room where I notice there are very few tables for two. Most of the diners are in loud, raucous groups of four or six. I'm not sure this was the best choice of restaurant for the dinner of conversation and encouragement I've been looking forward to all week with my best friend.

She fashions herself after Jane of the Jungle but with her big teeth and short croppy haircut she's really more of a Miss Jane Hathaway from the Beverly Hillbillies. Sensible, practical, and always a laugh, Jane can sometimes be a pain, but in a good way, I think, because I wouldn't want a best friend who just agreed with me about everything, would I?

The hostess is leading me to the far depths of the dimly lit restaurant.

Jane also happens to be a shrink, and although she doesn't always listen closely to me, most of the time she's the perfect person to talk to – full of advice and suggestions. But I don't see her or her animal print anywhere. I must've got here first.

Jane told me long ago to stop trying to control everything. "Life is just one disappointment after the next," she'd counseled when the DJ for my wedding failed to show. "The best thing is to grab the next vine and swing to the next tree." Then she'd seized the microphone and demanded to know who among my guests had a boombox. Everyone had scurried out to their cars and gathered up CDs and cassettes.

Finally the hostess steps aside, and I'm met with a wall of voices shouting: "Surprise!"

I freeze. Alarmed.

What's happening?

Jane rushes at me holding out a plastic tiara.

It takes me a moment to decipher the glittering letters across the band.

It reads: "JUST DIVORCED!"

The din in the restaurant hushes as everyone stares at me, waiting for my response.

Beyond Jane, cackling and clapping, is a table full of my colleagues from Lakeside.

I don't know what I'm supposed to do. Or say. I'm so confused.

Jane turns the tiara around and jams it down onto my scalp before her bony arms embrace me in a breathtaking hug. Diners around us resume their chatter and the spotlight swings away from me – a newly crowned divorced woman.

"Come on!" Jane says, breathlessly. "Aren't you *surprised*?"

I can't speak. My brain is scrambling to understand. *Why are they all here?*

I follow Jane, who's wearing skinny tiger-print pants and a black velvet pullover, while I'm wearing... Oh my gawd. I'm dressed for hot-chocolate and marshmallows in a ski lodge. I was not prepared for a dress-up event in a trendy restaurant.

She tricked me and thought it was a good idea to surprise me this way. Darn her!

Even if we have been friends since kindergarten, it feels as if she doesn't have a clue who I am or what I've been going through. It's been five years since Lydia left her; I guess she's forgotten how it feels.

I squeeze down into a chair in the middle of a row of pushed-together tables. All around me, my fellow shopkeepers from Lakeside are squealing and laughing. Suzy from the quilting store next door to my bakery; Jessica, the young woman who runs a fashion store down the street; Debbie, Lakeside's resident manicurist; Sylvia, interior decorator; and so on – I can't take them all in. I'm flabbergasted, and bewildered.

These women came out during a snowstorm to celebrate my *divorce*?

Since when do we throw divorce parties?

Especially for me, a person devastated by her marriage's shipwreck.

Yet here they all are decked out and jubilant, congratulating me on what has been the most painful, humiliating, and fattening event of my life.

I didn't know they all knew about Xavier dumping me.

The cork blows off a bottle of champagne and a waiter pours pink bubbles into a flute in front of my place setting.

"Congratulations!"

I blink back humiliated tears, clinking glasses and tossing the whole thing back in one gulp. Bubbles sting as they rush up my nose. I'm not accustomed to drinking champagne. Or being the center of attention.

"Speech, speech!" Debbie calls, dinging the side of her glass. The clatter rises to a terrifying level in seconds.

Jane nudges me but it's too cramped to get to my feet, so I just continue to sit as they all quiet down to listen. Blushing and tongue-tied, I blubber some thanks to all of them for coming, even though I'm too confused and unhappy to think straight. I'm terrible at speech stuff but my brief words seem to satisfy their need for me to acknowledge what a perfect blindsiding they've pulled off and their yakking resumes.

Debbie gushes, "My divorce was the *best* thing that ever happened to me!"

"Like being let out of prison!" agrees someone else.

"Men stink!"

Suzy counters with, "I'm married to a *wonderful* man!" and Debbie frowns at her pityingly.

Jessica nods, defending Suzy. "They're not *all* bad."

"Marriages or men?" Jane retorts, and then they're all laughing and talking at once again.

I'm glad the attention has swiveled away from me, leaving me alone in my usual role of listener and observer. It's safer this way. Meanwhile, inside, my brain is churning, struggling to keep up with the blab-fest.

As they screech with laughter and chat over each other I pull myself together. Come on, Trudy, don't be a spoil sport. This ludicrous 'party' will be over soon.

Plainly there won't be a chance to talk with Jane tonight – but I'm a little ticked at her now anyway. At times like this I wonder why we're even friends. She's like the box of cookies I don't want to eat but then I start with one nibble and soon, somehow, I've devoured the whole darn thing. Over and over.

Where is our waiter? I fish my reading glasses from my purse and set them on the table in anticipation of the menu.

Am I the only one thinking about food?

The cookies I gobbled down before leaving work today didn't curb my appetite at all.

And plowing through all that snow on the way here has made me extra hungry.

Still, I hesitate to dig further into the basket of baguette parked on the table in front of me, even though it is helping to distract me from painful thoughts.

No one else seems to be eating it. And they don't know what they're missing. It's crunchy on the outside, fresh and chewy on the inside.

I've had two pieces already.

I wonder where The Smokehouse gets it. Or do they bake it here?

It's delicious.

Soon enough, amid the chattering, my companions start waving their phones around. I'm amazed at how acceptable it's become to have your phone out at a dinner party. But I've come to accept that cell phones are ubiquitous these days. Another fashion accessory beyond the bracelets and rings attached to the end of every woman's arm. Except mine. My phone is sensibly tucked away in my purse.

Finally, from the end of the table, a waiter interrupts, asking, "Have we decided, ladies?" He still hasn't handed out the menus.

Some of the women hover their phones over a white sticker in the center of each table.

Jane nudges me. "Get out your phone – it's a QR code."

Baffled, I dutifully extract my phone from my purse. To save the battery I don't usually turn it on, but tonight I did because Mother might need me.

Weirdly I never worried about her needing me when I lived with Xavier.

"Now, switch on your camera."

Hurriedly I put on my reading glasses.

I hunt for the camera icon on the screen.

"Turn it on," Jane urges, as I flail.

I've never taken a picture with my phone and as I tap on the icon I stare at the blurry screen as it tries to focus itself on the knife and spoon at the edge of my table setting.

"Now, aim it here," instructs Jane, tapping at a black squiggly square on the table. "This is the QR code."

I do as I'm told and suddenly my camera lens captures the QR code, and The Smokehouse menu magically appears on my screen.

I stare in amazement. And not just because since when did they put menus onto phones, how did I miss *that* development? But also, because the menu is chock-a-block full of scrumptious sounding food that I would never *dare* order. Who would have the nerve to order Lobster Mac & Cheese, or a Hot Meatloaf with Smashed Potatoes Burger in *public*?

My stomach wants to order something piggy but instead I force myself to hunt on the small screen for the salad section.

Each woman murmurs her order to the waiter as he goes around, and then side conversations prevail while we wait for the food.

Next to me, Sylvia Martin, the interior designer with a helmet of ash blonde hair, is as usual, dominating the conversation at our end of the table, describing to everyone within earshot her daughter's recent breakup from her boyfriend. The couple only just moved in together before Christmas last year – I know because I was at their house-warming party – but the girl is already moving home to her mother's. It shocks me how fast things become obsolete these days.

"I'm considering turning the basement into an apartment for her. You know me – always redoing the house," Sylvia brandishes her swizzle stick. "And I have two more daughters younger than her, so...who knows?" She pauses to take a sip of her drink.

In the interim, someone else tries to take the floor. "Did you hear about Biz Buzz?"

Suzy asks, "What's Biz Buzz?" But Sylvia Martin is a mighty foe and she effortlessly hijacks the conversation again.

My attention drifts from her enumeration of each of her daughters' love life, school performance, and job prospects, and I think with a pang about my daughter, Madison.

I miss her, my baby. She's been away at college these past three years. Because we couldn't afford to put her in a dorm, she's been staying with Xavier's parents during the school year. This year, her summer job took her right off the continent; she left about four weeks ago.

I'm worried that time is flying by too fast and I'll never connect with her the way I did when she was younger. Unfortunately, her teenage years were fraught with conflict, and since Xavier left, I haven't been able to talk to her about anything. I've been an emotional wreck and she's always so busy with school and friends and now her job.

I only had one baby. Xavier didn't want any more after she came along.

I sip at a tall, fruity turquoise cocktail that has somehow replaced my glass of champagne.

I've not been as involved in Madison's life as Sylvia seems to be in her daughters' affairs. Maybe because I was working so much in the bakery but also because Madison shut me out, complaining that I was always prying into her life. Well, yes, isn't that a mother's job?

Whenever I suggested anything, she'd roll her eyes and dismiss me – even if she turned around and did exactly what I suggested. Straight out of high-school, she'd enrolled in culinary school and when I expressed delight that we shared the same interest in baking, she'd scoffed and said, "I'm not *baking*, Mom. It's *real* food!" which hurt my feelings. I bake real food, don't I?

After a long wait, our dinners arrive but before digging in many of the women pick up their phones, one more time, and take pictures of what they're about to eat.

"*Bon Appetit*!" Debbie shouts above the din.

My leafy green salad is piled high on a square white plate, smothered in creamy dressing, and dotted with red grapes, toasted slivered almonds, and frizzled onions. It would never be considered diet food but it's a salad, and I'm secretly grateful it's so big because I'm starving.

Beside me, Sylvia has moved on to gossiping about an incident she had with a demanding decorating client, and I notice she's pushing the food around on her plate with a fork but isn't eating it. That's willpower.

Jane, never concerned about her figure or what anyone thinks, ordered a basket of sweet potato fries along with her radish and strawberry salad, and she keeps nudging me to share it. As my hunger diminishes, my annoyance at her simmers down, and I dip into the crispy deep-fried sweetness in the basket between us, over and over. I only wish she'd ordered mayo to dip them in. Jane prefers ketchup.

"How's everyone's food?" she asks to the table at large. "Good?"

It's unanimous. Not a single complaint.

I scrape up the last of the dressing from my plate, my tummy full and happy, and wonder if the dessert menu will also be on the QR code. Do I dare take a peek now?

Tonight of all nights, I deserve a dessert, but I'm not going to be the first one to mention it. Surely others will want to try The Smokehouse's offerings. I know Jane will. She has a sweet tooth, that one – she can always squeeze in dessert.

Our plates are cleared away and in their wake the waiter places a tiny laminated card before each of us. Printed in swirly silver writing are a list of delectable sounding sweets.

Jessica is the first to announce the requisite: "I couldn't eat another bite."

"Do you want to split something?" chirps someone else.

I eye the menu, waiting to hear what others will declare before I say anything. Some are negotiating sharesies but to my surprise many are throwing their usual dieting-caution to the wind and ordering something decadent. A few add the virtuous, "Two forks, please! We're sharing!"

Jane does not offer to split anything with me and studies the menu intently, the monkey tattoo at the base of her thumb bobs and weaves as she gnaws at her thumbnail.

Whatever was in the turquoise cocktail may be responsible for loosening my reserve, or maybe it's hearing the others order, but when the waiter leans over my shoulder I point to the Banana Cream Pudding with toasted almonds, whipped cream, and cookies.

"You only get divorced once!" I quip. And then feel ridiculous when no one other than the waiter seems to hear, and he doesn't laugh.

THREE

At this point in the evening, my friends appear to be growing tired of entertaining each other with never-ending stories about their undeniably ordinary lives. One by one, they pick up their phones and begin to scroll. Photos of dogs and cats are flashed around the table.

I wish I'd thought to take a picture of the kitten I rescued earlier. It was so sweet how the poor little thing dove into the saucer of milk. I wonder if there's a store open where I can buy a can of cat food on the way home?

Photos of grown children with new babies begin to make the rounds to a chorus of oohs and coos. Becoming a grandmother isn't the sign of impending doom it once was. I remember when the expected response was, "You can't possibly be a grandmother! You're too young!"

Moving along to vacations and travel photos, some women open a social media site that has dozens of photographs – their own, and other people's. I don't have social media thingies on my phone. I don't even know how to get them. I just use my phone to...well...phone. And even then, only in an emergency, of which there has been none since I got it in January.

Debbie flashes a photo of Madison at me from across the table. "Tell us, Trudy! *What* is going on with Madison this summer?"

In the picture, my daughter stands barefoot aboard a yacht in a tiny bikini, her broad smile gleaming, and her hair streaming in the wind. I'm puzzled that Debbie has a photo of *my* Madison on her phone, but I answer the question. "She took a summer job as a cook on a boat in Croatia."

"Wow, that's adventurous. Wasn't she going to school for something?"

"Culinary," I answer, and inside, a wave of pride swells.

"Following in Mom's footsteps?"

"Mm hm," I nod, even though I know Madison wouldn't describe it that way.

It's nice to have something to brag about at the divorce party. My life isn't a complete flop. No one else's daughter is doing anything quite as exciting. And although I had little involvement in Madison's summer job decision and didn't actually even know about it until she asked me to pay for her plane ticket, I don't let on. I welcome the brief minute of admiration and follow-up questions until someone asks: "When are you going to visit her?"

I wave my hands around non-committedly. "The bakery's pretty busy right now."

"But this is your chance to go to Europe. Aren't you going to grab it?"

"Definitely," I answer, nodding, doubt growing rapidly in my tummy. The thought of a seven-hour flight over the Atlantic Ocean unsettling me.

"I have a friend who just got back from Croatia!" pipes up a woman down the table with short hair and tattooed arms who I have yet to be introduced to.

"Trudy, have you met Coco?" asks Sylvia. "She's opening up right across from you."

The tattooed Coco asks, "You're Honeywell's Baked Goods, right?"

I nod. "Yes, it was originally my grandfather's, Alexander Honeywell."

"Cool, cool..." Coco replies, but then her words are swamped by other women who already know my background and how I inherited the bakery from Grandad and probably don't want to hear about it again.

I haven't been out with these women socially lately, but most of the time I feel as though I belong among them. Especially since Madison is away and I'm living apart from Xavier, and really need friends. I bury myself in the busy-ness of the days at the bakery and in all the goings-on with the business community – everyone knows everyone on Maple Street.

Desserts arrive and as each dish is set down in front of, or next to its intended devourer, she holds her hand to her chest, picks up her fork, and groans, "Oh my gawd, I don't know if I can eat all this!"

Down the table, Coco isn't having dessert, but she's located photos of her friend on a yacht in Croatia and is flashing them around. It's the same gorgeous blue sea and dazzling white sails I've seen in the photos Madison occasionally emails to me. I can't see Coco's pictures clearly from my spot at the table, and I completely lose interest when the double-banana pudding is docked before me.

The buzz at the table changes considerably as forks and spoons scrape at the bottom of the dessert plates and bowls. Absorbed in the soggy cookies at the base of my banana pudding, I'm barely aware that the laughter around me has subsided, replaced with low murmuring and worried tones. I look up to see faces glancing away from me.

Uh oh. What have I done?

But it isn't me, thank goodness. The others are shushing and instructing Coco to put her phone away, flashing sympathetic shots at me.

"What's going on?" Jane demands to know. She's often savagely direct, which at this moment I appreciate very much.

Some of the women look down guiltily at the dishes before them while Coco holds up her phone and says, "It's a picture of my friend Zelda and her fiancé. They got engaged in Croatia recently."

Jane snaps her commanding fingers, which are decked out in a swath of wide silver rings. "Pass it down so I can see it."

Obediently, the women pass Coco's phone as though handling a holy grail, one manicured hand to the next. I lean over Jane's arm to get a good look.

"Oh, I know her!" I say, recognizing Zelda, the dental hygienist who's been cleaning my teeth for years.

Usually kind of homely and thin in her scrubs and mask, she looks very attractive in the picture – tanned, dressed in a stylish summer outfit, her arm around the waist of a man.

Jane enlarges the picture with her fingers, and I peer closer.

The man, wearing sunglasses, a floppy hat, a Hawaiian shirt, and heavy brown sandals, I realize in dismay, is...oh my God, it's Xavier.

In hushed tones, the implications of Zelda and Xavier are being explained around the table, but I understand immediately: *My husband* is Zelda's fiancé. *They're* engaged!

Shame burns like a fire on my cheeks.

Now I know why he was in such a hot rush for me to sign the papers that finalized our divorce.

I'd argued it was too soon, I wasn't ready.

I thought things would work out and that he'd regain his sanity when he realized he missed me and my home cooking.

My lawyer explained it was a financial bugaboo. In order for Xavier to continue being the sole supporter of Madison we needed to finalize the divorce; I needed to sign off on spousal support. Something about me owning my own business disqualified me, even though I'd never drawn a pay cheque from the bakery. We'd relied entirely on Xavier's salary from the TV station, which was adequate, considering we live in Toronto, and could never afford to buy a house. Honeywell's would have to start paying me now. I trusted my lawyer, I trusted Xavier, and I wanted the best for Madison, so, I signed.

But *no*! The real reason was *he's remarrying!*

Zelda!

The woman who's been picking at my teeth for the last ten years!

"Did you know?" Jane demands of me.

Every woman at the table seems acutely interested in my response.

I squirm in mortification.

Why didn't he tell me?

I can't believe this is how I am finding out.

Betrayal and jealousy, embarrassment and heartbreak, swarm around me like a host of gnats. My bladder pinches and I realize I have to pee very badly but I don't dare budge. I don't want to look like I'm fleeing. Instead, I sit in cuckolded agony.

Jane is still waiting for an answer to her question, did I know?

I don't want to sound like the stooge I am.

"He told me he was seeing someone," I lie, trying to sound like it isn't strangling me to utter the words.

Up until this very moment, I believed Xavier was having a midlife crisis and that after regaining his senses he'd come back to me.

Jane eyes me suspiciously.

If I knew, why didn't I tell her this news?

But the rest of the women accept my falsehood at face value and resume their chatter. Not about Zelda and Xavier and their now scandalous trip to Croatia where it's painfully occurring to me, they must have visited Madison.

"Who has to work in the morning?" Jessica asks, pushing away from the table.

"Me!" Debbie says, picking up her phone and beginning to tap at the screen with frosty pink fingernails. "But first...I'm leaving a 5-star review for the new Smokehouse. Who's with me?"

FOUR

Blue emergency lights flash across Jane's face as a rumbling snow-plow scrapes along Maple Street. While we were inside The Smokehouse eating, the sky ceased snowing, but a nasty east wind is still blowing.

One by one, my colleagues teeter off down the street in high-heeled winter boots, or begin digging the snow off their car windshields. Jane stands with me on the freshly shoveled sidewalk in front of the restaurant watching them go.

Even on a stormy night like this, Maple Street is alive. Couples scurry past, arm in arm, and groups of young people slide by in a blur of street-talk and odd haircuts, no hats. A slow but steady stream of cars snakes along the slushy main street of Lakeside.

I feel exposed, as though there's a flashing neon arrow pointing at me: Here she is, folks – the frumpy fat baker who Xavier Asp dumped for a thinner, more fascinating, dental hygienist.

Who knows how long they've been carrying on? Or how many in Lakeside already know?

The snow has stopped but I'm blanketed in shame. Nothing feels safe. I need to stay silent under the rock where I am hiding.

Jane, possibly from her training as a psychiatrist, or possibly because she realizes what a colossal disaster her stupid surprise divorce party was, for once isn't prying. Usually she probes at me, making piercing observations. Not tonight.

Standing on the street to the bitter end, her steady arm grips my shoulder as the guests, *her* guests, depart. It was *her* party. I didn't ask for this!

"I'll get you an Uber," she says, taking off her mitten and swiping the screen of her phone a few times.

I've never been in an Uber, but I know what one is – they replaced taxis a few years ago. We used to be able to stand on Maple Street and flag down a taxi, but now there are none to be seen. I only live a few minutes away, but it's all uphill, and I have no will to live anymore, let alone walk.

After several minutes, a snow-covered car, looking like a normal sedan, pulls up, and Jane makes her way through the heap of snow at the curb to open the back door for me. Silently, I climb inside.

"I'll talk to you tomorrow," she says, giving me a weak smile before slamming the door. She taps on the roof of the car as though all's well that ends well.

It's not.

I slump in the cramped over-heated back seat, holding my breath in hopes of making all the feelings go away. I refuse to cry in front of this driver, this stranger. In excruciating silence, he U-turns, and drives me the few blocks home.

Pulling up in front of Mother's house, I don't tip him, which feels odd, but Jane said it was all taken care of on 'The App'. I need to accept that these apps are taking over the world.

I struggle my way out of the car with a brief, "Thank you." The Uber drives off, leaving me to clamber across a bank of snow and up our un-shoveled walkway. I'll have to contend with all this snow in the morning.

All I want now is to crawl into bed, bury myself under my pillow, and die. The banana pudding was the worst thing I could've eaten – it's sitting like a blobfish in my stomach. I'm bloated and queasy.

I look up at the house. Every single light is on. This can't be good.

I hustle up the porch steps and open the front door, setting my purse down on the table beside the radiator. "Mother?"

There's a muffled response from the living room, "In here."

I kick off my boots and peek in through the doorway. She's sprawled face down on the floor. "What are you *doing*?"

Sweeping a broom back and forth under the couch, she answers, "I'm trying to get this darn cat out of here."

My body freezes but my mind is woozy and scrambling. With everything else tonight, I'd forgotten all about the kitten.

She continues to manhandle the broom while explaining to me. "It's a kitten. He was locked in the laundry room meowing to wake the dead, but I suppose you know something about that." She sweeps back and forth with a horrifying velocity. "I'm sure you'll be glad to know he got upstairs, got up on my bed, and wet his pants, all over my covers! I can't get him out of here."

"Stop swatting!" I cry. "He must be terrified."

Getting to her feet, she hands me the broom and says, "Maybe you'll have more luck. I'm going to bed. Got to get my beauty sleep."

Using an armchair to steady myself, I get down on all fours, my head spinning and my knees burning as I crane my neck to see under the couch. There, at the far corner, is the small, shadowy form of the kitten.

The poor little thing is petrified. He won't be coming out from under there any time soon.

I can't deal with any of this. My heart is broken and I'm rattled. The kitten is safe now that Mother has gone upstairs. He'll come out when he's ready.

Padding around the main floor in my socks, I check that the doors are locked, switch off the lights, and then begin the climb to my bedroom. The staircase seems taller and steeper than ever.

Mother calls. "Are you coming up here?"

"Just a minute," I answer, gripping the railing, one step at a time, my brain sloshing in blue drinks, my knees whining, me and my miserable heart climbing the stairs.

A floorboard creaks at the top and I look up. She's at the top of the stairs holding a bedspread. "Should I just throw it down?"

Before I can respond, the heaped comforter lands in my face nearly knocking me down the stairs.

"Oops."

"Mother!"

Hanging onto the banister with one hand, I wrestle with the damp pee covered blanket.

She's disappeared back to her room.

Cursing under my breath, I lumber back down the steps, careful to not slip and fall.

The blanket needs to go into the washer tonight and then the dryer so it won't go moldy in the machine.

Mother is a menace. She's trying to torture me, punishing me for daring to rely on her for some shelter while I'm in a stormy part of life.

From the darkened dining room beyond the kitchen, I spy the kitten peering at me as I fiddle with the knobs on the washing machine. His curiosity beat out his fear.

"Hello, troublemaker."

Staying close to the baseboards he sidles his way to my feet.

"Are you a little rascal?" I ask, bending down, a little wobbly, stroking his tiny head.

He rubs against my ankles in response and my heart melts. I've always wanted a kitten.

Xavier was allergic.

Ugh. *Him.* I feel the agony anew. I wish I could forget my million years of history with him.

The kitten mews, "Now?" A sweet high innocent little question.

I don't care what Mother says. I'll tackle her tomorrow. I am not turning this poor little thing out in the snow, in the dark. I'm not cruel like her.

I refill the saucer of milk, but he refuses to come into the laundry room where the washing machine has begun gushing and filling with rushing water. He stays safely in the kitchen staring at me, so I move the saucer to beside the sink. He rushes for it.

"Just don't get too comfortable," I caution him, watching him lap furiously at the milk. "When Mother wakes up and finds you still here tomorrow, she'll probably start charging you rent." He ignores me. "Never mind, don't worry, I'll take you to the humane society, or post notices on telephone poles, or...something. Where do you live? Don't you want to go home?"

Irresistibly cute, the kitten scrunches closer to the saucer, impervious to my questioning.

"I suppose you need a litter box of some sort if you're staying the night. No more peeing on beds. Do you know how to use a litter box?"

The cardboard base of a pop can carton will do until morning. But what can I fill it with? Mother's collection of houseplants lines the dining room window. I find a gnarled geranium that looks half-dead and pull it from the pot by its stem. Turning the pot upside down, I shake out the dirt into the shallow box.

"There," I say, taking it into the laundry room. "This is where you 'go' if you need to—"

Paying no attention to me, the kitten saunters from the kitchen into the hallway toward the stairs. I hurry behind, watching in awe as he scampers up the staircase like a tiny kangaroo.

I wish I could do that.

I follow as fast as my knees will allow. But when I reach the top of the stairs, he's nowhere in sight.

Mother's bedroom door is shut, thank goodness, and her light is off, no TV blaring.

I close myself into the bathroom.

My image in the mirror reflects exactly how I feel emotionally. Smeared make-up, bleary eyes, lumpy sweatshirt and ugly pants. What was I thinking?

I snatch up the makeup remover and begin swabbing my face. Why do I even bother? I'm a wreck.

Stripping down, deliberately avoiding catching sight of myself in the mirror, I pull on the nightie that's hanging on a hook on the back of the door. I brush my teeth, hoping the mintiness of the toothpaste will soothe me, but every time my mind wanders over the topic of Xavier and Zelda, my heart contorts, reminding me of what a fool I am.

I can't believe I didn't notice my husband of twenty-one years had lost interest in me.

I can't believe he took up with someone else.

I can't believe everyone knows about it.

I reach for a towel, wanting to howl. Pressing it against my face, freshly laundered, the towel exudes a clean reassuring smell that makes me want to cry even harder.

The laundry.

I've got to put Mother's stupid comforter into the dryer. Is the washer finished?

I pad down the hall and stand at the top of the stairs sniffling and listening. The spin cycle is in the midst of shaking the washer like a mean mother shaking a naughty daughter.

Please don't tell me it's off kilter. Do I have to go down there and intervene?

All I want is to crawl into bed and escape from the scenarios of Xavier and Zelda in my head but I can't until this relentless cycle finishes.

In my bedroom, I lift my laptop from the dressing table and climb into bed. I punch the pillows a few times, trying to settle in. The kitten startles me, clawing his way up the side of my box spring.

"Hello, little fella." I tickle his head. "What's your name? Casper? Snowdrop?"

He climbs over my thigh and walks straight onto the keyboard.

"Oh no, you don't!" I snatch him off and turn him to face me, feeling a wild purring motor in his throat.

"You funny little thing. Someone must be missing you like mad."

My heart aches at the thought.

I set him beside me on the bed and tap on the laptop keyboard to bring up the desktop.

"I'll show you how to use a laptop," I tell my new friend, who has taken up licking his chest. "It's easy once you figure it out. If I can do it, you can do it."

The kitten swipes a few more times at his chest then settles onto his haunches, his eyes beginning to close.

"Go to sleep, good idea. Don't worry about me. I'll just check and see if I have any emails."

His eyes are fully closed though I can still hear him purring.

"Do you want to know something ironic?" I ask, but he doesn't move a whisker. "I was forced to learn the computer when I hired a divorce lawyer. How about that? First thing he said was, 'You don't have a computer?' So, Jane helped me, and here we are."

The house fills with silence – the wash cycle concluded. I lug myself out of bed, rousing the kitten from his slumber. He takes a wild leap off the mattress and accompanies me back downstairs.

In the laundry room, I wrangle the now thousand-pound comforter from the washer and heap it into the dryer. The kitten watches in wonder from the kitchen.

"You mistook me for a weakling, didn't you?" I ask him. His gray eyes are wide awake now.

"How about a snack to ward off your hangover tomorrow?"

He blinks at me.

"I'll take that as a yes."

I pour more milk for him, and though he dips his nose in, he doesn't take more than a lick.

"Tired of milk?"

He wanders around the kitchen, rubbing his back against all the cupboards.

"I'll get you some real food tomorrow."

I stare into the fridge for a few moments wondering if he'd like a slice of bologna.

"I'm hungry," I tell the kitten, although it's not true. At least, I'm not hungry in my *body*. Something inside me is calling out for food, something sweet to soothe me. I pour myself a glass of milk and take a box of cookies from the cupboard. Just a light snack before bed.

Climbing the stairs again, this time, both hands full, I promise the kitten, "I *will* phone Dr. Gertie about my knees tomorrow, no matter what."

Back in bed, he curls up next to me and I wake up the laptop. Clicking on the email icon, I munch through a few cookies, waiting for the inbox to display.

"Let's see if there's anything from my daughter tonight," I say, brushing crumbs off my nightgown, hesitating for a moment before scattering them onto the floor.

I'm always hopeful for one of Madison's messages, wishing she'd say more about how her job is going, whether she likes it, is she making friends? Has she met anyone special?

Sometimes she sends photographs, and I gather she's having a wonderful time...

Xavier went over to Croatia.

The nasty fact bobs up through the surface of my mind.

He most likely saw Madison.

Now it's stinging me like a sea urchin.

He went with Zelda.

Stop! It hurts!

He proposed to her there.

The wound is so painful I can hardly see straight.

What did Madison think of it all?

She didn't mention it. Not in any of our brief conversations.

Does that mean she's okay with her father's new relationship?

It must have been horribly awkward for her. Zelda's been cleaning Madison's teeth since she was a little girl, and now the woman is sleeping with her father!

The email program opens and the top email is from Madison.

The subject line paralyzes me: `Guess who's getting married?!`

Why would she think her father's remarriage is something to share with me in an email?

I hear from her so rarely and *this* is what she wants to communicate about?

I'm angry, but I have to read it.

I click open the message, expecting her to 'break the news' to me. Too late, Honey, it's already been broken. And now I'm broken too.

But I'm shocked by what I read.

In answer to the question, "Guess who's getting married?!" she's written:

`I am!!!!!!!`

FIVE

My doctor shares space at Lakeside Medical Center with some other healthcare professionals. Her name is Gertrude Philips, but everyone calls her Dr. Gertie. A combination of efficient and kind, I've been a patient of hers since I was pregnant with Madison.

The only problem is her office is at the back of the building, which is nice for her because she has a full view of the park, but it means I have to pass by the dentist's office to get there, and today that means risking being seen by Zelda.

It's been several days since the divorce party and Madison's baffling email, and I feel like I've finally calmed down, but I don't need an encounter with Zelda.

The medical offices all have large windows facing the hallway. Sometimes their vertical blinds are shut in such a way that you can't see inside, but most often they're not. As I scurry by, I hope, hope, hope Zelda isn't in the dentist's reception area.

Success. She's not there. I pass unnoticed, and hurry further down the hallway toward Dr. Gertie's.

Up ahead and to my right, the door to the bathroom opens and just my luck, a tanned, sun-kissed Zelda steps into the hall, directly blocking my path.

Adrenaline surges through my limbs and I almost turn and sprint for the exit. From the expression on her face, I can tell she's as surprised as I am. She regroups, and it's clear – we're going to fake civility and act like there's nothing wrong with her stealing my husband.

"Trudy! How nice to see you," she lies, her eyes flicking over my body.

I wish I'd worn something else, but I dashed over from work and under my unbuttoned jacket I'm wearing the same thing I always wear to work – a large white blouse over gray checked pull-on pants – it's professional and I have five of these outfits. In the bakery, I also wear a dusty blue Honeywell's apron. My staff do too. Thankfully, I remembered to take off the apron today before I came over here.

What am I thinking? She's in a uniform too – head to toe in pink teddy-bear scrubs. In the past I might have thought her choice cute, today it makes me gag.

She says, "You must be so excited about Madison's wedding!"

She's going there. She could've passed on by and gone back to work but no, she's going to stand in the hallway and try to converse with me about my one and only daughter's sudden wedding announcement, which, awkwardly, I know next to nothing about.

I affirm the lie. "Yes, very excited."

The truth is exactly the opposite. I'm not excited – I'm anxious and worried. I'm trying to accept that at twenty my daughter has become an adult, who can make her own choices, and that she probably has a very good reason for not answering my frantic emails or phone messages. But I don't want to talk about any of this with Zelda.

I have no idea *why* Madison is suddenly getting married, or what she's planning, but if it's a wedding ceremony on a beach somewhere in Croatia that requires me to travel to Europe, I can't go!

The very thought of a transatlantic flight turns my legs to jelly. I hate planes. I hate flying. People get blood clots in their legs from sitting so long. I have enough trouble with my legs, hence my appointment today with Dr. Gertie. Also, planes crash *all the time*.

Zelda inquires, "Has she set a date?"

"Not yet," I fudge. "But we're close to nailing it down."

In fact, I've received scant information from Madison. Since her announcement the other night, she's replied to me exactly once, and the details were sketchy.

At least I know the groom's name: Matt Brown. She told me he's an Australian she met through her job.

I look at my wristwatch. "Oh, I better get to Dr. Gertie's."

Nosey, Zelda pries, "I hope nothing's wrong."

"No, no, just a check-up."

She looks as though she's in perfect health. I never noticed before how fit she is. She's always worn tennis shoes, but I thought they were part of her uniform. Maybe she's a member of the fanatics who jog around Lakeside in all weather. There's even a store catering to them now – The Runners Walk – full of the most expensive shoes ever. As she moves aside for me to pass, I glance down at her feet. She's wearing a regular pair of white sneakers.

It's not a long wait in Dr. Gertie's office. After giving the receptionist my change of address, I take a seat in the waiting area. There are plenty of magazines to flip through. I'm skimming an article on beginning a yoga practice, and trying not to think about Madison's wedding...or Zelda and Xavier...flip the page...or Xavier and Zelda...or Madison's wedding...when I'm called in for my turn.

"It's been a while," Gertie greets me warmly, pulling the curtain across her office doorway. She perches on a tall swivel stool behind her desk – empty except for a sleek fancy-looking computer screen which she taps into action. "Last time you were here was..." Her eyebrows rise. "Wow, Trudy, I haven't seen you in *three* years."

"Yes, you have," I remind her, grinning. Gertie Philips is one of my regular customers. She loves Granny's Grains, and often treats herself to one of my éclairs. "You've seen me at the bakery!" I remind her.

She grimaces comically, "Mea culpa," she says, before donning a serious doctor face. Over her shoulder, through the large south facing window, I notice the barren park, the snow of last week has melted away completely but the grass is still brown and the trees showing no sign of leaves. "So, what are we doing today? What brings you in?"

I explain to her about my knees. "They're mostly fine, except when I'm going up stairs."

She taps a few notes into her computer as I describe the twinging and pinging and throbbing.

"Let's take a look," she says.

And now I'm glad I'm wearing my elastic waist work pants, but when I try to slide them up, the leg holes are too narrow for my thick calves, so, I have no choice but to pull them down, exposing my large pink underpants. Gertie prods and pokes; has me straighten my legs and bend them. Then she indicates I can pull up my pants.

She says with a sad smile, "I think we need to lose some weight, Trudy."

What?

Surely, she doesn't mean *both* of us. She's a little chunky, but nothing like I am. She means me.

I'm shocked and embarrassed.

"I *am* going on a diet," I tell her sincerely, trying to sound like I haven't just committed to sensible eating again after skimming an article in one of her waiting-room magazines.

"Good for you," she says with enthusiasm. "How much do you weigh? Let's get you on the scale."

I don't want to get on the scale. It's located outside the patient cubicles, in the common area of the clinic, where anyone walking around can see it.

She pulls open the curtain and I reluctantly follow like a sad trained elephant at the circus.

It's a new-fangled scale that flashes the kilograms on a screen at eye level, including all spare grams and micrograms. I step on it and the numbers skyrockets. For a moment I wonder if there's been a malfunction. I've never seen it go over ninety before, not even during pregnancy.

I step off, deeply perturbed, and start calculating. If a pound is point four five of a kilo, then ninety-three kilos is—

"When was your last period?" Gertie asks, interrupting the alarming arithmetic in my head as we settle back in her office.

"My period?" I ask, with no idea why she's prying into all this extra stuff – I just want my knees fixed. "I don't remember," I tell her. "It's been a while."

She raises her eyebrows at me. "How long?"

I think back. When was the last time?

I recall now.

"It was just before Christmas...a couple of years ago."

I hadn't had my period in months. I thought I was finally finished with them – yay, menopause! Then on the morning of my mother-in-law's Christmas open-house, I'd flooded the bed and had to wear pads all day, and mope around my in-laws' house feeling sorry for myself. The only good part was the incredible food my mother-in-law spread out on her dining room table. I distinctly remember she made homemade mallomars. I would kill for one of those right now.

Dr. Gertie taps some information into her screen. "It would seem you're in menopause. Any spotting?"

She's really hung up on this menstrual cycle thing, which seems beside the point to me.

"I was wondering if physio might help my knees," I say, steering her away from my lady-parts. "Or yoga?"

She looks at me with sympathy. "Perhaps," she agrees. "But I think we'll follow up with an X-ray and an MRI. I have a feeling you might have some arthritis developing in there. It's not uncommon at your age."

I hang my head. I was hoping for a referral for a physiotherapy session or two. And since reading the article in the waiting room about yoga, I pictured myself lying blissfully on a purple mat, or sitting like a lotus flower with my hands poised against my chest in thankful prayer.

"And bloodwork. I want to take a look at what's going on in there."

"No!" I clap my hands over my mouth.

"Relax, Trudy. It's standard. You know that. And you haven't been in to see me in *three years*. I'd like to see how your bloodwork looks."

On the laundry list of things I hate, blood tests are right next to flying.

From a little machine beside her desk, she prints out a prescription for a single Gonzepam tablet. "Take this before you go for the bloodwork."

She remembered.

Taking a single Gonzepam for my anxiety got me through all the pregnancy blood tests.

I appreciate her kindness.

But a part of me wishes I hadn't come in here today and stirred up this trouble. Now, I have a to-do list a mile long: get an X-ray and an MRI, and blood work, which she wants me to, ugh, fast for. That means a hollow, aching tummy, and a late morning.

I just have sore knees. Surely a pain-killer, or a few stretches, would do the trick.

Gertie prints off the requisitions. "I want a mammogram and a stool test as well," she states, laying out an array of papers and an envelope with a lump in it. "That's the stool test," she says, patting the bump.

This seems really excessive. "Where do I get all this done?" *And why are you being so unreasonable?*

"You can get everything done at the Bingham lab. Call them and tell them your tests – they'll schedule you in. Plan to be there for the day."

"The day?" I object.

I don't know if I like Gertie anymore. I thought she was efficient but she's gone overboard.

"We'll call you back in to go over things once I see the results, okay?"

"Fine." I say through clenched teeth, wanting to knock over the jar of tongue depressors on the shelf behind her.

How did this happen? I felt perfectly fine this morning.

Well, except for my knees.

Now, I'm suffocating. It's hot and stuffy in this cubicle.

Gertie opens the curtain and a reviving gust of air from the open office brushes my cheeks. I scurry out and down the hall toward the building's exit, pulling on my jacket as I go, glancing through the dentist's window as I pass. Zelda is leaning against the reception counter with her back to the window, her petite derriere in its Teddy Bear scrubs wagging back and forth, mocking me.

Six

·˙·◆·˙·

J ane meets me in the bakery at lunchtime.

"This is some weather, eh?" she says, remarking on the abrupt change from winter to summer that has occurred in a matter of days.

A customer smirks and says, "Welcome to Canada."

Jane shoots him a big toothy grin, then asks me, "Where are we going to eat?"

Between baking, deliveries, and serving customers, I've been on my feet all morning. "Somewhere close," I plead. The last thing I want is to traipse half-a-mile down the street to lunch on these knees.

I wiggle my fingers goodbye at Eve, my counter-help, and step through the bakery's doorway – bam – right into the back of Jane's zebra pattern t-shirt. She's stopped, staring straight ahead, and I have to maneuver to get around her.

The hoarding on the building across the road has come down – they've been working on removing it all morning. A new sign is being erected. "Coco Nuts Gluten-Free Bakery."

I stand beside Jane, my jaw dropping open.

She asks, "*What* is a gluten-free bakery?"

I answer, stunned, "I have no idea."

Then I notice the tattooed woman from the divorce party, what's-her-name, Coco, waving at us, and things slowly start to make sense. *This* is the business she said she was opening across the road from Honeywell's.

A bakery right across the road from my bakery.

I return a limp wave, not knowing what else to do.

Jane hauls me off down the street, past the jeans store, past the used book shop, across the cross-walk, to our favourite restaurant, a diner with a black and white tiled floor, red tabletops and banquette seating. They serve homey diner fare: hamburgers, clubhouse sandwiches, and fried chicken. It was crazily busy when it first opened but now it seems to have gone out of style and it's easy to get a seat. I bet people don't realize there are tables in the rear with a view of the park.

Jane is wordless until we are safely and privately ensconced at the back, then she demands to know, "What are you going to *do*?"

"Do?"

"Yes! You've got to *do* something. It's not fair. What the hell, Trudy?"

I stare at her, slowly shaking my noncomprehending head back and forth. I'm not sure what she expects of me.

"Are you *okay* with Coco… and her coconuts?"

I laugh nervously. "Do I have a choice?"

She frowns. "A competitor like *that*, right across the road? This could be a disaster!"

Jane might be right. I've never had a competitor before. But what can I do about it? I can't force Coco to close, or move her business.

I try downplaying it. "I'm not worrying about Coco. Honeywell's is a Lakeside institution. Always has been." She looks skeptical, but my own logic persuades me. "I'm just surprised no one at The Smokehouse last week mentioned that Coco was opening a *bakery*."

"Exactly," Jane agrees. "I bet they all knew, those…those…B-words." She's only half-serious, but her loyalty is heartwarming. She slides a menu across the table to me and says, "Let's decide."

Since the fiasco of the divorce party, this is the first chance we've had to sit down for a full debrief. I'm looking forward to hearing Jane's take on the whole Xavier and Zelda debacle. Because that's what it is, a debacle – which I'm finding impossible to accept. I'm a big ball of pain – it's embarrassing.

And I hate that ugly Zelda.

I'm not sure if I *should* feel any of these feelings. Is it normal, months after a divorce, to still want my husband back? To still love him? Am I supposed to have moved on by now? Clearly, he has. Jane will know.

"This could be a problem," she says, drumming her fingers on the table. She's got a different amber ring on each, even her thumbs.

"What could be a problem?"

"Coco's Nuts."

I scoff. I don't want to talk about Coco.

Jane peers at me the way she always does when she's got her psychiatrist binoculars on. "You seem awfully unconcerned. Is business so good that you're not worried about competition?"

"Sales are a bit down." I squirm, pretending to search in my purse for something. "But they'll bounce back," I answer, off-handedly, and then joke, "People need to eat, don't they?"

I don't want to discuss business with Jane. I want to talk about Xavier and Zelda, and why, why, why, are they doing this to me?

Our waitress pours coffee. "What are we having today, ladies?"

I order the Corned Beef on Rye. They heap on the meat here and it sogs up the bread, just the way I like it. As soon as the waitress leaves, I say to Jane, "Guess who I bumped into at the doctor's office?"

"Who?" She leans closer, ready to dish.

"Zelda."

"Ooohhh. Interesting. What was *that* like?"

I tell her about my conversation with Zelda in the hallway, and like a good friend, Jane is completely sympathetic, understanding why it's so awkward, nodding her head all over the place.

She throws her hands in the air. "Why couldn't he have chosen someone we don't all know?"

I freeze.

Is she implying it's acceptable for Xavier to start a new relationship, mere months after our split?

Isn't the important question, *why* did he have to choose anyone at all?

Wouldn't it have been seemlier to wait a few years, before diving back into a relationship?

And they're *engaged*? Why? Why not just date for a while?

Or have they been dating all this time behind my back?

If I voice any of these questions, and Jane disagrees with me, I can't bear to hear it. I need every morsel of sympathy I can suck up. I need someone who understands, and I thought that was Jane. When I told Mother that Xavier was getting remarried, she said, "I knew it! You're going to be here forever."

Maddeningly, Jane changes the subject, "Why were you at the doctor?"

I answer, as dismissively as possible, "Just my knees bothering me,"

She nods as our meals arrive and I realize how hungry I am. She's having the Fish 'n' Chips and I momentarily regret my sandwich as I watch her squirt ketchup all over her glistening golden food.

She picks up a fork. "What did Dr. Gertie say about your knees?"

I've just taken a big bite of juicy corned beef so I chew for a few moments before I answer. "She sent me for tests. An MRI and an x-ray in case I pulled a tendon or something."

I dab at my mouth with my napkin, and do not tell Jane about the other tests Gertie ordered, the blood tests and the poo test, and how bothersome it all is. Nor do I tell her about the Gonzepam the doctor prescribed, because I know she'll start lecturing me about getting addicted. We've had that conversation before. It's just one little pill for blood-test anxiety! That's all Gertie ever prescribes. She suggested Gonzepam years ago when I was pregnant and too freaked out to have blood drawn. It's the only way I can get through the blood-letting without fainting.

Jane nods as she eats. "And have you had the tests done?" She knows me too well.

"Not yet. But I will. Next week."

She frowns, overly concerned and meddling as usual. "Better take care of yourself, Trudy."

I want off this topic too. I've avoided calling the Lettuceville Clinic where they do the testing because it's in a seedier part of town and I can't picture it. I'm nervous about going to new places. Maybe Jane will offer to go with me. But she doesn't.

"Now, tell me about Madison's big wedding plans," she says. "When's the date?"

Ugh. Another topic I'd rather steer clear of.

I wonder for half a second whether I should confide in Jane that Madison has told me next to nothing. But it's so embarrassing to admit I barely hear from my daughter overseas. Jane will tell me to *communicate* with Madison – tell her how I *feel*. She's always harping on about communication.

"We haven't nailed anything down yet," I say instead, because as far as I know, it's the truth. I've tried calling Madison, but she doesn't pick up, and her phone goes immediately to an answering machine.

I could call Xavier and ask him if he knows anything, but I'd rather stay in the dark than risk talking to him again. Last time, I got so upset I started crying. He hates it when I blubber.

"It's exciting, though, right?" Jane points her fork at me. "*You* are the Mother-of-the-Bride." A swarm of butterflies roils in my belly and my eyes open wide. "It's big!" she exclaims. "The Mother-of-the-Bride has *a lot* of responsibilities."

Now, I'm really alarmed. "Like what?"

Jane has no children. About five years ago, she and her longtime partner, Lydia broke up, and she hasn't dated anyone since, so, I'm not sure why she's suddenly an expert on wedding etiquette. But then Jane always knows everything about everything. She asks, "Have you thought about a dress?"

"You mean for Madison?"

Knowing my daughter, she probably has a dress already chosen, with no help from me."

"No, silly. For *you!* The Mother-of-the-Bride's dress is the second most scrutinized gown at a wedding!" Jane shovels chips into her mouth and chews, watching me.

I've suddenly lost interest in the remaining fries on my plate.

The very idea of being the center of attention distresses me – I'm so fat.

Finally, I whisper my admission, "I don't think I can go."

"Why?"

"What would I wear? Where would I ever find a dress to fit?"

Jane, who is tall and lean and built like an egret, proceeds to tell me all about shopping for a wedding outfit. "There are stores that specialize in it, silly. I'll go with you."

"Will they have anything to fit *me*?" My cheeks begin to heat.

I'd rather not talk to Jane about packing on the pounds during my years of hot flashes, brain fog, and the change. In her psychiatric practice she specializes in nutrition-related mood disorders. She's always telling me I'm eating my feelings. It's so annoying and I usually binge the minute I get away from her.

She asks me, "You think you're the only one who's put on a few pounds?"

SEVEN

W ith a half-sweet (I'm on a diet now) maple latte from the café down the street, I plunk myself down in my cubby-hole of an office in the backroom of the bakery. It's the beginning of May and I've been neglecting the office work for days. But the bills need to be paid so I tear into the pile of envelopes on my desk and sort them.

Opening the brown vinyl cheque-book, the same one my grandfather, Alexander Honeywell used before me, I catch a whiff of his comforting campfire smell and for a moment I savour the feeling of safety he always brought me.

It's just momentary though, because if he could see these sales numbers, his hair would catch on fire.

After tallying April's cash register tapes, I'm shaken to see that sales are worse than ever. Turning to the ledger at the back of the cheque-book, I pencil in the steadily declining sales figure.

I don't know how long I can flip flop along this way and I'm not sure what to do. Sales have never been so slow. On my own now, without Xavier, my only income is from Honeywell's.

My desk is tucked into a corner of the bakery's backroom where I can still hear the door to the street opening and closing, and the sound of voices as my helper, Eve, serves the counter. Customers still shop at Honeywell's, but it's nothing like the days when they crowded in en masse for their morning donut or Danish.

Nowadays, people buy more bread than pastries, especially the ancient-grain recipe I learned from an employee a few years back. I'd had my doubts about a loaf full of bird seed, but customers gobbled it up, and Granny's Grains has been a steady seller ever since.

Maybe I should ask Eve, and the other helper who comes in on the weekends, if they have any recipe ideas.

But I don't dare infuse the business with a whiff of failure. I haven't let on to anyone how low I am on funds. I'm not about to confess to my staff that I'm a wreck in this department of life too. They already know about my divorce, and that I've moved in with my mother.

Financially, the saving grace, once again this month, is Crumb-less cookies – a daily seller I personally carry around to several clients on the street. When I add up the sales from the Crumb-less cookies alone, it's exactly enough to cover the rent. If not for those cookies, I'm sure I'd have to close up shop. And then what would I do? I don't want to go back to a job cooking chicken-fingers in a daycare.

I invented Crumb-less cookies for Suzy, who runs Suzy Q's, the quilting store next door. She's hooked on my baked goods. A few years ago, she got on a kick about having a yummy smell in her store, something she read about it in a business magazine. It turned out she's allergic to smelly candles, so she tried setting out a plate of my fresh-baked cookies in her shop. It wasn't long before she had to stop that too because of oily fingerprints on her quilting fabrics and crumbs all over the place.

"If only you could make a crumb-less cookie," she'd lamented, draped across my counter.

So, I invented one for her. I tested and retested the recipe, dropping fresh cookies onto a paper napkin, tweaking the recipe until finally, my Crumb-less left no butter residue and no crumbs. They're the size of large buttons, just a bite or two, and I pack them in cute cupcake boxes. They're becoming kind of famous on Maple Street, and without even trying I keep getting more clients: Dressica, the fashion boutique; Peepers, the eyeglass store; and Paper Porpoise, the card shop; among others.

Fortunately, there's enough money in the bank account today to send a cheque to my landlady in Florida, pay for the ingredients from last month, and keep the lights on. I scribble out a cheque for Eve, and one for my weekend girl, but I'll have to shave a bit off my own take-home pay again to keep all these other cheques from bouncing.

I can't keep scrimping this way.

I've got to find a way to make enough so I can move out of Mother's house. Living with her was the last thing I wanted to do, but the alternative was paying the rent on the condo by myself. Jane assured me I could handle Mother for a few months, just until I got on my feet financially, and she even went with me to explain the situation to Mother. Basically, Mother made me grovel, and was so smug about it all.

Living with her, rent free as it may be, is a threat to my sanity. The longer I stay with her, the more cuckoo I feel. I've got to get away.

I sip at the maple latte and overhear Eve in conversation with a man. Little Eve is notoriously shy so my ears prick up when I hear a burst of laughter. I take off my reading glasses to listen better.

Who is she talking to?

The animated conversation continues and, dying of curiosity, I hoist myself from my desk to go see.

Emerging from the backroom, I bump into Eve.

"Trudy! I was just coming to—. This gentleman wants to talk to the owner."

He's dressed in a stylish, slim fitting, bright blue suit with a brown leather satchel over one shoulder. His pants are narrow and short and he's wearing argyle socks above his leather lace up shoes. Men's fashions are so odd these days.

With a shoulder raised, he reaches out his hand and sidles toward me as though he already knows me and is delighted to see me again.

"Trudy Asp? Hendrick da Vinci, Biz Buzz." He reaches into his jacket pocket with two fingers and pulls out a business card.

I glance at the card, but without my readers, I can't make out what it says. I look up at his face into startling blue mascara, which actually looks fantastic on him. He may have prettier eyes than I do.

"I love your bakery!" he gushes, waving his hands around. "It smells absolute-ly—"

His suit matches Honeywell's color scheme, or did, back when the paint was fresh and not the dusty-blue it's now faded to. He asks, "How long have you been here?"

I feel uncomfortable divulging information to someone who's just dropped in from the street. I have no idea what he wants to talk to me about. I respond vaguely, "A long time."

Customers come in and out of the shop.

"It's busy!" he nods with approval.

And before I know it, I blurt out, "Not like it used to be—"

I clamp my mouth shut before I can utter another word.

I didn't mean to disclose the fact that business is slow.

Now that it's out, I feel as if I'm on the deck of the Titanic, and it just tilted, I'm sliding into the sea.

He nods slowly, appreciatively. "Is there somewhere in this delicious place we can talk?"

I can tell he's flattering me, trying to sell me something.

My heart skitters.

But darn it, I'm curious.

Yet reluctant, not knowing what it's about.

Leading the way into the backroom, I drag over a chair for him so we can both squeeze into my office space. I sink into my swivel chair behind the desk while he sits and takes a long look around at the vast kitchen and stockroom.

"Wow. This is the real deal," he says, taking in the ancient oven, the cooling racks, the shelves of pots and pans and sacks of flour. "A *real* old-fashioned bakery."

"Of course, it is!" I huff. "What'd you expect?"

"Most places bring in everything frozen," he says, lowering his voice as though letting me in on a secret. "They may bake on the premises, but they don't *make* the dough. Did you know that?"

"I suppose," I lie.

I actually don't know how other bakeries run. I've been busy minding my own business, which has been more than enough, thank-you-very-much. And this year, I've been a tad distracted with my husband dumping me; my daughter leaving the country for the summer; and by moving in with a loony drunken woman.

Hendrick sounds genuinely interested when he inquires, "How did you get into the bakery business?"

I don't know why I'm giving this guy the time of day, but there's something charming about him, and it's not everyday someone wants to talk to me about my work.

"My grandfather," I tell him, tapping my knuckle on a framed newspaper-clipping on the wall behind me. It's a grainy photo of me and Grandad, taken outside on the sidewalk in front of the bakery. "He won an award because of his daily bread donations to the women's shelter."

"Is that you?"

"Yes. I'm about thirteen. I worked here on Saturday mornings."

"Adorable."

While other girls went to ballet or figure skating lessons, Grandad had me lifting blueberry buns off the pans hot from the oven and arranging them in rows on a tray for the window. He always let me eat one as I worked.

"I take it that not much has changed around here," Hendrick observes. "Is your grandfather still alive?"

"No, he died about fifteen years ago, and left the business to me."

He nods, thoughtfully.

"The window in that picture looks like it's brimming with goodies. That must have drawn in a lot of customers." He cocks his head at me "*Your* window only has a couple of cardboard wedding cakes." He pauses, as though waiting for an explanation.

"Grandad also had yellow fly tapes dangling in the window...so..."

He reacts in horror.

Miffed by his insinuation that I don't know how to run my own bakery, I inform him: "People want their food packaged up and sanitary nowadays."

"I see. So, I'll tell you why I'm here." He leans forward, in a confidential way. "A group of business owners in Lakeside are pooling together to see if they can, you know, improve their businesses."

They are? I'm surprised to hear this. "You mean businesses around here are struggling?" I thought I was the only one.

"Don't be silly," he scoffs. "Everyone wants to improve! Don't you?"

He opens his satchel, and hands me a flier. It's a funny picture of a woman with charred hair, dark ringed eyes, her mouth hanging open. The headline reads: *Burnt Out?*

How many times since January, have I peered at myself in the dim bathroom mirror feeling exactly how this woman looks?

"Can you relate?" he asks smugly, assuming I can.

"Not exactly," I lie.

He continues, "I coach groups of people, just like yourself. We meet once a week and work on an aspect of small business operations. It's called Biz Buzz."

Really? I've never heard of such a thing.

"Is there a cost?" I ask, frowning, because after writing out the cheques for the month, I can't afford another thing, no matter what my business buddies are doing.

"There is," he admits. "But I have a money back guarantee. If you find there's no improvement to your business after three months – I will give you your money back." He sits back in his chair, as though he's clinched the deal. "And I'll tell you what, I've never had to refund a soul."

He's so sure of himself it's ridiculous.

"Oh, I don't know," I say, pushing the flier back across my desk toward him.

I can't afford it, refund policy or not. And it sounds stupid, like a lot of trouble. Meetings, coaching, improvements. I have too much on my plate as it is.

"I tell you what, Trudy," Hendrick says. "You keep this." He steeples four long fingers on the woman's burnt-out face, and pushes it back toward me. "Think about it. Discuss it with your neighbors. I don't want you to miss out."

I don't want to miss out either, but I'm doubtful anyone I know is actually joining. News and gossip fly up and down Maple Street like crumpled napkins in the wind. No one's said a word to me, and we're a close group.

Or did someone mention it at that stupid divorce party?

My memory is hazy.

"I'll think about it," I fib, feeling annoyed with this guy for wasting my time.

He doesn't make a move to leave, so I squeeze myself up from my chair.

"Our first session is Wednesday night," he says, rising and following me from the backroom. "I'll pop in before then to see if you've made a decision."

My chest tightens. I don't like pressure tactics. I wish he'd just hurry up and go. He's trying to come across all nicey-nice, but he's pushy, and no one likes pushy people.

Who does he think he is coming into my bakery and telling me what to do? What could a guy like him possibly teach me about running a 'good old-fashioned' bakery as he called it?

All I need is a few new recipes.

Or maybe I'll implement half-price Tuesdays. That seems to work for the movie theater.

Or muffins. I've resisted jumping on the muffin bandwagon. Maybe it's time for Honeywell's Muffballs.

Hendrick wiggles his fingers and says, "Tootles!" The door to the street closes behind him.

Eve and I exchange looks.

She's not bold enough to ask what he wanted, and I'm not in the mood to talk about it. I'm already late for delivering today's Crumb-less. They're stacked on the counter ready to go.

But Eve is so jazzed by her interaction with Mister Blue Suit & Mascara that she's bursting to say something. "He was funny, though, wasn't he?" she says, eagerly, seeking my agreement.

She's a sweet girl, I hate to burst her bubble and tell her he's just a smarmy salesman.

"Mm hm," I agree, non-committedly, plating myself a brownie for some quick energy before I set off down the street. The walk will burn off the calories.

EIGHT

·▾·▾·▾▾·

othing looks right!

I toss another dress onto the pile of rejects growing on my bed.

It turns out, according to Jane, every single one of my friends and colleagues has signed up for Biz Buzz.

The next dress won't even go down over my shoulders. And now my hair is stuck in the zipper!

I can't afford Biz Buzz, but when I was outside sweeping the sidewalk this morning, I saw Coco across the street unfurling her crisp new navy and white awning. She waved, and I fumed. My customers are swarming in and out of her Gluten-Free Bakery like ants to a sugar cube over there.

Unlikely, but it's possible I could stand to learn a few new tricks, and maybe Biz Buzz will help. Besides, if everyone else is willing to give Hendrick da Vinci a try, I have a nagging feeling I can't afford to miss out. However, I'm darned if I'm showing up, dressed like the frump I was at the divorce party.

I'm going to look sharp, and with it tonight, and slimmer than I am, but I can't find *a thing* in my wardrobe that looks right!

When I was married, I made a point of getting dressed up and going out with girlfriends, every month. A magazine article I read said it was a fun way to keep your husband interested – keep him thinking you have your own life. Obviously, it didn't work – he left me anyway.

Ugh. Don't think about him. Concentrate on tonight.

My hair and makeup look good, I just need to choose an outfit to wear. Why does nothing fit right anymore?

I dash through the hangers in my wardrobe again and try on a stretchy, no-zip skirt. It looks like a sausage casing on me. I tear it off and kick it across the room.

This morning, I worried I was too late to sign up for Biz Buzz, but when I called Hendrick, he came to the bakery straightaway to pick up a cheque. A post-dated cheque.

"Trust me, Trudy," he said, opening his satchel, sliding the cheque into a leather folder. "This will be cashable sooner than you think."

He's awfully cocky, but he really is a likable guy, evidenced by him graciously accepting a PDC from me. And if Biz Buzz is a con job, well, I'm not the only sucker.

It's late. I hurry.

A slinky floral blouse with tiny fussy buttons gapes where one's missing at the bust. I struggle to pull it off over my head, mussing my hair.

For the three-month Biz Buzz fee, we get weekly sessions with the whole group, all about marketing and stuff, and then monthly private consultations with Hendrick about our own specific businesses. It seems like a good deal, it's just that I have no spare money right now.

But if I can increase sales at the bakery, it will be worth it, and hopefully I'll be able to afford to move out of this house. Maybe get a place of my own until, unless, Xavier and I reconcile before then. I've been thinking lately, this engagement of his can't be serious.

I tug on some black jeans, the fly straining as I inch it up over my tummy and suck in my gut to get the top rivet fastened. I dig around in the closet for the long-sleeved shirt I saw a minute ago. Pulling it over my head, I take a peek in the mirror, hoping the black on black will work its slimming magic, but instead, exposed by the V-neck, there's a distressing expanse of cleavage and doughy double-chins. When did *that* happen? I snatch a silky turquoise scarf from my dresser drawer and tie it around my neck, hoping it stays in place.

Working in Honeywell's was always just something I did to pass the time after Madison started school. I never put any thought into marketing – I don't even know what marketing is, if I'm being honest. Xavier thought the bakery could be a big success when I first inherited it and took over from Grandad. That's when we painted it blue. But I just kept it going the only way I knew how, and it worked, until now. Now, it's failing. I'm a good baker, but even I don't know how to rescue a fallen cake.

Rifling through my jewelry box for a pair of earrings, my collection of rings winks at me. It hurts, the way that traitorous engagement ring mocks me. I slide it face-down in its slot. One day I will wear it again, but for tonight I'll wear a different ring.

After Xavier left me, Jane encouraged me to ask the condo landlords to sublet, and they found someone immediately. A few weeks later, I crawled in here with Mother.

"Just until Xavier gets over his..." I waved my hands around. "...his midlife crisis. Or whatever this is."

Mother had said, "As long as it's temporary. You don't want to get dependent on me, and I can't afford to have you hanging around, cramping my style."

"Your style?" I laughed. "As far as I can tell you never leave the house. Whatever happened to Sabrina, and those ladies you used to lunch with and play bridge?"

She didn't answer, just walked away to fix herself another martini.

That was in January, when Jane told me 'temporary' was endurable. Now, it feels interminable.

I select the brilliant blue topaz Grandad gave me, years ago, before I was even married, and twist it onto my pinky, the only finger it fits anymore. But the pinky bulges and turns red, so I twist it off again, and toss it back in the box.

This is ridiculous. Absolutely nothing fits.

Over the eerie sad opening theme song of *The Bridge,* I hear Mother calling from her room. "Don't forget to feed the cat."

I hurry out of my room and down the stairs shouting, "Yes, my liege."

Now that we have a kitten – yes, we have a kitten, I'm fifty-two years old and I'm finally allowed to have a kitten – Mother is more exasperating than ever.

Since the night of the snowstorm, I've had to pick up every kitten gizmo in the world on the way home from work. Mother keeps coming up with them, phoning me at the bakery with her latest idea. She gave me her credit card to buy a battery operated no-smell litter box; cute matching water and food dishes; toy mice; catnip; a collar; a harness; a round bed; scratching post; a feathery bird on a rod; ping pong balls; and toy mice, this time with the catnip *inside* them. I've never seen her spend so recklessly, she usually has very deep pockets. And, I don't know why she can't go out during the day and get these things herself, but she won't. She just fools around with the cat all day, and drinks martinis.

"His name is Wallander," she declared.

"Why do *you* get to decide what his name is? I think it should be something more – more kitty-cattish."

"It's Wallander," she insisted.

"That's not a good cat name."

"Why not? He's smart and smooth like Wallander, and he likes it. Don't you Wallander? Mr. Puss Puss McCutey-pie." The kitten, sitting on her lap, closed his eyes in bliss as she stroked his chin and forehead. So, Wallander it is.

I zip the top off a tiny tin of cat food and following the aroma of salmon-delight, he rushes for it and begins feasting, his tiny eyes squinting in pleasure as he eats.

It's mind-boggling how endearing he is. I crouch down, to tickle his head while he eats, my jeans straining.

In an instant I can tell there's too much stress on the fabric. I need to get to my feet fast!

But I can't.

I feel the seam rip...right up my bum.

Crispy-critters! Maybe I'll just wear my bathrobe to Biz Buzz and be done with it!

I struggle to my feet.

Can I get away with a ripped bum seam?

I pull down on the top. It's nice and long, to my thighs, and I very much doubt anyone will be checking out my butt. It's okay.

"I'm glad to see you're making an effort." Mother startles the heck out of me, standing in the kitchen doorway with an empty martini glass. "But those jeans look..."

"Look what?" I demand.

"Never mind." She crosses the kitchen to the bar cart in the dining room.

Ugh, she's right, I've got to get these jeans off. I can barely breathe. I rush back up to my room as fast as my knees will take me, and search through the closet one more time.

At the far end, hiding behind an old blazer, are some black slacks folded over a hanger. Hello. What are these?

They look roomy. I don't even remember buying them.

Rubbing with my fingernail at the dusty crease that will fall across my thighs, I wonder if I have time to give them a quick spritz and a press. Will anyone notice? Or care?

The black pants slide easily over my hips and I turn to peer at myself in the mirror over my dressing table. Do they really fit?

Over the stretchy waistband, my midriff puffs only slightly. These pants are comfier than the jeans I had on. I twist and turn.

But they're awfully baggy. Do they look like clown pants?

Suddenly I remember where they came from.

I bought them when Xavier's grandmother died.

We'd attended her funeral.

Twenty-one years ago.

Why did I not notice and throw them away a few months ago when I packed to move in here?

I peer into the mirror.

The extra poundage on my body is distributed differently now than it was back then. However, there's no denying it. These pregnancy pants fit.

I look at my jeans, discarded like a wrinkly snakeskin on the floor. Wearing them actually hurt.

Will anyone notice I'm wearing maternity clothes?

NINE

The Lakeside Realty's boardroom, where the first session of Biz Buzz is meeting, is on the second floor. Next to the hum of a busy glassed-in real estate office, full of agents on phones and the clickety-clack of computer keyboards, a wide stairwell reaches up into darkness. It's about three times taller than the staircase at Mother's house.

I curse under my breath as I begin the ascent of my own personal Kilimanjaro.

Jane actually went over to Africa to climb the famed mountain. She trained for months at the gym so she could scale it and back with a group of other climbers. When she got home, she showed me reams of photographs, and of course, her monkey tattoo.

If sales really do improve, maybe I'll invest in a gym membership, as Jane has been urging for years. Possibly after Physio. Or my yoga practice. I'm not sure. All I know is I need to exercise these knees.

Halfway up the stairs, I pause, chest heaving, knees and thighs burning, begging me to stop. I glance over the handrail on my right, down into the Realtor's office, hoping none of them are watching the fat lady lug herself up to the second floor. Thankfully, they all seem occupied.

Shouldn't a swanky real estate office have an elevator? Surely, their clients and staff aren't able to all trip up these stairs, fandango.

"*What* are you doing?"

It's Jane. She's come in through the street door and is now standing below me in the hallway between the office and the staircase.

"Hey," I gasp, glad to see her. "What does it look like I'm doing?"

She crosses her arms and suddenly, I'm worried. Did I misread the location of the seminar? "It's in the second-floor boardroom, isn't it?"

"It is – but why are you taking the stairs when there's an elevator right here?" She points to her right, at what, I can't see. "I'll meet you up there," she says, disappearing.

I force myself up a few more stairs.

Why didn't I investigate the entranceway when I arrived?

I've never needed to come inside this building before.

Never bought or sold a house.

And I'm not acquainted with any of the people who work here who are a world unto themselves, driving fancy cars, wearing stylish clothes and haircuts. I know some of their names from signs around the neighbourhood, but I don't *know* any of them.

I climb a few more steps.

Not unlike the medical building's offices, the realtor's boardroom is glassed in by windows. Thankfully, as I reach the summit and traipse by, the vertical blinds are shut. Jane, dressed in a sleeveless leopard-print shift is waiting for me by the elevator.

I motion that I need a beat to catch my breath before we go inside.

I put my hands on my knees, instantly reminding myself that I've been reduced to wearing maternity pants. Or rather, the opposite – I've been *enlarged* to wearing them. It's mortifying. What if someone notices?

Hendrick swings open the door and makes a big fuss over Jane's dress.

A few businesswomen from Lakeside are already seated at the table, engaged in the usual shoptalk and gossip.

"Hey, Trudy!" Jessica calls. She runs Dressica, a trendy clothing store, and I'm amazed she's here. I deliver Crumb-less to her every other day and her shop always looks fantastic. I wonder what she expects to learn at Biz Buzz – she seems to know what she's doing. If I could fit into her sizes, and had money, I'd be spending up a storm.

Debbie, from Debbie Does Nails, barges through the doorway past me. "Jane, Trudy, hi!" She's dressed as if she just stepped out of a jeans ad, wearing open-toed strappy sandals, showing off her perfect pedicure.

Sylvia Martin is talking earnestly to Suzy who looks at me, wiggling her fingers in greeting.

They're all here. I'm glad I came, even if I am still perspiring and breathless. I squeeze past Jane and Hendrick's doorway conversation and into the delicious coolness of the boardroom. Pulling out a puffy black office chair, I sink into it gratefully as it lets out a long, loud, filibustering, fart.

Oh, my gawd! What next?

Suzy snickers but Sylvia Martin, deaf to anything but her own voice, prattles on.

Behind me, the elevator dings, and more shop owners from Lakeside, mostly women, crowd into the room and take seats.

I don't know whether to be relieved or nervous that Coco is not here.

On the hour, Hendrick steps to the top of the table, leans his long-tented fingers on its shiny surface and says, "Okay, who's ready to take control of their business?"

For the next 30 minutes he speaks at a dazzling pace. Branding. Positioning. Awareness. He tells us he's an expert in Gorilla marketing, and I laugh, but I'm the only one. Jane shoots an annoyed look at me. Apparently, he wasn't trying to be funny. I'm not sure I understand what's going on here.

Hendrick evangelizes:

"You must.... You should.... You have to.... You need."

All around me participants nod and scribble notes on the pads of paper in front of them. The cold temperature of the room is keeping everyone alert.

But I'm having a hard time keeping up with all the concepts and jargon he's throwing at us and into his anecdotes about businesses that have skyrocketed after implementing his strategies. I'm thankful when he finally stops and says, "Let's take a ten-minute break, shall we?"

Everyone crowds toward the refreshment table in the corner of the room, chattering like school kids. When I finally get close enough to see what's on offer, I'm disappointed. There's no food, just juice bottles, coffee and tea in tall white urns, and boxes of herbal teas for those who prefer it. Then I remember – I'm on a diet and wearing pregnancy pants. I should be thankful there are no snacks. But I'm not.

I select a *healthy* cranberry cocktail and pour myself a cup of coffee to warm me up. I'm stirring in a packet of low-cal sweetener when Suzy sidles up and says, "So...what do you think?"

"I'm..." I struggle to find a word that will sound positive, and at the same time won't reveal how dumb I am. Hendrick's presentation is leading-edge, I'm sure, but how does any of it apply to me and my little bakery?

Suzy confesses, without a shred of self-consciousness, "It's going right over my head."

Great! I'm not the only one.

Jane squeezes in beside us to fix herself a peppermint tea, and Suzy asks, giggling, "What are *you* doing here? Do shrinks need marketing?"

"Actually," Jane tells us in a serious, self-important tone. "My landlord asked me to attend on his behalf. He's paying for it. *My idea.* He wants the Wellness Center to attract more practitioners, so here I am – his eyes and ears."

Suzy and I nod.

Our two businesses are in leased shops next door to one another. Mrs. Landi, who owns our building, is an old woman who moved to Florida and hasn't been back to Lakeside in years. She probably hasn't a clue how Maple Street is changing and developing. More than one person has remarked to me how lucky I am to have a long lease because rents are going through the roof.

"Lots of fun stuff, huh?" Jane asks, with a nod toward Hendrick, who is now fussing with a laptop and a screen at the head of the table.

"Mm hm," I agree, but I can't open the cranberry juice while holding my cup and saucer, so, I turn and motion with my head toward our seats. Suzy leads the way through the throng of talking, laughing, women.

The second half of Hendrick's presentation takes a different tack. He shows us an impressive slideshow of before and after pictures of storefronts, and a few interiors. We all murmur and gasp in appreciation at the transformations.

Finished with the slides, he flicks the overhead lights back on.

I rub my arms; they're covered in goosebumps. It's too cold in here.

"Now, let's talk about *you*." He starts at the top of the table, and one by one, asks each person a different question about their business. When he comes to me, he asks, "Trudy, what is your target market?" When I stare at him, baffled, he rephrases. "Who does your bakery cater to?"

"Oh, I don't do catering," I answer.

Everyone laughs.

He tilts his head at me and his brow puckers. "No. I mean, what kind of customers do you appeal to?"

Ohhhh. Why didn't he say that in the first place?

I think of my customers. Suzy. Dr. Gertie. People who come in every day, or a few days a week at least. I've known most of them for years. They're like me, I suppose, regular people. Maybe *I* am my target customer? That would be handy.

I must look too dumbfounded, because he doesn't wait for me to offer a response.

"That's a problem," he says. "And I'm going to help you nail down your target market. All of you!"

My cheeks warm.

He moves on to Jane and she engages intelligently with him about something-or-other.

How was I supposed to know the answer to his question? I've never thought about this stuff before. I've just gone into the bakery every day for the last fifteen years and done what needed to be done – as my grandfather did before me. What's wrong with that?

I hate being put on the spot.

It's true, the bakery is experiencing a rough patch, but I'm trimming expenses wherever I can. I've tried sourcing less expensive suppliers for ingredients – but

I have to keep my quality up to snuff, my customers expect it. As my lightbulbs burn out, I'm switching them over to LEDs, which cost an arm and a leg compared to the regular kind, but apparently, I'll see an impact soon on my hydro bill. I cut back on staff, which means I have no choice but to cover the counter more often, but that's okay. It's not like the days when Madison was in school and I had to be home for her. I can stay later every day, now that there's no one to cook dinner for.

On the other side of the equation, I know I need to increase sales. But that's the problem. Lately, it's been impossible. I don't know why. Probably it's a cycle I just need to wait out. Maybe everyone's on a diet.

"So," Hendrick says, after he's finished grilling everyone at the table. "Who here has a Social Media presence?"

Heads around the table swivel as some raise their hands while others look panicky or puzzled.

"Okay, Debbie. Tell us about your campaign."

Debbie's always trying to look younger than she is. Tight pants, high heels, dyed blonde hair, and of course, the nails. "My daughter told me I could attract clients with a FlipFlop account. So, she set me up and all I do is send photos and videos to it every day and it does the rest." She punctuates the table with her silver fingernails. "It's fun. And clients *love* posing their fingers after a great nail-job. I snap, send it to FlipFlop, and presto – I'm gaining travelers *galore*."

"Splendid!" Hendrick says. "You see how easy that is?"

Everyone nods, but I think, how ridiculous. I've heard of FlipFlop.lol, of course. It's something for teenagers and silly cat photos.

"Homework, ladies!" Hendrick announces, clapping his hands. "By next week, I want each of you to open a FlipFlop account and add me as a traveler: @The-Hendrick. Post at least *one* picture. It's a first step! Easy, peasy." He snaps his fingers. "We'll be working on your brand manifesto and targeting over the next couple of weeks, but this is something you can start immediately. Any questions?"

I'm not going to admit I have no idea what he's talking about, and even if I did, it's ludicrous. Suzy looks at me and crosses her eyes. I stifle a giggle. I assume she's not doing the homework either.

How can sending photographs to a mindless social media site for teenagers possibly improve sales at Honeywell's? And where am I supposed to find the time? I'm up every day at the crack of dawn baking, and serving customers at the counter whenever Eve isn't there. When I get home from work, I tidy the house and look after Mother and her nonsense. I'm too tired to take evening classes. I regret signing up for this. I don't know if I want to come back next week.

"One more thing!" Hendrick announces. "By next session, I want a written paragraph from each of you on your target market. Over the next few days, take a good look at your customers, *and* at your competition's customers. Who are they? Why are they your target? Got it?"

That seals the deal. None of this makes sense, and I don't have time for it.

Yet around the table there's no dissent, and I wonder – are they all really going to do what he says? Or are they keeping their mouths shut because it's so flipping cold in this air-conditioning and everyone's dying to get out into the warm evening air like I am.

When he opens the door and releases us, people start down the staircase in gaggles and pairs. Jane links her arm in my elbow. "Elevator?" she says. I'm grateful for her.

TEN

Though I'm considering dropping out of Biz Buzz, and asking "*the* Hendrick" to tear up my cheque, I can't stop wondering about the effectiveness of FlipFlop. Could it really help Honeywell's?

Maybe I'm completely out of the loop about what it does. Oh sure, I've seen pictures on other people's phones when they flash them in my face. Cats, dogs, dresses, babies. Even Jane took a picture of the two of us at the divorce party and put it on FlipFlop. She somehow turned her camera screen around and snapped a picture of us together, giggling like teenagers, our heads tilted toward each other.

That was when the plastic tiara was still upright on my head, before I got sloppy and overheated and my makeup started melting.

That blasted party. My cheeks still sizzle when I think of it.

Never mind.

It can't hurt to investigate a FlipFlop account for the bakery. Surely, I don't need to pay Hendrick a wad of money to do it. Jane told me 'The App' is free.

In the privacy and comfort of my bedroom, I open my laptop and search for FlipFlop.lol. Right away, the website pops up. I click on the sign-up screen and enter my email address.

I wait.

A message pops up, telling me I must go to my email and click on something there.

I launch my account.

There's an email from Madison!

I open it eagerly, hoping she's answered my questions about her wedding. When is it going to be? *Where* is it going to be?

But all she's sent is a photo of herself, driving a motor boat. Behind her in the turquoise and white sea, a water-skier waves.

I'm hurt. Why is she freezing me out? Is she sharing everything about her wedding with Xavier?

I sigh in annoyance, at the same time reminding myself to think positively and stop fretting. My daughter is getting married and, as Jane pointed out, I'm the Mother-of-the-Bride! She may be a little young, but it will be wonderful. We'll reconnect, and no matter what, I'll make sure she has the wedding of her dreams.

I examine the photograph filling my screen. Madison is driving a boat. I'm proud of her, and thrilled. She doesn't even have a license to drive a car. She's growing up so fast in Croatia.

I too used to drive a boat – long ago. My grandfather's family owned a lakeside cottage and every summer I spent a few weeks there with my cousins.

Grandad taught us all about motorboating. He took us fishing, showed us how to start the engine, and how to refill the gas tank at the marina. One year, he bought water-skis and taught us how to get up on the surface as he zipped us around the small lake. They were smooth-bottomed banana skis, and I think he bought them because they were short, and we were kids. He didn't know that learning to ski would've been a lot easier with fins on the skis. Gradually, as the summer days went by, we each learned to let the yellow rope suspend our weight behind the boat – be one with the pull – get up on top, and keep the skis steady on the water.

"Tips up!" we'd yell at whichever kid was in the water readying for their turn to ski.

I got pretty good at skiing. I even learned how to drop a ski and slalom. I marvel at it now, studying Madison's photo. I was once like her – out on the water, the wind in my face, happy to be conquering life.

I try, without success, to push from my mind the incident.

It happened when I was twelve and just beginning to get curves. Mother was preoccupied with my weight, always watching me when I ate, always shaking her head at me. At the beginning of that summer, she went shopping *without me* and bought my first two-piece bathing suit. It was yellow.

"I'm surprised it's so loose," she said, tugging at me, turning me around, giving me a playful smack on my rear end. "Don't worry, at the rate you're going, you'll fill it out in no time."

The bottoms were slack in the seat, the cups gaped in the top, and the color was hideous. But my swimsuit from the previous summer was too tight, practically cutting me in half up the bum, so I had no choice but to wear the ugly yellow two-piece.

The sun was high, the water icy cold, and for the first time that year it was my turn to ski.

With the life-jacket on, I jumped from the boat into the water. Brr. Shocking, refreshing, exhilarating.

Grandad threw me the rope as I pulled on the skis – not an easy task while floating and struggling against the tug of a life-jacket. Finally, the rubber footholds felt snug around my bare feet. I braced myself in the water holding tight to the rope's handle.

"Hit it!" I yelled joyfully.

I felt so free at the cottage, so thrilled to be alive, it was my thirteenth summer and my cousins and Grandparents loved me. With a roar of the fifty-horsepower motor, the boat pulled me out of the depths and as I found my balance, I shook the water from my face and hair. The skis rumbled across the wake.

Though tingling with the glory of my body defying gravity, I felt the bottom of my bathing suit begin to slide down my bum. Holding the ski-rope with one hand, I grabbed at my bottoms before they could slide any further. Grandad was facing forward in the boat, driving, so he didn't see what was happening, but my cousins had front-row seats and they were pointing at me, laughing hysterically as I skied along grabbing at my sagging bathing suit.

Once more, I twisted to grasp it, and that's when the tips of my skis caught the wake and I launched forward, flying through the air, my ass to the seagulls. My legs tangled, a ski flew off, and I landed with a face full of hard bubbly water rushing up my nose.

Underwater, I struggled to free my other foot from the buoyant ski. The life-jacket pulled me to the surface and I sputtered for air, nose stinging. The boat, I could see, was heading back toward me. The skis floated nearby as I waited, humiliated, for my grandfather to circle around me.

The other kids were still screaming with laughter and pointing to the left of me as the boat drew near. I turned and saw the yellow bottoms of my swimsuit floating a few yards away.

Grandad cut the engine and I swam toward the boat, which was bobbing in the lake.

One of my cousins jumped in as I freed myself from the buckles of the life-jacket. She collected the skis, and my swimsuit, and flung it like a banana peel into the boat. The other kids laughed their heads off.

I clung to the ladder at the back of the boat, cringing with embarrassment. Finally, my grandfather held a towel for me and I scrambled up into the boat. He wrapped it around me, and retrieved the shriveled yellow bikini bottom.

I shudder to think about it.

I wish I could forget.

After that, I refused to wear the bathing suit ever again. The traitor.

My cousins loved to tell the story over and over. I tried to shrug it off, let it roll off me as just a funny anecdote, water off a duck's back, right? But it was excruciating, and now, all these years later, I still wince as if reliving it.

I close Madison's email and try to remember what I was doing before I read it, and who I am now.

Oh, yes. FlipFlop.lol.

After carefully reading the directions, I click on the link, and I'm back to the first screen where I must enter my email, again, and a password.

It rejects the password I come up with: waterski. It wants a number, and a special character.

What's a special character?

I reread the directions. It's an asterisk, a dollar sign, etcetera.

I try a new password: 1water$ki. Very clever.

Now it wants a capital letter.

Argh.

This is why no one uses these dumb apps!

Except, that's not true. *Everyone* uses these apps. It's just me who can't figure them out.

Part of my mind is still dragging along on the water-skiing episode.

When Mother found out I'd bared my bum to the world, she scolded me, forbade me from skiing.

I cried, but I knew she wouldn't be able to enforce it – she was just being a disciplinarian to me to show off in front of her friend Sabrina who was visiting. Skiing was the focus of my summer holiday and nothing could keep me away from it.

Aunts, Uncles, and Sabrina took turns teasing me, or soothing me. While Mother kept repeating, "It wouldn't have happened if she hadn't been *grandstanding*."

Grandad took me aside and told me I was a very different type of fish than my mother, which for some reason made me feel good.

Anyway, Mother forgot about it, and made no effort to keep me from the water. She was busy tanning and chatting with the adults. I wore a t-shirt and cutoff shorts for the rest of the summer and continued to enjoy everything to do with the lake – skiing, fishing, swimming.

"Fat floats," I overheard Sabrina say to Mother with a shrug of her shoulders.

Like a kaleidoscope, the FlipFlop website opens in front of me. "Welcome Trudy Asp!" It prompts, "Add a photo. Add some travelers."

What?

I stare in bafflement as videos pop up and instructions with flashing arrows tell me to take a tour.

I don't need this aggravation.

I snap shut the lid on my laptop, push away from the dressing table, and flop face forward onto my bed.

ELEVEN

It's stressing me out that Xavier, and therefore Zelda, are probably fully briefed on Madison's wedding and I'm still clueless. It should be *me* who knows everything before anyone else – *I'm* the Mother-of-the-Bride.

"You need to call him," Jane says, when she pops into the bakery to say hello.

"I know," I answer, miserably. "But I don't want to."

"Why?"

"Because if he knows all about the wedding, and I call asking questions, he'll know I don't know. And I don't want him to know that I don't know. I don't want him to know I'm..." I pause.

"You're what?"

I look away, feeling really sorry for myself. "I'm left out."

Jane puts her ringed fingers on my shoulders and studies me. "Remember the day you bumped into Zelda in the doctor's office?"

"Yea," I answer, wondering if she's about to start shaking me.

She lets me go and asks, "Have you booked those tests, by the way?"

"Not yet," I snap at her. "What about the day I bumped into Zelda?"

"You told me, she didn't seem to know anything more about the wedding than you did." Jane shrugs. "Maybe Xavier doesn't know anything either."

She could be right.

But that was a couple of weeks ago.

He probably knows more now.

"There's only one way to find out, Trudy."

I wait until my lunch-break to call from the phone on my desk in the backroom. I don't have to look up his phone number – it's the same one we shared for twenty-one years. I'm not sure how he wangled it, but suddenly the phone in the condo was disconnected, and he was using our old number. He simply got custody of it without telling me.

That's when Jane took me shopping for a cell. However, I don't use it for this call.

As I press in the number, I'm flooded with memories of our condo, picturing the phone jangling on the end table beside the couch. Some odd recess of my brain believes Xavier still lives in our old home, which of course he doesn't. I packed up the whole place alone, forced to deal with all the stuff he left behind – his hockey magazines and board games, our wedding gifts and mementos, family photographs, a picture of him and me in my grandfather's boat – stuff he didn't take with him.

His phone rings and rings before finally, an answering service clicks on.

My blood screeches to a halt when Zelda's voice croons: "You've reached Xavier and Zelda, we're not—"

No, no, no!

I slam the receiver into the phone cradle.

I will not leave a message!

I sit frazzled in the back of the bakery, kneading over my marriage, wondering for the millionth time, what went wrong?

I'm supposed to want to move on, but I don't. I just want him back. If he'd just give me a chance...

I pick miserably at pieces of my 5-grain sandwich and pop them into my mouth. Occasionally, I take deep draws on a tall mauve smoothie, concentrating on calming down. Finally, when practically all that's left in the wrapper are tomato slices and lettuce, I notice Dr. Gertie's requisition slip propped against the lamp on my desk. Argh, I still have to book an appointment for my tests.

Polishing off the last of the sandwich, I call the number on the top of the slip, which has been on my desk now for well over a week. In a matter of minutes, I have a day of tests booked. No eating the night before. I anticipate the miserable morning I will have that day. Not unlike today.

Getting up from my desk, I fetch a broken cookie from this morning's batch. Eating it makes me feel better the way only a cookie can. I really do bake the best cookies in Lakeside. I wonder, half-heartedly, what they're selling over at Coco's? I could go over there and take a look. But I don't want to. I'd rather not know what she's up to.

Like a demon compass, my mind swivels back to Xavier, and it dawns on me that it's safer to call him at his office. He's a sports announcer at a television station and I know his schedule like I know my own. Usually, he takes his lunch break around one o'clock.

Like an epitaph, his work number is also chiseled in my brain.

When his assistant Michelle answers, her voice is like that of a long-lost friend, and I'm struck again by everything I've lost.

"Michelle, it's Trudy!" I greet her, feeling the comfort of reconnecting with a woman I spoke to over the telephone daily, though I only met her in person a few times at Christmas parties.

"Trudy?" she answers, as though trying to place me. "Oh Trudy! Yes, hello." She sounds less enthusiastic to hear from me than I feel about her, which is embarrassing. How naïve of me to believe we were friends.

I get to the point. "Is Xavier around?"

"I'm sorry, he's not," she says, offering no further explanation. I'm pretty sure she used to reassure me that she'd tell him I called, but she says nothing like that to me now.

My face tingles, as though I've been caught doing something bad.

Why am I calling him? Why am I worrying about all this wedding stuff? The event isn't imminent, or I'd know about it. Why am I rushing things?

Finally, into the silence of the line, Michelle asks, "Do you want him to call you?"

"Sure," I gasp, grateful she's finally come to life. "It's not important. Not an emergency. Just have him call. At the bakery, or on my cell phone." I leave my new number; in case he's lost it.

For the rest of the workday, I carry my phone in my pocket, something I swore I'd never do. Cell phones don't belong at work. They belong in purses.

I check it a thousand times.

Make sure it's on.

Make sure the volume is up.

Between customers, I check for missed calls.

Is he really going to ignore me?

Is he really not calling me back?

TWELVE

_{▾·▾·▾·▾·▾}

In the window of Dressica is a skinny mannequin wearing a fuchsia tulle dress with a floppy sun hat and white sunglasses. I wish I could wear something fashionable like that.

Jessica, behind the counter, is sorting through boxes of sunglasses. She pushes all the junk aside so I can set down her box of Crumb-less, and asks me, "How goes it this morning?"

"I'm hanging in there," I tell her, and she smiles, continuing to unwrap sunglasses and set them in the spin rack beside the counter.

Truthfully, my knees are really hurting. I don't know how much longer I can keep doing these morning deliveries. I might have to send Eve out to do them. Yet it feels like I need the social contact, however brief. Living with Mother makes me restless. And I need the exercise – goodness knows I don't have time to do anything like go to a gym.

I look around Jessica's shop. A summer sale has turned the place upside down. The racks are messy, and the folded t-shirts jumbled, but I drink in the bright colors of the season. She has such playful taste – I only wish she stocked larger sizes. There must be a market for women like me.

I can at least shop for sunglasses. I begin looking over the selection, wondering what would suit my face.

Jessica is sipping on a tall green concoction. "What's that?" I ask as I try on a pair of white frames with dark lenses like the ones I saw on the mannequin in the window. They look preposterous on me and I snatch them off before she catches a look.

"Kale smoothie," she answers between draws on the straw.

Ick, revolting.

"Really?" I ask, "Is that good?"

"Oh, yes. And packed with nutrients. I blend a ripe banana, a scoop of protein powder, two cups of soya milk, and a handful of kale. Delicious. I can write down the recipe for you if you want."

"Oh sure," I agree, even though there's a full fridge at home that has none of those ingredients in it. I just grocery shopped last night and filled my cart with diet foods: salads, menu-lite dinners, apples, grapes, low-cal soda, low-fat yogurt, and cottage cheese. No kale, no soya milk. What even is protein powder?

I try on a pair of glamorous oversized glasses. They look quite amazing from what I can tell in the tiny mirror at the top of the spin rack. Strangely, the movie-star-look suits the sweep of my hair, parted on the side, and my full cheeks.

Something vibrates against my thigh, and I think for a moment we're having an earthquake. I look at Jessica but she's calmly unpackaging sunglasses. With another vibration I realize it's the phone in my purse. I scramble to answer.

It's Xavier. Finally, after two days, he's calling me back.

To my breathless, "Hello?" he responds, "Hey, what's up?" The familiar words and timbre of his voice in my ear turn me into a jellyfish.

I probably ought not talk to him within Jessica's earshot, but I think it's okay, she's distracted straightening up the folded t-shirts on a table display, and a customer has come into the shop. I turn my back to both of them and look out the window at Maple Street, my heart pounding.

Pressing the phone to my ear, I say, "I wanted to talk to you about Madison's wedding."

"Oh that," he replies, and I can almost hear his eyes rolling. I'm surprised – I thought he favoured snap-decision weddings.

I ask, "What do you mean, 'Oh that'?"

"Nothing. Nothing," he answers. "I just think it's a bit rash. Don't you?"

"Of course, I think it's rash! She only went over there six weeks ago, and already she's met someone and is getting married? It's incredible."

"Surprised the hell out of me."

I ask. "Have you met the boy?"

It's painful for me to make mention of his trip to Croatia with Zelda, but he may as well know that I know. To retain my composure, I must pretend I'm okay with it all, not rocked with hurt and jealousy. I don't have a chance of reestablishing a relationship with him if I'm weepy, or shrewish.

"Yea, I met Matt," he answers, nonchalantly. "A nice kid. But then a couple weeks later, she dropped it on me that they were getting married – I was bowled over. I didn't know they were even dating."

The event that precipitated *our* decision to marry swims to the surface of my mind. A morning in bed when we were visiting friends for the weekend, and I'd forgotten to bring my sponge – Xavier gently insisting, "One time, Babe. It'll be fine."

It was not fine.

I missed two periods before I finally got up the nerve to tell him.

I whisper into the phone, "I hope she's not pregnant."

"Me too!" he agrees emphatically, in a way that suggests he doesn't want for his daughter the fate that befell him. Biggest mistake of his life, or something like that. My eyes sting a little.

"Has she given you any idea of a date?" I ask. "A location?"

"Uh..." he stalls. "Not really. I think it'll be the end of August; an island called Vis; a place called King George's Garrison."

So, it *will* be overseas. My stomach drops.

Xavier pauses. "We're trying to talk her out of it."

Wait. What? *We?*

Now, his voice lowers. "I'm not sure I should be talking to you about this."

Feeling a little panicky, I interrogate, "*Why not?*"

"Uh...it's just..." He stalls again.

I know him inside out. There's something he's not saying.

Finally, he spills it. "Zelda is planning a destination wedding too."

The blood in my veins slows to a thick, cold, sludge.

"So...?" I wait for him to elaborate on the significance of Zelda's plan.

There's silence on the line for a few moments. My cheeks begin to flare and my recalcitrant eyes tingle with tears. This can't be real. I cannot be talking to the husband I still love about his upcoming nuptials with someone else. This cannot be happening.

"Zelda *loves* Croatia," he continues, digging the knife in a little deeper. "And she is thinking of having *our* wedding there at the end of August. So...it's not possible for Madison to have hers at the same time." He chuckles, enraging me, "I can't be at two ceremonies at once."

It's not enough she's ruined my life, that damn Zelda is now interfering in Madison's! How dare she? I'm so furious I'm unable to form any words.

It feels as if someone bumped me right now, I'd capsize.

My lips pressed tightly together – I stare out the Dressica window as shadowy pedestrians pass by in the mirage of bright morning glare.

"Trudy? Are you there? Hello?"

"I'm here." I breathe.

"I should go," he says. "I'll let you know when I hear something. Okay?"

The line goes dead. I feel like screaming. If I could reach through the phone and gouge his eyes out, I would. How dare he leave me? How dare he hurt me? How dare he abandon me? I hate him!

Jessica's hand touches my shoulder and I jump out of my skin. "Are you okay?" she asks.

I spin around, right into her sympathetic expression and burst into angry tears, realizing as my hands cover my face that I'm still wearing the glamorous sunglasses I haven't paid for.

"Oh, Honey," she says, gathering me in.

The bell on the door jingles as the customer, probably sensing an emotional tsunami is cresting, scoots past us. Jessica holds me as I weep against her shoulder, right there in the middle of the workday, in the middle of her store.

"Come on," she says. "Wipe away those tears. Was that Xavier? Come sit down over here."

I follow her to behind the counter and hoist a thigh onto one of her tall stools. Setting the sunglasses on the counter, I gather my purse onto my lap and search around in it for a tissue.

Jessica perches on the other stool and pats my knee. She must have overheard my side of the conversation and filled in the blanks. She probably knows the whole sordid story by now anyway, if not from me then from someone else. It's the gossip topic of the month around town. Xavier and Zelda. And poor Trudy was the last to know.

She asks, "Do you want to know what I heard?"

I sniff, swiping at my runny nose. "What?"

She hesitates, and suddenly I don't want to know.

I don't want to get sucked into the whirlpool of Lakeside gossip and backstabbing.

Especially if it might hurt me more. But it's too late to stop her.

"I think you should know," she tells me, leaning forward. "I heard that Zelda is planning a double wedding for her and Madison."

What?

I clap my hands over my mouth, as though that will help me from hearing Jessica's words.

"It's just talk, Trudy. Who knows if it's true." She pauses, but there's more. "The *other* thing I heard, was if they don't do a double wedding, on account of your fear of flying, Zelda said she will stand in for you. In case you can't make it over to Europe yourself."

THIRTEEN

Alone in the Lakeside Realty elevator, I push the button for the second-floor boardroom. This time, I won't be all hot and sweaty when I get up there.

The elevator dings, the doors glide open, and I realize I've arrived for the second night of Biz Buzz early. At least it's warmer in here than last time – they must've fixed the A/C.

I'm determined to stick with Hendrick's group now. I *need* Honeywell's to pay me a good salary now, so I can fly to Europe for Madison's wedding. There's not a snowball's chance in Hell I'm letting Zelda force Madison into a double wedding ceremony *or* stand in for me as Mother-of-the-Bride.

I don't know how I'll survive the plane ride, but I'm determined to fly!

Maybe hypnosis. I could ask Jane if she has a colleague.

But that would cost.

All the more reason to give Biz Buzz my full attention.

No one else is here yet so I have a clear view of the snack table. Tonight, there is actual food on it, which I'm glad to see, because if I'm spending this money on business lessons, I might as well get my money's worth on the snacks.

Under a sheet of cellophane are some nice-looking muffins, cookies, cannoli, and lemon squares. I'm tempted to pile an assortment onto a plate, but then, oops, I remember, I'm on a diet.

I'll resist for now and wait until coffee break before I partake.

A hot drink isn't necessary tonight, it's warm enough in here, so instead I just take a sparkling raspberry-lemon. The cap twists off with a satisfying fizz. I pour the bubbles into a tall glass, and take a seat on the opposite side of the table from where I sat last week. Someone else can sit on the farting chair.

Everyone arrives and the class begins with what Hendrick calls Show & Share. He goes around the table, and to my surprise my fellow store owners have *all* done their homework. I'm not sure what miracle they're expecting, but at least I understand the way they describe their customers – they're not using the million-dollar marketing words that Hendrick does. When it's my turn, if I can summon the nerve, I'm just going to say, "Ditto – what she said."

But, of course, when he gets to me, I don't dare have the nerve and I find myself babbling about my Crumb-less cookie customers and how they're my best. My target. Whatever.

"And your competition?" Hendrick asks, an eyebrow arched.

I begin to sweat. It's really warm in here. I think I preferred last week's ice box.

"My competition..." Think. Think. What am I supposed to say? "There aren't any other bakeries in Lakeside." I shrug, then I remember Coco's. "Except, a new bakery opened across the street from me. But it's a 'gluten-free bakery' so..."

Hendrick swirls his hand at me. "Go on."

I'm rattled. I haven't looked into finding out what a gluten-free bakery actually is, so I just relate how Coco came into my shop the other day to ask about my Crumb-less cookies. Her black-lined eyes bore straight into mine as she told me: "I ate one of your cookies at Dressica. They're awesome. How did you do it? No crumbs."

"She asked for the recipe," I tell the group. "Which I'm not going to give her. *Obviously.*" I wonder if this is what Hendrick means by outmaneuvering the competition. Cut throat tactics. Secret recipes. Maybe I *do* know how to do this.

"Okay," he says. "Any other competitors you've identified?"

Didn't he hear me when I said there are no other bakeries in Lakeside?

I shrug, wishing he'd move along to someone else. "Not really."

"Can anyone help Trudy out? Any ideas who her competition might be?"

There's a moment of silence in the room. We haven't been asked to do any brainstorming up until now, although Hendrick has warned it will be included.

Finally, Debbie taps her fingernails on the table and says, "The coffee shop?"

I snort.

The coffee shop!

They sell coffee and sandwiches and muffins and stuff.

They aren't my competition.

"The grocery store?" Jessica suggests, and instantly I'm insulted.

Doesn't she realize I sell *quality* at Honeywell's?

Sylvia Martin states, nodding authoritatively, "Crosstown Pâtisserie." A few women make the "Mmmm," sound.

Crosstown Pâtisserie? They're...they're all the way across town!

Hendrick nods, as though he agrees with all of these stupid stabs in the dark, and then snaps off the room lights. He clicks something on his laptop so a screen illuminates behind him with a picture of my FlipFlop account. Oh no! He's about to publicly humiliate me.

"I want to highlight this," he says, stepping to one side so everyone can get a good long look.

I've only sent four pictures to my account so far. One got stuck at the top, and I don't know how to make it small again like the other ones. Every day I take a few pictures of a particularly delicious looking piece of baking, and email them to myself. When I get into bed at night, before I fall into an exhausted sleep, I send the best one to FlipFlop. So far, nothing is happening. I can't understand how it's supposed to help my business.

"Trudy, you've done a tremendous job here," Hendrick says. "You've really captured the flavour, pardon the pun, of your bakery. See, here, in the background of this pansy flower cupcake, your girl, Eve, is serving a customer. This is an exceptional photograph with fantastic depth. Look at the spectacular detail of the cupcake, while the action beyond it is hazy; and yet we can make out that some sort of inviting, friendly business is going on. What kind of camera do you use?"

Stunned by his praise, I stammer, "Um, I just used my phone."

"Amazing. It must have a really good camera."

Jane pipes up, "I chose it for her."

Hendrick continues, "I think, in addition to baking, you have quite a knack for photography. Bravo! Your FlipFlop is, sorry to the rest of you, the best I've seen so far from this group. A round of applause for Trudy, please!"

Now, I'm self-conscious as my friends clap politely. They all put effort into their homework. I did the minimum, and somehow, I did better than everyone else.

"You've missed an opportunity, though," Hendrick continues, snapping the overhead lights back on. There's an audible groan. I think some at the table may have been snoozing in the warm darkness. "Hashtags," he hisses dramatically, tenting his polished fingers on the table. "What's missing are your *hashtags*."

I have no idea what a hashtag is. I've heard of them, but I don't know. I hope, hope, hope he doesn't ask me.

"Any suggestions for Trudy?"

Around the table my colleagues pull out their phones and start scrolling FlipFlop. I'd do the same but I wouldn't know what I was looking for.

"Hashtag Bakers of FlipFlop," Debbie calls out.

Someone else chips in, "Hashtag cupcakes! Mm."

Okay. I still don't know what hashtag means, but I nod and pretend to be following along.

"It's quarter to," Hendrick says. "Are there any questions before we take a break?"

Jane chimes in, "Yes. Could you do something about the air-conditioning in here? Last week we froze our asses off, this week we're melting. I can't take it!"

I'm puffed with pride as I head for the refreshment table. I may not have a firm grasp on this competition thing, but my FlipFlop was the best. Maybe Biz Buzz isn't beyond me. Imagine what I could do if I tried really hard, or knew what a hashtag was!

I rush over to the snacks before they're all gone – it's time for a celebratory cannoli.

Pressing my way through the crush of sweaty bodies, everyone reaching for bottles of water floating in a tub, I find a plate and serviette and place my cannoli in the center. It's magnificent. A work of art. Cannolis are not something I've ever dared attempt. I wonder where Hendrick found these?

And it's scrumptious, the brittle pastry crunches and crumbles as I bite through to the creamy custardy center. Oh my, it's heavenly. My lips stick to each other, and a gentle snowfall of icing sugar drifts onto my blouse. I'll just finish this, before I brush it off.

The cannoli is so good I must have another.

Jane arrives at my side. "Holy Cannoli, what do we have here?" Her silver-ringed hand hovers over the goodies until it finally lands on the row of cookies. She's munching on one when she says, "Almost forgot. I have something for you."

"Mm?" I reply, my mouth full of pastry.

She motions for me to follow her back to our seats. I grab a can of diet-cola and follow.

"Here," she says, smacking a copy of *Mother-of-the-Bride Magazine* onto the table between our seats.

"Ooh, what's that?" Hendrick comes around behind our chairs. "I love weddings! Who's getting married?"

I sense the room quieting, as if a taboo has shattered. The most recent wedding announcement, which apparently everyone in the world has heard about, is Xavier and Zelda's.

I probably shouldn't say anything, but maybe it's already common knowledge, so I tell them: "My daughter, Madison."

Now, everyone is congratulating me, and asking questions, to which I have very few answers.

"It's all in the works!" I say, waving my hands around, trying to sound like I know all the details.

"Anyhoo," Hendrick interrupts. "If you need advice, I'm here for you." He struts toward the head of the table. "I designed Sugar-D's wedding, if you saw any of *those* pictures. And of course, my own sister's wedding, two years ago, so I am *up to date* with weddings, should you need my help."

There are murmurs of awe around the room while I wonder who Sugar-D is, but Hendrick raps his knuckles on the table. "Okay, people, let's get back to the business of *your* business."

As we settle down, he turns to me again. "One last question for you, Trudy."

All heads swivel toward me. Jane snatches up her napkin and swipes at her mouth, nodding at me to follow suit. Oh crap, I've got sugar all over myself. I wipe blindly at my chin as Hendrick asks, "Why did you not travel with me on FlipFlop?" He pierces me with his blue mascaraed eyes. "It was the second part of the assignment."

I don't know what he means by 'travel with' him.

"I'm your only traveler," he continues, tilting his head to the side. "No one knows you're there. Unless you travel with others, no one will travel with you."

I suppose he thinks what he's saying makes sense, but it just doesn't. He's using words I understand, but I have no idea what any of them have to do with my pictures of tortes on FlipFlop.

I can suffer in silence for a few moments and just dumbly return his stare, or I can admit I don't have a clue what he's talking about. I blink. Surely, he's spent enough time on me for this class and will move along.

My colleagues have faithfully done their homework. I'm the only one who slacked off – although Suzy Q isn't here. More and more, my friends are moving on to things I know nothing about: computerizing their inventory; using tablets for cash registers and little machines for payments. Maybe I need to modernize. I don't want to become obsolete, like my mother. If it wasn't for Jane, I wouldn't even own a smartphone.

Finally, feeling my already warm face notch up to scorching, I ask Hendrick, "What do you mean by 'travel'?"

He blinks once or twice. I take a quick sip of my cola, careful so it doesn't fizz up my nose. I swipe the napkin across my lips again and wait.

"Okay, get out your phone," he instructs me.

I fish around in my purse and pull it out. "I just have to turn it on," I tell him.

For some reason he guffaws loudly. "Okay, okay. While we're waiting for Trudy to *turn on her phone*, let's move on to Alex."

He's teasing me, and I have no idea why. He adds, "We'll get back to showing Trudy how to *travel* with me afterward. It's '*the*Hendrick' by the way, for anyone who's forgotten."

Jane raises her hand. "I'll show her how to travel," she volunteers.

FOURTEEN

Every day now, when I get home from work, Wallander trots up to greet me at the door. After a long workday, he's a comfort to come home to, and my mother seems finally satisfied with his level of playthings. I pick him up for a quick cuddle and hear him purr.

Mother is at the kitchen counter, martini in hand, flipping through *Mother-of-the-Bride*. Oh boy – now I'm in for it. She'll have a zillion opinions about everything.

"I'm glad you're home," she says, not looking up from the magazine.

I narrow my eyes. If she's being nice, she must want something from me.

Still not looking up, she says, "The ice maker is broken."

I knew it.

One of Mother's main concerns is the temperature of her drink. She makes a big production about pouring the liquor over the ice in a tumbler, stirring it rapidly with a tall metal spoon, before straining it out through her fingers into a proper martini glass. She then licks her fingers.

I open the freezer and take out a couple of frozen dinners.

She waggles her finger at me, as if I'm the one who's tipsy at six o'clock in the evening. "No, the ice maker!"

"I'm getting to it!"

Lifting the ice maker's cover, I see the switch is set to off again. I don't know how it happens. It's possible the ice maker goes on strike from use and abuse and shuts itself down. I switch it back on.

"Now, give it a minute," I implore. "Let it make some ice before you go bashing at it again. Or better still, why don't you wait until tomorrow?"

"Pshh," she says, waving me away.

I start our meals in the microwave before going upstairs to have a shower.

She calls after me, "You're a genius."

After eating my dinner at the dining room table, I take the wedding magazine to my bedroom and settle in under the covers. I've only glanced through it a couple of times but now I have some time to concentrate.

The magazine smells sickly sweet from all the perfume samples tucked into the advertisements and I taste a horrid bitterness when I lick my finger to turn the pages. Pages and pages of women in gowns – women who look younger and thinner than me. How can these women be the mothers of brides?

According to the magazine, when it comes to choosing a dress for the MOB – for that's what I've learned I am now, a MOB – what matters most is the time of year the wedding will be held.

Madison hasn't given me a date, and Xavier hasn't updated me on anything. Despite begging for more information in emails to Madison, she just hasn't responded. I have to believe she's too busy with her job. So, until I hear differently, I'm assuming it's at the end of the summer.

Halfway through the magazine my eye is caught by an article titled: "The Groom and His Family."

I wonder about the young man she's decided to marry. She didn't go steady with anyone in high-school. At least, not that she told me about. She had friends, and her best friend Laura, and they often socialized with a crowd of boys, but Madison never seemed to be going steady with anyone.

Admittedly, she did keep stuff secret back then, especially from me, because I seemed to have committed the terrible crime of being the mother of a teenage girl. There was crying and door slamming and silent treatment on her part, but I assumed it was just the terrible teens.

I wish I knew now how she suddenly found someone she loves enough to marry – all in a matter of months. And I hope beyond hope that it's not because of an unplanned pregnancy.

I don't know if I'm up for any of this.

I flip further through the magazine, searching for reassurance and guidance.

According to *Mother-of-the-Bride,* online communication is crucial for the MOB, handier than the telephone because emailing can be done at any time of day, and light-years ahead of pen and paper and the postal service. Thankfully, I've mastered email, which I admit now, is handy. I don't know why I resisted it for so long. It's easy. Everyone should use email.

There's a spread on engagement rings with dreamy photographs of brides-to-be leaning against stucco walls, Mediterranean views in the background, their left hands displayed against their tanned throats; or lifting wine glasses in toast with other beautiful loose-haired women around colorful outdoor cafes.

I notice engagement ring styles haven't changed over the years – after all, how creative can you be with a big glittery rock and a gold band?

"An unconventional bride might search out vintage rings in antique stores and pawn shops – something old, something new," reads the text beneath a photo of a fussy, intricate ring.

I think of my simple solitaire, hiding its face in my jewelry box. I suppose if Biz Buzz doesn't work, and I get desperate for airfare, I could pawn it. My heart twinges. I can't imagine parting with the most meaningful gift Xavier ever gave me. Biz Buzz has got to work!

Does Madison have an engagement ring?

"Many brides-to-be post ring photos on FlipFlop as a way of announcing their engagement," the magazine informs me.

Did Madison do that? I better check.

Once again, I've forgotten to charge my laptop so the battery is dead. I go downstairs to retrieve my phone from my purse then climb the staircase back to my room, every painful step reminding me that it's a good thing I booked the appointment for my tests.

Mother is safely ensconced in her bedroom, watching something with, oddly, loud rock music. Her television is blaring.

I settle back in my bed and turn on my phone, hoping to remember Jane's instructions on how to find someone on FlipFlop.

When I get to my account there's a big red dot that's never been there before. I touch it and it tells me I have six new travelers. I peer at the list of names and photographs, recognizing my friends from Biz Buzz. They're all traveling with me!

I touch the top one, Debbie Does Nails, and there's Debbie in her nail salon with her daughter. I touch the anchor above the word "Travel" and blink, I'm traveling with her! It was easy.

I return to the list and add another and another.

My screen fills with my friends' pictures and videos and I spend a long time scrolling and reading all the comments – some fawning and clearly insincere, some hilarious, and some downright crude. I'm fascinated, and almost forget that I opened FlipFlop to find Madison.

Concentrating on the small screen in my hands, I try to remember what Jane said about searching for someone. I try a few options but just end up on screens that don't get me any closer to Madison. Is it too late to call Jane?

I see it. The binoculars. Search! That's right, that's how you look someone up.

Touching the binoculars, I begin to type Madison's name but before I'm even finished, her picture appears in a list. I touch it, and there she is. My beautiful daughter sitting in a lounge chair drinking a tall fruity cocktail.

I travel with her. And instantly I'm in Madison's world.

She's posted dozens of photographs. Group shots and selfies. Many, many bikini shots with no self-consciousness at all. Holy cow, she's got a belly-button ring!

When I reach a series of pictures of her dad, my heart stops, and my stomach sinks.

It's painful to look through the photos, but look I do.

It appears they spent about a week together in Croatia.

I'm relieved Zelda isn't in any of the photos, although that might be her bony shoulder in one of the selfies of Madison and Xavier.

My eyelids sag with sadness – a feeling of rejection weighing me down.

I scroll on through Madison's FlipFlop, half-heartedly looking for an engagement ring photo, but there's nothing.

I do, however, now know that her fiancé, Matt, looks like a koala bear, just as I expected for a boy from Australia. They appear to be having the time of their lives. It's amazing to me that she's being paid to be there, partying on a yacht in the Adriatic.

I learn nothing about the upcoming wedding. She still hasn't announced it publicly.

I turn off my phone, set it on my bedside table, and toss the magazine on the floor. Mornings come too soon and I need to get some sleep.

I switch off the light and sink into my pillows.

I dream I'm at Madison's wedding.

Except it's me standing at the altar, waiting for my groom to walk down the aisle toward me.

The church is full and Madison is sitting in the front row with my mother.

I'm wearing a pink satin dress, which is wrapped around me like a big shiny bandage, uncomfortably tight. When I look down, all I see is my cleavage.

The doors at the back of the church open and Xavier's grandmother starts down the aisle in a black dress and veil. I can't see the groom following behind her but when they reach me, his grandmother melts away and Xavier and his bride appear before me. Zelda is wearing a white headdress and a lacey gown. Xavier is handsome and young in a gold tuxedo.

Mother hisses at me from the front of the church. "Trudy, sit down!"

I'm confused. This is *my* wedding.

"Trudy, sit down! You're making a scene!"

I wake up with a start.

It takes a moment in the dark to remember where I am. I'm not at home in my bed with Xavier. I'm in my room in Mother's house. Xavier is gone.

I roll over in misery.

My whole being is filled, once again, with grief and regret. I wish I could change *everything*. I wish I could go back in time and make Xavier love me.

I reach for the light on my side table and switch it on.

All is as usual. My pink terry robe hangs on the back of the door. *Mother-of-the-Bride* is splayed across the floor. I check the clock. 2 AM. I've got to get back to sleep. There are only three hours before my day begins.

I reach into the drawer of my nightstand and feel around for my peppermint patties. They always calm me down. I unwrap one and pop it in my mouth, letting the dark chocolate melt in the middle of my tongue. After a moment, the cooling flavour of the peppermint begins to ooze and soothe me. I turn off the light knowing I should go brush my teeth again, but I don't. I roll onto my side and stare into the darkness of the wall, blinking.

FIFTEEN

D r. Gertie was gentle but firm when she told me the results of all the pokes, prods, and scans.

"You are pre-diabetic," she said, looking up from the computer screen on which she was reading the reports.

I nodded, because that sounded like good news. It's seriously bad to be diabetic – you can't eat sugar. Thankfully, I'm only *'pre'*.

"How's the diet going?" she asked.

"Fine. Good," I told her, nodding, but honestly, it's hard to stick to a diet – I'm so hungry!

I didn't tell her I keep cheating, because it's not like I'm *quitting* the diet – I'm sticking with it! And I've made so many changes in the right direction. Half-sweet drinks, for example; whole grain buns, whenever I can; sweetener instead of sugar; and only outrageously expensive but super healthy kettle roasted chips.

What I was most anxious to hear about was news about my knees, and as it turns out, there's something amiss with the cartilage in both.

"I'm referring you to a very good orthopedic surgeon," Gertie informed me, tapping at her screen. "His name is Dr. Arnot."

It's odd, but I was relieved to hear this. For some strange reason, I'm not afraid to go under the knife. The surgeon will get in there, fix whatever needs fixing, and presto, my knees will be as good as new.

I left Gertie's office with a bit of bounce in my step, or maybe I was just bounding past the dental office so I wouldn't see Zelda. When I got back to my cubby hole of an office, and made a phone call, it was easy to book an appointment with Dr. Arnot for the following week.

They told me to arrive early to fill in some forms, but it took less time than I anticipated to get here and now I have time to kill. Next to the aging red-brick building that houses Dr. Arnot's office, is a funky little coffee shop with the door propped open, folksy music pouring out.

I wasn't required to fast before this appointment, thank goodness – the blood test a week ago was brutal. A wreck without my morning coffee and toast, the only thing in my stomach was the single Gonzo and a little sip of water to dissolve it. But then the drug kicked in, and I forgot all about being hungry and terrified.

I order a frozen cappufrappé from a barista with a scruffy beard around the edges of his chin, and settle in by a window looking out on the street, drawing the creamy mocha froth into me with a wide straw. Even if it is only half-sweet, it's as delicious as a milkshake. A milkshake for grownups. Just what the doctor ordered.

I wish.

I imagined an orthopedic surgeon would have a swanky high-tech hospital/clinic type of setting, but Dr. Arnot is in an aging office building in a rundown part of town. The coffee shop is busy, however, so maybe Lettuceville is up and coming. It seems like the whole city is slowly getting spruced up. I sip, watching people walk by, noticing fewer moms with baby carriages, fewer joggers, but just as many dog walkers as Maple Street.

When it's near my appointment time, I make my way to the building next door and down a dingy corridor until I find Dr. Arnot's office. His door opens into a dark waiting room flanked with chairs. About four or five other people, some with walkers and canes, are already waiting. They look up at me as I enter, eyeing me, assessing what's the matter with me. At least, that's what I do when I'm in a doctor's waiting room.

I approach the receptionist who slides a window aside, asks my name, consults her computer screen, then requests my health insurance card. She types some entries into her computer and hands me a clipboard with a pen attached by a string.

"Fill these in, front and back." She nods toward the seats in the waiting area.

Finding a chair with empty seats on either side, I set my purse down on one of them and look around for a flat surface for my cappufrappé. There's only one table, and it's messy with shabby-looking magazines.

Dr. Arnot's waiting room does not instill confidence, and it smells like sweat and fear. I'm no longer so jazzed with the idea of him cutting into me.

I fill in the forms, which are more intrusive than can possibly be necessary. Height; weight, which somehow went *up* two pounds between Dr. Gertie appointments; current medications; past operations; allergies; do I smoke, no; do I drink alcoholic beverages, yes. How much daily? Well, not daily, like my mother – I never want to be like her; drug abuse, no; pain management, well, aspirins, I guess; flu shots; tetanus vaccine; heart problems; cancer; history of stroke; ulcers; hypertension; diabetes, no.

So many questions!

And on the reverse, they want to know my family history, followed by a list of tick boxes about my eyes; my urinary system; rashes; psychiatric issues – memory loss & confusion, nervousness, depression, insomnia – what do those have to do with my knees? Finally, there's a box about Musculoskeletal – the obvious reason I'm here at an Orthopedic Surgeon for heaven's sake. I circle KNEES, and tick all the boxes for joint pain; stiffness; swelling, check; muscle pain and cramps, check; difficulty climbing stairs, CHECK!

"Recovery from knee replacement surgery is incredibly painful," Jessica told me the other day.

I focus on, and fast-forward past the actual operation and imagine myself dashing up the stairs to get my final suitcase on my way to Madison's wedding. I can't wait for that day. If only I didn't have to fly.

Or the day I nimbly climb up to the rooftop patio that opened last week atop The Smokehouse. Everyone's raving about it. Or to scramble up the ladder on the back of a boat after an afternoon of floating on the Adriatic Sea in an inflatable unicorn raft—

"Trudy Asp?"

A nurse with a clipboard leads me to an office behind the glassed-in partition. There are about six offices back here, some with closed doors. It smells slightly fresher, a bit antiseptic.

I take a seat, nervously, my cappufrappé sweating in my hand.

I wait and wait, studying the laminated posters of the skeletal system on the wall – various joint diagrams, hips, shoulders, knees. On the desk before me is a model of a knee. Skinny bones, attached where their bulbous blue knobs meet by plasticine-like strips the color of a pink hot water bottle – tendons or ligaments, or something.

Dr. Arnot swoops into the room, a white coat over his blue shirt and tan pants. He plops down onto the chair in front of the computer screen and swivels to face me.

"Oh my, you're a heavy one," he observes, tapping me on one of my knees. "That's going to be a problem."

I am so shocked I don't know how to respond.

"What?" he laughs at my silent, stunned reaction. "You didn't know?"

My last shred of hope sinks like a deflated unicorn, and I reach for my purse. I will not sit here and be insulted. I am walking out of this appointment.

My knees protest as I try to rise from the seat.

"Now, settle down…" he swivels in his chair, checking the computer screen for my name, "…Trudy. I'm not here to coddle you, I'm here to *help* you. And…" He taps the computer and an X-ray appears on the screen. He pulls a pen from his breast pocket and uses it to point at the screen. "You see here?" His pen swings back and forth across the middle of what are apparently my pitiful knee bones. "This is where you should have nice fat cartilage. But this is your problem. Your fat is in the wrong place, Trudy. Your cartilage is all messed up."

He's really going to throw the 'fat' word around as often as possible. He's a horrible man. How would he like it if I told him I can practically see my reflection in his shiny bald head?

"Trudy, you've got one choice." He keeps using my name, as if we're pals. "You've got to lose this weight. It's crushing your knees. I can do the surgery, but it won't help until you *slim down*." He looks straight into my eyes then down at the cappufrappé on my knee. "Get rid of that," he directs me.

I grip it harder. My sweet, sweet friend.

He pulls a trash can from under his desk and shakes it at me.

Only an idiot would throw away a $7 drink when there's still a half an inch left, but I won't be finishing it near him. The suction sound when I drew up the last of the deliciousness from the bottom would be unthinkable.

With reluctance and great sorrow, I drop my cup into the outstretched can.

There's a wet ring on the knee of my pants where I was clutching it.

"First step," Dr. Arnot says. "Admitting you have a problem. And I'd say you have quite a problem, Trudy."

It feels like the world has gone bananas. No one is hearing me. I just want my knees fixed.

"So, you're not going to help me?" I plead. "I'm here for knee pain, not because I've put on some weight over the years."

Unexpectedly, he looks sympathetic, and interested. It was right to assert myself, he's paying attention.

Gently, he asks, "When did it start?"

Finally, he's prepared to listen.

"It's been about six months now, especially when I go up the stairs or—"

He interrupts. "Not the knee pain. The *fat*. When did it start accumulating?"

His insensitivity is shocking.

Does he talk this way to all his patients?

Some of the other people I saw in the waiting room were as large as me.

One man was larger.

I'm not sure whether to stand up on my poor knees and hobble out of here or stay and finish this debilitating conversation. I stare back at him in cold silence, my lips pressed tightly closed.

"I'm betting it was gradual," he murmurs, searching through a file on his desk. "Here it is! Here's the plan. Take it, embrace it, it's the only way. Then we'll look after those knees," he assures me, handing over a sheaf of papers titled, *Metabolic Food Plan*.

"How long will it take?" I ask him. "I'm planning a trip to Europe at the end of the summer. I was hoping to have the surgery over with by then."

"Call to book another appointment when you've lost sixty pounds," he answers, matter-of-factly.

Sixty pounds?

I stare at him in disbelief.

"How am I supposed to lose sixty pounds in two and a half months?"

"One bite at a time," he says, getting up from his desk and breezing from the office.

I hear him greeting a patient in the next examination room.

My knees hurt more now than they ever did, and it takes a moment to hoist myself from the chair. Blind with angry tears, I make my way from the building and out into the brilliant sunlight.

As soon as I get home, I read over the food plan. I knew something was wrong as soon as I saw his office building. Why would Dr. Gertie recommend a quack like him? I'll have to call her and get a referral to a different orthopedic surgeon.

The *Metabolic Food Plan* ludicrously recommends eating red meat every day, and staying away from fruit, and bread, even healthy bread. It has so many absurd suggestions I stop reading. It's a wonder he still has a medical license. Eggs every day! As if on top of all my other problems, blocking up my arteries is a good idea. I toss it into the recycling bin.

But he might be right about my weight delaying any surgery. So, I will lose some. How hard can it be? I'll just eat less and move more. That's what I'll do. I'll lose the weight, get a new referral, and get myself a new set of knees.

SIXTEEN

"**I**f you're going to Croatia, you need a new bathing suit," Jane insisted. "You won't be able to buy one over there."

"Why not?" I asked.

"Because..." She made a Pillsbury Doughboy shape with her hands. "They won't sell your size. All those European women are as skinny as sticks."

Bathing suit shopping is not something I want to tackle today, but Jane asked me to spend the day with her, shopping, and lunching, and she's hellbent on dragging me into this gigantic store called The Beach House.

Jane assumes I'm jetting over to Europe to attend Madison's wedding, but the truth is, even if the bakery's sales increase from the tactics I'm implementing from Biz Buzz and I manage to scrape together the money, I don't know if I *can* fly.

Of course, I *must* go – I'm the MOB after all. And there's no way I'm letting Zelda 'stand in' for me, whatever that means. But the rumor spreading around town about my fear of flying is, regrettably, true.

The first time I flew I was nervous to start with, and then the roar of the plane rumbling down the runway at the speed of a racing-car was almost too much to bear. I never signed up to be a race-car driver. I gripped the arm rests, held my breath, squeezed my eyes shut, and whispered, trying not to sob, over and over, "Please don't let me die!"

It was terrifying, and it took me hours to calm down when I got to Florida. So, right from the beginning, I didn't love flying. I may suffer from claustrophobia; I can't stand the thought that I'm locked inside a space with no way out. But the frosting on the cupcake happened when Xavier and I were once again traveling to Florida. Our plane got stuck on the runway during a snowstorm. The captain kept telling us they were de-icing the plane and we'd take off soon. It went on and on for hours.

If the monstrous 747 was so icy, I reasoned, why are we even attempting to take off. Let us off this plane!

It's cringey to admit, but I freaked out, begged and pleaded with the crew to let me off the plane.

"Trudy, sit down," Xavier hissed at me. "You're embarrassing yourself."

I think actually, I was embarrassing him.

I was panicking. A jittery mess. I staggered back and forth to the bathroom about five times. I was terrified even to lock myself into the tiny room, but I had to close the door – I didn't want anyone to see me throwing up into the weird grey toilet, or sitting down on it to...you-know-what. Xavier was so mad.

Eventually, the flight got canceled and the plane returned to the terminal. The storm was so severe we had to stay in an airport hotel overnight. The next day, I refused to reschedule. I ruined our vacation, and I've never been on a plane since.

I'm staring down the dilemma of how to get over to Europe with as much courage as I can muster. I have a feeling Madison and Zelda have locked horns. Apparently, Madison wants to go ahead with her wedding at the end of August, even though that's when Zelda has booked something in Croatia for her own nuptials. I can't bear it if it's a double wedding and I have to sit through the humiliation. I refuse to let Zelda win. She stole my husband – I'm not letting her steal my daughter's wedding too.

But I cannot even think about being suspended midair over a large body of water without wanting to throw up. All I can think of is how terrible it will be when we crash in the middle of the ocean and I die a freezing-cold, watery death, clinging to a flimsy life preserver, while everyone around me screams for help and drowns.

Xavier knows I'm phobic. He must have told Zelda – who is now telling everyone in town that I can't get on a plane, or go to my own daughter's wedding.

Fear of flying sounds ridiculous, even to me. Thousands of people fly every day, I know, I know, but I can't help it, I freeze. Even contemplating it now my mind frets about every little thing – crashes, terrorists, diarrhea.

Madison's wedding plans may be nebulous, but I am firmly in her camp. I am the one and only Mother-of-the-Bride, and I will get myself over there, somehow, someway, even if the quickest, easiest, and most obvious way petrifies me.

Filled with trepidation, Jane right behind me, I cross the threshold of the Beach House and am met with a mass of Caribbean colors, giant posters of tanned women in gorgeous locales, with plenty of palm fronds thrown in for good measure. The number of swimsuits is staggering. Tankinis and bikinis line the back wall and the rest of the place is a smorgasbord of cover-ups, sarongs, fancy flip-flops, and one-piece swimsuits.

I stand a few feet inside, gaping at the selection. There's got to be something for me in here, but I don't see a Plus-size section anywhere.

"Grab a few and I'll meet you in the change rooms," Jane says, disappearing into the jungle of waterfall racks.

With faint hope, I scan the one-piece suits for anything that might permit me to be seen publicly in a bathing suit.

I dread a salesperson pouncing on me, but no surprise, none do. They can probably tell from across the store that I'm a hopeless case and they don't need to waste their time on a woman that looks like me.

Pawing through racks makes me sweaty, so I take off my jacket and drape it over my arm. Purse and jacket on one arm, I grope through the crammed hangers for anything in my size.

Some suits are number-sized in US, some in UK, and some with letters only. Am I an XXL or an OX? I don't know, and it's precisely this indignity that has kept me from shopping for the past few years.

"How are you doing over there?" Jane yoo-hoos from across the store. "Found anything?"

I shake my head, dismayed that she's directing attention toward me, but at that moment, across the aisle, I spy what might as well be signed: FAT LADY

SWIMWEAR. It's a round rack of bathing suits with skirts, stripes, big flowers, and enormous bosoms. They're hideous but I paw through and pick out the least ghastly of the bunch: a solid gray suit of slinky material with a frilly polka dot peplum around the midriff. I traipse across the store to the change rooms where Jane is waiting.

A tiny blonde woman, in a fuzzy white sweater and trendy faded jeans, greets us and unlocks the cubicle doors. Her name tag reads: Polly.

"Let me know if you need another size," she says, winking at me and closing me into the little room.

Anxiety zings and my heart speeds up as I set my purse down on the small triangular bench wedged into the corner. I'm hot, and it's cramped in here. Mirrors cover two walls. At least I can unlock the door and walk out of here if I need to.

Am I really going to do this? Strip down to my undies and pull this slippery bathing suit onto my sweaty body?

I struggle out of my clothes, regretting that I let Jane talk me into this. As I draw the suit over my ankles, there's a tap on the door. Panicked, I look up and see reflected a thousand times in the fun-house mirrors, the back of my jiggly dimpled legs.

"Everything okay in there?" Polly asks.

"Just fine," I lie.

"Let me see how it looks when you get it on. Don't hide in there... Or tear it off."

How does she know that's exactly what I intend to do?

I squirm further into the suit, which is atrociously tight. There's no way I'm opening the door.

I hear Jane's voice. "How ya making out in there, Tru?"

"Fine," I lie again.

"Let me see!"

I hesitate.

Jane is making conversation with Polly, blabbing the details of my personal situation. "...she's going to Europe for her daughter's wedding and *needs* to buy a bathing suit. There's no sense trying to buy one over there. You know what those European stores are like."

Polly pitches in, like a good saleswoman: "Nowhere has a better selection than here at the Beach House."

I open the door a crack and peer out. Jane is wearing a snakeskin-print, bandeau top bikini with laces that rise from between her small breasts and tie around her neck. Polly is showing her that she can also wear it strapless. Jane is twisting and turning to see what it looks like from behind – the high-cut bottom reveals half of each of her scrawny butt cheeks.

"Come on out," Polly says, catching my eye in the crack of the doorway.

"No." I keep the door mostly closed.

"Come out, let's see. I can't help if you hide in there."

Jane snaps her long fingers at me as if I'm a naughty puppy. "Get out here!"

With reluctance I open the door, step into the passageway between the change rooms, and stand unhappily in my bare feet as the two of them scrutinize my body.

"Yup," says Polly. "It's all wrong." She waves me back toward the change room. "Hang tight, I've got an idea."

"Jeez." Jane chews on her thumbnail, her monkey tattoo bobbing. "Who designed that thing?"

Her eyes meet mine in my misery, and then begin to dance. A curve starts on her lips.

"Shall I take a picture? Post it on FlipFlop?" She doubles over, cracking up.

"Don't you dare!" I cry, hopping back into the change room and slamming the door.

But I also laugh, in hysterical release. I know she's kidding. She would never do something so mean. She's just trying to make me laugh like she has a million times over our lives.

But it's not funny.

What's happened to my body is a nightmare. Somehow, over the last few years, I've packed on an insane number of pounds, even though I don't eat more than I ever did. In fact, since starting my diet, I've been eating less, and of course, moving more, just like all the magazines advise, but the blubber isn't budging.

Still laughing on the other side of the door, Jane gasps, "You look like something from Marineland in that suit."

I look in the mirror. She's right, I'm a walrus clown.

I strip it off and hear Polly bustling back into the area. She flips a bunch of black separates – tops and bottoms – over my change room door.

"Oh, I can't wear a two-piece." I plead, "My stomach."

There's a girth of fat encircling my waist. No one is going to see it flopping around between a top and bottom.

"Trust me," she says, her fingers tapping on the handful of hangers over the edge of the door. "Try them on. Mix and match. I want you to find a top and a bottom that work for you."

I could refuse and just walk out of here, but Jane will argue and nag me until I do what she wants. I might as well get it over with. She'll see nothing works and we can go eat.

My stomach is growling. I'm hungry. All I want is to go have a nice lunch and talk.

Surprisingly, the first piece I try on, a high-waisted bottom, fits me superbly. It has a wide waistband that holds in my tum, and it doesn't cause the flab to bulge over the edge like an overfilled muffin tin. I turn and twist and look at myself in the mirror. These bottoms aren't half-bad. Progress is being made.

My arms and legs still look like pale lumpy dough, but there's nothing I can do about that except get some sun this summer. I heard Sabrina hurtfully say to Mother one time, "She's lucky fat tans so nicely."

I wasn't even fat back then! Not like I am now.

I try on the tops, hoping for a match. The first one looks like I'm wearing S&M bondage armor, and the next two are too skimpy. I refuse to reveal that much of the girls, thank you very much. In fact, right now, I'd prefer to reveal none of me. I think it's time to go.

Someone taps on the door. It's Polly. "What's happening in there?"

I release myself from the stranglehold of a twisted piece of black fabric. "Sorry, nothing's working,"

"Oh, that's too bad." The disappointment in her voice is genuine. She must be on commission.

"Are you sure you're the best one to judge?" Jane remarks, and I picture her standing on the other side of the door with her arms crossed, waiting for me to appear so she can evaluate me again.

These bottoms do look good.

There's one last top hanging on the door. One more. Then I can honestly say I tried everything and we can go for lunch.

I slide it from its tiny hanger. The wide straps tie behind my neck. The front is cut in a vee with a broad band encircling my ribcage, almost touching the top of the bottoms. The whole outfit reminds me of swimsuits movie starlets wore in the 1940s, only theirs were usually white and mine is black. I dig into my purse and pull out my new sunglasses. Looking back at me from the mirror is a mature woman I barely recognize but like very much. I wonder if she can be me.

I open the change room door.

A look of triumph beams from Polly's face. "You *see*?"

Jane, already back in her street clothes, is lounging on a chair, flipping through a magazine. She shrieks when she looks up. "You look amazeballs!"

"I've got one more thing for you," Polly says, unhooking a knee-length ecru crocheted cover-up from a hanger. She holds it out like I'm a queen, and I have no choice but to let her draw it up over my arms and shoulders. I turn and stare in the mirror at the goddess I've become since donning these stunning garments.

Jane and Polly whoop, and I blush, but I'm so pleased I almost hug Polly. "How did you know?" I cry. "I would never have put this all together."

"Let me show you something," she says, conspiratorially. She scans the store over her shoulder, as though making sure the coast is clear, before pulling her phone from her pocket. She scrolls through a few things then turns her phone to me.

On the screen is a photo of an obese woman. I look at it, wondering why she's showing it to me, and then slowly the face of the woman comes into focus, the blonde hair looks familiar.

"That's me!" Polly says, swinging the phone so Jane can get a good look too.

"No way!"

"Yup. That's me about a hundred pounds ago."

I'm shocked. She's a tiny thing now. Short and pretty and graceful.

"How'd you *do* it?" Jane pries.

SEVENTEEN

Whichile waiting for Polly to leave The Beach House and meet us on her lunch break, Jane and I browse around in a kitchenware store. Polly told us to meet her here; she said it was one of her favourite stores.

I'm staring at a wall of silicone gadgets. Lemon squeezers and tongs, egg slicers and garlic presses. Everything is either lime green or aquamarine, unless it's purple, or coral, or egg yolk yellow.

Jane is studying some expensive bakeware behind me – daringly lifting lids off the pots, exclaiming over the prices, and replacing the lids with a nerve-racking clatter. If she breaks one of them, it's going to be a whole scene. I don't want a scene. What I want is to know how Polly lost a hundred pounds. I need her secret!

I wonder if it will be one of those plans with the shakes and bars and meals that come in a big box and cost a small fortune. Yet if the results are as good as they appear to be – I'll find a way to pay! I charged the swimsuit and cover-up to my credit card, which makes me a little nervous. I wasn't planning on having another bill to pay next month but it's even more incentive to work hard and restore Honeywell's to its glory days.

At last, a bell tinkles and Polly enters the store. She chats for a moment with the woman at the counter. They must be friends.

"Let's go eat," she says, greeting me and Jane.

I wonder where she's taking us. Or is she brown-bagging her diet bar, and Jane and I will grab some takeout, and sit with her at a picnic table in the park or something? Not what I had in mind for this lunch with Jane, but Polly is harboring a secret that I must know now.

The woman at the counter comments, "Aphrodite's has souvlaki on special today."

"Let's go there," Polly urges. "You'll love it."

"Greek okay with you?" Jane asks, turning to me.

"Oh sure," I agree, reminded of the delicious baklava Xavier and I used to take home from Mr. Athens in the old days. It was Xavier's favourite restaurant. Mine was Luigi's Italian. The tiramisu. My mouth waters just thinking about those desserts from yesteryear.

Aphrodite's is not far away, which is a relief because my knees are aching from walking all over The Beach House and trying on bathing suits. Shopping is vigorous exercise. I avoid it because nothing usually fits, but I should do more of it. It would probably cost the same as joining a gym.

We walk into Aphrodite's and it's obvious the waiter is on a friendly basis with Polly. He leads us to a choice table by the window overlooking the street. The menus are tall laminated folders with the daily specials paperclipped inside. Jane and I begin to study.

Polly waits, her hands folded on her closed menu.

Jane asks, "You already know what you're having?"

"The special. You can't beat their souvlaki and Greek salad. It's the best in Toronto."

"Sounds good!" Jane agrees, closing her menu. "You?"

They both look at me as my eyes swim over the foods I adore: hummus, dolmades, grilled pita-bread with garlic, moussaka. They all sound healthy to me. Everything is so hard to resist. The words jump off the page into my mouth, filling me with tingling anticipation.

Polly is ordering the souvlaki, so I should have what she's having, even though besides Caesar, Greek salad is the fattiest salad, isn't it? I should just get fries with mine. I'll only eat a few.

The waiter returns with our coffees. He looks at me. "Decisions?"

Before my brain can jump in and order something else, I say, "I'll have the souvlaki special."

"With Greek salad?" he asks, pencil poised.

I look at Polly. Her blue eyes laser into mine and she nods.

"Yes, with salad," I say, fearing I'll regret my choice, as I often do. The moussaka made with potatoes sounds so good, and I still might be hungry.

The minute the waiter steps away from the table, Jane says, "Now tell us. How did you do it? How did you lose all that weight? I know it's not easy – I see reams of obese patients."

"Oh? You're a doctor?"

"Psychiatrist," Jane explains. "But I've always taken a special interest in the way a person's diet affects their mood."

"It's true," Polly agrees. "Food used to make me happy while I was cramming it in my mouth. But all the extra weight made me miserable. Every time I stood up, or saw my reflection in a store window, I wanted to cry."

That's me!

I ask, jumping in before Jane can rattle on about her patients and her helpful, fulfilling, professional career, "How did you lose it?"

Polly leans toward me over the table. "It's really simple," she says, and I feel a glimmer of hope. Simple is good. "I eat only low-carb foods. It's called a LOBO lifestyle." She holds my eyes steadily, and enumerates: "No bread, no pasta, no potatoes, no fruit, no sugar."

Jane gasps and I cringe, withering under Polly's steely blue gaze.

No bread?

"Hm," Jane says, with a whole lot of skepticism. "That doesn't sound very healthy. Are you following some guru?"

"No," Polly laughs. "Unless you call Dr. Arnot a guru, which I doubt anyone ever has."

Dr. Arnot?

I'm stunned.

Jane asks, "You mean, the orthopedic guy?"

"Yes, he did my hip. You know him?"

"I do," Jane says. "And Trudy here—"

I interrupt. "I saw him about my knees last week, but I'm not going back. He gave me the craziest—" My mouth snaps shut as I utter the words. Dr. Arnot's insane food plan is *exactly* what Polly is talking about. She's lost a hundred pounds eating all that meat and cheese. Her arteries must be clogged like a kitchen drain. I can't believe she's sitting here breathing and talking.

There must be more to it. I wait for her to explain, but she just smiles as our heaped plates of souvlaki and salad arrive.

EIGHTEEN

A fter lunch at Aphrodite's, I race home and dig through the recycling bin to find Dr. Arnot's food plan. Smoothing out the crumples, I read through it thoroughly. On the very last page of the plan, he cautions that I might feel lousy at first, but this is normal and should pass within a few days as my body adjusts and detoxifies from the sugar.

Days later, my body is not adjusting. Or if it is, it's putting up a mighty battle.

Working with and around the sights and smells of Honeywell's all day is killing me. If eating LOBO works, and I manage to lose a single pound, I will deserve a medal for doing so while working in a bakery.

It's day three, and my head has been achy and buzzing all day. On the way home from work, all I can think of is how unfair life is, and how I long to dive headfirst into a bag of cheesies.

The moment I open the front door of the house, Mother calls to me from the living room, "I'm in here!"

Most days, the only one to greet me is Wallander, but today, even his cute little straight-up tail trotting toward me isn't cheering. I just want to kick the shoes off my swollen feet, fix myself something to eat from the Bonjour Bacon foods that were delivered yesterday, and go to bed.

Mother is on the couch in the shadows, her stocking feet up on the coffee table, a tragic look on her face, martini in hand.

Either this is something, or this is nothing. Warily, I ask, "What's the matter?"

She puts her hand to her heart in a grief-stricken pose. "Sabrina died."

She hasn't mentioned Sabrina, in eons.

"How did you find out? Did somebody call?"

"Shirley-Jean. Do you remember her? She called. Apparently, she and Sabrina were still playing bridge with some other women, until recently, when Sabrina became too ill." She tilts the martini glass back – to capture the last drops. "I wonder why they never called me? I'm not the best bridge player but you'd think…" She trails off, gazing into the air, contemplative, wistful, full of friend-widow self-pity. The victim of exclusion from her friends' lives and now with the excuse of a death to drink her head off.

There are loads of pictures of Sabrina in the wedding album, which now sits open across Mother's knees. She always wore bright red lipstick, which was often on her teeth when she grinned. She had no children and lived with her husband in a mansion on the lake. Sometimes, Mother would drag me along for visits, but she always let me bring Jane. After first offering us ginger-ale in fancy glasses, and bridge mixture – the ickiest candy ever invented, which I gobbled down anyway – Sabrina would shoo us out of the room so she and Mother could privately gossip and shriek with laughter.

Because of all the mean things she said to me when I was young, as though hurting my feelings was an impossibility, I never liked Sabrina but Jane and I had fun exploring her massive house, finding the servants' staircase at the back of the kitchen, sneaking into hallways and rooms we weren't sure we were supposed to be in.

I'm about to sit down in the chair beside the couch, to hear how Sabrina died, when I notice a small shadowy lump on the seat. At the exact moment I turn on the lamp on the end table, Mother says, "Don't sit there. The cat left that."

It's a dead mouse.

I leap away in horror. "Oh, my gawd! Why didn't you—?"

She *knows* I hate mice.

She gazes at me and takes another sip of her drink.

"Ew, ew, ew!"

I don't even want to look at it, but there's no way Mother is going to get up and dispose of it for me. If I don't take care of the situation, no one will.

Shuddering off my mouse-revulsion, I fetch the dustpan from the kitchen. The thought of mice creeping around the house makes my skin crawl.

"I didn't know we had mice. Did he catch it inside?"

Mother shrugs, sipping her martini.

Wallander, the killer, paces back and forth on the back of the sofa. When he passes close to Mother, he sweeps his tail across the back of her head. I don't think she even knows he's there.

"It was cancer," she calls after me, as I return to the kitchen carrying the dustpan and corpse at the end of my extended arm.

Compost or garbage?

Opening the back door, I step out onto the deck and fling the tiny dead creature into the back border of lilies, then return to Mother.

I inspect the chair for remnants of mouse murder before I sit down. "You and Dad socialized quite a bit with Sabrina and her husband, didn't you? Did he die?"

She nods slowly and smiles. "Yes, we had some wonderful times with them, Lewis and I. Poor Sabrina. She married well, bags of money, but she's been alone all these years."

I can tell she's talking about herself and I'm aware that she too has been alone for many years. Now, I've become her unwitting companion. Well, me and Wallander.

Poor Mother, life can be so empty for women without husbands.

In the beat of a heart, I'm reminded that *I* am a woman without a husband. And mine is still alive!

In moments like this I feel so desperate. I want him back. I want my life back. To make the world feel right, I need my husband and me back in our condo. Where there were no mice.

I try to dismiss the longing, and not go wandering along that pathetic trail. I can't let Mother's melodrama suck me in. It's sad that Sabrina died and all, but right now, what I really need is to fix something for dinner. My lunch of takeout cheeseburger – no bun – with a salad seems like a long time ago. Dinner will require more effort from me than simply ordering takeout, and I can't just throw a frozen dinner into the microwave the way I used to do.

Polly recommended a food service while I'm getting the hang of cooking and eating LOBO. So, with her guidance, I ordered 6 nights worth of dinners from Bonjour Bacon. They arrived yesterday, veggies chopped, cheese grated, oil measured, protein ready for cooking. All I am required to do is unseal the containers and follow the directions on the lids.

"Did you eat?" I ask Mother. It's a silly question because of course she hasn't eaten.

She waves her empty martini glass at me and asks, "What are you having?"

"I'm going to cook up one of those meals I got."

She harrumphs. She told me yesterday I was out of my mind. "You silly goose, you *need* carbohydrates!"

I fear she's right. I feel dreadful, and the thought of cooking right now is nauseating.

On the second day, when I told Jane how dizzy and sick I felt, she also tried to talk me out of LOBO. "It's whacko, Tru. You're gonna eat your way into a heart attack!" She told me a bunch of clinical stories about vitamin deficiencies and cases she's seen in her practice, and how muddled people get when they don't eat properly. She got really worked up. In a condescending shriek she concluded, "I specialize in this type of thing!"

But how can I disregard the evidence of Polly's 'before' picture? I'm not far off from carrying an extra hundred pounds myself. That's ten sacks of flour. Imagine climbing the stairs carrying ten sacks of flour. No wonder it's so hard. My poor knees. 60 pounds, Dr. Arnot said.

Leaving Mother lost in thought on the couch, I stir-fry veggies and chicken in a pan and scroll through my phone. I'm beginning to understand why people enjoy their smartphones so much. Mine gives me the weather, the news, and hey, there's an email from Madison!

Hi Mom. Sorry I haven't written. So busy. Love you.

My heart soars as the chunks of chicken turn a golden brown amid sizzling vegetables in the pan. I read the short missive over again. No mention of a double wedding.

Mother wobbles into the kitchen, hands outstretched toward the fridge and counters in case she stumbles. "Smells good. What're you making?" she asks, heading for the bar cart in the corner of the dining room.

I'm smiling. It's been a while since my cheeks smiled this hard. My heart is singing. Madison loves me!

I tap the wooden spoon on the rim of the pan. "A healthy stir-fry, Mom. You want some?" I feel like sharing.

The tall metal spoon rattles the ice in her martini shaker.

"I'm good," she says.

NINETEEN

Polly doesn't live in Lakeside. She lives in Lettuceville, but she heard about The Smokehouse and wants to try it. She invited me to meet her for Sunday brunch, which I happily accepted because I need tips for sticking to this outrageous diet. The queasiness is gone, but it's impossible to stay away from the sugary temptations dancing like visions of sugar plums every day. How does she do it?

If I hadn't seen her 'before' picture, I wouldn't believe it. But she's lost a hundred pounds so I've decided to listen to her. Nothing else has worked, and I'm desperate to lose the weight to get my knees fixed, not to mention looking fabulous in a MOB dress at the end of the summer.

Before meeting Polly, I didn't take dieting seriously, even with two doctors' warnings. Everybody gets fatter as they get older, don't they? Ten pounds a decade is normal, isn't it? Yet now, I notice how many of my friends are battling the bulge, belonging to gyms and running groups. And Jane, the skinny-mini, complained so loudly last week about the decadent desserts Hendrick puts out during Biz Buzz, that this week he also set out a platter of veggies and dip, and they were a big hit.

My other motivation is Xavier.

It didn't occur to me before, but it has now, that he may have left me because I was gaining so much weight. He didn't say anything directly, but he often hinted that I should get exercise.

"Why don't you ride a bike to work instead of driving your car?" he suggested more than once, though I didn't even own a bike.

When we met, he was very athletic – active and fit – but after years of marriage, we both got a little tubby around the middle, a little sedentary. I thought it was normal. Xavier's knees were hurting long before mine, and a few years back his knees couldn't tolerate playing hockey with his buddies on the weekends. He blamed it on his weight, and he started trying to lose it.

"You're killing me with this food!" he'd moan as he chowed down on seconds of lasagna. I took it as a compliment. He couldn't resist, and he always cleaned his plate. And he looked fine to me, even if he did sport a bit of a beer belly.

Anyway, it's possible, if I lose sixty pounds, and start looking like I did years ago, he'll see I'm the same Trudy he married, dump that stupid Zelda, and we'll get back together.

But I'm weak. I have no will-power. I give in to my impulses daily. On Monday, there were a couple of leaking jelly donuts at work. Can't sell those. Down the hatch. On Wednesday, I made it through the entire day until I encountered the magnificent iced walnut-brownies at Biz Buzz – who could resist them? On Thursday, I went over to Coco's bakery, to do some market research, as instructed by Hendrick, and ended up buying a tiny, expensive cello bag of gluten-free cookies – which were extremely bland and far too sweet. Every baker knows that too sweet is as bad as not sweet enough. It's basic, and obviously Coco doesn't have the magic touch.

I wasn't impressed, but the point is, I ate them all anyway, while Coco was explaining to me that gluten-free means she only uses rice flour and barley flour and I think she even said garbanzo bean flour – ew –and something-or-other about elastics and an ingredient called, xanthan gum. I don't think she's my competition, my customers don't want to eat that stuff, do they? I think it's just the novelty of the new bakery – it does look spiffy in there with its beachy decor.

Anyway, I am consumed with guilt about all these cheats. I don't know how to control myself. I'm hoping Polly has some magic formula.

I arrive at The Smokehouse before her. It's crowded and I'm disappointed to find out there are no tables on the rooftop patio. This place has really hit on a winning formula here in Lakeside. It's a wonder Hendrick hasn't had the owner as a guest speaker some night at Biz Buzz.

Waiting for Polly, at a table for two, I order a coffee from a waiter who barely acknowledges me. He's tall – his thighs, under his white apron, lean against the edge of my table – as he scans nearby tables, not looking at me. He asks lazily with a Mediterranean sounding accent, "Cream and sugar?" He gives my table a quick swipe with a cloth, scattering grains of salt onto the floor.

I answer, yes, reflexively, because ever since my grandfather fixed it for me, with cream and sugar is how I've always taken my coffee. Grandad told me: "Coffee should be as smooth as cocoa, and sweet, but not overwhelming. You want to taste the coffee flavour." He was a connoisseur of many things in life. He savoured all the moments. I miss him.

Dressed in white summer pants and a flowy sheer top, Polly sails through the crowded restaurant. "So good to see you!" she greets me, landing at the table like a beautiful swan, her blue eyes dancing. "How's every little thing?"

She's so enchanting and stunning in her snowy outfit I'm drawn instantly into her aura. No wonder she seems to be friends with everyone. Her focus on me alone makes me feel like I'm elevating from my chair – right this moment *I* am the most important person in Polly's orbit.

Flustered, I don't know where to start. How's every little thing? Well...

The waiter plunks my coffee down, sloshing it into the saucer. No sign of cream or sugar.

"Coffee?" he asks Polly with the same indifference he paid me.

"Tea," she answers. "What kinds do you have?"

He sighs, audibly, and says, "I'll be right back."

There's no chance to ask about the cream or sweetener for my coffee.

Polly stares at his back as he retreats. "He's rude."

I agree. But let's not focus on the jerky waiter.

She exclaims, "He didn't even bring menus!"

How proud I am to jump in and point out the QR code in the middle of the table – and even more so to show her how to aim her phone's camera to get the menu up on her screen. It would seem I'm not the only dinosaur. Polly scrolls through the choices.

I don't know what to order. I certainly won't be having the mascarpone stuffed French toast with Grand Marnier sauce. I chew my lip and glance at Polly.

"Fantastic, they've got Eggs Benny galore," she says. "They're a life saver in a place like this."

I scroll down past the pancakes and waffles and she's right, there certainly are a lot of different ways to get Eggs Benedict.

"What about the English muffins?" I ask.

"Order without," she says simply. "Just ask for what you want. It's less food, not more. They can't object to that."

Good advice.

The jerk brings Polly a steaming hot carafe of water, a cup and saucer, and a tiny box filled with colorful envelopes of tea.

"Ready to order?" he demands.

"Go ahead," I tell Polly.

"I'll have Eggs Benedict with strip bacon, not back bacon, no muffin, no home-fries, no fruit."

He doesn't write anything down. "You?" he asks, and I wonder if he even heard Polly.

"I'll have the same." It's easier that way, though I do like back bacon. Just go with the flow.

I take a sip of the black coffee. Yuck! How do people drink it this way?

Polly asks if I received my order from Bonjour Bacon, and I begin to tell her how my week has been. I feel guilty about holding back from her, but I can't bring myself to admit to all the pastries and cookies I dipped into on the side, or the bowl of popcorn I devoured the other night watching *This Is Us* reruns.

The waiter brings food to the tables on either side of us and I can barely keep my eyes off the mound of waffles drizzled with chocolate syrup, topped with whipped cream and strawberries at the next table.

"This is so hard. How do you do it?"

"It gets easier," she assures me. "Eyes on your own plate."

Right. Good advice. I focus on her as we talk.

When my food arrives it's beautifully arranged on the plate with a side salad but there's an English muffin nestled under each mound of rich yellow poached egg and hollandaise sauce.

Before the waiter can take off, Polly holds up her plate. "I said no English muffin."

He stares at her meal. He's movie star handsome – young, dark. Automatically, I look for excuses for his mistake. Perhaps with that accent, he didn't understand her when she ordered.

Nervous, I pick up my roll of cutlery, but don't unwrap it. I'm frozen. I hate conflicts. Couldn't we just scrape the eggs off the muffins?

The waiter may be thinking the same thing, because he doesn't take Polly's plate, so she thrusts it toward him and raises her voice. "Will you *please* take this back to the kitchen and get me what I ordered!" People at nearby tables look over at us. She's making a scene.

Now, a hush falls over our end of the restaurant as everyone watches Polly versus the jerk. I'm trembling and anxious. I don't think I'm hungry anymore. Suddenly, I dislike this restaurant. And I'm not sure about Polly anymore either. My appetite has vanished.

Finally, he snatches her plate and glares at me. "Is yours all right?"

I wither under his punishing eyebrows and glance at Polly who raises hers, waiting for me to show some gumption.

I swallow the lump in my throat and pick up my plate. "Mine too, please."

The jerk grabs both plates and stalks off. Polly laughs and I sense diners around us expelling breaths of relief, resuming their usual clatter and chatter.

A minute later the hostess flutters over to our table. "Everything okay, ladies?"

I'm about to ask if she can please bring some cream and sweetener when Polly says, "I hope he doesn't spit in our food."

My eyes widen. A man at the next table guffaws.

The hostess murmurs something incomprehensible and darts off in her high-top runners toward the kitchen.

Polly takes a sip of her green tea. "I'm done with jerks. I had a husband like that. Always controlling and gaslighting me. Telling me I didn't say what I just said – that I couldn't possibly like what I like. I'm done with it. No more."

I'm awestruck. She's so clear about who she is.

I lean across the table. "Mine may have been cheating on me."

I can't believe I voiced it, but I did, and now that my biggest suspicion is out from under the bed, I can't stop talking. My voice low, so I'm not overheard, I fill her in with broad strokes on the Zelda and Xavier affair, careful not to paint Xavier as the bad guy, but wondering: how long had their affair been going on?

"He sounds like a jerk too," Polly says.

I want to argue that the reason he lost interest in me, may be understandable – I may have let myself go – but it's too shameful to admit.

It's possible I wasn't paying enough attention to him. And if, I mean *when*, we get back together, I'll mend my ways. We'll return to how things were at the beginning, before Madison came along. I'll be so grateful and relieved to live together again, I'll be able to stick to all my convictions.

I don't tell Polly any of that.

"Ex-husbands, they're the worst." she says. "But they're in the past and there's only one way out." She lifts her teacup and toasts, "To the future!"

There's no arguing with that. I lift my cup and take a sip of bitter coffee.

She tells me she's started to experiment with online dating. "It's a whole trip," she says, shaking her blonde hair. "You wouldn't *believe* how many fish there are in that sea."

The hostess, not the jerk, brings our food and waits to make sure everything is perfect before she disappears. Dragon slayed. Yay, Polly.

"Where do you work?" she asks, as we dig into our egg dishes.

"You're not going to believe this but I own Honeywell's Baked Goods."

She sets down her knife and fork and stares at me. "No!"

"I didn't mean to," I defend myself. "My Grandad died and left it to me." She resumes eating, listening. "I actually wanted to go into counseling, like Jane." She nods, and I'm surprised I've also divulged this little nugget about my long-ago ambitions. I never told anyone, not even Jane. "Then the bakery was suddenly mine, and Xavier really encouraged me, and it enraged my mother that Grandad left it to me and—"

"It must be awful, working around all those carby foods."

I look into her eyes. "It's impossible," I say, almost beginning to cry. "I don't want it to be impossible, but it is when the smell of baking is all around me."

She nods, understanding, and for a moment I think she's going to let me off the hook and tell me it's hopeless, I might as well give up. But she doesn't. She says, "I love the smell of things toasting or baking."

"Yes! Exactly! I can't resist it."

"Do you like roses?" she asks.

"Roses?"

"Yes. Do you like a bouquet of roses?"

I think about the gorgeous bunch of peonies and roses from the garden that Mother placed on the dining room table a couple of weeks ago. They were stunners and the pinky-orange roses smelled glorious. "I love roses," I answer.

"Do you like how they smell?"

"Mm hm."

"Do you eat them?"

I laugh. "What?" I hope she isn't adding flowers to the crazy food list. "Eat roses?"

"My point is," she explains, "just because roses smell good, doesn't mean you have to eat them."

It's a strikingly simple statement. Just because something smells good doesn't mean I have to eat it. This woman is wise! Maybe I will be able to do this.

"You can enjoy the smell of your baked goods and not eat them. Just leave it at, smells good. And make sure you don't let yourself get too hungry. Hunger is a trigger."

Duh.

She asks a bunch of questions about what I've been eating and drinking over the past week, giving me pointers about electrolytes, which I'd never heard of until now. Apparently, they're minerals floating around in water and we need them in our bodies.

"It's why you were feeling so rough the first few days. Be sure to keep up your electrolytes."

I nod dutifully, not fully understanding, but I'll be sure to drink lots of water from now on. I take a sip from the glass in front of me.

"And stay satiated," she counsels.

I like that word, satiated.

"Not food coma. Not stuffed. *Satiated*."

I nod. "Okay, so it's not about starving myself."

"Definitely not! No starving. The theory is, your body will burn up the fat it's already stored and you'll lose weight."

We discuss packing on pounds in middle age – apparently, we were both only moderately overweight until menopause, and then, Pow!

Polly asks, "How many kids do you have?"

I get out my phone and show her a picture of Madison aboard the yacht in the Adriatic.

"That's right! That's why you were shopping at The Beach House. I love Europe. When are you going?"

There's that terrifying question again. Every time I think about it, I feel queasy.

Polly's eyes are so reassuring. Though I barely know her, I think I can tell her everything.

"I'm afraid of flying," I whisper, and it feels good to get it out. I've been lying and brushing off people's questions for weeks now. It feels freeing to finally say it out loud – like being released from the waistband of too tight jeans.

"Me too," she says, and resumes eating.

"You're afraid of flying *too*?" I can't believe how much we have in common. Our weight, our divorces, and now our aerophobia.

She says, "I take a little pill before I get on a plane. It does the trick. You should try it."

TWENTY

I'm sitting in Doctor Gertie's waiting room, my purse in my lap, staring at a jungle poster on the wall, a tiger's face gazing back at me. I don't want to read magazines today – they're too triggering. Too many ads for junk food. Too many articles and ads about how to lose weight.

I used to think I enjoyed flipping through magazines. I didn't realize I always ended up feeling bad about myself, thinking I wasn't good enough, or else hungry and ready for a binge.

I *am* going to Europe. The decision has been made. I've heard nothing more about a double wedding. I'm charging it all to my credit card, and come hell or high water, I'll pay it back. I am not missing my daughter's wedding.

The thought exhilarates – and terrifies – me.

It's silly that I didn't think of it before, but I've used the 'take a pill' method many times over the years to calm me down before a blood test. There's no reason it won't work for flying in a plane, suspended over a vast ocean, for hour upon hour upon hour.

Stop thinking about that!

I will book the flight, take a taxi to the airport – pop the Gonzo along the way – and float through baggage check, security, customs, whatever. I'll be fine. Polly says she's been doing it for years.

I just need to get to the travel agent to book the flight.

I wonder how much it will cost.

It occurs to me that I can probably look that information up right now.

I dig my phone out of my purse, turn it on, and find the search bar and type: `Flights to Croatia end of August.`

Swarms of sites pop up. Deals and 'Book your hotel' banners flood the small screen. I scroll until I see a listing that looks vaguely reputable.

I click, but to go further I'm required to fill in a bunch of perplexing boxes, like airport code from departure city. And airport code for destination city. How am I supposed to know that?

I back out of the website and try another. Why is everything so complicated?

Finally, on a different site, I fill in my departure city and the dates I'm looking at. It thinks for a minute, then a list of flights appears on the screen.

Holy cow! It's way more expensive than I thought it would be. And that's without a hotel.

Maybe I can just go for three days – zip in, zip out.

My heart sinks. If I'm traveling all that way, I should stay for a week or two and have a look around.

But I don't have the credit limit, and I still haven't paid for the swimsuit and cover-up I bought at the Beach House. They cost a small fortune. Sales haven't increased enough yet to give me hope.

Maybe this whole thing is a ridiculous fantasy.

I should take the swimsuit back and get a refund. That will help. But it said everywhere in the store – in the change rooms, at the cash register, on the receipt – All Sales Final on Bathing Suits.

Maybe Polly can help me.

Maybe I'll just take back the cover-up.

Or else explain truthfully to Madison why I can't come.

And let Zelda stand in for me.

No way I'm letting that happen. Not today, sugar!

Yet what am I supposed to do? Go and spend money I don't have?

I wish there was a guarantee, other than Hendrick's verbal assurance, that the strategies I'm learning in Biz Buzz will work. On his suggestion, I made an appointment with the bank to see about getting a card reader. He laughed when he found out Honeywell's has only ever accepted cash. I didn't tell him that back in the day customers sometimes paid with cheques.

I still have my doubts that people will use cards to make small purchases, but Hendrick promises my sales will increase immediately.

I hope so, because I don't want to take my purchase back to the Beach House. I've got dreams for that black swimsuit and elegant cover-up. I'm imagining a pair of gold sandals with glittery stones over the toes. Not to mention Xavier's reaction when he sees me in it, looking svelte and beautiful.

The receptionist says, "She'll see you now, Mrs. Asp."

I make my way back to Doctor Gertie's cubicle.

"Trudy! So good to see you back so soon. You're looking wonderful. Everything okay?"

"Thank you, and yes," I say bashfully, uncomfortable with her compliment. "I'm actually here to get another prescription for Gonzos."

"What for? You don't have any more blood tests." She frowns. "You can't fool around with these pills. We don't want you to become dependent."

I'm puzzled. And a little embarrassed. No one wants to be 'dependent' I guess, but I don't really know what she means. I wasn't anticipating resistance to my idea. She's usually so amiable.

"I'm not fooling around," I plead. "I need to get over to Croatia for Madison's wedding."

"I heard she was getting married. Congratulations! But what's that got to do with Gonzepam?"

"You know how I'm afraid of blood-tests," I explain. "It's the same with flying. I *cannot* get on a plane. I feel sick even thinking about it right now. But I want to get to my daughter's wedding. I can't very well take a boat."

She nods thoughtfully, and suddenly I'm worried she's going to try to talk me into something whacky like a cruise ship, or aversion therapy. I just need the darn pills!

"Okay. I will write you a scrip," she relents. "Just for six tablets. After that, no more. You hear me?" She taps a few words into her computer and a prescription form prints out beside her. "I must say, you look marvelous, Trudy. Are you sleeping well or something?"

I don't know whether to tell Gertie about LOBO. "Don't call it a diet!" Polly instructed me. "A diet implies there's a beginning and an end. This is different. This is a lifestyle change."

And it's been going well for the last little while. I'm not sick or foggy anymore. I don't want to jinx it by telling anyone else. I learned my lesson with Jane and Mother.

Gertie, however, is the one who recommended Dr. Arnot. She may already know about his food plan.

"I've been eating a little differently," I tell her. "Home cooking, mostly, no junk food."

"That's awesome!" She grins. "Hop on the scale."

Polly also warned me against weighing myself too soon: "It's just a number. You don't want to get all obsessed about it. And sometimes it can be discouraging."

Dr. Gertie is up, smiling, and holding open the curtain for me, so I follow her like an obedient little prisoner. Stepping onto the scale, I close my eyes and hold my breath.

"Trudy, you've lost 8 kilos since you were last here! That's some home cooking!"

I open my eyes and stare at the number on the screen before me.

Is the scale broken? How did *that* happen?

TWENTY-ONE

"I want to sit in your mother's glorious garden," Jane says, inviting herself over for lemonade in the backyard.

Lemonade in the garden conjures up ladies in lacy frocks with parasols, nibbling on cucumber sandwiches and petit fours, drinking from beaded crystal glasses full of delicious lemony sweetness.

I can't do any of that now.

Not that I ever did before.

But I do want Jane to come visit, if only to tell her the amazing news about the weight I've lost. In your face, doubter!

Plus, bonus, for the first time in ages, Mother went off this morning for something-or-other across town. She told me as I was showering, shouting at me through the closed bathroom door. I couldn't hear what she said, and she was gone when I got out. Home alone! Yay!

I mix up a can of frozen lemonade and arrange a plate of store-bought cookies for Jane. Mother keeps her favourite treats in a cupboard over the stove. I'm trying to forget what's lurking there behind the closed cabinet door, but today, her stash is coming in handy. Mother's cupboard is full of the stuff she likes to eat, and she hasn't even noticed I stopped bringing home day-olds from the bakery.

Obviously, she wasn't the one eating them.

It's amazing how much day-old inventory there is to sell now that I've stopped gobbling it all down. And customers love the bargains. They snap them up by 11 o'clock, every morning. Hendrick thinks it's great.

Jane arrives in a camo t-shirt and chinos and we arrange our lawn chairs in the shade of the tall pines lining the south side of the backyard. It really is delightful back here. I don't know why I don't spend time sitting and watching the birds and insects doing their day's work among the flowers and shrubs.

I sip on a glass of iced bubbly water, garnished with lemon and lime slices, and a sprig of mint Jane plucks from the garden. Amazingly, I'm not envious of the wafers she's crunching through, brushing her crumbs into the grass for the ants.

"I've lost 8 kilos," I announce proudly. "That's 17 pounds."

She nods and waves her hand dismissively. "Water weight," she mumbles between cookies. "Your body is expelling the water it's been retaining."

I'm crestfallen. She can't possibly be right. Dr. Gertie didn't say a thing about 'water weight.' But Jane does know about this subject.

The plate of cookies is starting to call to me now.

To distract myself, I focus on the birdfeeder. A pair of goldfinches grip the side of the black mesh, pecking at tiny seeds.

Now, I know why Polly warned me against weighing myself. Or talking to others about weight loss. I feel as though the wind is gone from my sails.

I change the subject to Biz Buzz, and our friends, and as we have for our entire lives, we chat about every other topic under the sun. I complain to Jane about the exorbitant price of airline tickets to Croatia, even though I'm sort of bragging about going at the same time.

"It's going to cost a fortune." I list off the expenses I'll incur going to the wedding. "There's the hotel, my food, the dress. I'll have to buy shoes! I'll be paying it off for years."

She clucks her tongue. "What're you gonna do?"

Before our conversation can go any further, Mother bursts through the sliding screen door on the back-deck. Wallander darts out from between her feet and dashes into the garden, chasing a bird he's probably been stalking through the dining room window all morning.

Rising from her seat and crossing the lawn to meet Mother, who's making a beeline for us, Jane says, "Carole! How wonderful to see you! Shall I pull over another chair? Your garden is amazing!"

Mother acts like she doesn't even see Jane, and plows straight for me, her eyes fixed on my face. Oh no, what have I done?

When Mother plunks herself down in the chair where Jane had been sitting, Jane drags over another one.

"You will *never* believe what's happened," Mother says, catching her breath.

It's been so long since I've seen her sober and ambulatory, I'm enthralled.

"I told you my lawyer called this morning," she starts, and I nod, guiltily. Lawyer? I wasn't even trying to listen when she shouted through the bathroom door. What did her lawyer want? "He said it was important, and to meet at his office straight away, so I drove across town and you're never going to guess what happened." She slaps her thighs. "I'm rich!"

"You're rich?" Jane shifts her lawn chair closer, all ears. "What?"

"Oh, hello, Jane," Mother says. "When did you get here?"

Jane waves off the question – impervious to Mother's addled mind – and asks, "What do you mean you're rich?"

"Sabrina! That rascal. She left me her estate – I'm rich!"

And I'm gobsmacked.

Sabrina and her husband were swimming in money.

It's too incredible. She left her estate to Mother? Why? And how much money are we talking about? How is this possible?

"Sabrina died?" Jane asks.

Mother rubs her knobby knuckles back and forth over her thighs and asks, "What are you girls drinking?"

Fixing drinks, I watch from the kitchen window as Mother gives Jane a tour of the garden. They amble around, seemingly discussing the rose bushes and the lush border of perennials along the north side. Mother has a delighted smile plastered on her face. Apparently, she's no longer grieving the loss of Sabrina.

Birds dive down into the bird bath, splash around, and take off whenever Jane and Mother move nearby. The sun, high above, shimmers through a thin cover of clouds. I stir Mother's gin and tonic. I suspect she didn't request her usual martini in front of Jane because it's still early in the day. She attempts to behave normally when other people are around, which is a nice break for me.

"I've always wondered what is the first thing I'd do, if I won the lottery," Jane ponders as we settle back into our chairs under the trees. "I mean, besides pay off my mortgage."

"New car!" Mother says. And I stifle a laugh. She's been out of the house exactly once in the past few months, as far as I know, and that was today to go to the lawyer, but she thinks she needs a new car.

"What kind of car?" Jane asks, obviously delighted that Mother is willing to play this game.

"Mustang," Mother answers, and Jane and I both crack up.

Jane probes. "Why a Mustang, Carole?"

Mother takes a deep drink of her G & T. "Muscle car," she says, plucking a napkin from the tray to dab the corners of her lips.

Through her mirth, Jane asks, "And why do you need a muscle car?" She's always enjoyed my mother. Ever since we were teenagers, she told me my mother was a scream. I never thought so, but Jane loves egging her on. Anything for a laugh.

"I just think it would be nice. And I've always wanted one." She says to me, "Your father bought such boring old sedans. I'd like something fancy now. Red. I'd like a red Mustang. Can't you just see me racing down the freeway with the top down?"

Jane chortles. "Oh, it's a convertible, is it?"

"Yes. And I'll wear a kerchief of course, like Grace Kelly."

I shake my head, imagining the DUIs she'll collect. She doesn't realize she's drunk half the day. It's surprising she was able to maneuver her car down the driveway, let alone onto a crosstown highway this morning.

Wallander pads his way across the lawn toward us, his back covered in confetti from the spirea bushes.

Jane exclaims, "Is this the new kitten? Isn't he cute!"

Wallander makes the rounds, sniffing our toes, rubbing against our sandals. "Give him something to eat," Mother says, snapping her fingers toward the cookie plate.

"He doesn't need anything to eat," I tell her, exasperated, realizing how much of a food pusher she's always been. Always telling anyone thin, like Jane, to eat up, but frowning whenever I said I was hungry.

"Will you sell your house? Move somewhere new?" Jane asks. "Leave this beautiful garden?"

"I don't know," Mother answers, thoughtfully. She drains her glass, then rattles the remaining ice cubes at me.

I can't hide my irritation. "You want *another*?"

I'm up and down like a servant. This was supposed to be *my* visit with *my* friend but now it's the Carole Show. She's wealthy now, so I guess she's also the queen.

Jane grins at me, rattling her glass. "Me too."

It's past lunch time now, and I'm hungry. "Hunger is a trigger," Polly said. "Don't let yourself get too hungry." Refilling the cookie plate with store-boughts is a dangerous place to be.

I open the fridge and peer inside.

Yesterday, I hard-boiled some eggs for snacking, so I can easily mix up some egg salad.

"Anyone want a sandwich?" I call out to Mother and Jane who are having a gay old time under the trees.

Jane calls back, "Yes."

Mother shakes her head, no.

So, I peel the eggs, add green onion, mayonnaise, and a sprinkle of paprika, and spread it on a slice of bread for Jane. For myself, I drop a glob onto a bowl of mixed greens. It's probably not enough food, but it will get me through Jane's visit.

"Guess what?" Jane says, when I bring out our lunch and drinks. "Carole here is paying for us to go to Madison's wedding!"

I stare at my mother, who looks up at me, chin raised, as if it's the most natural thing in the world for her to be flinging money around. This, after a lifetime of complaining about how much my existence has cost her.

"Um, no," I say, setting the tray on a table.

At the same time, they both shriek: "What do you mean, *no*?"

I shoot a dagger at Jane. She knows very well the fraught history I have with my mother. There are strings attached to everything Carole Armstrong pays for. When I was growing up her favourite expression was, "There's no free lunch."

I hand them their drinks. "What I mean, is I'll pay my own way to Croatia. I'm not taking your money, Mother. Or Sabrina's."

Jane's face clouds over into a sulk, and she slouches in her chair, rattling the ice in her glass, staring off into the garden.

"Don't be a brat," Mother scolds. "Jane here *wants* to go with you. And I want to pay. I'm treating you girls. I've never been rich before!"

And I've never seen her so giddy. She's like Ebenezer Scrooge in his bare feet and nightgown dancing around on Christmas morning.

"Forget it," I repeat. "I don't want any part of this inheritance."

"But Sabrina always *liked* you," she lies, trying out the guilt card on me.

"Ha!" I respond.

"How about you, Jane?" Mother says, grasping Jane's forearm. "Didn't you just tell me you'd like to go to Croatia for Madison's wedding."

"Actually…" Jane answers, brightening. "I'd love to."

In all the weeks I've been talking to Jane about Madison's wedding, she's never once suggested she would like to come along, or that she'd accompany me, pay her own way. But now that Mother is dangling a free trip, Jane is all in.

"There you go, Honey Bun. Are you going to deprive your best friend of a European vacation?"

She hasn't called me by that endearment in a thousand years. Obviously, the gin is talking. But I don't trust her and I'm not letting her fish me in.

I pass Jane her sandwich and we lock eyes. She's as roused as Mother is; she really wants this free trip. The pair of them are levitating from the thrill.

"Think about it, Tru," Jane says. "You don't have to get a refund for your bathing suit. Or try so hard at Biz Buzz."

My brow furrows. "But I *want* to try hard at Biz Buzz."

"Perhaps Carole could invest!" Jane suggests.

"Invest in what?" Mother asks.

"The bakery."

Mother snorts. "Fat chance, that place is a lost cause."

"It is not!" I object.

She looks at me with pity and I turn away in anger, more determined than ever to make Honeywell's prosper. I wouldn't accept her money if she gave it to me on a silver platter. She's never been supportive of the bakery. She was pissed off when Grandad's will was read, and stomped out of the lawyer's office tossing over her shoulder, "Great! He left my daughter an albatross!"

She says to Jane, "We'll have *so* much fun, won't we?"

My head swivels around so fast I hear my neck crack. "*We?*"

"I'm not going to miss my granddaughter's wedding."

I stare, silently fuming, as the pair of them plan excitedly.

Why am I so angry? If she wants to pay for the trip, why don't I just let her?

But I can't shake the feeling that she'll just snatch it away the moment I accept it. This is all too sudden and confusing.

"Don't be a downer," Jane says. "If Carole wants us all to go to Madison's wedding – we all go to Madison's wedding!"

They clink glasses and look at me in triumph, but I'm not celebrating. I'm imagining my drunken mother getting thrown off a plane at Heathrow as we change flights.

"Hurray," I say, drooping back in my chair, feeling like cramming a thousand cookies in my mouth.

TWENTY-TWO

Jane leads the way into Debbie Does Nails, our friend's salon, for our ten o'clock appointment. Debbie is nowhere to be seen this morning, but her employees, lead us to the big cushiony massage chairs in the back of the store.

Warm water swirls around my submerged feet and I lean back into the chair, trying to relax.

"I could get used to this luxury," Jane murmurs.

"I'm glad you're comfortable," I answer, with a trace of sarcasm.

We spent hours on the phone last night debating about Mother's inheritance and what it might mean for me. Jane is far more comfortable than I am, with me, *and her*, spending my mother's newfound fortune. I never suspected that Jane would have such a laissez-faire attitude, but maybe it's because she doesn't understand how mercurial Mother can be; how she suddenly changes her mind as soon as she knows you want something, and immediately reverts to her penny-pinching ways.

I'm wary of what I perceive as Mother's charity. It's bad enough I'm living in her house. I hate feeling indebted to her.

Jane asks, "Did you find out how much Carole inherited?"

"No. For some reason, she's keeping that a big secret. But it must be a lot – Sabrina's husband made a fortune on the stock market. You remember their house? It was a mansion! I did find out she left Mother half. The other half is going to an animal foundation."

"Imagine that," Jane says, shaking her head.

"I know. So unbelievable."

The massage chair kneads at my lower back as the young gal at my feet begins the pedicure.

I used to paint my own toenails but it's become difficult to reach them, so, for a few years now, I've been doing without polish. I wonder how long that will be the case? Water weight or not, the pounds are melting off me like butter, and despite Polly's warning, I weighed myself again today. Seeing the number drop again motivates the heck out of me.

The pedicurist tickles my soles with a pumice stone and I flinch. This is the worst part – this and the big grater. Jane doesn't seem to mind. She leans back in her chair, her long legs in their skinny tiger jeans relaxed, flicking through her phone as shreds of dead skin fall from her feet onto a black towel.

"So," she says. "Who's on the list?"

She's referring to Mother's offer to pay for me and my friends to go to Europe, which, after our hours of discussion last night, I've agreed to accept. So far, the only demand from Mother's side is that she gets to come too. I suppose if she's paying, it's only fair, and she is Madison's grandmother.

Noticing our friend Debbie, the salon owner, at the front counter talking on her phone and peering at a computer screen, I don't answer Jane, but silently nod toward Debbie. Jane follows my eyes and interprets my meaning: let's not talk about free trips to Europe within Debbie's earshot. I'm not sure yet if Debbie is on 'the list.' I like her, but can I spend a week or two with her?

"So far, there's you, me, and Mother," I tell Jane, counting off on my fingers. "It's hard. I don't want anyone to feel left out."

Jane deadpans, "I'm glad I made the list."

I smack her arm. "You did, because *you* are Mother's chaperone!"

We both laugh, but I'm serious.

Debbie catches sight of us and clippity-clops over in her high heels and skinny jeans. "Hey! How are you two? What's shaking?"

Jane responds, "Oh, you know, just a little R & R."

Debbie takes a seat in an empty massage chair and proceeds to talk our ears off about her ex-husband, his gambling addiction, a car accident he was in, and how she's so glad he's out of her life now.

"TMI," Jane says out of the side of her mouth after Debbie returns to the front of the salon.

I don't know what she means by this. "Huh?"

"Too much information!" she hisses.

Right. So true. Debbie never stops blabbing all her personal stuff. She's definitely not on the Croatia list. I couldn't tolerate a week or two of her.

When our pedicures are done, Jane and I are shuffled in flip-flops over to the manicure station at the front of the store, our feet placed in tiny drying igloos under the table. Jane readies herself by removing a pile of silver rings from her fingers.

"No polish for me," I tell the manicurist when she fans out the cards of colors for me. "I work in a bakery."

"Nonsense!" Debbie intervenes. "You can do shellac."

"No, no. In all my years working in the bakery, I've never worn nail polish, or rings. Not even my wedding rings."

Pang.

I wish I could stop thinking about stuff like wedding rings.

"Shellac doesn't chip." Debbie insists, grabbing a different ring of samples.

Jane waggles a card with greens and blues at her manicurist. "This one," she says, tapping a bright shade of pickle. "With white orchids on my ring fingers."

"Aren't you worried it will look like gangrene?" I ask.

"Shush, you," Jane says.

The shellacs have fewer color options so I point to a summery, peachy pink that will match the color I chose for my toenails.

"Ho hum," Jane comments, but I ignore her.

"It really won't chip?" I ask Debbie, seeking reassurance. "I don't want flecks of nail polish in the scones."

"Guaranteed," she says, rat-a-tat-tatting her white fingernails on the tabletop in front of me. "Hard as diamonds."

When the soaking and filing and painting and drying is completed, Debbie snaps photos of Jane and I posing with our fingers splayed across our chests, giggling like we used to do in high school. A minute later, when I pull Mother's credit card from my pocket to pay, I'm careful to not smudge my shellacked fingernails, but I find, to my surprise, they're already dry.

"Haven't you ever heard the expression: 'Don't look a gift horse in the mouth'?" Jane asks, as we window shop along Maple Street, stopping at The Runners Walk to stare in at the array of shoes.

"I just think her reaction is *way* out of character," I repeat for about the tenth time. "She's *always* been so stingy with money. And thrifty. When I was a kid, she'd only take me shopping when the sales were on. Today, she's throwing money around like there's no tomorrow."

My eye is caught by a pair of mint runners with aqua highlights and turquoise laces. I've never seen running shoes quite so alluring.

"Maybe there is no tomorrow," Jane says. "Maybe today is all we've got. *Carpe diem*, and all that stuff." She turns to look at me and I see playfulness glinting in her eyes. "Let's go in and buy something. Quick, before Carole takes her card away!"

I laugh, rubbing my finger over the card in my pocket. She insisted I take it this morning and told me to go buy myself something. "And take Jane with you so you don't end up with anything ugly."

She also mused, assessing me from the side, that I might want to join a gym, but I am *never* joining a gym now. I did, however accept her card and the offer of a treated shopping trip.

We go inside.

Everything in The Runners Walk is beyond expensive. I've been in hoity-toity shoe stores before where I couldn't afford a shoelace, but I didn't expect it from a running shoe store on Maple Street. I scan the wall of footwear for the minty pair that caught my eye in the window. They're on the top row, and the price is over $300. For running shoes!

Jane nudges me. "Are you going to try them?"

She's holding a trio of ankle socks in her hand. Her big purchase.

"I don't know," I answer. "They're so expensive."

"So what? What's the worst thing that could happen? You take them home, show them to Carole, if she freaks out, bring them back." She looks around for a salesperson and shouts across the store, "Do you give refunds?"

Mr. Salesperson knows a buying signal when he hears one, something I learned about in Biz Buzz, and he waltzes over to us. "Ladies. What can I help you with this morning?"

He's smarmy – outfitted in a slinky short-sleeved top and tight black knee-length shorts. I take an instant dislike to him. I'm touchy about store sales-people – they see a big woman and instantly write me off, as if overweight people aren't worthy to buy their wares.

"She wants to try on *those*," Jane points a finger with a green fingernail at the exquisite runners on the top shelf.

He blinks a few times before coughing out, "Good choice."

I can tell he thinks I can't afford them. I fiddle with Mother's credit card in my pocket. I'll show him. I'll buy two pairs. I'll buy Jane a pair!

He disappears into the stockroom to retrieve the shoes in my size, while Jane and I giggle as if we're caught up in something naughty.

With a stack of boxes, he returns and informs me, "I brought an 8 and a 9 in Mermaid, but I only have 8½ in Ferrari." He drops them onto a chair and motions for me to sit.

Opening the top box with a flourish, he retrieves the precious shoe from the tissue, whips out the toe stuffer, and settles in front of me. My toenails shimmer with new polish.

Holding the shoe aloft, he asks in horror, "Did you just have those done?"

"It's dry," Jane says with authority. "It's shellac."

He's not convinced.

I struggle to reach my big toe and dab at it. It's still a little tacky. "Umm," I say, looking up at Jane. "I didn't get shellac on my toes."

The salesman immediately tucks the shoe back into its box as if I'm one of Cinderella's ugly step sisters and the glass slipper is not coming anywhere near my big hoof.

"Why not come back when your nails are dry, hm?" he suggests, but he sounds as if he couldn't care less if we do.

Jane throws her socks on the counter as we leave the store. "We'll be back!" she says. And it sounds like a threat to me.

Over lunch, my heart becomes set on the cool green shoes. When we finish eating, and my toenails are dry, we return to The Runners Walk so I can try on the red pair, which are my correct size. I must admit, they fit perfectly. In fact, I've never felt shoes so weightless and at the same time so stabilizing. I look up at Jane for advice.

She demands of the salesman, "What about another store? Could you transfer in a pair of the Mermaids?"

"The Runners Walk is *not* a chain," he sniffs, all snotty and stuck-up. "We don't have *other stores.*"

I get up and walk around in front of the mirror. They certainly are red.

They're like fire engines with laces and smoky flames on the sides.

"What do you think?" I ask Jane. "Are they too much?"

She's standing beside me, one arm crossed, chewing on a thumbnail, and gazing at my feet in the mirror.

"They are bright," she agrees.

"I mean the price!" I hiss, because the salesman is lingering nearby, eavesdropping. I don't want him to think I can't afford them, even though I've never spent so much money on shoes in my life.

"The price doesn't matter," Jane says.

But I have my doubts.

And the red may be too much for me.

I don't have any other red clothes.

But they feel so good.

I ask Jane, "What if I buy a red track-suit to go with them?"

She answers, "Um, no."

TWENTY-THREE

To deliver the Crumb-less on Monday morning, I pull on my new runners, encasing my feet in tight, squishy mattresses. These shoes are so comfortable!

I only wish they weren't bright red.

My heart keeps lamenting over the lost Mermaids I could've had if only my feet had been a little smaller, or a little bigger. But no, I'm stuck with the red runners, and I'm determined to appreciate them.

After the cookie deliveries, I walk further down the street past the dry-cleaner and the delicatessen and the flower shop toward Christabel, the travel agency. My feet are happy campers, and I feel like I'm walking at a good clip.

According to the scale this morning, I've now lost nearly 20 pounds and my knees are already grateful for it. Two sacks of flour down. Four sacks to go.

Mother has always been a client of Christabel Travel, so it shouldn't be a problem to use her credit card to book the tickets. I can barely believe it, but Mother went to the bank and ordered a supplementary card for her account *for me*. It won't arrive for another week or two, so I'm hoping Christa will personally handle the trip.

The money seems to have partially thawed Mother's cold, cold heart. The only comment she made about my new shoes was: "Jane let you buy those?" She didn't ask how much they were, or if I kept the bill.

Christabel is on the corner by the bank in a two-level stuccoed building. I'm surprised to find the door locked even though it's midmorning. I peer in through the window. It's dark, but as my eyes adjust, I can see that except for a couple of metal desks and some cords lying on the floor, the office is empty.

I step back and squint up at the sign, which is still there – a big blue sign with a white silhouette of the Parthenon. Yet Christabel is gone.

"She retired," says Hendrick, popping up beside me and startling me. "I tried to get her to join Biz Buzz but she was already packing up shop."

"I didn't know that."

Usually, I know everything that happens in Lakeside. Chit chat with customers in the bakery keeps me up-to-date, not to mention Jane. She must not know about Christabel. How is that possible?

"Booking a trip?" Hendrick asks.

"Uh huh."

He cocks his head, waiting for me to elaborate with some details, but I don't want to tell him. He takes a stab, "The wedding?"

"Exactly," I tell him. "Do you know another travel agent?"

"Oh Trudy, you don't need a travel agent," he scoffs, smiling his patronizing smile. "Just book it yourself. It's easy. Just go online."

He's always saying this type of thing to me, but nothing is ever easy! Recently, I've figured out quite a few things on my own, but none of them were simple, and booking airline tickets online seems extremely risky.

"Go on, try it," he urges. "It can't hurt."

Hmm. I'll think about it.

After dinner, I plunk my laptop down on the kitchen counter and pull over another stool for Mother. If I'm ordering plane tickets online, I need a witness, even if it's only her, in case it turns into a disaster.

Hendrick gave me the name of a website, and said I should order the tickets and book the hotel all at the same time. I've got it up on the screen when Mother joins me.

"Scooch over," she says, tapping my hip with the back of her hand, hoisting herself onto her stool.

Ignoring the insinuation that I'm taking up too much room *on my own stool*, I slide the laptop so it's between us.

She peers at the screen. "What are we looking at?"

"This is the hotel where we'll be staying."

"Mm. Looks nice. Is that where the wedding is going to be?"

"No, I think the wedding will be at a place called King George's Garrison."

At least, that's what Xavier told me.

Cynically, she says, "A garrison doesn't sound very romantic."

"Actually, it is. I looked it up." I switch tabs to the King George's Garrison website. On the front page is a photo of the setting sun in a wide burnished vista and a bridal couple kissing in front of a stone wall.

Mother takes a sip of her martini.

I scroll down through photographs of the ocean view; rows of white chairs set up under a canopy of exotic trees; a beautiful bridal dinner table glowing with tealights and wrought iron candelabra.

"Go back, go back," she says when I scroll past some wordage giving historical details about the site. Mother is a British Monarchy buff, fancies herself akin to Princess Anne, because they were born in 1950, though she's really enamored with Princess Margaret. "Hm," she comments after reading the text. "Built by George III. I don't know if that portends well."

"What do you mean?"

She looks at me like I'm dense. "George III. *Mad* King George? I don't know that I'd want to get married at a place named after *him*."

"Fortunately, it's not *your* wedding, is it?" Her cynicism annoys me. I switch tabs, back to the hotel booking site.

"How much are the flights?" She asks, tapping a fingernail on her credit card, which is lying on the counter next to the laptop. The pot lights above the sink reflect off the silver chip on the front of it.

I pull up the screen showing the ticket prices for each fare to the airport in Split, Croatia and tell her, "From Split, we'll catch a ferry to the island, but it says we should book the ferry once we're over there."

She gasps. "Are those first class?"

"Of course not."

"That's the price of a single ticket?" She adjusts her giant eyeglasses and leans closer to the screen.

"You didn't think it was going to be cheap, did you?"

"I had no idea," she says, fanning herself.

Here it is. She's backing out. Giving with one hand, and snatching away with the other.

I take a deep breath and my chest hurts. I'll have to go back to financing my own trip to Madison's wedding. Less extravagantly, to say the least. I may have to stay in a hostel. But it's not like I didn't expect Mother to rescind.

It will be so embarrassing to tell Jane and Polly and Suzy and Jessica that the trip is off.

"Well? What are you waiting for?" she asks, flapping her hands at the screen.

My eyebrows shoot sky-high. "You mean you want me to book the trip? Tonight?"

"I'm not thrilled there's no official invitation, and you're not sure of the actual wedding date, but..."

I ask point-blank. "Can you afford this trip or not?"

She takes a sip of her drink. "Don't worry about that, Pussy Cat."

I study her for a moment before proceeding, feeling a bit like a mouse approaching a hunk of cheese in a trap. If I knew how much money had landed in her bank account, it might help me understand this baffling generosity of hers. But she seems to be enjoying keeping that secret from me. If she thinks I really, really, want to know, she will never tell me to her dying day. Literally.

She looks at me with her big googly eyes. "Go on!"

"Okay, let's go back to the hotel site and take a look at the room prices." I navigate back to another screen feeling rather proud of my burgeoning internet skills. Next to me, Mother watches keenly, breathing her boozy breath as I tap on various menu items.

Dates: Last week of August.

Number of rooms: Three.

She asks, "Why do we need three rooms?"

"We're not all sleeping in one!"

"I know that," she says. "But there's you, me, Jane. Who else is coming?"

I sigh.

I told her all this earlier but she retains nothing.

"Polly is confirmed. And—"

"Who's Polly?"

Now, I'm exasperated. "I told you, Mother. She's a friend I met recently. A friend of mine and *Jane's*." I emphasize Jane, because in Mother's eyes, Jane can do no wrong. Except for the red shoes – she's blamed for those.

"I don't know why you have to invite someone we barely know."

It is odd but I feel a bond with Polly that I've not felt in a long time, maybe ever. She understands me. She's interested in me. She encourages me. And most importantly, she eats LOBO like me and doesn't think I'm out of my mind.

I told her about Mother's windfall, and the imminent trip to Europe, and I worried aloud, "I don't know if I can eat like this in Europe. How can I go to Rome and not eat pizza?"

"You breathe in the smell of the crust, and then you peel off the toppings and enjoy them without the carbs," she laughed, tossing her head. "Then you lick your fingers."

She's got everything figured out. I love that about her. It was then that I asked her if she'd like to join us, and she almost fell off her chair. "Of course, I want to join you! The last time I was in Italy, I was so overweight I almost sank a gondola!"

"Okay," Mother says. "That's four of us. So, why do we need three rooms? Unless, I'm getting a room to myself. Is that what you're planning? Stash the old lady who's paying for everything behind a locked door?"

I laugh. I have to. It's either laugh or kill her.

"That's a good idea," I answer, "but I was thinking the third room would be for Jessica and Suzy."

Mother squeals, "Suzy Q is coming?" Obviously, she approves of my longtime friend.

The screen returns a result: Rooms not available for selected dates.

Oh no.

"Are you sure you know what you're doing?" Mother asks, taking another swig of her drink.

"Shhh! Let me think."

"We should call Christa. I have her home number. She'll know what to do."

"Wait," I say, impatiently.

I try adjusting the dates, removing the first day of the trip. We could stay somewhere else for a night, I imagine.

Again: Rooms not available for the selected dates.

Mother drains her martini. "You should've booked this weeks ago."

I almost lay my forehead on the keyboard and cry.

Pointedly, I ask, "How could I do that when I didn't know when or where the wedding was going to be?" I tap furiously, grumbling, and setting the dates narrower and narrower. "Not to mention I couldn't afford to go until a few days ago."

She slides off her stool. "I suppose I should've asked Sabrina to die earlier."

"Don't be morbid!"

I'm frustrated. Suddenly, I have access to the money I need, but because Madison left it so long before providing any details, I can't book a room. And even then, according to Xavier, she still doesn't have a firm date. She just said the last week of August. I bet Xavier and Zelda have rooms. I bet they have a date for their wedding.

"I need a nightcap," Mother says, and I soon hear ice falling into her glass martini pitcher.

Bam! I land on the magic combination of nights. If I book Friday, Saturday, and Sunday nights for three rooms, there are exactly six rooms available.

Mother looks over my shoulder at the screen, her boozy breath wafting into my face. "Wow-wee, that's a pricey hotel."

"Are we booking or not?" I'm exasperated, but I'm also terrified that we're actually booking the trip. "We don't need to do this, you know? It was your idea."

"Why don't you buy the airline tickets?" she suggests. "We might have trouble getting a flight."

I return to the first screen and begin filling in the forms. My chest tightens as I follow the website's instructions, entering my name and address. I've never spent so much money in my life. My palms are sweating as they move around the keyboard.

Filling in a similar form for each of us, I then click through to the next screen. Passport details. Uh oh. I didn't realize I'd have to fill in those to order the tickets. I click around, trying to see if there's a way to bypass it for now, but no. For an international flight, I need everyone's passport information.

"I'll go get mine," Mother says, but she leans against the stove for a couple of moments before heading for the stairs.

Defeated, I tell her, "Don't worry about that right now."

I was doing so well with all this crazy internet stuff. Now, it's beaten me.

"We'll book it tomorrow," I mutter, partly to her, partly to myself. "I'll get everyone's info and we'll do it again."

"What about the rooms? There were only six left."

She's right. Even in her drunkenness, she's making sense.

I go return to the page with the hotel details, but the screen says my time has expired. Argh! Now what do I do?

"I'm going to bed. Beauty rest," Mother calls, already climbing the stairs with her drink.

I open a new tab and try the site again. Luckily, even though my decision time elapsed, the website has remembered where I left off. I punch in the dates again: Friday, Saturday, Sunday for three rooms. The site swirls for a moment and then informs me there are now four rooms available. A minute ago, there were six! If I'm going to book them, I better do it now.

My heart pounding, I pick up Mother's credit card and begin punching in the numbers, double and triple checking that I get them right. It would be terrible to accidently charge someone else's card for the hotel.

Finally, I press enter and sit back, expelling a sigh of relief as the screen flashes a thank you message. At the same moment, I hear a ping as an email notification flashes across the bottom: *Confirmation from Hotel Majka.*

Success! I did it! I punch the air in victory. I should celebrate with a big bowl of—

I catch myself.

I should celebrate with a big glass of bubbly water. And lime – I'll toast myself with that. And a carrot.

I'm humming as Wallander sits on the drainboard, watching me peel delicate orange strands into the sink.

I sing to him, "When the moon hits your eye like a big pizza pie, that's amoré..."

Twenty-Four

I'm wearing the red shoes and bouncing my toes together under the table at Biz Buzz, waiting for the coffee break to end.

I wonder what happened to Jessica? She was supposed to bring her passport details tonight but she hasn't shown up yet.

The Biz Buzz coffee break is hard for me, watching everyone else standing around nibbling, or returning to their spots at the table with goodies and drinks. I could have some veggies and dip if I wanted, but I find it easier to just avoid temptation. I stay in my chair with my fizzy water.

When I delivered the Crumb-less cookies to Suzy this morning, she told me the bad news.

"I can't go," she'd said. "I can't leave my store that long."

It's a ridiculous excuse. Suzy has a half dozen staff. She even has crazy quilt ladies who come in and volunteer their time. Her quilting supply store is always busy, which might be why she doesn't need Biz Buzz.

"Oh, come on," I pleaded with her. "You deserve a vacation."

"I know, I know. But there's Mark," she admitted, looking a little coy.

Mark is Suzy's husband, who she absolutely dotes on. She confided to me, back when we found out about Zelda and Xavier, that she watches Mark like a hawk when other women are around. "They're all over him the minute I turn my back."

I almost laughed in her face. Mark is the most ordinary middle-aged accountant in the world. Pasty, dumpy, an untidy fringe across the back of his head like a friar.

No one is after Mark. Suzy thinks he's a heartthrob, and it's usually cute to hear her talk about him, but today he's holding her back.

"He won't let me go," she explained this morning, like it was a point of pride.

"That's unfair." I frowned, thinking of the hotel rooms I'd already booked with a non-refundable reservation fee.

"Not really," she said. "He plans to take me to Europe, so he doesn't want me to go with 'the girls' and spoil it before I go with him."

I love Suzy, but she's delusional if she thinks her husband of thirty-odd years is going to suddenly get off the couch and do something adventurous for their marriage. Looking around at my fellow Biz Buzzers, chatting and laughing and having a good time, it occurs to me that perhaps the reason Suzy didn't join us for is she can't leave Mark alone in the evenings. It's as if she's addicted to him.

I sip on my fizzy water. For the first time since my divorce, I feel grateful for my freedom. I used to make *all* my decisions based on what Xavier was doing, or on what he wanted. I'm astonished to realize, I'm free of that now.

Hendrick is readying his laptop at the front of the room. Jane and some of the others are taking their seats when Jessica hustles into the boardroom.

"Sorry, I'm late," she says, breathless from jogging up the stairs. "I just got the greatest news!"

I'm relieved she's finally here. I was beginning to worry she wasn't coming tonight. I need her passport details to book the flights.

She announces: "Mackenzie and I are going to Brazil!" Everyone turns to listen as Jessica continues. "Wilson Souza moved back there, as you know." She's always referred to her ex-husband and Mackenzie's father by his full name, Wilson Souza. It's so quirky, but now everyone calls him that. Or did, until he moved back to Brazil. They have the strangest estranged relationship I've ever heard of – they're friends! "His grandmother is turning a hundred, so he invited Mackenzie and me. We're going to South America!"

Jessica loves Brazil. She lived down there for years when she was young. That's how she met Wilson Souza.

She comes around the table and leans down between me and Jane, squeezing my shoulders. "Sorry, Trudy. I can't go with you to Croatia."

Oh no!

I look at Jane, wide eyed, whispering, "We're down to four."

She nods with a questioning look toward Debbie across the room, gabbing away with Sylvia Martin.

I don't know. Inviting Debbie now would be awkward. She'll know she was on the B-List.

"I should've found out from everyone if they could go, before I booked the rooms," I say, cringing.

"Ya think?" Jane retorts. She calls over to Hendrick, "Have you ever been to Croatia?"

He whirls around. "Who me? Croatia? Yes, I love it there. Did you know that's where they filmed Game of Thrones?"

"How would you like to go with us? A spot just opened up," she announces, looking at me, nodding eagerly, like, good idea, huh?

I'm aghast.

Hendrick, wearing purple mascara tonight, flutters his eyelashes with interest. "What are you talking about?"

Before I can prop up my jaw, which has fallen open in shock, Jane is explaining to Hendrick the whole plan in detail: Trudy's mom Carole is paying. It's already booked. Five nights on Vis. End of August. Madison's wedding. Yada, yada.

I talked to Jane briefly this morning, but she was busy and preoccupied, and I didn't have time to tell her I'd done it myself on the computer. "Wait, wait," I object. "I haven't booked it yet."

"You haven't? Isn't that why you need the passports? I thought you went to Christa's?"

"I did go, but she's not there anymore."

"Christa retired," Debbie chimes in, taking her seat across the table. Obviously, she's overheard part of our conversation, but fortunately she's not glaring at me like, why wasn't I invited?

"Christa retired?" Jane asks, amazed there's something she didn't know. "When?"

"A while ago."

"Are you talking about Christabel Travel down the street?" Hendrick interjects. "She closed weeks ago." He can't help himself. He must turn this into a teaching moment. "Travel is a tough business these days, what with terrorists and pandemics and online booking. Who can survive all that?" He looks at me. "Did you go on that site I told you about?"

"Yes," I answer miserably, because it's hard to lie when so many people are looking at me.

"And?" He waits for me to answer. "Wasn't it easy?"

"Um, no, actually," I say, and it feels as if the whole room is listening. "All I managed to do was book the hotel rooms."

"That's right!" Jane jumps in. "We've got three rooms and two people have dropped out, so there's space for you, Hendrick! If you want to go."

He looks delighted, and I feel terrible. I may have to kill Jane. Shouldn't Debbie have been invited before someone we barely know? Why did I hesitate to include her?

"I'd *love* to accompany you ladies," Hendrick says, taking a small bow. "Let's talk about it after class."

He fires up his slideshow and turns off the lights.

"He can't come with us," I hiss at Jane as everyone scrambles to their seats. "It was supposed to be a girls' thing. Plus, Mother."

She waves me off. "Oh, he's one of the girls."

TWENTY-FIVE

The months between May and August fly past, and on the day of our departure, before packing it in my suitcase, I check my laptop one more time for an email from Madison. I'll check FlipFlop again on my phone at the airport to see if there's a post from her. That's how I'm figuring out this whole wedding – dribs and drabs of information from Madison's FlipFlop, her infrequent responses to my emails, and the rare phone-call with Xavier.

I'm not sure why I'm bringing my laptop, but you never know if I might need it.

Madison's indifference hurts today as it did when it began, back when she began high-school. I remember how bewildering I felt when my little teenager turned hostile and downright dismissive toward me. At the same time, her relationship with Xavier deepened, it was just me. He continued to dish out attention and affection to her, finding all her chatter entertaining, and I confess, I was jealous. She was young and pretty, while I, approaching middle-age, was becoming lumpy and boring.

But in embracing my role as Mother-of-the-Bride, I've become caught up in the excitement of the wedding, a sentiment reinforced by the magazines and blogs I've been reading over the summer.

"A wedding is a time for special bonding between a mother and a daughter," I've read over and over.

I just don't think Madison is seeing the same articles.

She hasn't let me in on any specific plans, or asked for any advice, but she *is* on the other side of the world, and working at a busy job cooking for a yacht full of people everyday, so I'm telling myself her incommunicado is understandable. In any event, I am showing up for the wedding. And hopefully, once we're together, everything will sort itself out. I want my daughter in a lifelong bond. I don't want to end up estranged from her, like I am with my own mother, who doesn't seem to understand me at all.

I lay my precious black swimsuit and crochet cover-up in the suitcase. If nothing else, I'm looking forward to wearing them. Maybe I'll even let Polly take a picture of me.

I'm less enthralled with the MOB dress I bought at a big-box wedding store on the hottest day of the summer. 'Bare arms' is not a good look on me but when we were shopping, Jane reminded me it will be hot in Croatia, and I'll be grateful for bare shoulders. If I must cover up, I can always put on the little chiffon wrap that came with the dress. I cram them both into my suitcase.

A terrible rollicking crash on the staircase sends me rushing from my room. Mother is standing at the top of the stairs, but her suitcase is at the bottom.

"Oops," she says, holding up a broken leather strap. "It slipped from my hand."

Her suitcase is about a million years old. Last week when I suggested she buy a new one, she refused. "Waste of money," she said offhand.

"Hold on a minute," I'd said, astounded by her flip-floppiness. "You can pay for everyone to go to Europe, but you can't buy yourself a new suitcase?"

Hers is a monstrosity made of green canvas with leather straps and zipper pockets all over it. I swear it's the size of a card table, but at least it has rollers on the bottom so she won't have to lug it through the airport – unless the broken strap in her hand is the pulley.

"I hope there was nothing breakable in there," I say, thinking of my laptop and wondering again if it's a good idea to bring it. I should cram it into my purse.

"Of course not," she says. "Have you ever seen how they handle suitcases at the airport? I saw a documentary about it one time—"

She's still talking as I duck back into my room and switch my laptop to my purse.

I'm traveling with my sensible black case – the middle piece of a three-piece set Xavier gave me for our first Christmas. I guess he thought we'd be taking family vacations, before we discovered I had aerophobia.

My heart twinges at the thought of happy long-ago family Christmases, just the three of us, but I take a deep breath and give myself a pep talk.

No thinking about your stinky divorce. And no worrying about your naughty grown-up kid. Things are just the way they are, for now. For Madison's sake, try to have a good time. Swing to the next tree.

The airport limo is booked to whisk us to the airport before the afternoon rush hour traffic through Metropolitan Toronto. Mother and I will meet the others on the plane. I glance out the window and notice it's already waiting in the street, causing me to panic a little and rush into the bathroom for one last pee before we go. Nervous, I drank too much coffee earlier in the day and now my pulse is hammering in my ears.

I grab my purse and recheck that my passport and Mother's are safely tucked inside – there's no way I'm letting her hang on to her own – also my wallet, my reading glasses, and a little bottle with six tabs of Gonzo.

"Are you ready?" I call.

"Almost," Mother shouts back. She's downstairs somewhere, and I hope that's not the sound of ice cubes I hear.

Slinging my purse around my neck, I lug my suitcase down the stairs taking it one step at a time.

The look on the baggage checker's face when he sees Mother's suitcase is priceless. "Ma'am, that's an oversize bag."

She stands before him, defiant. "I hardly packed a thing."

"That may be so, Ma'am, but it's too large." He gestures with outstretched arms.

"What am I supposed to do? I can't go home and repack. Trudy?" She turns around to search for me even though I'm standing right beside her.

"It's a hundred-dollar charge for oversize, Ma'am," the clerk says, leaning on the counter, waiting for her decision. "You can leave the airport and go repack in a normal suitcase, or pay the charge."

Mother sputters and is about to object when I slap down my freshly minted credit card on the counter. "Go ahead," I tell him.

Thanks to the bitter tasting Gonzo I choked down in the limo, having forgotten to bring bottled water, I'm parched but as calm as a summer breeze as we navigate through the security area. We get through customs finally after Mother tells the customs officer far more information than he cares to know about our trip to her granddaughter's wedding. Disturbingly, we are then waved over to the side, while other passengers stream past the Canadian flag toward the gate.

Our luggage is sitting on a table next to a gloved security guard. "Whose bag is this?" he asks, pointing at Mother's behemoth.

I push her forward, wondering if I'm feeling *too* casual about all this. Normally, I'd be a nervous wreck.

He unzips a side pocket and displays two full-sized bottles of drug-store quality shampoo and conditioner.

Oh brother.

"You can't bring these onboard," he says.

Mother protests, "But I'm checking my luggage."

"Oversized bags are stored in the cabin, Ma'am." His gloved hands rest on the top of the two bottles. "Do you want me to throw these out, or do you want to return to the terminal and buy smaller containers to pour them into?"

Mother sputters again and looks at me as though going back out and redoing this entire sequence of security steps is a reasonable option for two bottles of cheap hair products.

"Throw them out," I direct him.

There's a garbage bin beside him, and he lobs Mother's hair products in with a loud thump. Clearly, the bin was empty. Normal people understand they can't bring more than a couple of ounces of liquid on a flight.

The minute he says we're clear to go, I grab Mother's arm and hurry her along toward the corridor of shops and restaurants inside the terminal, telling her, "I need a drink."

"Super idea!" she agrees with a boatload of enthusiasm.

"Not that kind. Water."

As we discover a convenience store, Jane, in a safari-suit, bounces into the aisle in front of us. "There you are! I saw you getting searched back there. What happened?"

"It was this one," I jerk my thumb at Mother and smirk. "Too much contraband shampoo."

She eyes me suspiciously, knowing I'm usually anxious around Mother, not to mention all the rumors about my fear of flying. "You seem to be taking it well."

I laugh and shrug, thinking to myself: with a little help from my friends.

Linking an arm through Mother's, Jane gives her a squeeze. "I'll share my shampoo with you, Carole."

I duck into the store, grab a bottle of water from the cooler, pay, and breeze out past Jane and Mother, leading the way down the corridor toward the gate, as if I've done this a million times.

Twenty-Six

·▾·▾·▾·▾·▾·

We have three seats next to the window for Polly, me, and Mother. Across the aisle, in the center row, Jane is sitting with Hendrick. It's a big swanky jet.

I don't know how long planes have been like this, but there's a small screen in the back of every seat. The last time I flew, on the way home from Florida, we all watched the same movie on a big screen at the front of the plane. I still remember, it was *Beaches* with Bette Midler, and all the men on the plane groaned when it began. I don't know if I liked it or not, because I was gripped with fear. I couldn't follow the movie – I just stared forward in petrified silence, a prisoner of the doom-filled soundtrack in my own mind.

This time it's different. Thanks to Mr. Gonzo, things are going well.

Polly digs around in her bag and presents me with the gift of a seatbelt extender. "It's a fantastic gizmo for people our size," she says, showing me how it attaches to the regular seatbelt.

Mother scoffs and asks Polly, "Why would *you* need that?"

Polly doesn't answer her but says to me, "Someday, I hope you won't need it either." Acting as though she hasn't even heard Mother.

During takeoff, I sit back in the narrow seat, crammed between Mother on the aisle and Polly in the window seat. I close my eyes and try to ignore the roar of the engines and the rumble of the runway under the wheels. After only a minute or so, I feel the plane lift and after a few minutes, it levels off and I hear the ding of the seatbelt sign.

I did it! I'm flying and I'm not freaking out.

However, I am not undoing my seatbelt. Thanks to the seat extender, it's nice and comfy, and I may be relaxed, but I'm not *that* relaxed.

I just hope Mother doesn't get drunk, and embarrass me in front of Polly. I haven't yet told my new friend all the ins and outs of Carole.

Mother spies the drink cart starting down the aisle and huffs, "Finally!"

"Please, take it easy," I plead, but she shushes and swats at me. She has no idea how sloppy and ridiculous she gets.

"I'm buying!" she announces, loudly, and nearby passengers turn to look as the attendant approaches our seats. He's a handsome young man, smiling patiently as though he's accustomed to lushes like Mother.

He leans over, drops her tray, and lays out three cocktail napkins.

"Them too," Mother tells him, indicating Jane, and Hendrick who waves with a brilliant smile, batting his eyelashes, which are midnight blue tonight.

I wasn't planning on having a drink on the flight. Since I've been eating LOBO, I've been staying away from cocktails. I'll have a club soda.

Mother orders a gin and tonic. "Make it a double," she says.

I just know she's going to get tanked and make a spectacle of herself. I was doing so well not worrying about anything. The plane didn't blow a tire, or lose a wing, when we took off; terrorists haven't taken over the cabin with knitting needles and nail-scissors; and there seems to be enough oxygen to go around, at least, I'm breathing. Yet if Mother gets drunk, who knows what'll happen? She can cause a world of trouble.

I may as well go for a jolt of courage if I'm going to face the next few hours before Mother passes out, so I order a Bloody Mary – it's the only drink I can think of that isn't sweet. The attendant mixes it on his cart, complete with a stalk of celery. Good choice.

Polly orders a glass of champagne.

"Good idea!" Mother crows. "I'll have one of those too. Champagne for everyone!"

The attendant laughs, searches around in his cart, and says, "I'll be right back."

"Where's he going?" Mother complains as he disappears up the aisle. Other passengers around us laugh.

"Maybe they keep the champagne in First Class," Jane speculates.

"Why aren't *we* in First Class?" Mother demands to know, completely forgetting how she balked at the price of even the economy tickets. "It's so cramped in here. Planes weren't like this when I flew with Lewis."

I don't listen as Mother launches into a series of travelogues, stories of when she and my father left me behind with my grandfather. But she does have a point about the seats. We are jammed together, and for a heavy person like me, it's even worse. At least Mother's skinny butt isn't squished in between the armrests like mine is. There's no room to move my legs, especially with the tray down. I wonder if she'd mind if I lifted the armrest between us. How am I ever going to sleep tonight in this position?

The attendant returns with a bottle of champagne and Mother stops talking to watch him set plastic wine glasses on each of our trays. He pours in the golden bubbles without spilling a drop.

"Low carb, chin-chin," Polly says to me with a wink as we clink plastic glasses.

"Here's to Madison!" Mother says, raising her glass, happy now that she's got her booze.

"What movie are you going to watch?" Polly asks, fiddling with her screen and scrolling through the options. She shows Mother and I how to get our screens switched from airline videos to film selections.

There is so much to choose from, so many movies I haven't seen.

When Madison was little, I didn't go to the movies, other than the occasional weekend matinee at our local revue cinema when they were showing *Toy Story,* or *1001 Dalmatians,* or *Stuart Little*. And when she grew up, I only watched the odd film that showed up on TV when I was alone. Xavier was never a movie buff. He only liked watching professional sports, and there seemed to be a game on every night of the week, and all day on the weekends. It never occurred to me to get a television I could watch by myself in the bedroom.

"It's silent," Mother complains, selecting *Roman Holiday* from the Golden Age of Cinema section.

"You need headphones," Jane says, half-standing in her seat and snapping her fingers, trying to get the attention of our flight attendant, who is now at the back of the plane serving drinks.

"I'll get some," Hendrick says, rising from his seat, straightening his clothes. "Scooch," he says to Jane so she'll sit down again and give him enough room to get out of his seat. "I have to visit the little boys' room anyway." He touches his hair and marches off down the plane.

All settled – I'm starting to relax, almost as if I'm floating – when the smell of food wafts through the cabin. Our dinners. I forgot all about them. The food trolley rattles down the aisle. Mmm, I'm hungry.

With brilliant forethought, Polly had suggested I order the Gluten-free option when I booked the tickets. She assessed it would be the safest meal for us, but when we take the lids off our plates it's evident, they've given us the wrong meals.

"Oh no." Polly waves at the attendant before he can move on. "We ordered the Gluten-free dinners."

He looks puzzled.

"Aren't those Gluten-free?" he asks, surveying the meagre piece of breaded fish, the wilted green beans, rolls, and fruit salad. He scans a folded sheet of paper on his cart. "Ohhh, those are Diabetic meals. Someone's made a mistake."

Polly narrows her eyes at me.

"It wasn't me," I exclaim. "I double-triple checked *everything*!"

Around us, I sense other passengers getting restless.

"What's going on over there?" Jane demands, as though agitating for the hangry horde aboard the plane. "We all just want to get on with dinner. You're holding us up."

"It's not a problem," Polly says to the attendant, surprising me. I haven't forgotten her tangle with the jerk at The Smokehouse. "We will make do. Do you have any nuts?"

The attendant has a whole basket of salted almonds on the top of the cart. Polly takes eight packages and drops four on my tray. "We'll be fine," she says, sweetly, and reaches across me, asking Mother, "Would you like my fruit salad, Carole?"

A lover of mushy canned fruit, Mother accepts. "If you're not going to eat it…"

I copy Polly, passing my fruit salad to Mother, and picking the breading off my fish with the plastic utensils, revealing a white-fleshed absolutely tasteless mystery-fish hiding beneath. Following Polly's lead, I spread the pat of butter for the roll onto the green beans and eat them, though they're no longer hot and the butter doesn't melt. It's an unsatisfying meal, but my head is fuzzy and I don't really care. I lean back sleepily in my chair, the tray pressing against my belly.

I'm in a deep, dark, doze when I realize I'm being jostled.

Voices, muffled, yell my name and I wonder, lazily, have we been hi-jacked?

Yet I don't wake up.

Polly is shoving at me, trying to rouse me, but my eyelids are so heavy.

I just want to go back to sleep.

I sense Jane in the aisle waving, shouting, but she's underwater. It's impossible to understand her.

I turn to ask my mother what's going on, but she's clawing at her face, pointing at her throat, soundless, eyes bulging.

Oh, my gawd, Mother is choking. Someone needs to do something.

My hands flap at my seatbelt, but I can't find the buckle.

Beside me, hunched awkwardly, Polly is frantically stacking the plastic meal trays onto her seat. She pushes my tray up, trying to make room and is now crawling across my knees.

I hear shouting and uniformed folks fill the aisle. Someone in a cap leans down and pulls Mother up and out of her seat.

I can't undo my seatbelt.

I don't seem to be able to form words.

A flight attendant spins Mother around in the aisle. He flips up her arms and wraps his around her from behind. He heaves, and Mother flops around like a marionette, wordless, her eyes wild with panic. He adjusts his grip and heaves again. This time, out pops, a single, green, grape.

All around me I hear clapping and cheers but I'm mesmerized by the grape which is now rolling down the aisle.

Jane asks, "Are you alright, Carole?"

Mother is flustered, her face flushing as the blood rushes back into it.

I want to rise. I want to attend to her. But like a sandbag, I'm anchored in my seat. I can't move.

Jane looks at me. "What's the matter with you? Get up! They're taking her to the front of the plane; upgrading her seat."

"Shlshhhhhh..." is all that comes out of my mouth.

"Don't you want to go with her?" Polly asks.

I'm out of it. I'm bombed. I loll my head back and forth on my seatback.

Jane says, "Sheesh, Trudy. How many Gonzos did you take?"

Mother looks away from me in embarrassment.

The last thing I see is the back of Jane disappearing up the aisle toward Business Class.

Twenty-Seven

I'm a castaway at the luggage carousel. One by one everyone else has plucked their bags off the wide rubber belt, and have gone to sit down on a bench. There's no sign of my bag, or Mother's monstrosity.

Everyone is mad at me for getting so Gonzo'd on the flight last night and embarrassing them. I didn't know one little pill would react so badly with alcohol.

Jane confiscated the prescription bottle from me in Hamburg when we were waiting for our connecting flight, and Mother counseled me, "Really, Trudy. Try to control yourself."

By then, I'd sobered up a little, and while we waited for the 90-minute flight to Split, I managed to eat some scrambled eggs. Food in my system settled me down, and when we boarded the plane, I was determined to delay begging Jane to give me back my Gonzos. Enduring the racket of butterflies in my stomach, I survived the takeoff, and once we were up in the air, I told myself I could make it the rest of the way without help from my narcotic friends. I held tight to the armrests, and miraculously, I survived.

I'm a bit proud of myself, but everyone else is treating me like a pariah.

It's becoming apparent that there's a screw up with Mother's and my luggage. My throat feels tight, as though I can't swallow, and my eyes are beginning to water in anxiety. Everyone else is resting on benches and chairs over by the windows, waiting for me. All of us are hot and bothered and dying to get to the hotel in Split, which is supposed to be amazing. It cost an absolute fortune but it's only for one night, and everything else was fully booked. I'm excited to get there too, to look out at the beautiful Adriatic Sea, but here I am watching an empty luggage carousel go around and around.

Finally, an airport employee comes by, sweeping the floor into a dustbin on a long handle. Kindly, and in broken English, he tells me there are no more suitcases coming from our flight. He points out a baggage-service counter and I cross the nearly empty terminal to inquire.

"Ticket," the agent demands.

I rummage around in my purse and pull out my crumpled boarding pass. He opens it, looks it over, and says, "No, Missus. Your bag ticket."

I don't know what he's talking about and look around for help. Fortunately, Jane is already marching toward me in her safari suit. "What's going on here?"

"He says I need a bag ticket. I don't seem to have one. Did you get one?"

She digs into one of her handy pockets and finds her boarding pass and sure enough, stapled inside the flap is a luggage ticket. "Don't you have one of these?"

"No!" I cry. "Where's Mother? Maybe she has them."

We hustle over to the benches and ask Mother for her boarding pass.

"Sorry, I threw it out." She shrugs innocently. "No one told me not to. What do you need it for? We're here, aren't we?"

"Yes, but our bags are not!"

"What's that got to do with me?" She taps her ribcage with her fingers. "I'm not the one who organized this trip."

Jane and I trudge back over to the service counter.

"Look," she explains, "we don't have the baggage tickets. So, what happens now? We just got off that flight." She holds up her boarding pass and shows him. "Where are my friends' bags?"

The agent slides a form across the counter. "Fill out this," he says.

The document is in several languages. Fortunately, English is one.

I begin answering the questions. For the forwarding address Jane looks up our hotel in Split on her phone.

Description of bag #1: Black, medium size, soft case, no distinguishing features, although my home address is written on the tag on the handle, but I don't think that's what they mean.

Now, bag #2. That's another story. I could write a novel about Bag #2. Olive green, brown leather straps, noisy wheels, could feed a family of four on it, etcetera.

"Wait," the agent tells me. "I'll go look."

Jane sighs, and I can tell she's really fed up.

"Listen, Trudy," she says, putting her fingers on my shoulders and looking at me steadily. "It's too freaking hot in here. I'll take the others to the hotel. You follow us when you get this sorted out. Okay?"

"You're deserting me in a foreign country?" I panic.

I'm hot too!

In fact, I think I'm melting.

Jane is sweating profusely, her hair sticking to her temples like mine is. But my clothes are rumpled and damp while her outfit is somehow still free of wrinkles.

She says, "Carole needs hydration." And I can't tell if she's joking. I dare not laugh in case she's serious. She is, after all, an actual M.D., and has taken far better care of my mother on this trip than I have. Maybe it's not funny, and Mother really is exhausted, although I bet, she just needs a good stiff belt.

Hendrick joins us at the counter.

"If they don't find it now, you'll see, it'll be at the hotel by morning. I've lost *so many* bags," he assures me, launching into one of his ever-ready anecdotes. "One time, I literally *forgot* to pick up my bag. I just waltzed out of the terminal with my carry-on over my shoulder. Now, was it on account of the flight attendant I'd just met? Why, yes, that's a distinct possibility. We were meeting for a drink at his hotel and I completely lost my mind – he was gorgeous and—"

Jane wanders away with him as he chatters, returning to the window area where Polly and Mother are guarding the not-lost luggage.

I lean against the counter, anxiously waiting for the agent-guy to reappear, and watch as Jane guides my companions out into the warbly green and yellow world beyond the windows of the airport. They don't even wave good-bye.

"Sorry," the agent says, when he returns. "Nothing here."

"So now what?"

"I file the report," he says tapping his computer screen. "And they trace your bags. Two bags, no?"

"Yes, two bags. You can't miss the green one. It's huge."

"Ahh," he says nodding, as though I've explained everything now. "It will be fine, Missus. The bags will find you at the Hotel Park. Is a beautiful hotel."

Dejected, but trying to be brave, with my purse over my shoulder, I push through the airport doors into a wall of heat. It's like stepping into a pizza oven. I almost choke. How are people living in this?

Between tall tree-like sculptures, a line of taxis waits in the curve of the roadway.

My first glimpse of Croatia would be stunning, if everything wasn't wobbling in the heat.

Twenty-Eight

"We're down by the pool," Jane tells me when I answer the phone in the hotel room.

Because I arrived last, I'm sharing a room with Mother. Jane is shacked up with Polly.

Annoying.

I wanted to share with Polly. Or more accurately, I don't want to room with Mother. That's Jane's job.

Evidently, she's still ticked off about my negligence on the plane.

Can't she understand it was an accident? I didn't know the drinks on top of the Gonzo would spiral me into oblivion.

If it hadn't been for her and Polly, I would've slept, snoring and drooling, through the whole choking episode and my mother would've expired on a grape. I cringe at the thought.

My friends have both done enough for me – I don't dare ask Jane to swap rooms with me tonight.

You can handle your mother for one night. You're only here until tomorrow, then on to the island of Hvar.

Across the room, Mother has just popped an olive into her mouth. She's fixing a martini from the tiny bottles in the hotel room fridge. It's likely not her first. It took me a while to get here from the airport, check in, and locate our luxurious room in this grand hotel. By then, she'd made herself at home and apparently located a jar of olives, which are her main food group.

I hold my hand over the phone and ask her, "Jane wants to know if we want to go swimming?"

She waves me off. "Don't have a swimsuit."

Incredulously, I ask, "You didn't pack a suit?"

She shoots me a look of amazement. "Have you forgotten we've lost our luggage?"

Oh yea, I cringe, how did that little detail slip my mind? This heat is really getting to me.

I return to Jane on the phone. "I can't," I whine, feeling very sorry for myself. "I really want to. This room is boiling. I think the air-conditioning is broken. Is it working in your room?"

"Barely," she replies. "That's why we're down here by the pool. There's a breeze from the ocean."

I moan. "My bathing suit is in my suitcase."

"What a drag. I wish I could lend you one but..." She doesn't finish her absurd thought because she knows I would never fit into one of her skimpy bikinis. "Polly, did you bring a bathing suit Trudy could borrow?"

I hear Polly murmuring in the background but I can't make out what she's saying. It doesn't matter. I'd never fit into one of her suits either.

"Forget it," I tell Jane. "I'll just come down to the pool and watch."

You've got to stop feeling sorry for yourself! This is a fantastic trip – the trip of a lifetime – your daughter is getting married – and you can't let anything ruin it.

Not the air conditioning that feels like a dragon's breath? Not sleeping in a bed with an old drunk lady? How about lost luggage that's traveling on its own around Europe?

Light pours in through vaulted windows as I trudge through the lobby. Under my red running shoes, a beautiful floral carpet sprawls over a marble floor. Outside, beyond a stone railing, palm trees wave. Glittering chandeliers dangle over exotic flower arrangements on tables amid loveseats and velvet armchairs. Heads turn to watch me and it feels as if everyone is wondering, who is that slob in the creased, sloppy, outfit with the fire-engine red shoes?

To my right, is a gift and souvenir store. In the window are nose-plugs and a bathing cap. On the off-chance they also sell swimwear, I deke inside.

Oh, it's wonderfully cool in here. I stand in the cold air, lapping it up before approaching the desk.

"Do you sell bathing suits?" I ask the clerk.

She shows me to a shelf of bubble baths and soaps, mistakenly thinking I need a bath, which I do, but I shake my head and repeat my question, gesturing at my torso. I make a little dive motion with my hands.

She looks at me blankly, pulls her phone from her pocket and holds it toward me, motioning with her other hand. "Say again," she manages in English.

"Do. You. Sell. Swimsuits?" I repeat, enunciating each word.

Magically, her phone translates my words into something she comprehends and she says, "Ah!" and leads me to the back wall of the shop where a number of bathing suits hang.

She asks me something and gestures up and down my body, assessing my size.

How do you say hippopotamus in Croatian?

My cheeks, which had been enjoying the coolness, heat up again. It's unlikely she'll have anything to fit me. This was a stupid idea.

She rummages through the hangers and finally pulls out a very large, very red, tank suit emblazoned with the word, HRVATSKA across the bosom. "You take?" she asks, pushing it at me.

Incredibly, it just might fit. I don't know. I bite my lip and glance around the shop. Where am I supposed to try it on? I'll have to buy it and take it up to my room. "Do you give refunds?" I ask.

"Twenty euro," she answers in English, interpreting my question as a buying signal. I almost laugh. Wait until I tell Hendrick it's universal.

The swimsuit material is thin and cheap but very stretchy and amazingly, the ugly thing fits. I survey my image in the bathroom's full-length mirror. I look outlandish in matching swimsuit and shoes, both the same garish color. A nagging regret about the Mermaid runners resurfaces – if only, if only.

And I have no idea what HRVATSKA means – hopefully, nothing embarrassing.

"Let me see!" Mother yells from the bed.

When I'd returned to the room to try on the bathing suit, I found her lying down in her underwear in an attempt to stay cool, a wet washcloth over her face. She'd closed all the curtains and turned off the lights.

Now, cloaking myself in a plush terry robe from the back of the bathroom door, I step out and flash her. That's it. That's all she gets. I'm not opening myself up to her criticism.

"Going to the pool!" I announce, grabbing my room key. The door slams behind me, leaving her alone in the dark with her martini.

I need some light. I need some fun. I'm here in Europe for Madison's wedding. I did it, I flew without Gonzos (part of the way). Nothing can stop me now!

The pool area is lined with spiky date-palms and square white shade umbrellas. Beyond the stone railings of the hotel's grounds, I glimpse the dancing dark blue of the Adriatic Sea. Scanning the guests enjoying the late afternoon shade of the trees, I spot my friends, reclining on wicker loungers next to the pool. A server, who could be the twin brother of the jerky waiter from The Smokehouse, is handing down drinks to Polly, Jane, and Hendrick.

"None for me," I tell him before he can ask. I'm taking it easy on the booze from now on.

Jane asks, waving at my terry robe, "So, what are you swimming in?"

I may as well join the party and laugh at myself. Maybe it will ward off humiliations before they happen.

"Nothing, I'm skinny-dipping!" I answer, beginning to untie the belt. "Or whatever the fat version of that is."

For a beat, my friends look aghast, as though they believe I'm naked under the robe, until I drop it, revealing the ridiculous red suit. Then they laugh in hysterical relief.

"Where did you get *that*?" Jane cries.

"In the gift shop. You want me to get you one?"

More laughter.

"What does it say?" Hendrick asks, examining the big white letters across my chest while he sips on a blue cocktail that matches his eyelashes.

"It means: Croatia," Polly says, smiling at me. Her support means everything. There's nothing to be embarrassed about. I'm just a large lady who lost her luggage. I can still have fun. I can still go swimming in a hotel pool with my friends.

"Here goes nothing," I announce, turning to jump into the inviting blue water.

My bum bumps into something behind me.

I didn't realize anyone was there!

I turn and watch in horror as a server staggers, stumbles and tries to balance his tray of tall drinks. When I reach out to help him, he trips over my terry robe, and twisting, spinning, he flops into the pool with an enormous splash.

Water splatters me, my friends, and everyone else sitting nearby, on the pool deck.

The server's tray and a flotilla of capsized plastic glasses, bob on the surface of the pool, the drinks seeping into the water, red, orange, white; a cloud of Trudy's grandstanding.

The waiter comes up sputtering, whipping his hair to the side, and cursing, at least, I'm pretty sure, he's cursing. He glares at me and I can almost hear him thinking, "You fat cow!"

"I'm *sorry*," I plead, wishing I could just disappear through the pool deck.

Why was I being such a clown?

Why can't I just act like a normal person?

Twenty-Nine

E xhausted from our travels, and stuffed with a magnificent Croatian dinner, we stop by the front desk to check whether our luggage has arrived, but, no.

Instead, the clerk offers us toothbrushes and combs.

Listening in and lounging on the edge of the marble front desk, Hendrick assures me with his usual confidence, "Don't fret, Trudy. The bags will be here tomorrow, you'll see."

"And if they're not?"

"Then they'll send them on to the next place. Right?" He shoots a dazzling smile at the front desk clerk, who nods.

Hendrick leads me away, toward the elevator bank. "Where is the next place?"

As we wait for the elevator, drooping in the heat, I update everyone on our itinerary. "Tomorrow is Hvar, an island Madison's boat visits every week on Thursdays."

I'd figured out Madison's movements from her FlipFlop account. Every week there are new photos and videos posted from something called a White Party at a flashy nightclub in Hvar, everyone dressed in white, dancers glowing blue, arms outstretched, selfies of girls pressed cheek to cheek with enormous white smiles.

"Is tomorrow Thursday already?" asks Hendrick.

"I'm so jet-lagged I have no idea," says Jane.

Mother asks, "Are we meeting Madison there?"

"Yes," I answer as the elevator bell dings and the doors open.

But the truth is, I don't know if Madison is taking a break from her job this week, or if she's working right up until the weekend. I tried calling her but it went straight to her answering machine. "Hi. It's Madison. You know what to do." I left another message, and I've emailed, but she hasn't replied. Either way, Hvar is on the way to the island of Vis, where the wedding will be on the weekend. We'll spend a night in Hvar, go to the nightclub Madison always goes to and meet up with her there. The following day, we'll catch the ferry to Vis for the wedding.

Silent and melting, we disembark from the stuffy elevator into a stifling hallway leading to our rooms.

"I can't believe you picked the hottest week on record to drag us all to Europe," Jane says.

I stop dead in my tracks and stare at her. "I didn't order up the weather! How was I supposed to know how hot it would be?"

"Don't bicker," Mother says, as the others stream past us. "I have a headache."

"We're not bickering!" I protest, ready to defend my position.

Jane is so unfair, always blaming me for every little thing that goes wrong.

Polly and Hendrick already have their keycards out and in their door locks, fleeing from the airless hallway.

I need to take a cue from them, and not let a tiff with Jane cloud my evening.

I say a gruff goodnight to her and open the door into the darkened room I'm sharing with Mother. She's tipsy, but I wouldn't say she's drunk. She refrained from ordering hard liquor at the restaurant and stuck to the wine Jane ordered. She always manages to behave herself in public.

For myself, I didn't find it difficult to steer clear of the drinks, especially after, perfectly sober, I knocked a waiter into the pool.

"Too many carbs," I whispered to Polly at the dinner table, waving off the server – a different one, thank God – who was pouring wine for everyone. I'm adept at LOBO lingo now. Carbs are bad guys. Stay away from them.

Polly looks up the carbohydrate content of everything on the LOBO app. I may figure out how to get it for my own phone so I don't have to ask her all the time, but tonight's meal was easy: grilled swordfish and vegetables drizzled in citrusy olive oil.

Under the palm trees and candlelight, food never tasted so good.

Mother strips off her sweatsuit and dressed only in her old-lady bra and underpants, flops onto the bed we're sharing.

"Good thing it's a Queen size," she says. "I don't want you cuddling up to me on a night like this."

As if!

I lock myself into the luxurious white-tiled bathroom looking forward to a nice cool shower.

Although they won't dry out by morning, I need to rinse out my sweaty underwear, so, I bring my undies and bra into the shower to give them a shampoo. With any luck, our suitcases will arrive by the morning, but if not, I'll wear damp undies. Who cares? It's not like they aren't soggy with sweat as it is.

The shower is lovely cool, but the minute I step out and begin toweling off, perspiration beads on my upper lip.

How am I ever going to sleep tonight?

And in what?

It's unthinkable to sleep naked with Mother. Don't even mention it. And what am I going to wear to bed?

I consider the terry robe hanging on the back of the bathroom door, but it feels impossibly thick and heavy. I'm not even going try it.

The red bathing suit is hooked next to the sink. It's dry. It only got a splash when the waiter ended up in the pool.

I cringe, recollecting the drinks slipping away into the pool, polluting the water – milky pina coladas, bloody red Caesars, a green melon zombie.

No one could swim after that. They had to drain the pool.

"It wasn't your fault – it could've happened to anyone. And it did not happen because you are fat," Polly told me, when I started to cry.

Sitting in the red bathing suit in the dark, I flip open my laptop. Its glow illuminates the writing desk by the window. I'm hoping there will be a response from Madison now that she knows I'm here in Croatia.

Still, there's nothing. Only an email from Eve at the bakery.

```
Wally is fine. He's in thick with my girl kitties.
The bakery is busy. Have a wonderful vacay! Suzy Q
sends her love.
```

I smile, surprised to hear the bakery is busy. Maybe on her own, in charge of everything, it feels strenuous to Eve. Whatever, it's reassuring to know life at home is under control.

But I can't understand why Madison hasn't responded. The absence of her email brings a sting to my eyes. She's freezing me out.

It's true, since her teenage years I haven't been able to get close to her, but I've always tried. If only she'd give me a chance. I'm here in Europe, aren't I? Come on, Madison!

I open FlipFlop and begin scrolling through her account to see if I can find a clue of where she might be, or what she is doing. She's posted a new selfie, aboard the yacht. Surprisingly, the next photo is of Xavier, sitting, at the front of the boat, wind streaming through his hair.

I didn't know the two of them were together already.

I stare at the photo, feeling utterly left out.

He's here in Croatia, in touch with Madison, and she took him sailing. She didn't invite me.

He looks relaxed and lost in the peace and majesty of the sea and no wonder, the water is magnificent. I wish I was there!

I sniff, about to leave her account, too dejected to look any deeper, when another photo appears – freshly posted. It's Xavier and Madison, their cheeks pressed next to one another. He looks so handsome it takes my breath away. I don't want to look. It hurts. I study his face, drinking in the fullness of his tanned cheek, knowing how it would feel, the slight stubble at this time of night. His eyes are a bit blurry. He's drunk and relaxed. I wish—

Ugh! Stop!

Searching the screen for the way to exit I notice notifications at the top of the page. Clicking on the red dot, FlipFlop informs me that Zelda MacGillacuddy wants to travel with me.

Shut up! I want nothing to do with her!

Before my hand can slam the lid of the laptop shut, a prurient interest seizes my brain. Instead of closing the computer and going to bed like I know I should, I click on Zelda's profile picture and her account opens before me on the screen.

Why does it shock me that she's here in Croatia too? I knew she'd be here for Madison's wedding with Xavier, if not her own, but these photos of hers are devastating.

I shouldn't keep scrolling, but I do.

Photos of the pair of them dining at streetside cafes; hiking on rocky terrain against wide vistas of the Adriatic Sea beyond the edge of cliffs; Xavier waving off Zelda's camera lens, but grinning like he's high on the attention she feeds him.

Ugh.

One photo is a group shot aboard a yacht – a gang I recognize as Madison's colleagues, plus Zelda and Xavier, posing against a backdrop of turquoise water and a rainbow of sails and floating rafts. Xavier clutches the shoulder of a tanned, muscular man with dark sunglasses, black stubble over his chin, and a wide smile of brilliant teeth – he's tagged as Jakov Mihaljevic. Madison must've taken the photo because she's not in the picture. Everyone is laughing and happy.

Except me.

I close my laptop and the room disappears into darkness.

As noiselessly as possible, I pull open the curtain and stare out at the nighttime glow of golden light reflecting in ripples onto the dark sea. It's stunningly beautiful but I'm too bitter to appreciate it. A lemon of jealousy is twisting in my heart, flooding my veins. As hard as I try, I can't get past my husband of all those years leaving me for that vapid skinny b-word—

"What are you doing?"

Mother's voice scares me half to death.

She's lying on the bed – I thought she was sleeping.

"Nothing, nothing, just getting ready to come to bed."

"You were looking at pictures of Zelda and Xavier."

Damn. She caught me scanning Zelda's profile.

She rolls onto her side, and probes, "What are you looking at them for?"

Ignoring my internal warning system, that Mother is the worst person in the world to talk to about this type of thing, I answer, "I know it's not fair. She's probably not an airhead. But I can't help it, I hate her!"

"That's only natural," Mother observes, which I interpret as understanding, so I continue confiding.

"It's Xavier who deserves my wrath. If he was so unhappy in our marriage, why didn't he say something?" I turn in my chair to face her. "We could've worked on it. I could've changed. Something. Been more of what he wanted."

Mother flips her pillow in search of the cool side and rolls onto her back again.

"Maybe that was the problem," she says. "Maybe you were too much more." She spreads her arms.

What did she just say?

Did she just say out loud what a mean part of me has been telling me for months?

I know it's ridiculous. He didn't leave me because I got fat. I may not fully understand why, but it can't possibly be because of *that*! Can it?

I glare across the darkened room, wondering how hard it would be to smother Mother with her pillow.

Beyond the bed, the basket of snack foods on the top of the hotel room fridge beckons me. *Trudy, come eat us!*

I imagine the sound of the packaging crumpling in my hands, and the first whiff of cheesy goodness.

We're salty. We're crunchy. You'll lick your fingers. Come eat us!

THIRTY

At breakfast time, I accompany Mother to the hotel's outdoor dining room vowing that today, I will not allow her to burrow her way under my skin, causing me to eat things I instantly regret.

We're the first to arrive, but Hendrick soon joins us.

The same waiter that I knocked into the pool last night serves us this morning, pouring coffee and setting menus on the table. "You're safe," I joke with him. "No pool in sight."

He smiles politely, nodding in my direction, letting me know I'm forgiven, but not funny.

"I wonder where the others are?" Hendrick asks, looking around, sunshine streaming in through the open roof above the courtyard. "It's not possible they didn't hear Hell's bells tolling at six A.M."

He's referring to the symphony of church bells that rang out earlier today, rousing me from a restless and sweaty sleep.

"Woke me right up," Mother comments.

"I heard roosters!" Hendrick exclaims. "And dogs barking – please tell me they don't do that every day?"

I laugh. "Don't worry, we won't be here tomorrow."

"But where are Jane and Polly? How did they sleep through that cacophony?"

"Maybe they had their windows closed—"

Mother interrupts. "Let's not wait for them. I'm starving." She waves our server over.

I can't believe she's hungry after the dinner we ate last night, which was amazing and the definition of the word, satiating. Here in Croatia, it will be easy to stay in the LOBO lifestyle – they don't push the starchy stuff like they do back home.

Mother's porridge arrives and Hendrick digs into his fruit plate of figs, grapes, plums, and pears, drizzled in honey. It looks delicious. But fruit are "not on my menu," as Polly would say, and I'm starting over today. I'm determined to be satisfied with my rich dark coffee and at lunch time I'll eat.

I wonder if there will come a day when I'll be thin enough to indulge in a succulent, juicy, mango. I banish the thought from my mind. "Future-tripping will not help you," Polly said.

Between spoonfuls, Hendrick remarks to me, "Eve is doing a terrific job with your FlipFlop,"

"She is? Oh good, I haven't checked."

He chuckles. "I think you should."

"Right now?"

Mother shakes her head. "You people and your flip-flops."

"I'll show you," Hendrick says, pulling his phone from his breast pocket. "We wouldn't want you to have to 'turn on your phone'." He winks at me, still teasing me about my lack of technical prowess, which isn't fair. I've been getting really...competent. I keep my phone on now, and remember to charge it. And I've taken dozens of photos with it since we've been in Croatia. I just don't know what to do with them.

Hendrick turns his phone-screen toward me and I see the familiar blue Honeywell's Baked Goods banner of my FlipFlop account, which I was so proud of myself for figuring out. He scrolls down.

The most recent photo is the front counter, full of all the usual squares and cakes. Everything looks right, and in place. I feel proud of my little bakery. And Eve's taken a good photo. Clear, in focus, the counter glows, all the desserts shining colorfully under the lights.

"Notice anything?" he prompts me.

I look a little longer. I don't see anything until…

"Wallander!" I shriek.

Mother's head zips around on her neck. "Wallander? Where?"

"Look," Hendrick says, pointing at the screen.

There, on top of the bakery counter, is our cat.

Before leaving home, I arranged for Eve to look after him, and I also asked her to post a daily photograph to the Honeywell's account, but I never dreamed she'd marry the two. Or bring him into the bakery!

"Oh, my God!" I shriek. "She has Wallander at work? That's a health violation!"

"Very unsanitary," Mother agrees.

Hendrick laughs. "It's not real. Can't you tell it's photo-chopped?"

I stare at the picture again, trying to understand, but my mind is racing, imagining blue lights flashing and sirens wailing as official cars pull up on Maple Street outside the bakery; a contingent of Toronto health inspectors in white lab coats racing across the sidewalk to Honeywell's, their clip-boards and red premises-is-closed notices flapping.

Mother retorts, "It looks pretty real to me!"

"Look carefully, see here, the cat is walking on air above the counter. He's not actually in the bakery. Eve is very good at photo-chopping. Take a look at this one."

Hendrick scrolls to the next photo: a picture of Wallander, his nose pressed into a cupcake the same size as him. In the next one, wearing a polka-dot bowtie, his moustache and whiskers are dotted with milk, in the foreground is a tiny glass with a straw.

"Oh no! This is terrible!"

Hendrick laughs. "Your travelers don't think so."

I gawk in disbelief as he scrolls over the pictures, which have amassed hundreds of hearts. I'm lucky if the pictures I post attract three hearts.

"She's using a clever hashtag too," Hendrick adds. "Hashtag Wally Whiskers at Work. It's gaining a little following."

I pull my phone from my purse. I've got to see this for myself.

I check the number of travelers at the top of the account and I'm astounded to see it's in the thousands. When we left home less than a week ago, I had a dozen travelers.

Yet it can't be a good idea to have cat pictures associated with a bakery.

Polly and Jane join us at the table.

"I slept so good!" Jane says, stretching her bony arms over her head.

Ignoring her, and still panicky about FlipFlop, I tell Hendrick, "I'm going to tell her to stop. Delete those pictures."

"Tell who what now?" Jane wants to know as she takes her seat.

Hendrick shows her his phone screen. "Wally Whiskers has become a bit of an internet sensation while we've been away."

Polly leans over to look, "Oh, isn't that sweet!"

"It's not sweet," I object. "It's a *cat* in a *bakery*. It's unhygienic."

"I think it's cute," Jane disagrees.

"Trudy, calm down," Hendrick says, and I see red. Only a man would have the gall to tell a woman to calm down. Oblivious, he continues to needle me, "We've talked about ways to improve your business. This is one way. Awareness. It lets people know Honeywell's exists and it's got personality. Real people work there."

"With a cat!"

"Most people will be able to see that Wally is not really using a fork to eat this—" He gapes at the photo of a slice of my signature Decadent Charisma Bomb. "Oh my God, what is this?"

"His name is Wallander!" Mother corrects, but no one is listening to her.

Jane peers over at Hendrick's phone. "Chocolate mousse cake. It's delicious."

Polly leans across the table toward me. She can tell I'm upset. She looks me in the eye, and probes, "This all sounds exciting for you. What other plans have you got for your business?"

"Plans?" I stare at her, exasperated. Isn't the important thing right now, whether I should tell Eve to delete the Wallander pictures?

Polly is waiting for me to respond. She wants to hear about my business, but under the pressure and feelings of frustration, I'm drawing a blank. Everything Hendrick has suggested over the past three months has vanished. All I know is, besides posting stupid photos to FlipFlop, he's asked me to change just about everything.

"We talked about your target market," Hendrick prompts, nodding at me, encouraging me to continue.

Oh sure, in our one-on-one sessions, he suggested I try things my competitors aren't doing. Admittedly, it was news to me that I had competitors other than Coco's. According to Hendrick, *all* the coffee shops are my competition. They all sell baked goods, mostly big cookies and muffins. No wonder people aren't coming into Honeywell's first thing in the morning anymore. When I took over the bakery, there were no coffee shops on Maple Street. Now there are four.

I told Hendrick at the time, "I was thinking of adding muffins,"

He scoffed. "Leave the muffins to the coffee shops. Anyone can bake a muffin."

I was about to argue, when his next suggestion came along.

"You've got those great Crumb-less cookies, right?"

I nodded.

"Why not build on that?"

"You mean make stuff that doesn't have crumbs?"

"No, no," he laughed. Annoyingly, he's always tickled by everything I say, even when I'm serious. "I mean, corporate clients, business clients, B to B."

I must have looked lost because he'd explained. "You could start catering to restaurants. And other businesses like realtors – they love putting out an expensive tray of goodies in an Open House." He spread his fingers on his chest. "Or people like me who give seminars. You've seen the treats I put out for our classes. I get them from a place across town. I'd rather get them from you. I can't be the only one who needs catered dessert trays." I saw fire under that purple mascara. He was getting excited by his own idea. "Trudy, you've *done* the old-fashioned bakery thing. Admit it, it's not working anymore. You're a fabulous baker. You've got to expand. Weddings perhaps. Or corporate. I love that idea for you."

He loved it because it was *his* idea, but I had to admit the Crumb-less business was very good. And it did seem to expand on its own. I asked, "Don't restaurants make their own desserts?"

"Some do," he agreed. "I'd wager most don't."

I thought about The Smokehouse dessert menu, which had come around on a little laminated card. Did they bring those desserts in from elsewhere? How could I find out?

That conversation was months ago now, and I hadn't followed up. I'd become distracted planning our trip.

Now, there are these Wally Whiskers pictures...are they really okay? Are they actually going to improve my business?

No one, other than Mother, agrees the photos are concerning. That alone should tell me I'm off course.

The busboy takes away Hendrick's empty fruit plate.

"I'd like to see Trudy update the bakery," Hendrick says, smoothing the place-mat before him.

"Oh yes," Jane agrees, her mouth full of toast and soft-boiled egg.

I confront her. "Why 'Oh yes'?" She's never mentioned anything like that to me.

"You know – a spruce up! Everyone needs a spruce up now and then."

Mother says, "I've been trying to tell her that for years."

I turn to her, astounded. We *never* discuss Honeywell's – she's against *anything* to do with it. Unless I want a fight, I never mention it. "You have *not* been telling me the bakery needs a spruce up for years!"

"I don't mean the bakery."

I'm stunned.

"I don't like to say it, Honey Bun, but you've let yourself go."

She's truly unconscionable. She just says whatever pops into her head, no matter how hurtful. No matter how true.

"That's not fair, Carole," Polly scolds her. "Trudy's doing amazing on LOBO. She's lost, how much weight have you lost now?"

I don't want to talk about it. I'm coming apart at the seams.

"I'm just saying. Xavier might have stuck around if she'd started earlier," Mother says, fiddling with her placemat.

Jane shushes her. "Carole! That's just nasty."

Yet, I've thought the same thing, and the idea is excruciating.

"Don't listen to her," Jane coos across the table. "Xavier's a jerk."

Polly nods. And there's an awkward silence.

My friends think my husband is a jerk.

I didn't know that.

I'm hurt, but I suppose if any of them had told me before, I would have been angry at them.

"Okay..." Hendrick says, in a bright cheerful tone. "What are we doing today?"

THIRTY-ONE

Under a starry cobalt sky, amid sandstone buildings and thick spiky palms, tourists and couples jostle and mingle on the polished stone street. Cooking smells from streetside bistros blend with the ever-present scent of the ocean. It's all so incongruous, Hvar. The town, so ancient, is a relic from a history book, and yet it's vibrating with life, even at ten o'clock at night.

With Polly straggling along, Mother draped onto Jane's elbow, and Hendrick at my side, we approach a stony three-story building that's been converted into a nightclub. This is where the White Party is taking place. The façade, lit up by blue spotlights, glows and my spirit soars. In a few minutes, I'll be meeting up with Madison at last.

All day, I've been fussing about this party; finding out from the hotel's concierge where it takes place; finding a nearby restaurant for dinner; and making sure each of us has a white outfit to wear.

The White Party, I've learned from searching Madison's FlipFlop, takes place once a week at this nightclub in Hvar. The yachts from Dalma Sailing Tours, for which Madison works, dock in Hvar and deliver their guests to the White Party every week on this night.

I wish I could've found something fashionable for myself, like Mother and Jane did at a shop they discovered in Old Town. Jane is dressed in a flowy white on white leopard dress, and mother in a smart jumpsuit. I had to settle for a white t-shirt and a pair of baggy tennis shorts. The scarce stores on this island don't cater to women shaped like me. They're full of sizes for lean, fit, or skinny women.

I borrowed jewelry and makeup and did up my hair, so, from the neck up, I think I can pass for a middle-aged hot babe.

And it is hot.

Each time we step outside of an air-conditioned space, I droop like an old cut flower.

Nearing the nightclub, we hear the thump, thump, thump of the bass from inside, and every time the front door opens, we're blasted by the sound of electronic dance music.

Polly's face is green. She didn't eat a thing at dinner. Since the ferry ride over here to Hvar this morning, her nausea hasn't settled.

Jane peers into her eyes. "Are you alright in there?"

Looking distressed, Polly takes in the bustling nightlife on the street. "Not really."

I've never seen her daunted. Polly is usually ready for anything. She's my warrior sister, but now she's avoiding my eyes.

"Do you not want to go in?" I ask.

"I don't want to ruin anyone's night!"

Jane crosses her arms, tapping her ringed fingers. "You're not 'ruining' anyone's night! Personally, I'm too old for that kind of music anyway."

I look from one to the next, a feeling of panic rising. My daughter is on the other side of that door, and *none* of them are going to help me find her. I'm being stranded, once again, to navigate alone.

"Did Madison say she'd be here tonight?" Mother asks, dubious, scanning the young people, all dressed in white, streaming in and out of the club.

I almost shriek. "She's here every Thursday!"

Mother purses her lips. Polly looks at the ground. And Jane wraps her bony arm around Polly's shoulder saying, "Sorry, Tru. I'll take these two back to the hotel."

Honestly, she's like the coastguard, steering everyone away from me when I need them the most.

Hendrick clasps my forearm in reassurance. "I'll go in with you," he says, willing to be my knight in shining armor. He looks very chic in his slim white shorts and rolled-sleeve button-down shirt. Tonight, he's wearing dramatic black eyeliner with his mascara.

We make our way up the steps and into the nightclub.

The music is fierce, and so loud it's hard to distinguish what kind of music it is. A blue strobe light throbs with the beat as Hendrick and I inch into the crowd of bodies holding their drinks aloft, bopping to the music, up and down. Dancers glow white, then blue, their teeth and eyeballs gleaming, their faces disappearing into darkness for a pulse.

"I'll go this way," Hendrick mouths at me, indicating the left side of the room.

"Good idea," I mouth back.

I plan to search the edge of the crowd, and if I can, circle toward the stage where the DJ is conducting the gyrating throng. Madison is in here somewhere.

Bodies jostle me, and it feels as if I'm being swallowed into a pit of sweaty serpents. A few yards in, my eyes adjust and I glimpse tables along the perimeter. I change course, heading that way. Perhaps Madison and her friends are sitting down.

I'd like to sit down. Strapped into newly purchased leather sandals, my feet are red and puffy, screaming from all the walking and stair climbing we've done today. Hvar is all stairs!

I promise myself I'll soak my feet in cold water later, but right now, I'm on a mission. My daughter must be found. I am part of her wedding, whether she acknowledges it or not. I am Mother-of-the-Bride.

She's got to have a role for me. I can lend her something blue. Or fluff her dress. Or something.

I scan the individuals at tables, groups of young people glowing with health and festivity, drinking straight from champagne bottles, and shouting in each other's ears. Every few tables I see a girl I think is Madison and I rush over, but when I get close, I see it's not.

In the corner of the room, I spy the women's washroom. Perhaps I'll be lucky and find her inside.

A couple of girls stumble out as I press my way in through the door.

Inside, it's brightly lit, and a bit of a relief from the sound system and the shrieking of the crowd. The high notes of the music are muffled but I can still feel the bass booming in my chest.

A few girls lean over the sinks, smoothing their eyebrows and brushing their long hair in the mirror. I duck into a cubicle to pee, and when I emerge the girls are gone.

I look at myself as I wash my hands. Wash-out white is not my color. Nor is damp-T-shirt-material-clinging-to-rolls my style.

A cubicle door behind me opens.

"Mrs. Asp?"

I spin around and come face to face with Laura, Madison's best friend from high-school.

"Hey! What are you doing here?"

"I could ask the same thing!"

We laugh, stare at each other – so out of place – and embrace. I'm delighted to see her.

She explains, "I'm working for Dalma Sailing Tours – same as Madison!"

I'm so surprised.

"She didn't tell me anyone from home was working over here too. Are you with her tonight?"

Laura shakes her head. "I haven't seen her. But it's pretty crowded."

"I'm here for the wedding."

Laura tilts her head, looking puzzled and alarmed. "You're here for Madison's dad's wedding?"

"Of course not!" I correct her.

"Oh, good," she says, laughing in relief.

"I'm here for Madison's wedding."

Now, she looks confused. "Madison's wedding? What? When?"

"On the weekend! I can't believe she didn't—" The hurt and confusion crossing her face shuts me up.

She says, "No, well, she's kept that quite a secret."

"I'm sure it's nothing personal, Laura," I rush to reassure her. "She hasn't been very forthcoming about the whole thing – even with me."

Laura nods, as if she understands, but the look on her face is disconcerting, and doubtful. She asks me, "*Who* is she marrying?"

"Matthew. The Australian boy. Do you know who I mean?"

Again, she nods, slowly. "Yes...but he went back to Australia a couple of days ago. Are you sure it's the same Matthew?"

Now, I nod. But I'm confused. I hope I know the name of the boy my daughter is marrying. Darn her. Why has she been so evasive?

"I noticed on FlipFlop that Madison comes here on Thursdays, so I thought I'd run into her."

Laura turns to the sink and washes her hands. "We *all* come here on Thursdays. It's part of the tour, but I haven't seen her tonight. And I can't believe she's getting married." She dries her hands. "I did see Jakov. Her captain. He's here."

"Oh! Where? Can you take me to him?"

"I'll try. He was over by the bar. We can see if we can find him."

An eerie feeling washes over me. A premonition. *Something is wrong.*

Laura says, "Just to let you know, he's kinda a jerk."

"Who? The captain?"

"Yea. He and Madison do *not* get along. She's been trying to get off his boat since the summer began."

"Oh. I didn't know that."

There's so much Madison and I could've talked about, if only she'd written back.

"He hits on *all* the girls. Plays practical jokes and pranks. Madison told him where to go, so he's making her life miserable. But of course, he's 'only joking'."

"That's awful." I dislike this captain already.

"And, she's really into the plant-based foods. You knew that, right?"

I shake my head. Plant-based? "I recall you two dabbling in vegetarianism when you were in high-school. Is that what you mean?"

Teenage Madison had made dinner times very stressful for a while, declaring she couldn't stand watching Xavier and I eating the flesh of animals in front of her.

"Jakov gets really upset over the food she serves on board. He's a caveman – just wants meat, meat, meat, but Madison is a sensational cook, and she's been experimenting. Her guests love the meatless dishes – she gets rave reviews, but Jakov hates them and I heard they had a giant blowout recently." Laura's eyebrows rise. "Still want to meet him?"

I do, but my trepidation is through the roof. I'm worried about my baby, and have so many questions. Where is she? Why is Matthew now in Australia? What is going on?

Laura leads the way through the sauna of youthful bouncing bodies toward the bar and before we reach it, I recognize Jakov from Zelda's group photo on FlipFlop. He's leaning against the bar, shouting at the people he's with, waving around a bottle of vodka.

The rest of his party is laughing, swaying in and out of my view. One guy, a stupid half-smile slapped on his face, looks older and out of place here. Next to him, a woman in a sleek white gown with a gold bracelet snaking up her bicep, glows like a Greek Goddess. Laura leads me closer, and closer, as I catch glimpses of our destination. Suddenly, amid the bobbing bodies, I realize, the old dude ahead of me is my husband, and the woman on his arm is Zelda!

Laura penetrates the throng around the bar, and as surprised to see him as I am, she greets Xavier with a hug, before making introductions as best she can over the deafening music.

I didn't expect to bump into Xavier here.

This is not how I fantasized our reunion would go.

Not when I'm hot and sweaty and my mother's intuition is blaring like a siren. *Madison should be here but she's not. Something bad has happened to her!*

As though he's been dying to meet me, Jakov roars over the noise, "Turdy!" and reaches out a giant sweaty paw to pump my hand.

Did he just mispronounce my name?

Madison's other colleagues shake my hand and shout a confusion of names at me: Brittany, and Emmeline, Sam, and somebody-or-other, but I'm telescoped onto Xavier, who's obviously had several cocktails. I try locking his bleary eyes in mine, and demand, "Where is Madison?"

"Bad news," Zelda shouts at me, but before she can interject another word, Xavier steps between us and takes my elbow, escorting me toward the side of the room, stupidly, as if we'll escape the thunderous turbulence over there.

He turns and sloppily, pulls me close. I'm shocked by the familiar intimacy – suspended by the feel of his hands on me.

But he's not trying to embrace me – he leans in, and shouts in my ear, "Madison eloped."

Thirty-Two

"Eloped? Where? When?"

Xavier shrugs, but not with indifference. "If I knew..."

I can't hear him. We're both just lip-reading.

We need to go outside.

I point at the exit, and apprehension floods his face. He glances toward the bar. Toward Zelda. Infuriating me. Is he not allowed to be parted from her for a few minutes while we discuss our daughter's whereabouts?

She's watching us.

Xavier motions toward the door, and quickly starts snaking through the crowd. I'm panting trying to keep up with him. Finally, we burst through the front doors into an enchanted Croatian evening.

It's a minute before I can get my bearings. Sights and sounds are muffled, even surreal, after the maniacal interior of the nightclub.

Beyond the red roofs and stone walls of the town, the ocean dances dark and playful, the moon reflecting off small whitecaps. A breeze ripples tendrils of hair across my face. My updo has become loose, unraveling, and I reach behind my head, fussing with the hairpins, trying to secure it.

A jangly guitar player begins a song. Wafts of cooking from nearby alfresco restaurants drift by. A lime green Volkswagen passes next to a couple kissing by the sea wall.

It's magical and romantic and here I am with the handsome man who I am struggling to remember is no longer my husband.

As though moving in slow-motion and trying to speak underwater, I turn to him. "When did you last see her?"

He runs his hand through his hair and I notice his graying sideburns. Endearingly, he's getting older. Just like me. Doesn't he miss me?

"Yesterday," he explains. "Zelda and I went out for dinner – to the same restaurant Madison took her guests – and we met up afterwards."

At the mention of Zelda's name on his lips I feel a jab of jealousy, but I shove it aside. I can't let it get in my way right now.

"And the wedding was still on at that point?"

He shrugs, again, that same infuriatingly impotent shrug. "We didn't actually *talk* about it. Zelda is still upset—" As if on cue, the nightclub door swings open and with a blast of music Zelda emerges, quickly followed by Jakov.

"Turdy!" he shouts, rushing toward us. "I've heard so much about you!"

He *is* mispronouncing my name.

"It's TRUE-dee," I correct him, enunciating the two syllables.

Zelda looks sideways at me, as if I'm making a big deal out of nothing, which makes me feel foolish. And Jakov looks at me quizzically, as if he doesn't understand, but says, "You must come on the boat tomorrow! I will take you for a sail. Are you here alone?"

Oh gosh, I forgot about Hendrick. Is he still inside? "No, no, my friends are..." I flap my hands around vaguely.

"Xavier told you, yes? Maddy eloped. Just like that." He snaps his fingers. "Gone."

Madison detests being called 'Maddy.' She corrects anyone who dares shorten her name. No wonder she clashed with this guy.

I quiz him, "But how do you know she eloped? Did she leave a note? Maybe she's missing. Is her fiancé gone too?"

I'm not going to just sweep aside my daughter's disappearance, and I'm not discounting my distressing intuition. I can't shake the feeling. Something is wrong.

Jakov's eyes are the darkest I've ever seen. Not a trace of brown, they're black. I feel the hair on the back of my neck rise as another warm wind grazes my sweating skin.

He laughs, as though my interrogation amuses him. "No, he's gone too."

"Are you sure she's okay?" I appeal to Xavier. "Who is this fiancé? I have this feeling—"

"I'm so sorry, Trudy," Zelda croons, reaching over to stroke my arm, oozing insincerity. I recoil as if from a snake bite. "You came all this way," she continues, implying poor pitiful Trudy, always the last to know.

And just like that, the topic of Madison is dismissed.

"So," Jakov says, clapping his large hands together. "What do we do now?" He's their ringleader, orchestrating their activities.

Xavier shuffles his feet and studies the ground.

What is he thinking?

Finally, he meets my eyes and says, "Look after yourself, Trudy."

I'm stunned. What does he mean?

It dawns on me. He's taken a good long look – my unflattering outfit clinging to my rolls; my probably melting makeup. The ridiculous fantasy I had, that he would see me, looking leaner and lovelier, and fall instantly in love with me again evaporates into the cloying air. What a fool I am.

"Go home," he says. "Save yourself some money, and go home."

THIRTY-THREE

Discovering me standing with Xavier, Zelda, and Jakov, outside the night-club, Hendrick blunders into our circle with a hearty, "So, where's the bride-to-be?"

Flustered, distracted, and flooded with shame, I introduce him to the others.

Immediately, Jakov takes charge, informing Hendrick with confidence that "Maddy" has eloped, and no one knows where she is. He's arrogant and forceful and the more I hear him say it, the more I try to convince myself that I must accept it. There will be no wedding. I will not be Mother-of-the-Bride.

But where is my daughter?

The facts are these: she's not here with her friends. She's not here with her father and his fiancé. Allegedly, she snuck off and married some boy named Matthew in secret. According to Jakov, she was unnerved by all the attention we were giving the wedding.

It's at this point of him sketching in the details that I realize that I may have caused her elopement. *I* was the one pestering her with emails and phone calls. I couldn't leave her to plan her wedding with her father. I couldn't take a hint. I wanted her to want *me*. I wanted to squeeze into the middle of their relationship and make us the trio we once were. I wanted to be Mother-of-the-Bride. It's pathetic.

Most likely, Madison is embarrassed of me, and doesn't want to introduce me to anyone. And no wonder. Look at me. Next to Zelda, who's radiating like a goddess, I'm a dumpy mess. I came all this way to find out something I should've known back home. My daughter doesn't want me in her life. She doesn't love me. I'm a terrible mother.

After listening to Jakov's soliloquy, during which I'm holding back an ocean of tears, Xavier, Zelda, Jakov, and a few others who've joined the group, stroll off down the street toward who-knows-where. Over his shoulder Jakov shouts back, "Tomorrow, Turdy! We sail!"

Hendrick asks me, "What's that about?"

"Oh, gawd, I don't know," I cry in exasperation. "He wants to take us out on the yacht."

"Wow! That's exciting!" Hendrick gushes.

His face falls when he sees I have no interest in sailing with my ex-husband and his gang of new friends.

"I hate to ask you this, Tru," he broaches in his next breath, "but do you mind if I stay here at the white party?"

I glare at him.

Just like every other man, he really is insensitive. I want to smack him.

He rushes to say, "Unless you want me to walk you back to the hotel, but I think it's safe here."

"It's fine." I lie, numb with the pain of holding in all my disappointment and doubt. My feet throb, and my heart is cracking. I've never felt so shattered.

Oblivious, Hendrick gives my shoulders a squeeze and plants a quick kiss on my cheek. "There's the cutest guy in there who wants to dance with me!" He practically squeals with excitement, skimming right over the news of my daughter's elopement and this whole pointless European excursion. He is acting like he assumes I will shrug it all off as everyone else is doing.

I stumble away from Hendrick and up the cobblestone roadway toward the hotel, blind with tears. I just need to hold it together until I get to the hotel and find some privacy in which I can wail.

Rounding the corner of a church, a forceful gust of wind whips past me. The trees and planter boxes in the street flap wildly. Above the buildings, the sky darkens, and a mad scramble ensues – diners and evening strollers dashing for doorways and cover. Thunder, like a load of bowling balls dropping onto an alley floor, crashes against the blackening sky above me. Giant globs of rain begin pelting down, instantly soaking me to the skin. I don't know which way to go.

I think, I hope, I'm headed in the direction of the hotel.

"It's a Nevera storm!" I hear a man shout as he rushes his family toward the shelter of a restaurant door.

I have no idea what that is, but the wind is slamming, and rain teems, plastering down my clothes and hair. My new sandals squish and slosh in the water stream-ing along the cobblestones – they're going to be completely ruined. Fighting my way through the wind, I plunge onward, straining to see through the rain and darkness. Up ahead and to the left, I glimpse wavering orange lights from the lanterns outside our hotel. There is no bellhop, no doorman to greet me. I stumble forward, pulling hard to open the door.

Inside the opulent hotel with its twinkling chandeliers, florid carpets and marble walls, people are scurrying about, wet, dripping, laughing, obviously caught like I was in the sudden downpour. Through the vaulted lobby windows, courtyard palms with their strings of tiny white lights, thrash in the wind.

Praying I don't run into anyone I know; I rush to the open doors of an empty elevator and lean against the wall, inwardly sobbing, breathing painfully as I'm carried up to our floor.

Fumbling with the room card, I am beyond relieved to find the room dark and deserted, Mother nowhere to be seen.

I don't know what I would do if I'd found her here. I just know I couldn't deal with her I-told-you-so's and why-didn't-you's right now.

I throw myself onto the bed, burying my face in the pillow.

I don't care if I'm soaking wet or that my sandals are still on my feet, the buckles snagging against the bedspread.

To think, I imagined Madison would want my help, when in fact she was trying to stay away from me.

In my delusion I'd thought I would rock being the MOB, and that she'd appreciate me, and Xavier would too. He'd love me again. I believed everything would end happily ever after.

I'm pathetic.

Sobs roll over me like waves on the ocean. I clutch handfuls of the bedspread, and wail.

How ridiculous I've been – dragging my friends, half-way around the world, for something so uncertain and unconfirmed.

And where are they now? Off somewhere having a fantastic time without me.

None of them care whether I'm with them or not.

I let myself cry.

Does anyone even like me?

My misery moves on to maligning my companions.

Bossy-cow, Jane. Why did I even bring her? She only hangs out with me so she has someone to belittle and boss around. Who does she think she is?

And Hendrick – what a flake. He's so insensitive and he's going to find himself in real trouble someday, flirting with the wrong guy.

And Polly – what a pushover. Too nice, too sweet. Get real!

And Mother. Gawd. Talk about the worst woman on Earth. Nasty and hypo-critical. I'm a better mother than she ever was.

I never criticized Madison, or made her feel like an oddball, the way my mother did to me. At least I don't think I did.

I sniffle.

Why does Madison hate me so much?

It's so unfair.

And Xavier. *What the hell?* Does he not care about his daughter? Does he not wonder where she is?

Why am I the only one worried?

They're all so wrapped up in their own self-gratification they can't see that something might be terribly wrong.

I sniffle, roll over, and look around the darkened room. It's stuffy in here.

Unbuckling my sandals, I toss them toward the closet. They're probably ruined.

In bare feet, I pad to the window, crank it open and breathe in some fresh night air.

The storm has blown the humidity away and the wind has subsided. People are returning to the bar area around the pool. Hotel staff shake out cushions and push loungers and chairs back into place.

Thirsty, I cross the room to the bar fridge.

There, on the top, is the basket of snacks, looking as enticing and harmless as a child's Halloween booty.

I pull open the fridge door and scan the contents. Water, water, cola, booze.

I slide one of the tiny bottles of champagne from the door compartment and examine its label and pink foil top.

You shouldn't drink. Drinking won't help how you feel.

I put it back and firmly close the door causing the chip packages to rustle in the basket.

In one beat, I yank open the fridge door, rip the foil from the champagne bottle, wrench off the cap – it's not a cork – and rush it to my lips. Champagne fizzes over. Bubbles sting my nose.

You shouldn't be drinking this.

Why not?

After the night I've had, why the hell not?

I take another slug. It's really very good French champagne. I should get a glass and drink like a grown-up.

I am a grown up!

In the corner of the room behind the door, I spy my suitcase.

My suitcase?

Wheeling around I see Mother's case on the luggage rack on the far side of the bed. Our luggage arrived!

I could go home right now. Just pack up and go. There's nothing for me here.

I pull my bag onto the bed and unzip it. Inside, my Mother-of-the-Bride dress is completely squashed and wrinkled. Absolutely unwearable. I snatch it from the bag and fling the ugly thing across the room.

Beneath it, are a pair of stretchy black jeans, newly purchased a week ago especially for this trip. I yank down my soggy white shorts and kick them away. Rummaging through my case for a top, at the very bottom, my fingers catch on the crochet of my cover-up. I'd almost forgotten it was hiding there.

Thirty-Four

Alone in a swanky hotel room on the Adriatic Sea is a place I never dreamed I'd be. Yet, here I am.

I open another split of champagne and stare at the basket of snacks on top of the fridge.

I wonder if they taste any different than North American versions.

What would Polly say to you right now if she were here?

She'd say, "Get away from the snack bowl. Get it out of your sight. Think about something else."

A vision of Xavier flashes through my mind – looking up at me with that look on his face. What was it, pity? Disgust? Exhaustion? "Look after yourself, Trudy," he'd said.

I pop open a bag and am met with a waft of familiar friendly cheesiness.

Just one bag. No one will ever know.

I take the first snacky crunches, noticing they taste pretty much the same as the ones back home: a warm artificial almost dirty-feet tang tingles my palate.

I'll just eat this one bag, then no more. No biggy. I'm a grown up. I can eat a bag of junk food if I want to.

I munch as I dress, pulling on the black jeans and buttoning up a short-sleeved blouse. It's wrinkly but at least it's pretty, and doesn't smell like sweat.

It's getting late, and I wonder where Jane took Polly and Mother. Hendrick is probably still at the White Party, but I half-expect the others to come bursting in the door, catty-chatting about all the fun they've had while I was searching the night club for Madison.

I crumple up the empty snack package and search around for a place to hide it.

Fortunately, it flushes quite easily down the toilet.

After patching up my makeup, I comb out my damp hair and re-pin it so it's off my neck. As I fuss before the mirror, it crosses my mind that the bag of snacks caused absolutely no problems, but didn't quite hit the spot. I'm a little hungry, and I've already blown my diet. After the night I've had – I deserve a treat!

I pop open the second bag and crunch into the familiar taste of pretzels and salt. I've missed this so much. Cramming more into my mouth, I chew quickly, needing to finish them off and get rid of the evidence before the others catch me.

I've got to get rid of the greasy orange residue around my lips before I head down to the lobby and start searching for the others, but I'm reluctant to brush my teeth and wash away the flavour of sticky snacks that permeates my mouth.

Thank goodness Polly won't be able to read my mind. In fact, none of them will know the terrible things I've been thinking about them. Guilty feelings needle at my cheeks.

I wish I hadn't eaten those things. My stomach feels sick.

Stepping out into the hallway, I hear their voices and laughter and the ping of the elevator arriving. Jane, Polly, and Mother turn the corner and catch sight of me.

"Trudy! We were just coming to see if you made it back!"

"Were you caught in the storm?"

Their concern is genuine, and I feel guilty about disparaging them to myself.

Mother asks, "Did you find Madison?"

My throat tightens, and my voice cracks when I utter the one-word answer, "No."

"Oh Honey, what happened?" Polly grasps me around the shoulder, and Jane unlocks the door to their room, ushering me inside.

"She eloped!" I announce, flopping down onto a chair, reliving the misery all over again.

They flurry around me, turning on the lamps in the room, getting me a glass of water.

Polly asks quietly, "Are you a bit drunk?"

"No," I lie instantly, unwilling to divulge what I've been eating and drinking and flushing for the last hour.

I stare at the two beds in their room. She and Jane have two beds while I share one with Mother. How did this trip spiral so far out of control?

"We were downstairs having nice cocktails in the lounge," Mother tells me, fanning her face with her hand. "They have a wonderful lavender mojito. It's lovely down there. We should go back down, and you can tell us all about your night."

The others agree, and escort me to the elevator and down to the main floor. We emerge, just as Hendrick is sauntering across the lobby. He looks rumpled, but very pleased with himself.

"Where are you partiers off to, so late in the evening?"

Jane herds him into our group and leads the way to a table at the edge of the bar, overlooking the pool. The palms and the ocean beyond are dark and mysterious.

"I assume Trudy told you the bad news," Hendrick says, as we settle into our seats.

"Yes, what happened?" All eyes look to me to tell the story.

The night seems a little blurry now. I've come to, and subsequently discarded, so many distressing conclusions since Jane, Mother, and Polly left me outside the nightclub – I'm not sure where to start.

"Xavier was there, inside the White Party. With Zelda. And a guy from Madison's boat – he's the captain, his name is Jakov."

"Jack-off is right!" Hendrick snorts. "What a macho man. Did you ever? What's his deal?"

Everyone leans forward, their interest piqued. Mother asks, "Who?"

I answer, "I don't know, really, except Laura, that's Madison's friend from back home, told me Madison and Jakov do not get along. Apparently, Madison's been trying to get off his boat for months."

"Wait. When did you talk to Laura?"

"In the bar! In the bathroom. She was there. She's working for Dalma Sailing Tours too."

There's silence around the table as everyone digests this tidbit of information. "That's quite a coincidence," Jane observes.

"I know!"

A waiter places a jug of sangria and five glasses on the table.

"Oh, thanks but not for me," Polly says, and requests the waiter bring us a bottle of Jamnica, a fancy Croatian spring water. She looks at me with a question in her eyes.

I nod and hold up two fingers to the waiter. "Two glasses, please."

Mother asks impatiently, "Now, what's this about an elopement?"

I collect my thoughts, as well as I can after three mini bottles of champagnes and a regretful binge of junky carbs. "Jakov claims she eloped, but I can't believe it. Something feels off."

Jane's head cocks to the side. She's all about feelings and intuitions. "What feels off, Trudy?"

"Madison *knew* we were coming. And now we're here! She knows that. I've tried to contact her a bunch of times since we landed." I trail off, not willing to reveal how many messages have gone unanswered.

Mother looks worried. "Do you think something happened to her?"

"I don't know," I complain. "It sort of makes sense that she eloped, but I'm confused about her fiancé, Matt. Laura said he went back to Australia."

"And what does Xavier say about all this?" Mother demands to know.

"He believes everything Jakov says. They're pals."

Now, I feel churned up again, and I don't know what to think. I wish I hadn't drunk the champagne, or eaten the snacks. My stomach feels queasy.

Mother quizzes me in the semi-sarcastic, interrogative tone she used to whip out when I was a teenager. "So, you think, that even though she knew we were coming for her wedding, she just ran off at the last minute? Why would she do that?"

I look around at my friends, all sitting up, attentive, with quizzical looks on their faces, waiting for me to enlighten them.

I divulge what Jakov told me. "Her captain said she felt pressured about everything."

"Of course, she felt pressured! Every bride feels pressured," Mother huffs.

"I bet it was Zelda," Jane interjects. "*She* didn't want this wedding to happen in the first place. She must have said something to Madison to make her run off."

"You think?"

"Of course! What else would explain it?"

I should confess. I take a sip of the bubbly water and say, "Well...I did send *a lot* of emails. They may have scared her off."

"Pish-posh," Mother scoffs, shaking her head. "A girl only has one mother. And every girl wants her mother at her wedding."

Polly nods in agreement.

But I don't know – did I want my mother at my wedding?

Yes, I did. I remember.

I wanted her there to show her I wasn't the loser she thought I was. A man loved me enough to marry me. Our families and friends were coming together to celebrate. In your face, Mother!

Jane says, "That's true. You only have one mother, and I'm sure Madison will get in touch with you. However, right now, you need to accept she changed her mind about the wedding and eloped."

"That's right," Hendrick agrees. "Until we hear otherwise, that girl is a married woman."

My friends lean in, propping me up as we sit in the bar sipping our drinks.

When Madison was a little girl, *A Wedding Promise Barbie* was all she wanted for Christmas. She loved marrying Barbie to Ken. It was the only time he got out of the toybox. She'd insist I prop him up as Barbie hopped down the aisle toward him and the book he was standing on. They'd kiss their awkward hard plastic kiss and then Barbie would be off to change into something new for dancing the night away.

"In other news," Jane says. "We're off to the island of Vis tomorrow. Isn't that right, Trudy?"

To Vis, where we've got rooms booked in a beautiful hotel overlooking the sea.

"I suppose it makes sense to still go there," I answer. "Even though the wedding is off."

THIRTY-FIVE

fter paying for our Hvar hotel rooms, I wander around the lobby, waiting for the others to appear.

My sleep last night was restless, but I did a lot of thinking. Listening to the sound of Mother's whistley snoring, I realized, I need to make some changes.

Through the window of the souvenir shop, a pair of silver flip-flops with glittering beads on the thongs, winks at me. I must have them. No need to try them on, they're just flip-flops, I'm sure they'll fit, and if not, so what? I'll leave them in some future hotel room. I rush in to buy.

They cram without trouble into a side compartment of my suitcase.

I didn't pack the red souvenir bathing suit. I left it hanging under a terry robe on a hook in the bathroom. I didn't want any of its hideous vibes to rub off on any of the nice clothes in my suitcase.

Jane appears with the others trailing behind her, and we head outside to be met by an overcast sky, a pale gray with streaks of smokier clouds here and there. It's the first day since we arrived in Croatia that the sun isn't blazing down.

The concierge assured me that the best way to get down to the harbor is to walk, it's all downhill.

And today, I find it's actually easier to walk. Maybe I'm getting used to it, with all the sightseeing and tromping around we've been doing. Or possibly the weight I'm losing is contributing. Whatever the reason, my knees are quiet, no squawking or grinding, and my feet are happy in my comfortable Ferraris.

It's a new day – no nachos or pretzels for me.

When we get to the marina, there's a plethora of options to transport us to Vis. We can take the ferry – an idea that turned Polly green at breakfast. Or we can hire a speedboat or a yacht. I just want to get to Vis – I don't really care how we do it.

After what I went through last night, I'm looking forward to a few days in a beautiful villa, where I plan on coming to terms with my position in my daughter's life, which, I must accept, is negligible. She's an adult, making her own choices, and now that she's married, I'm fairly certain, I've got to stop interfering or intruding on her life.

My fantasy of becoming her beloved mother, the revered Mother-of-the-Bride, all of it, is gone. It's over.

I'm crushed, but I need to rethink what I'm doing in life, because who says I have to keep doing what I've always done? I could sell the bakery. I could do something new.

I don't know what, yet, but I know there's something out there for me.

For starters, I'm developing a new body – I'll try exercising for real! And I can buy nice clothes again. Wouldn't it be amazing if I could fit into something at Dressica?

The look on Xavier's face wouldn't be pity anymore.

I need a new frame of mind. A new way to fill my days. A few days on Vis, watching the sun setting into the ocean, some time to think, it's just what I need. And we're here anyway – I might as well enjoy it.

A row of sleek, modern speed boats is tied to the seawall.

Jane says excitedly, "Let's take one of *these*!"

"That sounds like fun," Hendrick agrees.

I look at Mother. "What do you think?"

She purses her lips and inspects the row of boats. I know she's about to say, "No." I'm reminded of our long-ago conflicts over Grandad's boat. She was always unreasonable about motor boats, and having fun.

"I'd rather go on one of those," she says, pointing down the harbor to a row of beautiful sailing yachts and catamarans, their tall masts poking the sky.

They are magnificent, masts naked, hulls gleaming, tiny flags snapping in the wind.

"A yacht it is!" Jane announces. "She who holds the gold...and all that."

Mother looks pleased.

Now we just need to figure out how to go about hiring one.

We make our way further along the seawall, dragging our suitcases.

"Turdy!"

I hear him before I see him.

Standing aboard a beautiful big yacht, waving at us as we approach, are Jakov; Zelda, holding down a glamorous floppy straw hat; and Xavier in Bermuda shorts.

We wheel our cases closer so we can talk to them.

"Where are you going?"

"To Vis."

"That's where we're going! It's a perfect day for sailing. Climb aboard."

But I balk.

I don't want to spend time in the company of him, or Zelda. I'm starting a new life and it doesn't include them.

Nevertheless, everyone else is wheeling their suitcases straight onto the boat and I seem to have no say in the matter.

"Come on!" Jakov yells, gesturing with his hairy arm. "Don't be a sport-spoil, Turdy!"

I really don't like this man.

Hendrick asks, as he lands on the deck of the vessel, "Wow, is this the boat Madison works on?"

"Yes!"

It's wider than our living room back home, lined with fashionable gray seating, sophisticated and beautiful, and I feel completely out of place. Zelda appears to fit right in.

Pointing at a staircase inside the salon of the enormous boat, Jakov commands: "Stow your cases in one of the cabins"

"I'll show them," Zelda volunteers.

She guides us down into a small passageway and swings open a door. We squeeze in past her, and leave our luggage inside.

Which of the cabins is Madison's bedroom? And is she coming back to work after her honeymoon? She doesn't like Jakov, maybe she'll be assigned to another boat.

The engines rumble and we make our way up to the cockpit where Jakov, hands on a giant chrome wheel, steers the yacht through the marina's channel, out and onto the wide choppy water of the Adriatic.

After we're in the open sea for a while, he switches a mechanism and one of the large triangular sails unfurls.

It's spectacular. Even though the sky is overcast and the water is a dark troubled blue, looking back at the Hvar shoreline is incredible. The breeze on my face, strands of my hair flying around, I realize I've missed this, boating. Besides the ferry, I haven't been on the water in years.

Mother announces: "How about a drink to celebrate?"

I'm not sure what she's celebrating, but everyone else agrees it's a good idea.

"Let's go back down to the deck," Zelda suggests, and turning to Mother asks, "Do you want to help me make some margaritas?"

"Aren't you sweet? Of course I want to help."

"Hang on to the rails," Jakov barks as we take turns, ladies first, descending the narrow spiral staircase. "Careful on those stairs while the boat is moving."

Down on the deck, I find a place to sit on the lovely gray seating. Mother and Zelda go inside the galley, and I can't help but be irked at the way they are getting along, laughing, and chatting, as Mother looks appreciatively over the well-stocked bar.

Xavier's legs appear on the staircase, last to climb down from the cockpit, his hair windswept. I wish he didn't look so handsome.

Hendrick asks him, "How long a journey is it?"

"Not sure." He shrugs. "Jakov said we'd take our time today and just enjoy the sail. Do you want a tour of the boat?"

Hendrick agrees, eager to explore.

"So, what do you think?" Jane asks me and Polly. "Is this great or is this great?"

"It's absolutely wonderful," Polly agrees. "This whole trip." She looks at me. "I don't know how I can ever thank you. And your mother. It's just beyond…"

I wave her off. I don't need any thanks. I'm grateful for her!

Aside from the forays into the snack basket, I couldn't have stuck to LOBO if she wasn't here. But I don't say anything in front of Jane because she doesn't understand. She thinks Polly and I are on an extremely unhealthy fad diet.

Jane pats her flat belly. "I don't know about you but I'm getting peckish,"

It's astonishing how much she eats. Now that I don't devour everything in sight, I notice how much she does. And inexplicably, it doesn't seem to have any consequences for her.

Zelda and Mother come back with drinks: tiny bottles of chilled Jamnica for Polly and me, and a foamy lime pitcher of margaritas for the rest.

"There's plenty of food onboard," Zelda tells us with a vague wave toward the kitchen. "Help yourselves."

Jane turns to me. "Shall we make lunch?"

"I'm game." I didn't eat breakfast, just my usual black coffee while the others ate, because I knew I needed to get back on the LOBO wagon, fast.

Now, I suppose it's around noon, and I'm ready for my first meal of the day. It's funny how LOBO works. Even the feeling of hunger is different. It's a feeling of, *sure, I could eat*, rather than, *if I don't eat right now, I'm going to chew my arm off!*

The tiny ship kitchen is ingeniously designed with every luxury imaginable tucked into the tiniest of spaces. Jane pulls open a refrigerated drawer, while I slide open the cupboards and cabinets. Mostly what I find are plastic containers of what appear to be grains, or rice, or dried beans – the kind of thing you'd buy at a bulk food store and would need time to soak or boil.

"There's not much here for lunch," Jane observes, and I peer over her shoulder into the freezer. Inside, are neatly stacked cryovac'd frozen meats, but not much else.

In the refrigerated drawer are cartons of juice, soya milk, almond milk, kimchi, and a package of sliced sprouted bread, whatever that is. No cheese, no deli meats, no lettuce, just a bunch of rubbery celery stalks, and an apple. There's nothing we can quickly throw together for a meal; Madison must have prepared *everything* from scratch.

"Did you see any peanut butter?" Jane asks, sliding open the cupboards to search them herself. On the counter by the bar, next to a tented card explaining the importance of 5-star reviews to the crew of the yacht, is a large wire basket packed with potato chips and pretzels. "Or we could have these," she says, tapping a ringed finger to her chin.

I frown. I am not eating chips. "I can't believe Zelda said there was plenty to eat. What are we supposed to have? Bowls of porridge?"

Jane laughs, and we resume our hunt.

"Aha!" I pull a crock of grape jelly from the bottom of the fridge just as Jane discovers a jar of almond butter.

Returning to the seating area with a tray of sprouted sandwiches, I ask Polly, "Almond butter and celery alright for you?" Her face is contorted and pale, her eyes a bit wild, as though she doesn't know where to focus. "Oh no, are you sick again?"

Zelda asks, "What's the matter with her?"

"She's seasick."

"I've got just the thing for that." Zelda jumps to her feet and disappears down into the cabins. A moment later she trots back up with a package of antihistamines. "These will do the trick."

Skeptical of such a simple solution, I glance at Jane, who's a doctor. Her arms are crossed as she watches Polly swallow the pill with a sip of fizzy water.

Polly says to Zelda, smiling. "I hope it works. I had no idea I would get so sick. I've never been on a boat before this trip."

I think back on my summers at Grandad's cottage when I practically lived on the water. It's been years and years, but the feeling of the boat under my body as it bounces and rocks gently through the waves feels natural to me, and soothing.

I feel sorry for Polly that she can't enjoy it the way I do, and suddenly, I'm aware that I am enjoying myself, despite the company, Zelda included. Can I think of her as my dental hygienist again, and not as the Jezebel who stole my husband? I don't know, I'm still pretty dismayed about that.

"How about some peppermint tea?" she asks Polly.

"I'm not sure. Let's see if the pill helps."

Returning with Xavier from his tour of the boat, Hendrick exclaims, "Ahh, sandwiches!" as though he hasn't eaten in days. "What kind?" His nose wrinkles when he finds out they're almond butter and jam.

"That's all we've got," Jane says. "Take it or leave it."

"I'll take it," he says, snatching one off the plate. "And I'll take one to our captain."

Why does everyone seem to get along with Jakov? He's such a jerk. Bossy and aggressive. And I believed Hendrick thought so too, but now he seems to have changed his mind and they're buddies.

I recall what Laura told me in the washroom of the White Party, after she told me Jakov was hitting on Madison. She said that he and Madison were fighting about the food she served. Now, as I bite into a bendy piece of celery smeared with almond butter, I wonder, what *was* Madison serving?

"I'm a vegetarian," Zelda is telling Jane as she nibbles on her sandwich.

"Oh? How long have you been doing that?"

"Since I was a teenager."

Xavier doesn't like nut butters, and I notice he eats nothing. Just sips on a margarita and gazes out at the sea. Sailing suits him. I had no idea he'd enjoy it so much. I wish I'd suggested sailing years ago.

Jane asks Polly, "Are you feeling any better?"

"Much better. It's a miracle. Thanks a bunch for the cure, Zelda."

"What's that?" Xavier asks.

Jane tells him. "Zelda cured Polly's seasickness."

"With what? Antihistamines?" He scoffs. "*I* taught her that trick a few months ago when we first came to Croatia. She was sick as a dog."

Instantly, I recognize Xavier's subtle undermining of Zelda. He used to do that to me, and I don't like it.

Zelda looks a little chastened, but she recovers quickly by gushing about their first adventure in Croatia. "It was, oh, so romantic. We just fell *in love* with it here!"

"Xavier," Mother interrupts. "When you were here in the spring, did you see Madison?" I'm surprised she's been following the conversation. She also didn't eat a sandwich, and she just finished draining the last of the margaritas into her glass.

"I did," Xavier answers.

"And was she getting married when you saw her then?"

"Uh, no—"

Mother jumps in. "I'd like to know how it all came up so suddenly. Where's that Jack? Maybe he can explain."

Xavier chuckles. "No, Jakov doesn't know any more than I do. Madison was here the day before yesterday; we were with her. We went to the White Party last night to meet up with her again, but she was gone."

He sure is throwing the 'we' word around.

"Hmph," Mother says, shaking her head. "Seems awfully strange to me."

"Not if she eloped." He shrugs with maddening confidence. "I'm sure you'll bump into her on Vis."

This is news to me.

"Why do you say that?" Mother asks.

"Which hotel are you staying at?"

Everyone looks at me for the answer. "Hotel George," I confirm.

Xavier nods. "That's where Madison is staying."

Zelda pouts. "*We* couldn't get a room there," she says. "They were all booked up. How did you manage to get rooms?"

"Trudy booked them," Mother boasts, not remembering that it was she, who at the last minute, prodded me to do so.

"Just dumb luck." I shrug. But I'm chuffed. I zipped in there and booked the rooms, scooping Zelda. Hendrick's room, which I'd so regretted, might've been hers, if I hadn't snapped it up.

"Land ahoy!" Polly shouts, pointing over my shoulder.

Sure enough, a group of islands appears in the distance.

As we approach, the sea calms, and we hear the engines start up. Hendrick and Xavier head up to the cockpit to confer with Jakov.

"We've got a great idea," Hendrick says, coming back down the spiral stairs a few minutes later, rubbing his hands together. "We're going to pull in to one of those coves and go waterskiing!"

Xavier, right behind him, adds, "Or wakeboarding," as though he knows a thing or two about the difference.

Oh, no we are not.

I am getting to Hotel George as fast as possible. Especially now that I know Madison will be there.

"I don't think so, Hendrick," I say. "I'd rather just get to the island."

I look around at the rest of my companions for confirmation. Mother is dozing in the shade, and Jane looks disappointed.

Polly flaps her hands at me. "Whatever you want, Trudy."

Hendrick's shoulders droop, and Xavier frowns.

I'm in charge and it bugs him. If I want us to go straight to the hotel that's what we will do.

But how often do my friends get to spend a day on a yacht? And Polly finally feels better. She's no longer green.

I question Hendrick. "How are we going waterskiing? You can't ski behind a sailboat."

Xavier responds, and Hendrick nods, "Jakov has a friend with a ski boat. He's nearby. He'll meet us and captain this boat, and Jakov will take us skiing. He knows how to drive a motor boat."

I'm not as impressed with this as he seems to be.

"What do you say?" Jane presses me, laughing. "You don't want to be a 'sport-spoil' do you?"

I suppose I don't. And it can't possibly take long. We'll be at the hotel by dinner time.

THIRTY-SIX

· ▾ · ▾ · ▾ · ▾ · ▾ ·

Here, close to shore, the water is a beautiful shade of aqua. Beaches line the coast, sparsely dotted with people. I'm in paradise and thrilled to the core. The yacht slows, coming to a bobbing rest.

"Letting the anchor down here," Jakov shouts from the cockpit.

The water in this bay is unruffled, and the air is full of the briny scent of ocean. Seagulls hover overhead and other yachts bob nearby. Around each, a flotilla of rafts and inflatable creatures, unicorns and flamingos and dragons nodding in the breeze.

Jakov comes down from the cockpit, taking charge. "Now, girls. Why aren't you in your swimsuits?"

Mother ignores him, but Jane, one eye closed against the bright sky, looks him up and down and says, "I'm considering it."

"Good." He smacks his hands together.

She continues, lazily. "But not because *you* told me to."

He grins. "Come on, Jane. You know you love it when I tell you what to do."

One of her eyebrows shoots up, but I can see she's enjoying this flirtatious battle.

I was not planning on changing into my bathing suit but soon Polly, followed by Jane, head down to the cabin where our suitcases are stowed. Zelda rises from her seat and pulls the thin t-shirt she's wearing over her head, revealing that she's already wearing a bathing suit underneath. I notice her ribs as her arms stretch overhead, and her sharply angled hip bones as she wiggles out of her shorts. To me, she looks *too* thin, but that's probably just my catty jealous eyeballs talking to me.

"Turdy? You're not swimming?" Jakov asks, not looking at me, but scanning the water around us with a set of binoculars. "I'm finding Marco. By now he should be here."

If I'm the only person not in a bathing suit, I'll feel out of place, so I relent and go down to the cabin just as Jane and Polly are coming out of it, giggling and barefoot. "Isn't this great?" Polly says, squeezing my arm with excitement as we cross paths.

Opening my suitcase, I lift several layers of clothes before finding my prized bathing suit. This is the moment I've been waiting for all these months. Xavier is going to see me in this amazing swimsuit. I'm so glad I splurged.

I kick off my red runners and disrobe in the cramped cabin, luxuriating in the air-conditioning.

The swimsuit fits better now than it did when I bought it. I'm still losing weight, but not at such a rate that the material is saggy. It's comfortable and I look at myself in the full-length mirror. Hmm. Not bad for a plump lady.

And now for the crochet cover-up – the spun sugar on the crème caramel, so to speak.

Pulling it out, I give it a shake. It still looks wonderful even though it's been crushed in my suitcase all this time. I slip it on and turn to gaze at my reflection.

It's a magical garment, transforming me into the woman I want to be.

And this is great timing. It wasn't what I imagined, or what I had planned, but *this* is the first day of the rest of my life.

I retrieve my new flip-flops from the suitcase and shove my feet into them. They fit. And they're cute. They slap my soles in a sassy fashion as I make my way back up on deck.

Jakov's friend, Marco, is tying his speedboat to the back of the yacht and climbing aboard. Xavier, Hendrick, and Jakov stand around watching him, their carefree chests bare to the elements.

"You need četiri," Marco says, holding up four fingers and waggling them at Jakov.

"Why? We have only three. The girls don't go."

"Četiri," Marco insists, counting off the personnel required for waterskiing on his thick, tanned fingers. "Jakov, you drive. One skis. One watches skier. One watches the water forward. It's busy day. Not like the other day. I told you!"

Jakov blows him off. "It's not busy."

Clearly, Marco is not as happy with this skiing arrangement as Jakov made it sound.

"Okay," Jakov relents. "Who is coming with us? Zelda?"

But she has wandered off to sunbathe at the front of the boat. She looks at Jakov over her sunglasses but before she can respond, I jump in. "I'll go!"

Xavier turns and sees me; his eyebrows rise in surprise.

I'm not sure why I volunteered, but I'm feeling feisty. Something in me wants to beat Zelda at something, anything. I want to get there before her.

Jakov looks at me, skeptically, like a fisherman weighing a fish, wondering whether to throw me back into the water. "Alright... Okay...."

It *will* be okay.

Boating today has lifted my spirits fantastically.

"Let's go!" Jakov bosses us, directing Xavier and Hendrick.

For the first time today, the sun breaks through the cloud cover, and all around us the water sparkles with a million diamonds.

Xavier turns and holds out his hand to me as I step from the yacht into the motor boat. My new flip-flops flash in the sun. His hand feels hot and firm in mine.

"You spot the skier," Jakov commands me, pointing behind the driver's seat to the seat that faces behind the boat. I sit, feeling titillated by spending time in my bathing suit, with Xavier, away from Zelda.

As they wrestle the skis and wakeboard from the hull, and begin unfurling the ski-rope, I gaze around at the rugged shoreline. The island of Vis rises from the water like a snapping turtle's back. I'm tingling with excitement. We're here and

I can't wait to get to the hotel and bump into Madison. Even if she doesn't want me, I want her, and always will. She's my baby.

"Which one goes first?" Jakov asks Hendrick and Xavier.

"I will," Hendrick says, donning the life-jacket.

I ask him, "Have you skied before?"

"A couple of times," he answers, flashing a grin before jumping off the back of the boat.

He may have skied before, but it takes him a great many tries to get up on two skis, with Jakov circling around, yelling instructions at him over the sound of the idling motor.

"Tips up!" I yell, as Hendrick finally manages to retain hold of the ski-rope handle long enough to allow the boat's force to pull him out of the water.

"What did you say?" Jakov yells at me over the roar of the engine. "Tits up? Turdy, you naughty girl!"

I don't turn to look at him, the idiot. I keep my eyes trained on Hendrick, as my grandfather taught me.

There are many boats and swimmers in the water and I need to keep my eyes on my skier for when he inevitably falls, or drops the rope. He's clinging for dear life to the ski-rope handle and grinning, his skis pounding along the bubbly white wake. Jakov takes the boat on a large circular course, coming terrifyingly close to the beach where children are swimming. The parents are alarmed and I spot angry faces and shaking fists as we head back out to the deeper water.

Hendrick doesn't ski long. He doesn't have the stamina, and after wiping out twice, he gives up and climbs back into the boat, exhausted, but clearly delighted with himself. I'm glad he's having fun.

By the time Xavier has taken his turn – trying, and failing to get up on the wakeboard – the midday heat is as oppressive as it has been on previous days. My forehead and upper lip are sweating unbecomingly and my armpits are slippery. I'm looking forward to returning to the yacht, and even more so, to the air-conditioned rooms of Hotel George. Whenever the sun glares, in and out between big cottony clouds, it's scorching. Sopping wet, Xavier climbs into the boat, and it's lovely when some of his water drips on me.

"I'm jumping in," Jakov announces. "Will you join me, Turdy?"

I decline immediately and laugh, as though it's preposterous that I would jump out of a motor boat, when honestly, I would love to be submerged in that ocean right now. If there's time, I may go for a dip when we get back to the yacht.

Jakov plunges from the boat causing it to spin away from him for a moment. He swims off to gather up the wakeboard, which has drifted a couple of yards away. Without a life-jacket to buoy him, he struggles, then uses the ski-rope to pull the boat back around toward himself.

"Help me reel this in," he orders, thrashing the yellow rope on the surface.

I lean over the back of the boat and start drawing in the rope in large neat circles, just as Grandad showed me a thousand years ago.

Jakov swims to the back of the boat and grabs the ladder with one hand. I look down into his tanned dripping face and fierce dark eyes.

"Thank you, Turdy," he says, extending his other hand. Instinctively, I reach for it, and he pulls. For a moment I struggle with him, thinking he needs me to help pull him into the boat.

I realize – too late – he's pulling me into the ocean!

Head first, I splash into the shockingly cold water.

I kick my legs, and the crochet cover-up tangles around my body.

I come up sputtering. "You—!"

Hendrick and Xavier rush to the stern, both shouting at me and at Jakov.

He's laughing as he climbs easily back into the boat with the wakeboard under his arm. "Turdy, you kill me."

I tread water and see my silver flip-flops bobbing on the surface a couple of feet away.

"Do you need help?" Hendrick shouts. "Should I jump in and get you?"

Jakov laughs. "No, no. Let her ski!" He tosses the two water skis into the ocean near me. He's getting a real kick out of this trick he thinks he's playing on me. What a bully!

Xavier comes to my defense. "She can't ski!"

Bubbles rise to the surface around me. "I'm fine," I mutter, beginning to make my way over to the boat, but the cover-up sleeves impede my stroke. I try to gather my flip-flops before they drift away.

"Get the skis!" Jakov yells, pointing. One of them has drifted a few yards away and I struggle over to retrieve it.

As I gather the skis, amid the tangle of yellow ski-rope, I'm immersed in sensory memory. The wide expanse of sky overhead. The smell of gasoline from the boat engine. The feel of the skis' weight in my fingers. The water on my face though these trickles taste delightfully salty like tortilla chips.

"If you want back in the boat, you have to try at least!" Jakov proclaims, his hands on his hips.

Xavier and Hendrick begin arguing with him. Xavier is touchingly upset. I know him well enough to recognize it, but Jakov is unconcerned. He's smirking and having fun humiliating me. The man is a colossal jackass.

I stroke toward the boat, irritated, but also full of regret.

If only the three of them could've seen me cutting the wake on one ski when I was a teenager. None of them would be laughing at me. Unless my bathing suit bottoms fell off...but no, I feel them nice and secure on my body.

I wish I could ski, even if just to prove my salt to Xavier, who has too often underestimated me, never mind Jakov, the jerk, but there's no way I could get up on skis now. I'm too heavy and out of shape.

Xavier hovers at the back of the boat, waiting to help me in. Jakov stands next to him, hairy arms folded, a look of triumph on his face. He's succeeded in humiliating poor old Turdy, yet again.

I grab a stray flip-flop and fling it toward the boat but I overthrow, and it disappears beyond.

I just know it's gone forever.

Thirty-Seven

Treading water on a beautiful summer day in the Adriatic, pissed that I've lost my new flip-flops, I'm seized with an urge to rebel. Why not ski? I'll show them!

Xavier yells, "What are you doing? Get in the boat."

"I've decided to ski!" I declare, pride beginning to swell, filling me with power. Or is it adrenalin?

My legs cycle hard beneath the water, keeping me afloat.

Xavier protests. "Trudy, you can't ski! It's too hard. Get back in the boat."

Just because he couldn't do it, he thinks I can't?

Jakov frowns for a moment, bends down in the boat, and the next thing I know a bright yellow life-jacket is flying through the air, landing, splat, in the water beside me.

"Here you go!" he yells, mocking me. "Put it on!"

The stunned, helpless looks on Xavier and Hendrick's faces are maddening. They're convinced I'm going to fail!

I kick hard and grab the life-jacket.

It won't be easy to get it on in the water and I'm not sure it will be wide enough to go around me but I can probably adjust the clips.

I'm still wearing my cover-up. My heart is pounding. There's no way I can get the life-jacket on, or ski, with the cover-up on. It will get all tangled up in my legs.

Defeated, I abandon my ridiculous idea to ski, and start swimming back toward the boat. I'll pretend I was joking all along.

"What? You're giving up? Turdy!" Jakov laughs, and starts drawing in the ski-rope. "You girls are so silly. Now let's get going. It's time for a beer. Right, boys?"

I stop and tread water for a few moments; thinking and thinking and thinking.

I don't want to lose my cover-up.

Thinking.

Especially just to prove a point to these obnoxious men.

Thinking.

Xavier looks relieved that I've changed my mind. Hendrick is worriedly examining his upper arms and belly – his skin is turning a flaming red. He needs to cover up.

I ought to get into the boat and let them get to their next bit of recreation. My legs swirl beneath me as I ponder my options.

A seagull flies over, squawking like a freaking-out woman, "Caw. Caw!"

I look up from the water at the three stooges who expect me to surrender. Not have any fun. Not try hard things.

A voice inside me whispers, *just let it go.*

I can't believe I'm doing this.

I tug the cover-up off my shoulders and kick it out of my way.

With an urgent struggle I wangle the life-jacket on, all the while, Xavier is shouting at me, "What are you *doing*?"

I grab hold of the ski-rope handle and clutch it in the crook of my arm while gathering the skis.

They slide easily onto my feet – the rubber foot holds are set at man-size. My feet slide around somewhat, unlike the life-jacket, which fits snugly, but not impossibly. I can breathe. And I can ski.

Jakov is gleeful to watch me fail, and returns to the driver's seat. He puts the motor in gear, jolting Xavier down into the spotter's chair. The boat moves slowly away from me, straightening the rope between us.

It all feels so familiar.

I lean back in the water and get my ski tips up in front of me, above the surface where I can see them, the yellow rope, safely between them. My legs are wobbling. The fear is thrilling.

The moment the rope goes taut, I yell, "Hit it!"

Jakov guns the throttle and the engine roars, propelling the boat forward, up, and out of the water. I hang on like my life depends on it, concentrating on keeping my knees bent and those ski tips up. Because my body is submerged, the water presses around me heavily, pushing me back against the forward motion of the boat. I cling, and pray, and as the boat levels off, my skis catch the edge and I'm pulled up from the water.

I can't believe it – first try, I'm up!

Straightening my trembling legs, I watch Xavier and Hendrick cheering like maniacs in the boat. Jakov turns back to glance at me with a look of wide-eyed disbelief.

I'm skiing! It's glorious. In your face, Jerks!

Jakov drives in a short circuit. I suppose he thinks I have less stamina than Hendrick, but I feel strong and I have no intention of stopping. As we circle around, I see my cover-up floating in the ocean like a fisherman's lost net. Farewell, dear friend.

I am not letting go.

It's midafternoon, and the sea is filled with swimmers and small watercraft. People curse at me as I ski past. "Sorry," I yell as I fly by. But I'm not sorry. Unless the boat runs over one of them.

Instead of circling back again through the busy water and all the swimmers, Jakov drives the boat onward into the next cove.

Here, the water is rougher, a darker blue, and I can feel it's colder. Clouds cover the sun so there's less glare off the ocean and I feel a shiver starting in my legs.

Just savour this moment, I tell myself. It will be over soon enough and you may never have this chance again.

My body feels weightless, and my spirit is soaring like a bird. I'm alive and it's wonderful, and my new life has truly started.

I will enjoy the scenery, and when Jakov circles back to the other bay, where our yacht is anchored, I'll call it quits. I'm not rushing my ski turn just because he wants to have a beer with the boys.

Yet he doesn't circle back.

He keeps going, and the shoreline becomes more rugged. Strangely, there are no people on this beach – they're all back in the other cove. This must be a remote location, not accessible by road.

Suddenly, a figure appears. Way down the beach. A woman.

I can tell it's a woman because she's wearing a bikini and has long hair...like Madison.

My eyes lock on, and I wish we were closer so her face would come into focus.

Why is she here all alone?

Abruptly, Jakov steers the boat away from the isolated beach, circling back to the other cove now.

The woman waves.

I stare at her as we veer away.

She waves both arms, as though she's signaling. To me!

It's Madison!

As Jakov drives away, heading to the other cove, I point frantically.

Xavier, who is supposed to be spotting me, is preoccupied, laughing and talking over his shoulder to the others.

I make slashing motions across my throat. Yelling, "Hey! Stop! We need to go back!"

None of them hear me. And none of them are watching me.

The boat speeds onward.

Should I just let go?

Will Xavier even notice?

My legs are exhausted and wobbly, the palms of my hands burn from clutching the ski-rope handle. I turn my head to catch one last glimpse of the girl on the beach and my body hurtles off balance.

In one spectacular moment, I flip over the skis, my bum bounces off the wake, and I sink into the bubbles and dark blue ocean. My nostrils fill with stinging water. I snort and slash at the enveloping sea. The skis slide off my feet, and I kick.

Underwater, it's deafeningly silent. Only bubbles rush past me.

The life-jacket pulls me up, up, up, toward the light.

I break through the surface, sputtering, and struggling to get my bearings. Where is the shore? Where is the girl?

Where is the boat?

All I can see is the back of it, in the distance, roaring away from me.

Thirty-Eight

Quiet. The only sound around me is the sloshing of the waves. I strain to hear the boat returning but it's gone.

The water is frigid, and my legs feel wonky, probably turning blue.

I try to stay calm, assuring myself – they'll come back. They'll come back.

Jakov might let me die, but Hendrick and Xavier will not. I think.

My hands trembling, I grab one of the skis and hold it straight up from the water. Jakov will be able to see it when he finally realizes I've fallen and he needs to come back for me.

Xavier and Hendrick are useless spotters, the idiots, but eventually they've got to notice there's no one on the end of the ski-handle that's bouncing across the water.

I wait and wait, my teeth starting to chatter.

I concentrate on remembering everything Grandad taught me about surviving cold water. Don't panic. Don't panic. Keep moving. Make your way toward shore.

It's brutally cold.

I kick my legs and try to stretch my head above the water, straining to find the shoreline. The water is choppy and the beach bobs only occasionally into view.

I'm certain the girl I saw was Madison.

But why would she be on a desolate beach all alone?

Was it her?

Holding one ski aloft, and the other tucked under my arm, I float, resting against the back of the life-jacket, kicking slowly toward the far off shore.

I don't think this is how Trudy Asp is meant to end. Here and now, on the first day of the rest of her life. I don't want to die like this, cold and alone and ignored. I want to be home. I want to be with my daughter and my friends. I want to be warm again. With people who love me. I want love. I want life. I want me. Please God, don't let me die today.

In the distance, I hear a motor boat, but I keep kicking toward shore in case it isn't them, or they don't see me.

No, definitely, a boat is approaching, and finally, after what feels like an eternity, it circles around me. Jakov cuts the engine and the boat comes to a bobbing stop. Scrambling to the back, he starts pulling in the ski-rope, as though he's more concerned about it than about me.

Xavier leans over the stern, guilt and fear rippling across his face. He holds out a trembling hand to me. "Hey, sorry. I didn't see you fall."

"I saw Madison!" I tell him, handing over the skis, grabbing hold of the metal ladder beside the engine.

"What? Where?"

"Didn't you see the girl on the beach? I was pointing!"

The ski-rope handle bangs against the motor as Jakov sweeps it into a neat loop before dropping it into the boat. "Let's go!" he barks as I'm hauling my leg over the edge.

Blubbery and numb, chilled to the bone, I'm aware that I must look like a mess, dripping, and desperate and covered in goosebumpy flesh.

"Your lips are purple," Hendrick says, wrapping me in a skimpy white towel he must have found somewhere in the boat to cover up his sunburn.

How wonderful it would've been to draw on my crochet cover-up like a cocoon right now.

Clutching the towel around my shoulders, my teeth chattering, I implore Xavier, "I'm sure it was her. We need to go back."

He looks at me, troubled, but he doesn't take me seriously. He's probably just glad they found me and I didn't get eaten by sharks, because that would have looked really bad on him.

"There's a path on that beach leading to the food trucks," Jakov informs us. "We get hotdogs sometimes," he says, hopping back into the driver's seat. "If someone is on that beach it's because they want to be there. Your eyes are blurry, Turdy. Perhaps saltwater doesn't agree with you."

"No! I saw her. I know my own daughter."

Now, I'm pissed.

The three of them observe me with something between skepticism and pity.

I demand of Jakov, "Where are those binoculars?"

He slides them from a slot beside the driver's seat and puts them to his eyes, carefully scanning the shore. "I see nothing."

"Let me have them!"

However, my hands are shaking too much, and I can't hold the binoculars steady. I smack them into Xavier's chest. "You look!"

He raises them to his eyes, fiddles with the focus, and scans the shore right and left and back again.

"I don't see anything," he says, handing them back to Jakov.

I crumple onto a seat, shivery, spent, and alone. I whimper, "I know it was her."

Hendrick pats me on the head and smiles. "Your skiing was amazing though! Where'd you learn to do that?"

Thirty-Nine

A t the marina, on the island of Vis, we disembark from Jakov's boat. Everyone is making a big deal out of saying goodbye. You'd think they were all
best friends by the number of hugs going around.

Turning my face so I won't have to smell her hair, I reach one arm around
Zelda's shoulder and give her a light pat. Her coconut sunscreen worms into my
senses anyway.

Xavier leans toward me and taps my back for a brief, meaningless gesture, and
when Jakov starts making the rounds, bear hugging all the women, I busy myself
with the straps on Mother's suitcase. There is no way I'm letting that guy hug me.
I don't care what any of them think. He is bad news.

"Goodbye!"

"Goodbye!"

"Goodbye!"

Zelda and Xavier remain on the deck with Jakov, waving. Apparently, they still
need to pack before they go to their hotel.

I turn away.

For the rest of us, it's uphill, pulling our suitcases to the street where Jakov
assured us we'd find a taxi.

Majka Town is like a toy village perched on the edge of the treed island,
reminding me of the wooden toy towns that came in net bags when I was a little
girl – red roofs, tan walls, black windows. This town has sailboats.

When we get to the corner, a taxi is easily hailed, but we can't all fit in one car
so Jane, Mother, and Hendrick take the first one. Polly and I will follow.

The air is sweet and salty at the same time. A hot breeze blows over us while we stand on the street admiring the scene, waiting for another car to appear.

It's the first time she and I have been alone together since the beginning of the trip, and I find myself talking nonstop, rattling on, trying to convince her that I saw my daughter on the beach, hoping she'll help me figure out how to go searching. Polly nods, and murmurs, but I can tell she's unsure of whose story to trust. If the others didn't see anything...

No one took me seriously when we returned to the yacht after skiing and I excitedly told them, "I saw a girl on the beach *who looked exactly like Madison!*"

Polly wanted to know what happened to my cover-up. And Jane insisted I explain how I lost both my cover-up and the glittery flip-flops.

"You should've seen the Trudster ski!" Hendrick gushed. "She was amaze-balls!"

Jane asked, "And you didn't film her?"

"Can you believe it? The one time I forget my phone..."

Mother scoffed and pulled the brim down on a large sunhat, which I presume she borrowed from Zelda. "Take a load off," she said to the group at large, waving a drink around.

The men disappeared to find beer, and frustrated, I sank onto a cushioned bench, giving up trying to persuade anyone. The skiing, and treading water, had drained me, though my mind was still zipping along at fifty miles an hour.

I sat, silently, stewing, and chewing my lip, watching the sea for the rest of the sail around the island to Majka Town.

There's a reason I didn't drown out there. My instincts aren't playing tricks on me. *Madison needs my help.*

It's disconcerting that Polly is humoring me now. Like everyone else, she doesn't believe me.

"Tell me again about the skiing," she says, steering me away from the subject of the girl on the beach. "I can't believe it! You skied?"

I relate the story of Jakov, the jerk, pulling me into the water, and how I was overcome with annoyance, and wanted to prove something to them all. "So, I got up and skied!"

"Amazing," she says, bopping me affectionately on my arm. "Yay, you. It must be the LOBO lifestyle. Your muscles are repairing. It's a miracle!"

I blush, waving at my face in the heat. She doesn't know about my snack attack last night.

She rhapsodizes, "People think *we* are missing out by not eating all that carbage – but I think *they* are the ones missing out – on feeling so good!"

I don't reply. If I tell her about the carbage I ate last night, she'll be disgusted with me. She won't want to be friends.

Instead, looking curious, she asks, "Is there something you want to tell me?"

"No," I lie, rubbing my forearms.

"Are you sure? You didn't binge last night?"

My eyes pop open wide. "What? No!"

But I can't look at her, I'm so full of regret. I stare at the ground. My heart pounding. She's caught me lying. She's going to tell me I'm unworthy of her friendship and she can't believe how weak I am.

"Honey, you had crumbs on your shirt," she continues. "And you smelled like booze. Why are you lying?"

I've never had someone so gently and kindly ask me why I'm betraying them.

"I don't know!" I wail.

"You're not a failure, you know? It was just a lapse. No biggy. You're back on track today, right?"

I nod, holding back tears. I can't believe she's not mad. You're not supposed to lie to your friends, but she seems unconcerned about that.

I laugh in embarrassment, though I'm about to cry.

"I feel so childish," I blubber. "I'm not usually emotional like this. It must be the heat. I'm usually slow and steady, never-rocks-the-boat Trudy."

She nods. "I know exactly what you're talking about. You've been stuffing down your feelings with food your entire life. I did that too," she reassures me.

We stand smiling at each other, a sob remains caught in my throat.

This day has been too much. Too turbulent.

"When we get back home," she says, "I want you to do something for me."

"Of course. I will." I'd do anything for her. "What is it?"

She holds my gaze, about to ask something very important of me. "No lying, okay?"

I nod vigorously in agreement, even though I have no idea if I can follow through. I seem to lie a lot.

She continues, "I want you to come with me to my UBMH meeting."

I look at her puzzled, with no idea what UBMH is.

"It's a support group," she explains. "It stands for Un-Binge My Heart."

"Ohhh," I say, still baffled.

"It's a funny name," she says, as if that explains it.

"But why do *you* go to a support group?"

She laughs. "To help me stay off the sugar."

This astonishes me. She's done so well. She lost all that weight. "But you don't have a problem, do you?"

"I still need support," she answers.

I nod, not really understanding, but deciding to believe her.

"Sure. Of course I'll go with you, if you'd like my support...for your support group."

She laughs again.

I don't return to the subject of Madison. Instead, we chat about this and that, melting in the heat, watching the sea, surveying the town, and after the seagulls have flown a few more laps around the harbor, the same taxi reappears and scoots us off to the hotel.

FORTY

· ▾ · ▾ · ▾

Hotel George is an ancient sand-block castle, charming and inviting like
something out of a fairy tale. Vines and plants trail along walls and window boxes, narrow walkways and stone staircases dip and curve, here and there.
The entrance is surrounded by iron gating and twinkle lights.

We step inside to soft music playing, a fountain trickling nearby.

Polly whispers, "Oh my gosh, Trudy. This is incredible!"

We approach the front desk.

"The others in your party have already claimed two of the rooms," the clerk
informs us. "You will be sharing the third?"

Polly and I exchange happy glances. Finally, we'll be spending some quality
time together on this trip.

With her, I have so much to talk about. Things I can't discuss in front of
the others – even Jane. I'm not sure when I began to feel a barrier intensifying
between myself and my 'best friend' but Jane irritates me now. *A lot.*

After a lifetime of friendship, I don't have the same connection I used to
have with her. Even though she's a shrink, and should understand, she's never
experienced the years of self-loathing I have. She doesn't know how it feels to live
inside an out-of-control body that's on a wild ride of its own. She doesn't get how
hard it is to deal with life's troubles without medicating them away with a pill, or
a drink, or a donut.

Polly does.

We are going to have the most soulful heart-to-hearts this week. I just know it.

However, I haven't forgotten my daughter, and I must know she's safe, and not stranded on some Godforsaken beach somewhere. Before leaving the front desk, I ask the clerk, "Has my daughter, Madison, checked in?"

She consults her computer screen. "Madison...? What is her last name?"

"Asp," I tell her, and reflexively, my left thumb reaches across my palm to stroke the base of my ring finger, but the ring that resided there, reminding me, and the whole world, that I am the woman Xavier Asp chose to be his wife, is gone.

However, Asp is my daughter's surname. And I am her mother. So, it's my name too. I'm not giving up Asp.

The clerk shakes her head. "I see no one at the hotel, besides you, with that name."

"What about a reservation? Are you expecting her?"

She checks the screen again and says, "Yes, we expected her yesterday, but she didn't check in."

My stomach quivers with nerves, and I picture the girl on the beach, arms overhead, waving at me.

"She must be at a different hotel," Polly assures me as we rise to our floor in the elevator.

"I suppose... it's possible...." Now, I'm humoring Polly, because that's not what I really believe.

Walking down the Berber carpeted hallway, I bite my lip in worry.

I can't help it – my mother's intuition is whirring again. Madison was supposed to be here and she's not. Where could she be?

"Look," Polly says, trying to distract me, unlocking the door of our room. "We've had a great day. Let's just relax tonight, and leave tomorrow to tomorrow."

We are sharing a swishy, modern hotel room, decorated in soft grays and whitewash with macramé accents. Between the two single beds, a light on a sleek ivory phone on the bedside table is flashing. "Looks like we've got a message," Polly says, examining the phone, a rotary model, but with buttons, she asks, "How do you use this thing?"

I take a stab at it, pressing the blinking light.

"We're in room 2-11," Jane's recorded voice tells us. "Call back when you get this."

There are tiny typewritten instructions beside the phone's buttons, only some of them are in English. I push 2-1-1 and watch the phone but it does nothing.

At the same instant that Polly says, "Pick up the receiver!" I remember how old-fashioned phones operate.

Laughing, at our ineptitude, I snatch it up and retry the buttons. "It's ringing," I tell her, and she shakes her head, incredulous that we both momentarily forgot how *all* phones used to work.

After some odd whirring buzzes, Hendrick answers. "You made it!"

"We did!"

"Are you hungry? We're starving. Those nutty butter sandwiches were not my jam."

I ask Polly. "Are we hungry?"

She laughs.

It's funny because honestly, after eating the almond butter and celery for lunch, I've barely thought of food all day, other than regretting the junk I ate last night. I had things on my mind but food was not one of them. Polly told me this would happen someday and I didn't believe her. I'm contentedly living off the fat amply stored on my body.

Now, as I imagine the delicious dinner they'll serve in the hotel dining room we glimpsed on the way to our room – I realize, I'm ravenous.

"Give us twenty minutes to get changed," I tell Hendrick, my mouth beginning to water.

The restaurant is on a sandstone terrace with tall palms and gnarled trees, smooth wooden furniture, and a view of the ocean. The maître d' introduces himself as Fabijan, and leads the five of us to a glass-topped table set with black linen napkins and woven straw placemats.

"I'll have a martini," Mother says to him the moment we sit down. "Dry."

Fabijan bows slightly. "I will tell your server, Missus."

Jane breathes across the table at Mother, eyes blazing. "Couldn't you wait for one darn minute?"

I stifle a giggle. Jane's about to find out. Living with Mother is no day at the beach.

The waiter sets menus before us: *King George's Feast,* a list of fresh fish, grilled meats, octopus, and local vegetables.

Ignoring Jane, Mother addresses me, "Now, where is my granddaughter?"

Folding the menu over my finger, I tell her the only fact I know, "She isn't here."

"She's not? Doesn't that alarm you?"

So, now, Mother is concerned. Doesn't that just figure? All day no one took me seriously, and now, finally, it's she who's paying attention.

She leans across the table toward me. "You said you saw her on a beach. Xavier said she'd be here. What's going on?" she demands. "We've come all this way to see her get married. I'm beginning to think this wedding is a hoax."

The server sets a tall triangular glass before her, momentarily suspending her interrogation.

Her shifting attitudes unsettle me. Dismissive one minute, deeply concerned the next. You'd think I'd be used to her by now, but I'm not. I'm always thrown off kilter.

"Madison is probably here on the island at another hotel," Polly speculates, waving her hand toward the ocean view. "Somewhere."

Hendrick nods. "More than likely."

"She's on her honeymoon!" Jane crows. "We won't see her for days!"

Mother's mouth goes tight. I don't think she likes what Jane is insinuating; that her granddaughter is holed up in a honeymoon suite with some man.

Admittedly, neither do I.

Only, I'm not at all convinced that Madison is in a honeymoon suite.

I believe she's stranded on a lonely beach somewhere.

Deep inside, my mother's instinct flickers. My child is in danger. I can't ignore the feeling.

I close my menu, and tell the group, "Tomorrow, I'm going exploring. To see if I bump into her."

"Leave her alone," Jane says, minimizing my decision, as usual.

Mother quietly gazes across the restaurant, sipping her martini. The rest of the table studies their menus. The waiter pours wine, takes our orders, and the topic of Madison and her whereabouts drifts away.

But I am not forgetting.

I take a sip of the Rioja. Too sweet. I set it down again.

I wonder if Madison has posted anything. I pull out my phone to check FlipFlop.

"Trudy Asp!" Jane exclaims. "Are you using your phone at the dinner table?"

Everyone looks at me, and I don't care. I'm concerned about my daughter. "I'm just checking to see if she's posted anything."

Jane snickers. "I'm telling ya. She's in no position to post pictures right now." Laughing, she makes the obscene hand gesture we invented in high-school to signify coitus.

Rolling my eyes, I respond, "Very mature, Jane."

Ignoring her, I check my phone, but sadly, she's right. Madison hasn't posted since the night she had dinner with Xavier when she added a photo of the two of them, pressed cheek to cheek for a selfie. In it, Xavier looks handsome and drunk, and Madison looks.... How *does* she look?

For the first time, I notice a faraway look in her eyes, and a forced smile. She's gaunt, and there are shadows under her eyes. Her skin is as pale as paper next to Xavier's tanned cheek. Even though I've looked at this photo a zillion times, I never noticed these things about Madison before. I was always looking at Xavier. I neglected my daughter because I was obsessed with him.

"Honestly, I'm worried about her," I say, putting my phone away.

I look to Mother for some backup, but in need of another drink, she's scanning the restaurant for the server.

"She'll be fine," Polly says, patting my arm.

I don't believe that. Polly has been right about a lot of things, but when it comes to my daughter, I know best.

The meal is delicious, just as expected, but when the dessert menus appear, I take the opportunity to visit the ladies' room. I don't need to hear a recitation of the sugary concoctions about to be ordered. On the way back, I notice Fabijan, the maître d' leaning against the bar, scanning his phone.

"Excuse me," I interrupt, and he quickly puts his phone away. "I'm just wondering if you could help me with something."

He snaps to attention. "Of course. Whatever you need."

"I'm wondering, actually, if you know if I could rent a boat to go around the island."

"A boat? You mean a sailboat?"

"No, I mean a motorboat."

His eyes light up. "I have a boat, Missus. I sometimes take tourists out fishing."

"Really?"

"Yes. When would you like to go?"

"Tomorrow." I can't believe my luck. "But not to go fishing. I want to go around the island, slowly, close to the shore."

"Okay," he agrees, but he looks confused. "Sight-seeing?"

"I'm looking for something I saw when I was out on the water today."

His eyebrows furrow. "What is it you saw?"

"A person, actually. My daughter."

His eyes widen, and he looks baffled. Obviously, it's an odd request. He responds, "I will take you. I work only at dinner tomorrow. If we leave early, we can go around the island, and see your daughter."

After thanking him, and exchanging details, I return to my seat at the table, declaring "I've hired a boat for tomorrow."

"What? No! I've had enough of boats," Polly protests.

Jane argues, "I want to explore the garrison."

"Oh yes, me too," Mother agrees. "I forgot all about mad King George."

I look at her in disbelief. We are literally staying in Hotel George and just ordered from *King George's Feast* menu. Her brain is pickled.

"Hendrick? What about you? Will you come with me?" He was my knight in shining armor at the White Party, perhaps he'll pick up the sword again.

He hesitates. "I wanted to check out the stores, and do some souvenir shopping." He taps his chin and studies my face. "But I can do that the next day. Sure, I'll go tomorrow. Are we skiing again?"

"No!"

He's taken aback by the forcefulness of my response, so, I reel it in a little, explaining, "My skiing days are now over."

"No way," he counters, grinning. "You were amazing! We should do it again."

"Someday, but tomorrow, I just want to see if I can find Madison, on that beach."

Hendrick's face falls, but he doesn't say anything about backing out.

Jane butts in, "Are you serious, right now? You saw a girl waving at you from some random beach, and you think it's Madison and you're going to go find her?"

It sounds far-fetched, and I know Jane expects her scorn will dissuade me, but finding that girl is exactly what I intend to do. I need to follow my intuitions, or they're going to eat me alive.

Looking steadily and defiantly into Jane's eyes, I tell her, "Yes, I'm serious. I'm going to find my daughter."

Taken aback, she pauses for a moment. "Then dammit, I'm coming with you!"

FORTY-ONE

The next morning, seagulls circling over the wharf while fishers head out in their boats, Hendrick, Jane, and I hunker down in Fabijan's fishing boat. It's a bare-bones vessel compared to the sleek ski-boat we were zipping around in yesterday – no ski-rope, no wakeboard, no ladder. Just a rough fiberglass hull and cracked vinyl cushions on the seating in the bow. All I care about is it's a boat and it floats.

"There are many coves that sound like that," Fabijan tells me after I describe the beach where I saw Madison. "Vis doesn't have many roads leading to beaches – there are a few, but they're dirt roads. Most beaches are reached by sea. We'll try to find it but it won't be easy." He asks me, "Why is your daughter there?"

"I have no idea, but I have to find out."

"It's possible it's not her," Hendrick says. "But Trudy saw someone. Whoever it is, may need our help."

At last, he seems persuaded that I truly saw a girl on the beach and wasn't imagining things. I'm relieved to finally have someone on my side.

Clearing the marina, the small boat increases speed and bounces through the choppy sea at a good clip. We watch the shore stream by, beautiful villas, long beaches, and stretches of large rocks with trees growing right down to the water. After a couple of hours, we're exhausted by the constant bouncing and the loudness of the motor and the wind, but then Fabijan points out a flotilla of yachts anchored offshore in the distance.

"That's it!" Jane says, pointing a long ringed finger. "I recognize it from yesterday."

Fabijan steers the boat toward shore and slows it down so we can scour the beach through his binoculars.

Each cove's beach is empty, just stretches of gray sand littered with driftwood and ocean debris. No people.

I'm beginning to worry we're too late. Madison is gone. I fight a mixture of sadness and panic. Where is she?

Coming around the point of yet another bay, I spot what looks to me like a figure on the shore. My heart leaps into my throat.

I point. "Am I seeing what I think I'm seeing?"

"What? Where?"

I keep pointing and the figure doesn't disappear.

I can't believe it, after miles of coastline, and thousands of pieces of deceptive driftwood, we've finally located the beach. And the girl.

Hendrick trains the binoculars on the shore, scanning until they land on the person at the water's edge.

He confirms, "It's a girl."

We draw steadily closer. Her face comes into focus. "It's Madison!" I shout.

Training my gaze on my daughter, I will her not to disappear. My eyes keep watering. I'm choked up in relief.

But I'm also frightened. How did this happen?

Jane, Hendrick, and I shield our eyes with our hands as Fabijan steers the boat toward the beach.

"Oh Trudy, I'm so sorry I doubted you," Jane utters, hoarsely.

On the shore, as if crumbling in relief, Madison sinks into a crouch, her arms wrapped around her knees.

The ocean beneath the boat shallows very quickly, ripples of sand clearly visible through the green water. Fabijan cuts the engine and tilts it up so the propeller doesn't hit bottom. He hands Hendrick an oar, and as fast as they can, they begin poling the boat toward shore.

"Madison!" I shout, waving my arms.

Her head comes up, and she looks toward me, but she doesn't rise or say anything back.

"What's wrong with her?" I ask, my worry taking on a terrifying new tack.

Before, I had a vague sense of danger, that something bad was happening to my daughter. Now, I'm petrified it's already happened, and we're too late to prevent it.

Jane looks worried too, her eyes glued on Madison.

When we're close enough to the beach, I scramble from the bow, churning as fast as my legs will take me through the knee-high water, toward Madison.

As I draw near to her, she doesn't rise, but I hear a word escape from her.

"Mommy?"

I drop to the sand beside her, enveloping her birdlike form in my arms. "I'm here now," I say, crying and pressing my lips to her forehead.

On her other side, Jane drops down and grasps Madison's wrist, checking her pulse.

Madison collapses out of her crouch position, sinking directly onto the beach, her thin pale legs unfolding in front of her.

The boat settles about ten feet from shore. Hendrick drops his oar and clambers over the side, while Fabijan stays in the boat, leaning against the windshield.

"How did you get here?" he calls to Madison. "There is no access."

At the sound of an unfamiliar voice, she looks up, her eyes struggling to focus on his face. Her lips, chapped and sunburnt, move. "I thought there was a path to the hotdogs," she answers, nonsensically, her voice raspy and hoarse.

"She needs water," Jane says.

I repeat Fabijan's question, "Madison, *how* did you get here?"

She doesn't answer. "Water," she whispers.

"C'mon," Jane says. "Let's get her into the boat. She needs medical attention."

Grasping her skinny arms, we hoist Madison to her feet, and lead her to the boat.

Hendrick scrambles in ahead of us and reaches out his hands. In his chipper, engaging manner, he says, "Come on ladies, right this way." He reassures Madison, grabbing her arms. "I'm a good friend of your momma, and Jane, and your grandma!"

"Grandma?" Madison repeats.

"Yes, Grandma," I encourage her, my mind swirling. "She's at the hotel. She wants to see you."

"Let's get into the boat," Jane urges.

After minutes of struggle, pinched thighs and arms, we're aboard. Fabijan passes around bottles of water, but Madison is too weak and uncoordinated to remove the cap, so I twist it off for her. She drinks deeply while the men pole us out to deeper water where the motor can be dropped.

FORTY-TWO

I n the white dusty gravel of the marina parking lot, Jane and I settle Madison into the back seat of a taxi summoned by Fabijan.

Hendrick, who always finds an opportunity to flirt, asks Fabijan, with a sly grin, "You're not coming with us? You could squeeze in the front with me."

Fabijan's cheeks color, and he shakes his head. "Not now. I'm taking care of my boat."

"Leave him alone," Jane chides Hendrick, his eyes in an amorous dance.

"Is the young lady okay?" the taxi driver asks, curious as a waif-thin Madison, sunburnt from forehead to coral toenails, and dressed only in a bikini, climbs painfully into his back seat.

"I hope so," I tell him.

A wave of relief had washed over me during the bumpy sea journey back to Majka Town. She'd been sheltering in my arms, taking occasional sips from her water bottle, and then about halfway, sat up on her own and started watching the shore, fussing with the hair blowing into her face.

"She's young," Jane yelled over the noisy motor. "She's rehydrating fast."

In Croatian, Fabijan fills in the taxi driver, gesturing at the sea and then at Madison. With an incredulous expression, the taxi driver asks a few follow-up questions, shaking his head in disbelief.

Hendrick stands next to the two Croats, watching their faces with rapt attention, even though I know he doesn't understand a word. After a few minutes of back and forth, Fabijan addresses Hendrick in English. "Should we call police?"

Hendrick looks surprised. "Police?"

"Yes, this girl. She was dumped on the beach by someone, no?" Fabijan lowers his voice, but I hear him say, "She could have died."

Madison, sitting in the back seat, stiff and still so as to not jostle her sunburn, stares forward through the windshield, wordless. Jane, having taken the seat on Madison's far side, is fussing over her, chatting, and encouraging further sips on the water bottle. I lean against the open car door, where I've been listening to the men talk before climbing inside.

Hendrick asks me, "How did she get on that beach, Trudy? And where's the groom? Do we need the police?"

Since finding Madison, and loading her into the boat, I've been wondering the same things. Well, not the police question – that didn't cross my mind before now – but the other two: how and why was she on that beach? And where is Matt Brown?

I lean into the car to ask Madison. "Sweetie, can you tell us how you became stranded on that beach?"

She takes a deep breath, as though it's going to be a giant exertion to tell us.

Fabijan comes closer. "This is *very* serious," he says. "You must tell us, and we will call the police."

"The police?" she reacts – whipping her head to face him, wincing in discomfort from the sunburn. "*Why?*"

"Because someone left you on the beach. Who was it?"

She flaps her hand dismissively. "He didn't leave me on purpose."

Jane asks, "Who's he?"

"Jakov."

I gasp in surprise, and Madison looks at me questioningly, as though trying to figure out why I'm stunned.

"He told us you *eloped!*" I tell her.

Annoyance flies across her face. "What? That jerk!"

I continue, "But I *saw* you yesterday—"

"You did? Where?" Now she's the surprised one.

"On the beach when I was skiing. I told everyone – I told *Jakov*! 'That's her,' I said! He told me I was loopy."

She waves her hands at me. "Wait. Wait. How do *you* know Jakov?" And before waiting for my response she adds, incredulously, "What do you mean *you were skiing*?"

I laugh. There's so much about me she doesn't know.

"I met him at the White Party," I begin to tell her. "I went looking for you but—"

"Wait!" she stops me again. "You went looking for me at the White Party?"

Her astonishment and the flood of appreciation on her face reaches deep inside me, squeezing my heart.

"Of course, I went looking for you, Sweetie. We couldn't find you!"

It's hot. I'm standing, half in, half out of the taxi, in the sun. All around gulls are circling, and calling.

The driver clears his throat, and Jane whirls her hand, interrupting the tenderness of this mother/daughter moment, trying to get Madison back onto her explanation. "We just need to know *why* Jakov left you on that beach," she says, in her matter-of-fact fashion.

Madison explains: "We were skiing with some guests, and Jakov was being...." Her brows furrow as she remembers.

"...obnoxious?" I finish her sentence, nodding, encouraging her to go on.

She smirks. "You *have* met him." We both laugh but Madison winces, and whines, "I'm so burnt!"

Hendrick leans into the car beside me. "So, then what happened? You had a big fight with him, or what?"

She huffs at his impatience. "He was *bothering* me," she explains, blinking, thinking back, taking a little sip of her water. "More than usual."

Over Madison's head, I exchange a glance with Jane, imagining what Madison means by 'bothering.' Hitting on her is probably more like it.

"Then what happened?" I press gently. "You were skiing with your guests. But how did you end up alone on the beach?"

She throws up her hands as if we're all dense. "There were too many people in the boat. It was too heavy – no one could get up. So, I volunteered to go ashore." She scowls, remembering, and continues, "I'd had it with Jakov. I told him, 'That's it – I'm *done*!' We yelled at each other, a lot..." She pauses, suddenly looking worried. "...in front of the guests. Mom, I'll probably get fired!"

"I don't understand," Fabijan interjects over Hendrick's shoulder. "She works with this man?"

"Yes, on a yacht tour," I explain.

The three of us are crowded around the back door in the unbearable heat. Fabijan asks Madison, "Did you think you could make your way over here to Majka Town in your bare feet?"

Jane spouts, "With no wallet? No cell phone?"

"I know! It was stupid. I admit it. But, Aunt Jane, I was so fed up." Madison slaps her thighs, and winces again. "And there used to be a path up to the food trucks, and to the other beach, but I couldn't find it! There were fallen trees everywhere." She shrugs, looking sad. "There was no way to get through. I just had to wait for someone to find me."

Looking up, her eyes shining with tears, she mouths, "And it was you, Mommy."

My heart pangs. I push Hendrick aside and climb into the car next to my daughter.

"I think she's right," he concurs, shutting the car door for me. "Jakov told us about the hot dogs," he tells the other two men, as though he's the authority on the veracity of Madison's tale. "No need for the police."

"We had a bad storm last week," the taxi driver agrees, rounding the front of the taxi, taking the driver's seat. "Trees down all over the place."

"But this man. He is very bad," Fabijan insists. "We should call the police."

The taxi driver leans across the front seat and looks out the window at Fabijan, sweat trickling down his temple. He says something in Croatian and Fabijan's eyebrows furrow.

He translates. "He says, the girl is fine, she's alive. The police will do nothing. But—"

"Whatever!" Madison says. "Can we *go*?"

FORTY-THREE

The hotel's doorman rushes to the cab, telling us, as we clamber out, "Your Mother and friend are waiting by the pool."

Jane says to me, nodding at Madison, "We need to get her some food."

I agree. My daughter is as thin as I've ever seen her.

"Are you hungry, Sweetie?"

"I'm not going to a restaurant like *this*." Madison gestures at her bikini-clad, sand-caked body.

The doorman holds the door to the hotel for us. Hendrick does an incorrigible little curtsy as we pass through.

"We need to get her some clothes," I tell Jane as we stand in the lobby.

"Give me your credit card. I'll find Polly and get her to go buy something."

"Good plan. But my purse is up in my room."

The bell to the elevator dings. We pile inside.

Hendrick pushes our floor number and as the elevator doors close, wiggles his fingers at the doorman.

"*You* order her some room service," Jane instructs me, as we rise to our floor. "And *you* can go buy some vitamins," she directs Hendrick.

"Excellent idea," he agrees. Turning to Madison, he brags, "I take vitamins for my eyesight. Most people my age need readers, but not me. That's why I spotted you right away on the beach."

"B-12 is what she needs," Jane interrupts, bossily. "Find a pharmacy."

"Okay, okay," Hendrick says. "I'll ask the doorman."

They wait in the hall while I let Madison into the hotel room and fetch my credit card from my purse. I can hear them arguing about which one spotted Madison first on the beach as they head back to the elevator on their missions.

"You relax," I tell my daughter, trying not to flinch as she lays down on my bed and her dirty feet disappear between the clean, brilliant white sheets.

I pick up the room service menu from the dresser and read out the options, holding back from adding my opinion of what I think will be best for her. I'm aware of being in Mommy mode overdrive, but I have to remember my daughter is an adult now, and I need to let her make her own decisions.

"A smoothie," she answers, rejecting the grilled fish, scrambled eggs, or bowl of oatmeal she might have chosen, that I might have chosen for her.

I pick up the phone's receiver and dither for a few minutes; finally figuring out which number to call for the kitchen and order room service.

In the meantime, Madison's eyes close, and after a moment her mouth falls open. She's asleep in a heartbeat. The poor thing must be exhausted.

While she naps, I pace the room.

She explained that she and Jakov often dropped people on the deserted beach when they needed to make the ski-boat lighter, I understand that. But why, when he knew I was looking for her and said I saw her, did Jakov not compute the danger she was in? He's either really dense, or really sadistic.

Whichever, I can't let him get away with what he did. I've got to report him. Even if the Croatian police don't care, I'm sure his employer will want to know.

I've got to do it before Madison wakes up, because she'll try to stop me. For some reason she's minimizing it.

I open my laptop and search for the Dalma Tours website. Who knew I'd be making so many clandestine searches while my roommates slept? There it is, and a contact us page, with a phone number, an address, and a box to send a message.

I jot down the number. But if I call now, it's bound to wake her up.

I click on the box and type quickly: `I would like to report some reckless endangerment by one of your captains, Jakov—`

I wrack my brain trying to remember his last name. Something that starts with an M.

Madison rolls over in the bed, and I freeze, waiting until she's sleeping soundly again.

I backspace over my previous message and resume typing, as quietly as possible: `On or about August 27—`

I've calculated the date as the day before the White Party – Xavier said he saw her the day before, which was Wednesday.

`Jakov M, Captain, recklessly abandoned hostess, Madison Asp on a deserted beach in Vis. She was left without food, water, and shelter for over 24 hours until she was rescued by a search party.`

I don't know whether I should say this last part when I don't know all the facts but I type it in anyway. `It is also suspected he harassed her while they were working.`

I type in all my contact information and click send, letting out a deep sigh of relief. Madison might not want to stir up trouble, but as far as I'm concerned, it's the right thing to do.

The other topic she's avoiding is her fiancé. She hasn't breathed a word about him.

Or the wedding.

I'm not exactly afraid to ask, but for some reason, I'm hesitant to raise the subject.

On the boat ride back from the beach, it occurred to me that Matt Brown, or whichever Matt it is she's engaged to, has left her on the eve of their marriage and broken her heart.

I hear a key slide into the lock and Polly enters the room with a stuffed shopping bag, followed by Jane carrying the smoothie – she must have intercepted the room-service waiter in the hall. No sooner has the door closed behind them, when there's another knock, which I expect will be Mother. I brace myself.

However, it's not. It's Hendrick, half hidden by a giant potted plant.

"It's an aloe," he grunts, plunking the spiky thing down on the dresser. "Perfect for sunburns."

"Did you get the B-12?" Jane drills him.

"Yes. Yes," he says, reaching into the back pocket of his shorts, pulling out a small, crumpled, brown paper bag. "Calm down, Doctor Bossy-pants," he says, handing it to her.

"How are you feeling, Sweetie?" I ask Madison, who's now waking.

"Do you remember how you got here?" Jane sits down on the opposite bed and pulls out the bottle of vitamins, quizzing Madison, "Do you know where you are?"

"Yes, Aunt Jane, I do," Madison assures her, groggily. "And I gotta pee." She lifts the covers, attempting to rise from the sheets, grimacing as she discovers, yet again, that she's fried to a crisp.

Hendrick breaks off an arm of the aloe plant and holds it out to her as she heads into the bathroom. "Just dab it all over."

Looking skeptical, she accepts the oozing frond from him.

"I'm gonna head out," Hendrick tells the rest of us, snapping another arm off the aloe. "Some for me." He winks, and slips from the room.

"I cleaned out a local store," Polly tells me, shaking out the contents of the shopping bag onto the bed. A pale peach t-shirt, a soft sage blouse, some khaki shorts – she even thought to buy a pack of underwear.

I pounce on Madison the moment the bathroom door opens. "How are you feeling, Sweetie?"

"I'm *fine*, Mom," is her peeved response, as though I've been pestering her all day.

I touch her winglike arm. "C'mon, Madison. I'm allowed to make sure you're okay, I'm your mom."

"I noticed," she smirks.

Jane and Polly stifle some laughter and I shoot glares at them.

Madison says, "I'd like to wash my hair, but you don't have any decent shampoo—" She spies the new clothes on the bed. "And I need something to wear."

"Those are for you," Polly tells her. "Your mom said those were your colors."

Madison holds up the package of underpants. "Sailor Moon, Mom. Really?"

"I'm sorry," Polly rushes to explain. "A child's XL was the only thing I could find. It was either Sailor Moon or Little Mermaid."

Madison stares at the undies for a moment, then tucks them under her arm and picks through the rest of the pile, selecting a few items. She shoots a quick smile and thanks at Polly before closing herself into the bathroom again.

I'd wondered how a few months in a real job, living so far away from home, might affect my daughter; whether it would mature her beyond recognition – but she's still the same Madison. A little headstrong, a little spoilt, a little feisty.

I hear the shower running and feel relieved. "Good sign?" I ask Jane.

"I think so," she answers. "She must be feeling stronger, but get her to drink that smoothie when she comes out."

I move the glass to the table by the window, and when Madison reappears, dressed in a cute summer outfit, her hair wrapped in a towel, I ask, "Ready for this?"

"What flavour is it?" She shuffles over to sit at the table.

My eyebrows rise. After surviving a night in the wilderness, she's already picky about the flavour of a smoothie?

I clamp my mouth shut, telling myself, now is not the time to correct her manners. If ever again. At the age of twenty – if she hasn't learned everything I have to teach her by now – I might as well give up.

"Go easy," Jane cautions, as Madison picks up the tall glass, and takes a few sips through the straw.

I pull over a chair so I can sit across from her. I've got to the question that I'm sure is on everyone's mind.

But there's another knock at the door, and as Polly answers it, I know, this time it's Mother.

Dressed in a chiffon caftan and lamé turban she makes a sweeping entrance and demands to know, "Where's my granddaughter?"

"Grandma!" Madison rises from her chair, and hurries, stiff-legged, over for a hug. Mother embraces her for a few seconds, then looks around for a place to plop herself.

Sinking onto the bed she begins interrogating Madison. "We came all this way to see you get married. *Where is your fiancé?*"

I hold my breath at the abrupt inquisition.

Madison sits down in her seat and picks up her drink. Taking a deep draw on the straw her eyes flick away from Mother, her cheeks flushing a deeper pink, slowly matching the color of the smoothie.

"She's revitalizing before our eyes," Polly says. "What's in that drink?"

Madison's eyes keep darting around the room as she sucks on the straw, keeping herself busy with the smoothie so she doesn't have to answer Mother's question.

"What happened?" I ask, gently. "Did Matt break up with you?"

Madison's cheeks flame pink again, and I know instantly, she's hiding something.

"And why did that man say you'd eloped?" Mother demands to know.

"I gotta go!" Madison cries, leaping to her feet, tugging at her shorts, and rushing into the bathroom. She slams the door.

"Diarrhea," Jane says, shaking her head. "I told her to go easy."

"But *where's* the boy?" Mother sputters.

Polly whispers in horror, "He dumped her?"

We all wait. We all want to know. My mind is busy filling in gaps, all the while knowing that Madison is withholding crucial information.

Finally, after the rush of water running, and shuffling sounds emanating from the bathroom, she emerges.

"What?" she says, when she sees us all staring at her. She picks up the smoothie and sucks noisily at the remainder.

"It's nothing to be embarrassed about," Jane offers. She's obviously arrived at the same conclusion I have – my daughter's been jilted at the altar, so to speak.

Madison puts down the glass and a loud, sharp, burp erupts from her gullet. She claps her hands over her mouth.

"Answer the question!" Mother says. "Where is your fiancé?"

"It's complicated!" Madison shrieks. "Why are you being so *extra* on me?"

Uh oh. They're about to battle in front of us all.

"We came all this way for your wedding, Sweetie," I say reasonably, trying to calm Madison down. "I think we have a right to know."

She clutches her belly, and bolts back into the bathroom.

"She doesn't want to tell us," Polly observes. "Maybe we should back off, give her time, until she's ready."

"It will do her good to talk about it *now*," Jane disagrees, hands on her hips.

"You should call Xavier," Mother advises. "He'll get to the bottom of this."

I look from one to the next, wondering what I should do.

No one should force Madison to talk. Yet we do need to know.

I hear the blow-dryer running.

Behind that bathroom door, drying her hair, is the child I held secretly in my womb at my own wedding. No one, other than her father, knew that fact. I never told anyone.

"You all go," I say, holding the hotel room door open. "I'll talk to her alone."

Mother sputters. "But, but..." she protests, looking around for support.

Polly gives my hand a squeeze and goes out to wait in the hall. But Jane stares at me, her face inscrutable. I can't tell if she approves or not of take-charge-Trudy.

"Come on, Carole," she says finally, taking my mother by the arm. "Let's go see if it's happy hour somewhere."

"Where'd everybody go?" Madison asks when she emerges from the bathroom.

I pat the empty chair by the window. "Come sit here, beside me."

Her hair falls, hiding her face as she sits down. Every nuance of her demeanor tells me this is a conversation she is unwilling to have.

"You know, Sweetie, we all have secrets."

She looks up slowly, smoothing her hair away.

"Are you pregnant?" I ask.

"No! Gawd, Mom, no!"

I let out a gargantuan sigh of relief.

Yet the relief lasts for only a pulse, because I still need to know what happened to her fiancé.

Before I can formulate the question, she asks, "What secrets do *you* have?"

I search my mind trying to come up with an innocuous secret, not quite as enormous as the one I would have shared with her, had her answer to the pregnancy question been affirmative.

"Okay, even though I'm on a special meal plan," I tell her. "I've binged on junk food on this trip, in secret."

She scoffs at that revelation. "Mom," she says, "It's no secret you like your snacks."

"But, but..." I stop, realizing this is not the time to try to explain my weakness for cheesies, and how I've been refraining. "Okay, I'll tell you a secret but then you have to tell me yours."

She swallows nervously, closing her eyes, but nods in agreement.

"You know on FlipFlop, how you can look someone up?" I ask her, and she opens her eyes. "I found Zelda's page." I blush with embarrassment. I can't believe how mortifying it is to admit this to my daughter. "And I looked at all her pictures."

"You *creeped* Zelda's page?" She giggles. "Mom, you bad girl."

I laugh in relief. I seem to be making headway. She's relaxing her guard.

"Help me understand," I plead with her. "What's so complicated? What happened?"

She gazes at me for a moment. She must realize she has to tell me eventually.

Almost in a whisper, she says, "There is no fiancé."

The shock closes my throat.

She covers her face with her hands, and sinks down in her chair, moaning. "There never was!"

My mind reels back over all that's happened, and I croak, "You *lied* about having a marriage proposal?"

"I didn't mean to," she cries. "It just happened!"

I stare at my daughter, astounded, almost speechless. "*What* 'just happened'? You made up a fiancé and a wedding? How does that 'just happen'?"

She cries snotty embarrassed tears.

I can't believe I got on a plane for this girl. I went bathing suit shopping because of her. How much more do I have to endure?

Finally, with her hands hiding her face, she blubbers: "One day I told Dad that I was getting married."

"*Why?*"

She shrugs, sniffling, wiping at her nose with her bare arm. I get up and bring her the box of tissues. "Madison, why on earth would you tell your dad you were getting married if you weren't?"

I never imagined she was *lying* all this time.

She blows her nose before she answers. "It felt like everyone was coupling up." She shrugs. "Everyone except me."

It's a terribly thin explanation, but something's dawning on me. "Was this when he and Zelda were over in the spring?"

She nods. "He told me they were engaged, and I was so upset I told him so was I. It kinda snowballed."

I almost laugh. *Snowballed?*

I'm mortified for her. All the lies she's told. And she looks so miserable.

She wails, "How am I going to tell him?"

I blink. Once, twice.

"How are we going to tell your grandmother?"

FORTY-FOUR

"Good morning, Mrs. Trudy," Fabijan greets me in the dining room doorway. "And Miss Madison, so happy to see *you* today!"

After yesterday's shared adventure, I feel akin to Fabijan, as though he's more of a close friend than our Maître d'. But I suppress the urge to hug him; I don't want to get him into trouble with the management.

He leads Madison and me to a table where Jane, Polly, Mother, and Hendrick are already drinking their tea and coffee and eating breakfast. Addressing Madison, Fabijan declares: "Anything you want." He spreads his arms. "The kitchen will make everything for you! You are my special guest this morning."

It's a bit awkward that he's celebrating Madison, but unlike the rest of us at the table, she hasn't bald-face lied to him.

And, as oblivious as only a person her age can be, she's quite comfortable being celebrated. As far as she's concerned, she said her sorries last night, so everything's forgiven. "I'd love some pancakes," she says. "Do you have those?"

"Of course," Fabijan says, clapping his hands. "Pancakes it is!" He rushes off to the kitchen.

Maybe it wasn't a bald-face lie, maybe it was a lie of omission. Certainly, Madison told the initial whopper to Xavier, that she was engaged and getting married. And she did send me the email, way, way, back, possibly to bolster the lie she'd told Xavier; however, she never offered me anything but the vaguest of details. In a way, I forced her to lie to me.

Why didn't I catch on? What kind of a stooge plans a trip half-way around the world without concrete details about the wedding they're attending?

One who was caught up being Mother-of-the-Bride, that's who.

And I'll admit I was a tad distracted by a bit of a rivalry with Zelda.

But then with Mother's windfall. Everything just fell into place.

Mother just about lost her mind last night when, reclined on her bed having cocktails before dinner, she found out Madison had concocted the whole wedding, including the fiancé.

"You *lied*?" she screeched.

Poor Madison stood there, her bony knees practically knocking together; she was so terrified.

And she cried and cried. It was pitiful.

The others, Jane, Polly, and Hendrick, weren't as miffed. Why would they be? They're enjoying an all-expenses-paid trip to Croatia.

Jane, however, did pull me aside and ask, "Do you think she's a pathological liar? I might have a colleague you could send her to."

The truth is, Madison was devastated by Xavier's engagement. It never occurred to me that it affected her so badly. Wrapped up in my own trauma and jealousy, I didn't consider how she'd feel. Certainly, I pondered it a little, but only because I wondered if she was on my side.

Last night, after her confessions were done, including a dreadful phone call to Xavier, and a subdued dinner in the hotel dining room, we had a long mother/daughter talk under the moonlight at the edge of the pool. Stars were twinkling, the palm trees silhouetted black against a midnight blue sky.

"Why did you divorce Dad?" she asked me.

Her question surprised me and my immediate response was, "What do you mean?"

She clutched the edge of her lounger. "I didn't know there was anything wrong. One minute I was away at school and the next minute – Dad moved out!" She leaned toward me. "What happened?"

"Oh Sweetie, it's complicated."

She made an annoyed puff sound. "Don't say that, Mom! People always say, 'it's complicated' when they're evading the question."

"I'm not evading the question! It *is* complicated."

I wasn't sure what to divulge. All the magazine articles say don't talk trash about your child's father. And I don't know if Xavier was seeing Zelda back then. I suspect he was, but I couldn't speculate about that to Madison. She's not my friend and confidant, she is my daughter. And she is *his* daughter.

I chose my words carefully, and told her what he'd told me. "Your dad felt we'd grown apart."

She huffed again in frustration. "And you? What did you feel?"

I covered my mouth with the back of my hand and looked out at the ocean, a thousand thoughts racing through my mind.

I couldn't tell her how deranged and isolated I'd been. How my every waking thought had been: How do I get my husband back? How do I make him love me again?

I couldn't tell her I'd eaten myself into a stupor every night.

I'd neglected my duties as a mother.

I'd abandoned her to cope with the divorce on her own.

Traces of transient clouds raced across the moon, disappearing into the night sky above the dark ocean.

"I haven't been a very good parent, Madison."

She shook her head. "What do you mean? You searched for me in a foreign country – and found me! That's more than Dad did. He's just been partying with Jakov."

I didn't expand on that topic with her. I knew she was still upset after her phone call with Xavier. He had not been forgiving, or understanding, about her deception. He'd yelled *a lot*. Ranting and raving about a hotel room he'd paid for. A venue he'd booked.

Defensive and crushed, Madison had fought back. "I didn't *ask* for any of that! You just did it!" She huffed, pouted, slammed the phone down, and threw herself on the bed crying.

She was still hurting, and I decided she didn't need to hear how little Xavier had considered her well-being when she'd disappeared in Hvar.

I reached over and stroked her arm. "What I mean is, I should have talked with you more about the divorce at the time. I should have made sure you were okay, that you understood. But you were away at school. And then off on this job – there never seemed to be an opportunity. I assumed you were okay. I'm *sorry*."

Madison brooded in the dark on her lounge chair, her arms folded across her chest.

"I wasn't okay, Mom. I was *devastated*. You think you're the only one whose heart was broken? I *believed* in you and dad. I thought you were forever!"

"I'm sorry," was all I could come up with. Silently, I agreed with her. I thought we were forever too, kiddo. But now we're not.

Eventually, the hotel staff came by and told us they were closing the pool area, so we went up to our room to sleep.

The hotel set up a cot for Polly in Jane and Mother's room, and Madison slept soundly in the bed next to mine, while I'd tossed and turned. Thinking of all the ways I needed to up my mothering game.

How do you mother an almost-grown human?

Why don't the magazines talk about *that*?

She looks like an adult, but she's still a child inside. She needs me.

Talk around the breakfast table is about the night just past. How did everyone sleep? And, of course, how is Madison feeling today?

She is, according to her, "More or less normal."

"The aloe worked, didn't it?" Hendrick nods.

Madison comments, "I just wish I had my phone."

Mother shakes her head. "You people are *addicted*!"

"Where is your phone?" Polly asks.

Hendrick says, "I can't imagine being parted from mine."

"It's on the yacht," Madison answers. "With all my clothes and stuff."

"How will you get it back?" asks Jane. "Do you know if you still have a job?"

"That's why I need my phone," Madison says, her eyes widening. "Without it, I don't know what's going on. I've got to contact my manager!"

Our server, followed by a bouncy, excited Fabijan, lays a plate of thick yellowy cakes before Madison. A Croatian version of pancakes made with cornmeal I surmise. Madison looks around the table, as if expecting a jug of Canadian maple syrup to magically appear.

"You'll have to use this, bambino," Hendrick says, passing her a crock of plum jam.

Madison hesitates before slathering it all over the cakes, digging in with relish.

It's buoying to see her eat.

"What are we going to do with the rest of our time here?" Polly asks.

"Good question," Mother retorts. "I was looking forward to celebrating at a wedding…"

Fabijan hovers at the end of our table, an eager smile plastered on his face. "I wonder," he says, clasping his hands in front of his chest. "If you would all join me tonight at a wonderful establishment up on the hill." He rushes to explain. "I'm not working *here* tonight and I'd love to show you the sights, take you up to King George's Garrison. Maybe you would like to have a celebration dinner up there?"

Mother's ears perk up at the mention of the garrison. "What are we celebrating?"

Fabijan looks momentarily confused and says, "Why, the rescue of this young lady by Mrs. Trudy, of course! If it wasn't for *her*, this girl might never be found."

Mother looks from Madison to me. It appears the gravity of the situation is only now sinking in to her. Fabijan's enthusiasm is forcing her to acknowledge that searching for Madison was the *only* thing to do!

If I'd been lost or missing, would she not have done the same for me?

"I for one would *love* to join you on the hill," Hendrick gushes.

"We all would," I announce for the table. "We'd be delighted. Our treat," I add, shooting a brief glare at my mother.

"Just got a text from Zelda," Jane interrupts. "She says she and Xavier are meeting up with Jakov later today."

Madison looks at me and purses her lips.

Jane taps a few keys into her phone. "They're getting Madison's things and bringing them here." Her eyebrows rise as she reads the reply. "Zelda says Jakov's on leave from Dalma Tours for a few weeks. He's going home to visit his family."

"What?" Madison says. "That's weird."

"Why is it weird?" Polly asks.

"How can he leave in the middle of a tour?"

"Isn't that what you did?" Mother questions her.

Madison scowls and jabs the last bit of her pancake with her fork, twirling it around in the jam on her plate. "And I'm probably going to be fired for it!"

I say nothing. My complaint worked faster than anticipated.

FORTY-FIVE

In the evening, after a day of mounting a million stairs, visiting a gorgeous baroque church, declining a trip to the Blue Cave – no more boats – and shopping for souvenirs in Majka Town, we climb into taxis and ascend the hill to King George's Garrison. As we disembark at the restaurant, the setting sun paints the stone building in a warm tangerine glow. I tingle with the ancient romance of the place. Fabijan points out the height of the garrison walls, and the sightlines of the lookout points as we enter the building.

A waiter ushers us down a hallway into a private room with wide windows overlooking the sea below. Candles flicker from wall-sconces, the table is smothered with glimmering tealights, and candelabra dangle low over the table. The room is beautiful and magical.

Fabijan rushes to the head of the table, drawing out a chair. "For Mrs. Trudy," he says. "The seat of honor."

Flattered by the commendation, I squeeze past Mother to take my seat. Fabijan tucks the chair beneath me, and rushes to the other end of the table. "For Miss." He motions to Madison.

From my perch at the top of the table, she looks like a tiny waif. My heart clenches – I came so close to losing her. I'm never losing sight of her again.

Everyone else scurries around the table, taking their seats as Fabijan orders champagne for all.

Polly is on my right, and we toast each other with our flutes of bubbly. She winks and whispers, "Yay, Trudy!"

I'm so grateful for her. A couple of days ago, I was looking forward to us sharing a hotel room, getting to know each other and talking over my worries and woes. I had no idea I was about to be swept away on an adventure to rescue my daughter. If it wasn't for Polly, I wouldn't have had the energy, or clarity. I'd have been stuffing my face with cream puffs and pizza and whining, "Where's my daughter?" I wouldn't have heard my inner guidance telling me to persevere to find Madison.

"Polly, without you, I'd be all fogged up on carbs." I squeeze her hand in thanks.

Hendrick uses his spoon to clink the side of his glass. "Here's to Trudy, our heroine!"

Everyone raises their glasses.

Fabijan calls, "Speech!"

My stomach flutters. I'm not good at speeches, and don't like being the center of attention. But they're all looking at me, holding their champagne, waiting.

I rise to my feet at the end of the table, glancing around at each expectant face.

"I'm just thankful for all of you," I stammer, getting choked up immediately, tears threatening, because I mean my gratitude so sincerely. "Madison, of course," I start. "Without you, none of us would be here."

"That's an understatement," murmurs Hendrick. Everyone titters, and I realize my gaffe. If Madison hadn't *lied* to all of us, we wouldn't be here.

Undeterred, I rush on thanking Fabijan for his boat and Polly for her friendship.

"Hendrick, you've been trying to steer me since we met, and I've been so resistant. Yet you kept at me, and I learned. I keep my phone on now!"

More laughter.

Hey, I'm pretty good at this speech business.

I continue addressing Hendrick, "You *knew* the luggage would arrive. You've been so helpful. Thank you!" I hoist my glass to him. "And Jane, thanks for—" I glance at Mother, who, champagne glass empty, is looking around for a refill, "—for helping with *everything*." I wink, and raise my glass to my old friend.

A waiter refills Mother's champagne, and she looks eagerly toward me. "And Mother, of course," I acquiesce. "Thank you, Mother, for paying for us all to get here!"

I finish, feeling vulnerable, but proud of myself for coming up with something meaningful to say to each and every one of them. I sit down to a chorus: "Hear, hear!"

All around the table there's clinking, and an interval of chattering, as the server takes our orders, and we wait for the food to arrive.

"Tell me again how you knew where Miss Madison would be," Fabijan says. He's really stuck on the events of yesterday.

I begin to retell the story: "So...it was when I was skiing—"

"At which she was fabulous, by the way," Hendrick interjects. "You should've seen her!"

"*You* should've filmed her!" Jane razzes him.

"At least he was there as a witness," I jest, but it *is* important to me. Despite the disapproval of Xavier, and my own self-consciousness and doubts, I proved I could do it. Hendrick was there to document it, even if he did forget his phone. "Anyway," I continue, "before I fell flat on my face, I caught sight of a person on the shore who seemed to be waving at me." I smile at Madison. "Do you remember that, Sweetie?"

She shakes her head slowly. "Not really."

Fabijan turns to her, his dark eyebrows drawing together. "Again, why were you there?"

Madison replies with indifference, "We often ski there. It's a quiet bay on that side of the island. Sometimes we let people off on the shore so the boat is lighter, faster."

"But who is this man driving the boat?" Fabijan is really digging. "Why didn't he come back for you?" He wants to know all the facts.

"That was Jakov," Madison dismisses.

Persisting, Fabijan asks, "And who is he?"

Madison looks squarely at him, and replies, "He's an asshole."

At the expletive, Mother spurts a mouthful of champagne across the table, and everyone bursts into laughter.

For a few moments, there's a commotion, as Hendrick wipes spray from his face. "Why don't you tell us how you really feel, Madison?" he jokes.

Mother resettles, coughing a little, dabbing at her mouth with her napkin.

Madison looks abashed. "To be one hundred percent truthful," she says, speaking quietly and looking meaningfully at me. "Jakov found out I'd told Dad I was engaged to be married, so of course he started teasing me relentlessly, calling me Mrs. Brown, and making rude insinuations about my wedding night..." Her face reddens in embarrassment. "I was so fed up with him, I wasn't thinking straight, I got off the boat."

"I never liked him," Jane says.

"Hear, hear!" Polly waves her glass around.

I agree. "The man certainly is..." I pause, disinclined to repeat Madison's word for Jakov. "He certainly is an ass."

"The scoundrel dropped her on the beach, pretended he didn't know where she could possibly be," Hendrick gushes, filling in the details for Fabijan, adopting the story as his own. "He concocted a tale about her eloping, knowing full well she was here on Vis!"

"He is a very bad man," Fabijan tells Madison. "If we did not found you in time, he would be in a hell of trouble." He turns back to me and says, "Thank God for you, Mrs. Trudy."

"I'm telling you," I repeat. "It was mother's intuition."

"And God made mothers," Fabijan says.

More pouring of champagne, more raising of glasses, more clinking.

I hope they bring the food soon. This preposterous toasting has got to end or we'll all be smashed.

"You know, I had an intuition one time," Hendrick says, straightening the cutlery on his place setting. "About a man. He tried to rebuff me, but I just *knew* he was the one for me."

"You're single," Jane says quizzically. "What happened?"

"Nothing," Hendrick answers. "It fizzled."

Now, it's Fabijan's turn to spit champagne.

Everyone is getting tipsy.

Jane declares, "*I* had mother's intuition one time."

Mother frowns. "Jane, dear, *you* can't have mother's intuition. You're not a mother."

"I *did*!" Jane dismisses her. "It was when Trudy was pregnant. I *knew* she was going to have a girl. Isn't that right, Trudy? Remember?"

"Vaguely."

Hendrick scoffs at Jane. "You had a fifty-fifty chance!"

"No!" she objects. "I had a *feeling*."

"Well, I had an intuition once," Mother says.

Everyone turns to her, giving her the floor.

And suddenly, I have a feeling she's about to resurrect the bare-bum skiing story of my childhood.

"It was in the summertime—" she begins, and I rise from my seat.

"Mother! Now is not the time for *that* story."

She blinks at me with annoyed eyes. "Why not? It's funny."

"You didn't think it was funny at the time!"

I may have to douse her with ice-water.

"What story is this?" Madison asks.

Everyone is curious now.

I remain standing, glaring at my mother.

Jane admonishes me, "Sit down!"

I sink with trepidation into my seat, and Mother continues. "Trudy was quite a skier when she was young; it's what we did at our cottage. Water sports all day long."

I can't believe she's going to embellish her participation in the cottage activities. She detested being at the cottage. When Grandad allowed it, she left me there for weeks on end, while she went back to the city with my father.

"I wish I'd been to the cottage," Madison says.

"Your great grandfather decided to sell it once all the kids were grown," Mother informs her.

"Not me, I wasn't grown!" She pouts a little. "I wish I'd known him more. I only have a few memories of the bakery – the gingerbread houses at Christmas."

"He was a real outdoorsman," Mother says wistfully. "Taught all of us to ski." She shakes her head, as though she's remembering her childhood. I'm skeptical, and full of scorn – Grandad told me she *never* skied. For the next part, she puts on a spooky voice, as if she's telling a ghost story. "One day, I don't know why, I had a feeling something bad was going to happen." The candles around the room shudder in the breeze from the open windows.

I have no idea where this story is going. That's not the way the day went, and she knows it. She's just going to go on lying, and if I interrupt and question her, I'm going to look like a killjoy, and possibly ruin this lovely evening.

Perhaps this time I can weather this cringey story. Perhaps tonight I'll see the humor in it.

When Mother gets to the part where my bathing suit bottoms slipped down, Hendrick shrieks, "So, your va-jay-jay was hanging out?"

All heads turn to look at me.

I laugh, reassuring them. "No, no, just my ba-bum-bum. The life-jacket covered the front of me."

"So, what did you *do*, Trudy?" Polly asks.

I finish the story. The real way it happened. I finish by telling them I never wore the hated bathing suit again.

"It was a yellow bikini," Mother interjects. "She didn't have the body for it."

Everyone laughs. Even me.

"It's true," I agree. "I didn't have the body for it because it was the wrong size, for heaven's sake!"

Mother purses her lips, and looks around. "Where's our food?"

In the very next moment, as if at her command, the food arrives, carried in by multiple servers, plates laid before each of us at the same time. The food is stunning, garnished with flowers and leaves and tiny glistening pools for dipping, arranged like artwork on our plates.

"Bon Appetit!" Polly says.

Before me is an exquisite piece of grilled sea bass. I don't dare look too closely at my companions' plates with their scoops of polenta, pasta, and sauces. I keep my eyes on my own plate, and Polly's. She's slicing into a tender medallion of beef.

Around the table, the candlelight casts a warm glow on each person's face as they dig in to eat and exclaim about the flavours. I lift my fork and break into my filet of fish, savouring every morsel.

"Speaking of intuitions, Trudy," Hendrick says between mouthfuls. "You could use yours to become a fortune teller if the whole bakery thing doesn't work out."

Everyone laughs, including me, and Jane jumps in to enthrall us all with a hilarious story of consulting a palm reader before deciding to become a psychiatrist.

After the main course plates are cleared away, the waiter comes around to tempt the table with sweets. And while the desserts are served, I excuse myself and meander through the labyrinthine garrison in search of the washroom. I'm off sugar, and I don't need to watch other people consuming it. My appetite is satisfied. I just need to pee.

When I finally find it, the ladies' room is small, and smells like lavender, reminding me of Mother's room back home. She bought a giant bag of lavender in town today to replenish her supply. I can't go on living with her.

She's never going to appreciate me, or treat me with respect.

I can't go through life subjecting myself to her criticism. When I married Xavier, I got away from it. I can get away from her again now.

As I wash my hands, I survey myself in the gold framed oval mirror above the sink.

Still a plump woman, I see. But a pretty one.

It's true, hurray, I've lost a few bags of flour – I'm not sure how many, I haven't encountered a scale in Croatia – but I'm still overweight, with a way to go. I'm not going to pretend any differently.

We leave for home the day after tomorrow and I'm beginning to think I'm not going to fit into my life back there.

I apply some lipstick and brush my hair.

I can't go back to being surrounded all day by flour and sugar. And all those delicious aromas. I don't know if I can take it. Accidentally licking blackcurrant jelly off my fingers, and setting off a binge is something I'm not willing to risk anymore. My mind is so clear nowadays. I can't return to the brain-fog, and the sore knees, of a few months ago.

But what on earth would I do instead?

My phone pings in my purse.

As I dig it out, my heart quickens when I see it's a text from Xavier.

`Trudy. X here. Just want to say u r a rockstar`

My eyes devour his words and letters, stuttering over his abbreviated texting style. We didn't text when we were married. I didn't have a smartphone. It feels so intimate.

`I see u r a changed woman dont think I dont notice. Sorry I shoulda listened to u. Imma fool.`

I read those last two words again.

And again.

Does he mean he was a fool about not taking me seriously about Madison's disappearance?

Or does he mean he's been a fool *about me*?

I chew over the text message.

What does it mean?

Is it some kind of code?

A part of me whispers: *He's into you. He's after you. He's playing games. He doesn't know what he wants. He's coming to his senses. He's running back to you, just like you knew he would.*

I scoff at myself and the ridiculously obsolete inner voice.

If any of that were true, who says I want him anymore?

This trip has been eye opening for me. I can have oodles of fun with friends and enjoy the adventure of new experiences. Madison and I can spend nourishing time together as grown-up mom and daughter. I don't want to let those things go. My soul is tugging me in a different direction – somewhere bold, and enlivening, that has nothing to do with Xavier.

I begin formulating a reply to him, when the door of the bathroom flies open, and Jane and Polly burst inside the small room.

"Trudy!"

"What are you doing in here?"

"We've all just received messages on our phones!"

Their panicky eyes travel down to my hands, fixating on my phone with worry.

"What? What's happened?" I ask, frantic.

With a stricken face, Polly maneuvers around Jane, and stands close to me, stroking my arm as Jane delivers the news:

"Zelda and Xavier's wedding is *here.* Tomorrow. We've all been invited!"

FORTY-SIX

At breakfast, Mother spends the entire time singing Xavier's praises, and trying to persuade Madison to attend her father's nuptials. "It's a beautiful day for a wedding!" she says, completely insensitive, as usual.

Petulant and unhappy, Madison insists, "I am *not* going."

There's a sadness to the fact that she is not the one getting married today. It feels as though Xavier and Zelda are dancing on the grave of her wedding. Even if it never existed. Even if I'm relieved that she's not getting married so young, or pregnant.

And it's maddening that their wedding is taking place today, while we're all here in Majka Town, so Zelda feels compelled, out of politeness I assume, to invite us all.

"Apparently," Jane had relayed last night, "Xavier already had the space reserved for Madison, so…" as though this baffling explanation made anything any better.

"I'm not obliged to attend my ex-husband's wedding," I inform the breakfast table, sipping my coffee. "You all go. I'll stay here."

Mother shakes her head ferociously at me, jerking it toward Madison.

"I don't want to go, if you don't want to go," Polly says, supporting my position.

"And I'm not going either!" Madison sasses.

"I'm neutral," Hendrick declares, waving his hands. "I'm absolutely Switzerland over here."

Jane chews the inside of her cheek, staying strangely silent, drumming her ringed fingers on the table. It's unusual for her to not have an opinion – Miss Wedding Etiquette Expert, and all that hooey.

"A daughter should attend her father's wedding," Mother states with authority, not in the least bit cognizant of how ridiculous she sounds.

"Grandma!"

"What? You should. Your father is moving on." Behind her enormous glasses, Mother's eyes dart around the table, surveying for support. "Zelda is a *perfectly* nice woman. You need to show some respect."

I feel Mother's words like a sharp pinch to my cheek. Madison's face goes white, and for a moment I think she might throw up. I reach for her hand across the table, it's cold and clammy.

"Mom?" she pleads, looking at me out of bewildered, teary eyes.

She shouldn't have to go somewhere she doesn't want to go, should she?

I'm unsure. I'm in uncharted waters.

I look at Jane. Why isn't she helping me, right now?

She asks, "You want my opinion, don't you?"

I made a rule, long ago, I don't allow Jane to give parenting advice. She's never been a parent, and I don't care how much education she has, some things can't be taught, or read about. I glance toward Madison, hoping Jane understands I'm concerned only with my daughter's wellbeing. I don't want this decision to screw her up forever.

"You know about these kinds of things," I plead to Jane. "And I don't mean wedding things."

She takes a deep breath. "Both of you feel that you don't want to go," she says, using her forth-right psychiatrist voice. "And Trudy, I agree with you 100% – you don't need to go. But…" Now she addresses Madison, "if *you* don't go, it's going to set up a bad precedent with your dad. And your new step-mother."

There's a gasp around the table as Jane drops the S-bomb.

My eyes go wide, realizing, after today, Zelda will be Madison's official step-*mother*.

"Don't shoot the messenger!" Jane says, holding up her hands. "You wanted my opinion."

"She's correct!" Mother says. "Madison, you've got to go."

Madison looks at me, her eyes pure misery. "Do I have to, Mom?"

Polly and Hendrick both shake their heads, looking aghast at the predicament, indicating that I should not turn to them for help.

I fiddle with the spoon beside my coffee cup, wishing I had another cup to toss back and help me think.

I see Jane's point. Madison will have to get used to having a step-mother – gack – eventually.

She thought her life was charted one way, but Xavier sailed off in a different direction. She's going to have to come to terms with it.

If I allow her to blow off what is a terribly special day for her dad, he'll be hurt, and their relationship will suffer, maybe irreparably. His daughter's absence will spoil the day for him. And Zelda will blame Madison forever for ruining her wedding.

I know what I must do. I need to step up, and be the best mom I can be.

"Tell you what," I say to Madison, looking intently into her eyes. "I'll go too. We'll stick together. I'll be your plus one."

Forty-Seven

S hampoo trickles down my forehead, stinging my eyes, so I turn my face to the shower spray, letting it zing courage into me.

Today, I must shepherd my daughter through what will undoubtedly be an arduous day for both of us.

At this moment, she's definitely more upset about Xavier remarrying than I am. Strangely, right now, I'm at peace with it. His decision no longer eats me up inside. I no longer see it as something he's doing *to me*. It's just something he's doing.

Yet I am still vulnerable, with ripples of fright fluttering through my heart. While there's a fierce protectiveness toward Madison, I'm also aware that by attending Xavier and Zelda's wedding I risk being slammed by heartbreak again, or being overwhelmed by jealousy, or anger. For Madison's sake, I'm willing to take that chance, and hope I can control myself if anything happens.

And maybe we can avoid another ocean of tears. Heaven knows, she cried enough last night.

I let the noisy blast of the blow-dryer fill my whole world for a few minutes. Hot and loud it's hard to think about much else. I watch my hair swirl around, and remind myself to let everything else go.

After breakfast, Madison showered before me, and put on the swingy turquoise dress Polly loaned her.

"I have just the thing!" I told her, rummaging around in my case to find my blue topaz ring. I was going to give it to her on her wedding day if she didn't have 'something old' or 'something blue.'

Sliding it on her slender fingers until she found one it would stay on; she hugged me and said, "I remember this ring!"

Thankfully, she didn't seem to associate it with the nasty fight we'd had when she was a teenager and borrowed the ring without asking. She'd ended up throwing it at me at the dinner table when I'd demanded it back. A mother and daughter squabble, now forgiven, and forgotten, at least by her.

"Mom, I just want to tell you," she said, solemnly looking at me. "I want you to know, it was *so* hard lying to you. Misleading you. One part of me was going berserk with the lie, while the other part of me was cringing in shame. *I'm sorry.*"

I gathered her in my arms. "It's okay, Sweetie. I understand why you did it."

"I got all your messages, Mom." She cried into my hair. "I'm so sorry I didn't tell you the truth sooner."

Now, when I step from the bathroom into the empty hotel room, Madison is gone. Since rescuing her from the beach, whenever I lose sight of her, my heart quickens and misses a few beats. I reassure myself now, she's safe.

She's probably gone out with Polly, or Jane. Or she's holed up somewhere on the hotel patio with her precious phone, which was delivered by a bellhop, along with her rucksack, to our door this morning.

As soon as she'd charged her phone, she got a text from her manager telling her she was welcome to rejoin the tour, as soon as she felt up to it. And of course, she heard from Laura, telling her Jakov had been fired, and all the hostesses were celebrating.

"He got fired, Mom," she'd told me. "Not visiting his family. The big liar."

Yay, me for reporting him.

The hotel room feels warmer than it has for the past couple of days so I give the ancient window air-conditioner a crank. It grumbles and finally whirrs out a coolish breeze.

Standing in my bra and undies, I contemplate the closet. I don't have much of a wardrobe to choose from. I consider wearing my black form-fitting jeans with a fancy top, but it's too hot for jeans.

I pull out the maroon MOB dress and give it a shake; the humidity has taken care of its wrinkles. Why did I ever let Jane talk me into this funeral-parlor color?

"You look *mature* in burgundy," she'd said, and I'd taken that to mean I needed to act my age.

Pulling it over my head, I wiggle into it. It's not too tight, but it's not exactly loose either. Since buying it, I've lost weight, so maybe it doesn't look as hideous as the clingy fabric feels. I twist to take a look at the rear view. There's a fancy lace cut-out between my shoulders, which hopefully will distract from my big bum.

I slide my feet into the burgundy satin shoes I bought for Madison's wedding. I haven't worn them before today but they were a good purchase – the heels aren't too high, and they feel comfortable.

Last step, cosmetics. I apply my eye makeup, managing a shimmery shadow; subtle, even eyeliner strokes; and pretty, dark, lashes.

It's too warm in this hotel room, but I try on the chiffon shrug and take stock in the mirror. With my shoulders covered, and my hair down, I must say, I can pass for a hot mama, which I am, literally.

Back in the bathroom, I add one more stroke of mascara, and try fluffing my hair in the clammy humidity.

I hear the hotel door open.

Madison slumps into the room and flops down on the bed. She's wearing Polly's turquoise dress, which is so lovely on her. "Do I *really* have to go?" she complains.

"It'll be over in no time. I promise."

I'm determined to stay upbeat in front of her and take this day as it comes. There's no sense in letting this day spoil the end of my Croatian adventure. Even though I came her for my daughter's wedding, it's my ex-husband's I'll be attending. How weird is that?

"Everyone is waiting in the lobby," Madison says glumly.

At least she's not crying.

When we emerge from the elevator, Hendrick whistles. But everyone is dressed up in the outfit they would've worn to Madison's wedding, so it's not like I'm the only one looking swanky.

"Backatcha," I say.

Pushing through the front doors of the hotel to catch a cab we're hit with a wall of humidity. I thought it was hot inside – it's a sauna out here.

"Ugh, the heatwave is back!" Jane exclaims.

The taxi driver blasts his A/C, but crammed in together – Mother and Hendrick in the front seat, Jane, Polly, Madison, and I in the back – we're sweltering by the time we get up the hill to the garrison and burst from the cab, gasping for air.

Fortunately, up here, on top of the small mountain, there's an ocean breeze several degrees cooler than down in town. Even so, I immediately peel the shrug from my shoulders and stuff it in my purse, wishing I hadn't brought it.

The historic venue looks different in daylight. Gone are the romantic shadows and soft colors of the mounted torches we encountered last night. Now, the midafternoon sun, reflecting off the stone walls, turns the building blindingly white. Insipid ribbons, strung amid spiky potted plants, line the pathway leading to the entrance. Our group, usually upbeat and noisy, is reserved and silent, not as we would've been had this been Madison's wedding – somehow, it's Xavier's instead. I feel almost as if I'm in a funeral procession.

En masse, we step across the threshold and stand adjusting to the indoor darkness for a moment. Soft music plays and around us there's the murmur of voices. I take Madison's arm and like blinded penguins in the middle of a pack of very hot penguins we shuffle along with the others.

"This way, ladies. And gentleman."

Our pack turns to the right, trailing the voice of a shadowy figure. I follow along, Jane's bony shoulder in front of me leading the way.

At last, there's light up ahead, the entrance to an outdoor courtyard, and on the other side of the arched doorway I catch sight of Xavier, watching our approach.

He's dressed in clothes I would never expect to see him wear, a modish, shrunken, linen suit with a pink tie, an anxious smile stretched across his face.

As we draw nearer, Madison clutches my arm.

Xavier's hair is buzzed up the sides, different and darker than it was the other day on the yacht. His gray hair has disappeared. He's dyed his hair! Since when does Xavier dye his hair?

He says, almost how I imagined he would in my delusional fantasies, back when I believed he would come to his senses and want me again, "You look beautiful."

But he's not talking to me. He's talking to Madison. And I'm okay with that.

She allows herself to be drawn into his embrace, but her arms hang at her sides and she doesn't hug him back.

I almost feel sorry for him. It's going to be a while before she's okay with all this.

Xavier draws Madison apart from our group, but I keep my eyes on them as he strokes her hair, speaking earnestly, pulling a small wrapped gift from his jacket pocket, and pressing it into her hand.

"What's with his hair?" Jane murmurs, and I swat her.

She and I have had far too many fits of laughter at inopportune moments.

"Don't you dare make me laugh!" I warn her, but every time I glance her way, hilarity threatens to boil over inside me.

Hot-cheeked, I fan myself, and look around, getting my bearings. We're in a luxurious outdoor courtyard under a sweeping ancient tree. In the distance is the ocean, dotted with white sailboats. The sun, now behind us, isn't glaring back here, so we won't roast under direct rays. There's a canopy over three rows of chairs and a handful of other dressed-up people milling about.

Hendrick mutters, "Gee, if *we* weren't here, there'd be no guests at all."

Madison rejoins us, a piece of crumpled wrapping paper dangling from her hand.

"That dress is darling on you," Mother says approvingly to Madison who's fiddling with a bracelet on her wrist.

Polly comments on it, "That's cool."

Madison's face is tortured as she holds out her arm for inspection. "It's from Zelda."

Mother twists it around on Madison's thin wrist marveling at the craftsmanship. "This cost a pretty penny."

Zelda should not be buying expensive jewelry for my daughter!

In a blink, the amusement I was feeling about Xavier's hairdo is gone. Instead, I'm strangling down feelings of possessive outrage.

"Do I have to wear it?" Madison whines to me.

I bite back my reaction, trying my best to reassure her. "Just for today, Sweetie. Try to—"

I can't finish my advice.

I have no clue what to tell her to "try" to do. She's in an impossible situation, and wants to be anywhere but here. She stands miserably at my side, enduring.

Slowly and steadily, my heels sink into the mossy ground beneath my feet. Even with low heels, my toes are pinched in these dressy shoes. I ask, hoping for agreement, "Should we sit down?"

Instead, we stand around awkwardly for another interminable stretch of time, fanning ourselves and exclaiming about the sensational view, wondering when the ceremony is going to start.

At the front of the space, a guitar player is strumming instrumental rock songs. We stand, while his fiddly and overly melodic renditions of "Californication," and "Smells Like Teen Spirit" float on the slight breeze.

"I'm just going to scoot to the bathroom," I inform my companions. It would be embarrassing to have to slip out of my seat after the ceremony starts.

Inside the building, I hunt hurriedly for the ladies' room, remembering the difficulty I had finding it last night. Rushing down one dim hallway after another, I finally locate the small room and dash inside.

As I pee, I check the time, careful not to let my phone fall in the toilet. That's all I need. Plus, I wouldn't want to lose all the mother-daughter selfies Madison and I took last night.

It's ten minutes past the ceremony start time.

I've got to get back.

Washing and half-drying my hands, I rush from the bathroom.

But the hallway is confusing.

Which way back to where I want to be?

A King George's Garrison employee is striding down the hall toward me. I flag him down, asking, "Which way to the wedding chapel?"

He points down a corridor, and I hurry off on my low wobbly heels toward the light at the end.

All the guests are quietly seated in rows on either side of a strip of green indoor/outdoor carpeting.

Mother and Madison, and a couple I don't know, are in the front row on the right.

Behind them in the second row, there's an empty chair, presumably for me, between Jane and Polly.

At least I'll be safely sandwiched by my two friends.

Ahead of me on the green carpet, walking very slowly toward the front, is a barefoot man with a gray ponytail. He's wearing faded jeans and a flowing, white muslin shirt. To my surprise, he steps up onto the riser and turns to face the gathering, holding a leather-bound book.

He's the officiant!

If I don't get into my seat fast, I'm going to be part of this ceremony.

I tap Jane on the shoulder, and she swings her knees to the side, so I can scramble past. It's a tight squeeze, and I feel my shoes sinking into the ground again. I wobble to regain my balance and hear Jane screech as one of my kitten heels crushes down on her toe.

"Sorry, sorry," I flap, stumbling into my chair.

Mother hisses, turning in her seat, "Pipe down back there."

"My goodness, they've crammed us in," Polly complains.

Hendrick on the other side of her whispers, "There are only a dozen people here, couldn't they have spread us out a little?"

I feel my chair listing to the left, and Jane shoves at me, growling, "What are you doing?"

"My chair is sinking!"

"Well, stop it!" She swats at me, unhelpfully.

I sit tilted on the chair, leaning to the right toward Polly, willing myself to weigh less, and praying, "Please God, don't let this chair collapse. Please don't let this happen here, today, now."

My heart clutches when Xavier joins the officiant on the riser. It feels other-worldly to see him awaiting the arrival of his bride, but if he thinks I'm going to stand by and watch while he and Zelda fawn all over my daughter, turning me into odd mom out, then they have not met the new Trudy.

I don't dare reach out to reassure Madison with a tickle on her shoulder. I don't dare unbalance my precarious seat.

The officiant starts. He tells us his name is Oh-Jay. At least, I think that's what he said.

With a lilting, rhythmic, voice he welcomes us to this "Sacred Event."

Out of the side of her mouth, Jane informs me, "Zelda found him in a yoga class."

I snort, trying to stifle my derision, and keep my eyes staring straight ahead. If I look at Jane, I know I'll start laughing. So far, this day couldn't be more ridiculous.

Instead, I concentrate on how odd it is that Jane is privy to so many details about Zelda's goings on.

They've become friends behind my back. Or was it right in front of me? I don't know.

And am I doing the same thing to Jane with Polly?

Anyway, isn't there a rule about not becoming friends with your best friend's ex's bride? Isn't Jane obliged to be on *my* side?

I'm not having very 'spiritual' thoughts while sitting here listening to Oh-Jay casting his blessings and angels all over us today.

I wonder where Zelda is. Isn't she the star of this rigamarole?

Suddenly, there's loud strumming from the guitar player, and the opening chords of "More Than Words" begin. Oh-Jay motions for us to rise and everyone stands and turns to watch Zelda's entrance.

She's wearing a tight scarlet dress with a slit up the front and stalking on impossibly high heels up the aisle. If it weren't for the indoor/outdoor carpeting, her heels would be sinking into the ground like golf tees.

A thousand catty thoughts and judgements swarm my mind. Who wears red to their own wedding? How can she be so thin and still have such big boobs? Who chose this song, and why? Everything seems absurd, and almost comical. I want to say something funny to Jane, but I don't dare. Not now. I must behave myself, for Madison's sake.

The music stops, and the officiant begins speaking as Zelda and Xavier join hands and stand next to one another. I can't see Xavier's face. I don't think I want to. I'm satisfied with the back of heads and hairdos.

Madison turns around in the row ahead of me. Our eyes meet. She smiles sadly, and turns back to face the front. My heart swells.

Oh-Jay is not using traditional wedding vows. He's reciting what sounds like someone's creative writing project about the meaning of love. I'm having difficulty following the words, or concentrating on anything other than wondering how long before this is over.

A hot-flash begins on my back, spreading up to my shoulders, rushing onto my face. I lift the hair from the back of my neck, and fan myself with my other hand while blowing down on my chin.

I'm melting.

Oh-Jay asks Xavier and Zelda: "Do you promise to witness every sunrise and sunset together?"

I don't hear their answers because I'm whispering cynically to Jane, "Don't trust him, Zelda. He barely comes home from work."

She snickers, and I squirm in my seat, the maroon synthetic dress sticking to me like suffocating saran. My chair tilts sharply to the left and the next thing I know, I'm sprawled on the ground. My face pressed against Jane's thigh.

The ceremony halts. Mid-vow.

Once again, mortification is trying to kill me.

Guests begin to titter and chatter.

But I refuse to die.

Pushing myself up off the damp ground, clinging to Polly's arm for support, I stagger to my feet. Embarrassment scrambles up the back of my neck, turning my cheeks crimson, I'm sure.

"Are you alright, Mom?" Madison asks, rushing to my side.

"I'm fine, I'm fine." I brush everyone away, and straighten my dress.

A staff-member of King George's hurries to replace my now bent legged chair.

Aware of an internal scolding running through my mind: *You're a clown show. You're too fat. You've made a spectacle of yourself. No one wants to be associated with you.* I hush that harpy voice and summon a kinder one. A voice that rolls with the waves, shrugs, and says, *Stuff happens. You'll survive.*

Before retaking my seat, summoning every ounce of dignity I can, and looking directly at Xavier, I announce to the gathering, "So sorry to interrupt."

Mother, swiveled around in her seat, stares at me, shaking her head in disapproval.

Whatever.

Madison retakes her chair beside Mother in the row ahead. The gathering quiets, the ceremony continues.

Polly on my right squeezes my hand and smiles.

Hendrick gives me a quick wink.

Jane stares straight ahead, and I can tell she's ready to burst.

If I nudge her, she'll explode in laughter. We'll both be goners.

A tight knowing smile takes control of my face.

I'm safe in the company of my friends.

The worst is over.

FORTY-EIGHT

The reception is held on a roofed patio adjacent to the wedding venue. Abutting the wall of the garrison, a table draped in a white cloth, holds a coffee urn and chilled bottles of Jamnica mineral water. Waiters circulate among the guests, offering flutes of pink champagne. Another table next to the entrance-way is laden with Croatian desserts.

That's it. No hors d'oeuvres, or tapas, or predjela as the Croatians say.

Mother grabs a champagne glass from a passing waiter.

"Ooo, what do we have here?" Jane says, pouncing on the dessert table and hovering over a platter of crêpes zigzagged with drizzled chocolate.

She and Madison flit around the table, while Polly and I drift to the edge of the patio, sipping bubbly water, and discussing the next 36-hours' travel plans. Our plane flies out tomorrow night from Split, so we have a whole day of ferries and transfers ahead of us. Polly is fully armed with antihistamines.

Jane and Madison clown around near the desserts, exclaiming rapturously over the flavours, their fingers sticky, their spirits soaring as the sugar floods their systems. Madison seems buoyant. I can't see that the ceremony upset her, or plunged her into despair, but I'm still watching carefully. Ready to steer her into calmer waters if things suddenly get stormy.

Hendrick mingles among the other guests, introducing himself, and doing his usual, flirtatious, Hendrick, thing.

"Did your dress rip badly when you fell off your chair?" Polly asks.

"A little...but sometimes fat comes in handy," I joke, lifting my arm to reveal the hidden flap of torn fabric.

"You could repair it," she suggests.

I scoff. "Oh, I don't care. I hate this dress anyway. I'm throwing it in the garbage the minute we get back to the hotel."

She giggles. "I was wondering. It's really not your color."

"No kidding!" I'm so glad Polly recognizes the color of my personality. I'm not a maroon person – I don't even like red. I favour turquoise and mint and cooler colors. "I don't know *what* Jane was thinking, way back when we chose this ugly thing. Or why I listened to her."

"She likes those darker colors," Polly observes, looking over at Jane, who's dressed in a cheetah print backless jumpsuit. No bra. No worries. Just her bony spine bent over the dessert table.

Now that I'm standing again, my poor toes begin complaining, so I slip off my shoes and stand barefoot on the cool stone floor, such a relief.

"You know what we should do, later today?" Polly says. "Once this is all over."

"What?"

"When we get back to Majka, why don't we go hang out by the ocean and go swimming?"

"Okay!" I love that idea. "Let's go to the beach near the promenade. Sand, sand, and more sand."

We haven't been to any swimming beaches on our trip. We've only been dipping into hotel pools, and of course, my plunge in the ocean on the day I waterskied.

Beyond the reception area, Xavier, Zelda, and Oh-Jay take turns signing papers under the tree in the wedding venue. They pose for photographs against the myriad of stunning backgrounds before the newlyweds finally join the rest of us on the patio.

I feel strangely detached. As though I'm attending a wedding as the plus-one of an invited guest.

This Xavier – shaking hands, receiving cheek kisses – with his mod outfit and buzzed hair, I don't know him. And, I realize, he doesn't know me.

Decades ago, when our lives intersected, I abandoned the real me, lost track of her. I hid away my real self, terrified if I let her be seen, my husband wouldn't love me anymore.

Yet these travel companions of mine, they've seen the real Trudy. They've seen me trashed, and clownish, frustrated, and wild with ferocious maternal instinct. And wonders, they all still seem to like me.

Well, almost all of them.

Mother has grabbed Madison by the wrist and is dragging her over to the newlyweds. I can't hear what's being said, but Mother is doing most of the talking, admiring Zelda's red bridal outfit, and playfully teasing Xavier about his haircut. She always liked him, and he her.

Good. They can have each other.

Madison is standing shyly, her legs and feet crossed awkwardly, her thin arms wrapped around her midsection.

Xavier says a few words to her, and suddenly she leaps forward and hugs him – hard and fierce.

When they release from the clutch, she steps back and says something to Zelda, who smiles and gives her a light embrace.

What on earth did he say?

"I'm getting hungry," Polly comments, not as riveted by my family triangle as I am. "How about you?"

Although I'm fascinated by what's going on over at the reception line, I realize my trembling nerves from earlier in the day are gone. The knot of stress in my stomach has dissolved. "I could eat," I answer her with a smile.

"We can grab a bite at the beach."

Immediately picturing a sandy hotdog in a foil wrapper, I ask, "Do you think they'll have anything?"

"I seem to remember a string of street-food carts along the promenade. I've been wanting to check them out since we got here. Maybe finally have an octopus burger?"

We discuss the various options we hope will be available, foods we've encountered in Croatia: veal rolls, ćevapi, bite size kebabs, barbecued chicken. All kinds of meat. We can just throw away any bunnage.

Eventually our buddies – all except Mother – drift over to chat with me and Polly.

Jane poses a question to everyone, "How did you like the ceremony?"

I'm not going to say here, in front of my daughter, that I found it a hilarious mishmash, or that I thought Oh-Jay was a hoot, the whole thing laughable.

"I didn't know Dad had it in him," Madison says earnestly, her eyes shining. "He's always been such a jock, you know? Today he showed a different side. I loved it."

I'm stunned.

Everyone murmurs some non-committal assent.

"The vows were interesting," Hendrick adds. "Watch the sunset together. Wow!"

Polly says, "And the musician sure added to things, didn't he?"

I don't know if she means she liked the instrumental heavy rock songs, or not. I don't know her well enough to know her musical tastes. I for one found it icky, one notch up from elevator music, but I keep my opinion to myself.

"The guitarist is an American," Hendrick tells us. "Just over here on a sabbatical."

Jane asks, "From what?"

"He's a professor of proctology," Hendrick answers. And we all turn to look at the man, sitting in the corner, still noodling away on his guitar. Jane snorts with laughter.

"What's proctology?" Madison asks.

"Never mind," I tell her.

Conversation ebbs and flows. Standing around is boring. A swim in the ocean is the exact thing to wash this day out of my hair. "Does anyone want to go to the beach with me and Polly after this?"

"This man does!" Hendrick jabs his thumbs into his chest. Madison and Jane nod enthusiastically.

We stand around some more. Minutes tick past. We admire the view, over and over again.

"Our flight is tomorrow," Jane muses. "So, when do we get home on Tuesday? I've got a week of clients to catch up with."

"Me too," Hendrick agrees. "All the Biz Buzzers are FlipFlopping me. They want their one-on-ones."

"I have to work for the next forty days and forty nights," Polly says, fanning herself. "So many peeps covered shifts for me so I could come on this trip, next week is payback time."

Madison slips her arm around me and lays her head on my shoulder. "I'm ready to go, Mom."

Delighted she's the first one to say it out loud, I'm also relieved. "You mean from the wedding?"

"Yup. And home-home too."

Now, I'm even more astounded.

"Really? Do you want me to get you a plane ticket?"

She shrugs with the insouciance of youth. "I don't have a captain to work with anymore. And the season's almost over. So, I might as well get back to Lakeside. Start looking for a job."

I survey the reception guests, locating Mother still talking to Xavier and Zelda and anyone else who approaches them, as though the ex-mother-in-law of the groom is a normal part of the reception line.

"We better say our goodbyes," Jane prompts, and we drift en masse toward the happy couple.

"You goin'? Already?" Mother says, slurring her words, swiping another glass of champagne from the server who's collecting empties from everyone else.

"We are," I tell her firmly. "And I think you should come with us." I stare at her meaningfully, hoping she'll get my drift from behind those giant glasses of hers. *You've had enough, lady! Time to lay off the booze!*

She just makes a sweeping motion with her glass and says, "You go on ahead. Jjh-avier will get me a taxi. I'm shurr I'll be fine."

Xavier smiles. "We'll make sure she gets back safe." He steps toward me and takes my elbow. "May I have a word?"

Oh my, a storm cloud passes swiftly across Zelda's face, then disappears.

She's jealous of me!

I can't believe how the tides have turned. I'm no longer jealous of her. She can have this guy as far as I'm concerned, and for everyone's sake, I hope her jealousy ends soon. We're going to be stuck together for a long time. I'll always be Madison's mother; and Xavier will always be her dad.

"I just want to thank you for bringing Madison today," he says, when we're a few feet away from the others. "She didn't want to come. She was texting me swear-words. She seemed really really upset."

"Can you blame her?" I ask.

He looks at me, clueless. "I guess," he says, then quickly returns to what he wanted to say to me. "Anyway, I know you must have talked her into it. Nothing else could have got her here today."

"She seemed to really like the ceremony," I tell him.

"Yea, she told me," he says, stretching his arms behind his back, and grunts, shifting his head back and forth as though cracking his neck, thrusting out his chest in an all too familiar motion of restlessness. He wants this reception over with as much as I do.

FORTY-NINE

T reading water, I turn back to take a good long look at the shoreline.

An assortment of dog walkers with their dogs are strolling along the boardwalk: a Basset Hound with a tall energetic woman; two tiny caramel puff-balls with an over-dressed senior; ye old faithful Golden Retriever plodding beside a mother and stroller. Dogless pedestrians dodge and weave through the leashes and animals; roller-bladers and bicyclists zip past it all on the bike path. On the beach, kids play in the sand with pails and shovels and the season's last sunbathers are stretched out on blankets and towels, grabbing the September sun's rays.

Polly pops up beside me like a playful porpoise. "A little chillier than the Adriatic, isn't it?"

We're swimming today in Lake Ontario. The water only gets warm enough from late August to mid-September. There won't be many days hot enough to brave these waters.

"Chillier, and with an absence of delicious street-food carts," I say, reminding her of our glorious final afternoon at the beach in Vis, noshing on ćevapi, delicious caseless sausages.

A lifeguard in a small boat rows past, warning us, "Not much further, ladies. The undertow is strong today."

We stroke a few yards toward shore, not liking the sound of an underwater current we can't see that might suddenly suck us down and sweep us away.

Nodding toward a zinc nosed lifeguard on the lifeguard stand, Polly asks, "Where do they get these guys?"

"You mean young guys who can go for hours, without looking at a smart-phone?"

She splashes me with water, and laughs. "You know what I mean."

I do. She means men far too young for either of us, who could easily be mistaken for Calvin Klein models.

Polly is the midlife equivalent of boy-crazy right now. Since we got back from Europe, she's been hitting the dating websites like mad, hell bent on finding a boyfriend by New Years. It seems she has a coffee date every time I call her. I was lucky to book her today, on her first full day off from The Beach House. It might be the last time this year we get a chance to swim in the lake. Plus, I need to talk with her. Not about anything in particular, just about life, and how life-y it is.

"Xavier was a lifeguard before he met me," I tell her, the thought popping into my head and out of my mouth for no apparent reason. I hope memories of him and our life together will fade from my mind and one day I won't be mentioning him all the time. "He told me it was a fantastic summer job while he was in high school and college."

"I imagine so – if you don't actually have to save someone," she muses wryly.

"There's that," I agree with a laugh.

Another thought jumps into my mind. "*I* should've been a lifeguard. It would've been the perfect job for me! Spending my time on the beach instead of in the bakery working for Grandad."

Polly nods.

"Why didn't I?" I ask rhetorically. "Do they let girls be lifeguards?"

"I certainly hope so," she replies.

We paddle around in the deep cool water, enjoying the sounds of summer: seagulls overhead, a speedboat engine in the distance, the gentle lapping of the lake.

"How's Madison settling in?" Polly asks.

I giggle. "Mother doesn't like the hours she's keeping. In and out at all times of the day and night. Is it bad I'm amused that Madison is annoying Mother so much?"

Polly laughs and says, "A wee bit vindictive."

"She's keeping me awake!" Mother had complained to me the week we got back from Croatia and Madison was reconnecting with her Lakeside friends. She'd shrieked, "Why is she out until 2 in the morning?"

"Why are you waiting up for her?" I'd responded calmly. She'd harrumphed.

"Has Madison found a job yet?" Polly asks. "I could put in a word for her at The Beach House."

"She's still looking." We are drifting in the strong off-shore breeze, so we keep having to stroke toward shore again but it doesn't interrupt our conversation. "I was considering offering her a job at Honeywell's, but I don't think it's a good idea. Can you imagine? It would probably be a disaster and ruin our relationship."

Polly looks thoughtful, her chin below the surface of the water as she treads, gazing at the shore and the courts of volleyball players. "But it might not be a disaster," she says, turning and squinting at me from one eye. "You can't know unless you try."

She might be right, but something is holding me back from mentioning it to Madison, an inkling, a feeling to which I'm paying heed. "She's trying to find a kitchen job at a high-end hotel," I tell Polly.

I don't want to influence Madison's decisions.

And she'd probably decline anyway. She prides herself on her culinary degree and wants to put it to use in her career.

"How were sales while you were away?" Polly asks. It's nice to have a friend who's also in retail, she understands how business ebbs and flows, and how important it is to measure it.

"I can't believe it!" I tell her. "The numbers soared after Eve posted the Wally pictures on FlipFlop. Within days a new crowd was coming in. Young customers, Eve's age. I heard a girl the other day say, 'It's so *vintage* in here!'"

"Really?" Polly sounds as amazed as I am. "I thought millennials were all health conscious, into gluten-free and all that."

I laugh. "Turns out a lot of them go for the gooiest, richest pastries we make. Within days, Eve was selling out of eclairs, and pavlova with berries. She started double and triple batching. We sell out every day!"

"Wow," Polly says. "Phenomenal."

My skin is starting to goosebump. "Are you getting cold? Do you want to go in?"

We swim toward shore, hobbling the last few yards over the stony bottom to the beach.

Unfolding our chairs, we unpack our picnic. I get out the cheese and pickles I brought, and Polly unwraps sliced salami and salted celery chunks.

"Don't forget," she says, "we've got a UBMH meeting this afternoon."

Un-Binge My Heart. That's the name of our support group. Today will be my second time. I got choked up and cried last time, couldn't even say my name. I was so moved by the honesty of the people there, sharing about their difficulties staying off the junky food.

Our conversation drifts back to our jobs: Polly selling swimsuits – she says the whole store is on clearance – and me selling what has essentially become contraband to her and I. Our jobs take up so much of our time, no wonder we can't get our minds off them for long.

"Eve's dad donated a wooden bench for outside the bakery," I tell Polly as we munch our lunch. "Customers tie up their dogs to it, but they also sit on it all day. It's incredible how those silly Wally Whiskers photos attracted new business."

"And do people expect to meet him when they come inside?"

"Some do," I laugh. "But Eve had a cardboard cut-out of him made, so it's up on the counter. Customers pose next to it and take pictures holding up their pastries."

"Wow! How did she find the time to do all that in ten days?"

"I don't know!" I shake my head. "The energy in these young ones is something else."

A couple of curvy girls in bathing suits are standing at the foot of the lifeguard station, chatting with zinc nose who also has a blistering smile, with dimples no less.

"Maybe you *should* ask Madison if she wants a job," Polly says. "She and Eve could team up. You could take time off."

I nod, but I'm skeptical.

"I'm serious!" Polly says.

I think about it momentarily. Having Madison at the bakery, working side by side, a mother-daughter team. Is it feasible?

"The thing is, I don't want her to feel like she *has to* work at the bakery. I don't want it to limit her options."

Polly lifts her sunglasses and squints at me. "The way it did yours?"

"Exactly. Don't get me wrong," I hasten to add, "I'm grateful for Honeywell's, and my grandfather trusting me to carry it on. And I love all the people I've met, all the Lakeside women, the customers, but it's barely supported me this past year." I frown, thinking about the day, way back in the spring, when I wasn't sure I could pay the rent. "That's changing now, but I've got to think about my sanity...being surrounded by all that sugar—"

I don't need to finish my thought. Polly knows what I mean.

Leaning back in my folding chair, stretching out my legs, I watch some kids playing with their dog by the edge of the lake. They're throwing stones into the water, which he's chasing as if they're balls. The stones sink and disappear and the dog swims around in a circle for a few moments frantic and confused. Laughing, the kids call him in, and they shriek as he shakes water all over them. He readies himself for the next stone ball. This one will float.

"Hendrick was right," I say to Polly, as another thought occurs to me.

"Hmm?" She's got her face tilted up to the sun, her sunglasses mirroring the wide blue sky.

"He was right about installing a card reader – those people don't use cash! And he was right about FlipFlop attracting a new clientele."

"I suppose so," she answers. "But wasn't it Wally Whiskers who attracted them?"

I consider that for a few moments. That and all the other things Hendrick has suggested I do. Some, like the card reader, I've done, but most I haven't got around to yet. His list is exhausting.

"I wonder if he'd have any advice on how I could *get out* of running the bakery."

Polly looks at me in surprise. "You want *out*?"

Now that I've said it aloud, I'm certain.

"I do!" I cry. "I want out! I can't take it anymore. All the smell-a-vision breads."

She laughs, and adds, "And surround-sound sweets."

"All those ooey-gooey carbs. It's torture."

She nods. She doesn't get all doubtful and practical, and ask me what I'm going to do instead, like Mother would, like Jane would. She just says, "I wondered about that."

FIFTY

T he elevator in the realty office has a note on the door: Out of Service.

Determinedly, I walk a few paces over to face the tall staircase up to the boardroom.

Even though I haven't attempted the climb since Jane pointed out the elevator all those months ago, I know I can do this.

I take a breath, grab hold of the railing reminding myself, one step at a time.

I was surprised Hendrick asked me to meet him *here* today, on a Sunday afternoon, but he said he had news for me, and he didn't want to meet in the bakery where we'd met last time.

I'd felt unsure about admitting to him that I wanted to hang up my apron, but I'd made the decision, and I wondered if he might have some suggestions on how I should proceed. With more than nine years left on my lease – how the heck do I get out of Honeywell's?

"But what about our *plans*?" he'd cried, dismayed, as I'd predicted he might be. "I thought things were going so *well*. You can't give up now!"

From a previous one-on-one session, when we'd returned from Croatia, he was ecstatic about the sales increases, and all the new customers, and I'd suspected he'd try to persuade me to keep going.

Summoning my inner GPS, I looked him straight in the blue mascara, and said, "I've given this a lot of thought, Hendrick. I don't want to do it anymore."

He looked so disappointed as we sat together in the back of the bakery amid the tins and sacks and ovens and rolling racks. I'd never seen his shoulders slump before. "But what about your grandfather? You've got a legacy to uphold."

I was prepared for this objection and had rehearsed a response. "Don't make me feel guiltier than I already do," I pled. "If Grandad were here, he'd understand when I explained: I *need* to move on."

Hendrick tented his fingers together, looking at me dubiously, shaking his head. "I've seen people make big moves like this then *totally* regret it a few years later."

I held my own hand on top of Grandad's vinyl cheque-book. "I'll take that chance."

After a moment of silent thought, his eyes blinking, Hendrick had slapped his thighs, snapping himself out of his funk. "Alrighty then." He looked around the backroom, as though assessing the bakery in a new light. "You've got a great lease," he mused, thrumming his fingers on his chin. "So, *that* is something a buyer will be interested in."

"But how do I find a buyer?" I'd asked, certain this was a difficult and costly problem.

"Hunny," he said, fluttering his eyelashes at me, "That is what I *do*. I help my clients any which way I can."

I began to believe. Hendrick really is a marvelous man. I've never met anyone quite so generous with their expertise.

Eager to brainstorm, I reminded him, "So, there's the legacy, as you called it. Fifty years in business, that's got to be worth something."

"Well…" he drawled. "Not necessarily. A new buyer might want to come in and change everything, you know, *modernize*." He stressed the last word, which I felt insinuated the way I ran things was hopelessly out of date. "Or they might just want the lease. Turn it into a shoe store or office space or something."

"I see," I said, suppressing my resistance to new ideas, new people coming in here and messing with *my* bakery.

"Our best bet," he said, tapping his lip, "would be to sell to someone who wants to utilize the kitchen facilities, so you can at least get something for all your equipment, a café… Or a dog bakery! They're popular."

"And you can find me a buyer?"

"I'll see what I can do," he'd said, gathering his satchel. He'd paused and asked, "Are you *sure* you can handle it if someone moves in here and changes *everything*?"

I swallowed. "I'm sure."

But I wasn't sure, and I felt so guilty.

Now, reaching the top of the realtor's steps, a little out of breath, my thighs smarting and my butt muscles squawking, miraculously there is no pain in my knees. Just a slight hint of strain, which if I hadn't felt stabs of pain in the past, I might not even notice. I can't wait to tell my pals at Un-binge My Heart about this victory. I don't think I need to go back to Dr. Arnot at all. No surgery for me, I'll just keep doing what I'm doing.

Hendrick, alone in the boardroom, welcomes me inside.

"I took the liberty," he says, gesturing at a cup of black coffee in front of an empty chair. "Sit, sit, I have good news!"

Before I can even take my seat and roll my chair closer to the table he announces, "I found you an angel!"

I look at him sideways, has he lost his crackers? "An angel?"

"Yes, an angel investor! Even better than a buyer." He explains. "An angel is an *anonymous* investor." He sucks in his cheeks as he says this, as if holding in a secret he's dying to tell. "They don't want recognition, or payback, or anything like that. Unless, of course, the venture takes off – and then they get paid back."

I'm incredulous. "Sounds too good to be true."

"I know, right?"

Even though he's given up caffeine, Hendrick appears to be vibrating. It's astonishing how much enthusiasm he puts into me, but probably every other client too. I can't believe I actually wanted my money back after the first night of Biz Buzz.

"So, what's the catch?" I ask, keen to find out more about this ethereal benefactor.

"There is no catch! In fact, there's a bonus!"

With trembling fingers, he opens a leather folder and slides a mint-green money order across the polished table surface toward me.

My eyes pop open. "Wow!"

The amount is higher than what Hendrick estimated I could get for the value of the lease.

"And here's the bonus," he squeals. "You get to keep the bakery. With a raise in salary! The angel wants you to stay on."

I stare at him.

And then at the money order.

Speechless.

It's a little warm in here in the late October sun and I squirm in my chair. I've never been in the boardroom during the daytime. Have they turned off their air conditioning for the year?

"I already obtained the property owner's approval," Hendrick continues, clearly pleased with himself, tidying the edges of the papers inside his folder.

"You did? How?"

· She lives in Boca Raton. How would he have got hold of her?

"Your angel happens to know Mrs. Landi," he informs me with a shrug and a satisfied smile.

"Really?" I'm flabbergasted. "How is that possible?"

"I know!" he says, not answering me. "And the best part is, we can keep working together and implement all our plans!"

I stare into the sunbeams streaming in through the south-west facing windows.

The conversations I've had with Polly over the last few weeks, everything I've been dreaming about crowds into my mind, clamoring for attention. A brochure for community college courses starting in January arrived yesterday. I circled a certificate course I could take to become a counsellor. Un-Binge My Heart is helping me, and now it feels like my calling to help other women who want to change their lifestyles, their bodies, their relationship with food. *That* is what I want to do now.

But this money order...

"You don't seem excited," Hendrick says. "I thought you'd be over the moon. You can carry on your Grandad's legacy."

I chew on my lower lip.

Polly and I have been looking for a house to rent. I was planning to use the money from the sale of the lease to cover my expenses for the coming year while I figure out what to do with my life. A little house with a garden for Madison, Polly, and me. We talked about getting a dog.

Who knows? I could start dating.

I fiddle with the corner of the money order.

Hendrick gets to his feet, and paces back and forth in front of me.

"Maybe this will change your mind—"

He reaches for the handle, and opens the door.

Madison is on the other side, a delighted smile on her face.

She rushes into the room, leans down, and grabs me in an awkward hug. "Isn't it *fantastic*, Mom?"

The room swirls as she pulls out a chair and plunks herself down with a big puff.

"What's happening?" I'm so confused. "What are you doing here?"

She grins, as Hendrick, bouncing on the balls of his feet explains, "So, your *angel* investor is *anonymous,* however they did have two stipulations: one, that the business remains a bakery; and two, that you and Madison run it together!"

He sits down in his chair.

I am without words.

Madison grabs my arm. "It's been *so* hard keeping this a secret!" Her eyes are dancing, and she looks like she wants to kiss me.

I look at Hendrick, my eyes wide, and back at Madison. They've hatched this plan for *my* future behind my back. "Hold on a minute," I protest as their fanciful piñata cracks open in my mind. "Does this 'angel investor' happen to wear a turban and enjoy her afternoon martinis?"

"Ha! How did you guess?" Madison laughs, jubilant.

"*She* came to me!" Hendrick claims excitedly, feigning innocence, which I find hard to believe.

I confront Madison, "I thought you wanted nothing to do with the bakery."

"What do you mean?" she asks, looking perplexed. "Mom. Aren't you happy about this?"

"When you enrolled in culinary school, you told me it was *different* from baking. You implied—"

"Oh, Mom, that was ages ago. I was probably just being a brat."

I stare at her. Not knowing what to say.

"Grandma's gonna be a *silent* partner," she assures me.

I laugh.

"She *promises*! And won't it be fun working together. You can teach me everything you know."

I laugh again. Fat chance a mother can impart *anything* she's learned in life. Unfortunately, a daughter needs to discover every mistake for herself.

I turn to Hendrick. "So, what are my options?"

"Options?"

"Yes, if I say no to this, can you find another buyer for the lease?"

Into a stunned silence he clears his throat, loosens his tie, and undoes the top button of his shirt. "Would anyone like a cold drink?" he asks. "It's awfully warm in here."

"What are you *saying*, Mom?" Madison cries.

"I'm just weighing *all* my options," I tell her. "I've already decided to move on from the bakery. I'm not staying."

"What about *me*?"

I smile at her. She's so young and inexperienced. I don't want to crush her plans, whatever they are, but I can't make my decisions for the future based on her. She's an adult now. As gently, but firmly, as I can, I tell her, "Well, Sweetie, that's what I'm just figuring out."

Hendrick plops a bottle of fizzy water and three glasses onto the table, and sits down. I can see I've shocked both of them, and I'm sorry about that. I twist off the cap and pour three glasses. I take a few sips of mine, wetting my whistle, I have news for the two of them.

"So," I ask Hendrick again. "What are my options?"

"Let me think," he starts, his eyes tearing up. Clearly, he's crushed that I'm not jumping on his brazen plan to trap me in the bakery until the day I keel over. "I suppose if you turn down the angel, I could keep looking for a buyer. There's lots of interest in a long-low-rent-lease on Maple Street, that's for sure." He taps the money order. "But I doubt you'll get this price."

Madison sits beside me, silently. She hasn't touched the water. "You're really gonna turn Grandma down, Mom?"

"I'm deciding," I tell her.

I could hold out for another buyer, thumbing my nose at Mother, or I could take the money...

Oddly, I feel calm inside, like I'm sailing on an open sea, the wind in my sails.

"Can I accept the money?" I ask Hendrick. "And stay on in a consulting role only?"

His eyes widen, and I can almost hear the beaters in his brain twirling.

"Of course, you can!" he claims with enthusiasm. "I mean, I think you can." He looks at Madison and says, blinking, "Why not?"

Now she's smiling.

"That would be *awesome*, Mom. I have a million ideas."

"I'm sure you do, Sweetie," I smile at her. "But, modernizing? I don't have any guidance for that."

She answers: "No way! We're leaning into the whole vintage thing. Honeywell's is perfect for it, isn't it Hendrick?" She leans forward, talking excitedly. "I saw this fancy old-fashioned cash register, all brass and ornate – it comes with a computer inside it! State of the art."

Hendrick nods his head enthusiastically.

I laugh. "So, what do you need me for?"

"For the recipes, Mom! And the baking. I don't even know how to make bread!"

FIFTY-ONE

⸺ ⸱⸳⸲⸳⸱ ⸺

This morning, I joined Madison and Mother in their Christmas food festivities with a frothy heavy-cream latte and crispy strips of bacon as a special treat while they devoured their French toast made with Honeywell's croissants and fresh maple syrup.

Madison, sitting on the couch in her new snowflake pajamas with Wally Whiskers on her lap, gripes at me, "You're going to a support meeting *on Christmas Day?*"

Her stocking is empty and she's finished unwrapping her gifts, which were copious this year on account of old Money-Bags, lounging in her recliner across the room. Mother is dressed in a forest-green velour housecoat, her hair in curlers festively covered in a red chiffon kerchief. "I'm going to a turkey dinner in the church basement," she announces.

"Grandma!" Madison exclaims. "You are? *Why?*"

After a doctor's appointment, about a month after we returned from Croatia, Mother abruptly quit drinking, declaring, "Cold turkey for Thanksgiving!" I suspect her GP gave her a dire warning, pleading the case for her poor liver – she wouldn't divulge the details. But I overheard her telling Madison at the time, "If *your* mother can quit 'pigging out' on junk food the way she used to do, how hard can it be to cut back a little on my martinis?"

I was outraged at being called a piggy, my efforts trivialized behind my back, but Polly helped me to realize, if my LOBO lifestyle had inspired my mother to join AA, who was I to condemn her?

Carole Armstrong went to her first meeting one night in October and hasn't been the same since – although she does go through the same amount of ice cubes, guzzling diet cola with a squeeze of lemon night and day instead of gin. At least the pop doesn't make her stagger and slur her words, or make me nervous to leave her alone in the house.

I remind Madison, "You're going to your dad's place today. What does it matter what Grandma or I do?"

She tickles Wally behind his ears and shrugs, "I mean…whatever."

I start gathering up crumpled wrapping paper and sticky dishes, shuffling out to the kitchen in the reindeer slippers Hendrick gave me. They've got antlers, eyes, and bright red balls on their noses – my toes.

Jane dropped by last night with a gift for me. "Open it now," she urged. "You'll want to wear it tonight."

I worried a little about what she'd chosen for me, the size, the color, the style, but it's a beautiful white nightie with pearl buttons and pin tucks. And it fits perfectly, a regular size extra-large, not extra-extra large, or ox.

Tonight, I'm hosting a Christmas dinner for friends. Hendrick has a new man, so he's not coming. He's meeting his new beau's family at their cabin up north – it must be serious. Jane is bringing a male friend of hers who she thinks Polly will like; and we'll be joined by a few other people I've met at Un-Binge My Heart who had nowhere else to go tonight. Jane complained about strangers at the Christmas dinner table, even though she's bringing one, and made me promise I won't invite any others. The food will be mostly LOBO, of course – I'm roasting a turkey stuffed with chestnut dressing – but at Jane's request there will be a small bowl of whipped potatoes and a secret yule log from Honeywell's stashed in the kitchen – just for her.

This afternoon, while the turkey is roasting, I'm going to UBMH for our regularly scheduled Saturday meeting. It doesn't matter that it's Christmas Day, and everything but the churches are closed. We bingers need support every day of the year. I've reached the stage where I can be at the meetings to help other members, just as I was helped when I joined a few months ago.

I cried a *lot* – during the group discussions, afterward as we stood around chatting in the parking lot, and on the way home in Polly's car.

"You're melting," she told me kindly. "Now that your diet is clean, your emotions are thawing out."

As I listened to other members share how they felt about not being able to put down the panzerotti, I became brave enough to speak myself. Some of the other members aren't even overweight, but still, they can't stop pounding the sugar once they start, and they feel sick and hate themselves until they find a way to clean up their eating.

Little by little, I dared to tell the group how long I'd loathed how my body looked in clothes, in bathing suits, in lingerie. I confided that I'd used peppermint-patties and cheesies to soothe my emotions and put myself into a food coma. I revealed my secret binges of cookies and pizzas and potato chips. The more I divulged, the freer I felt. And amazingly, the impulse to reach for food as a solution to anything other than legitimate hunger, diminished to the point where I barely ever notice it anymore.

It's a miracle!

To think I spent so much of my life ruled by my cravings for comfort.

I wish I could just forget it all, but I must continue to be honest about it. If my experience can help someone else, I'm not ashamed to talk about it.

I slide the key into the lock and open the door of the small space we rent for our bi-weekly Un-Binge My Heart meetings. There are a few minutes of preparation to do, brewing some coffee and filling the tea kettle, setting out a circle of chairs.

If this was years gone by, and a PTA meeting or church function, I'd have brought a big box of Christmas goodies from Honeywell's. Not this year. However, I still have the inclination to do something special – we Un-Bingers need to celebrate somehow. I nip out to my car and retrieve a box of tiny vases filled with holly and red rosebuds. I asked the florist to make sure they were the scented kind. We can enjoy the smell without eating them.

Polly arrives in her snowy white parka and stands by the door, welcoming the members who have ventured out on this Christmas Day.

The room is full of chatter and good cheer as everyone takes a seat, some with a hot drink, some without. Just as we're about to start the door opens and a woman that I don't recognize attempts to make herself invisible and sneak inside. Yet we're all aware of her. She's new. And on Christmas Day. Wow, brave.

"Come, sit down," I call to her and she slinks into the circle grabbing the first available chair. Her cheeks are ablaze with self-consciousness, her eyes are fixed on the floor. She pulls her jacket off and uncomfortably twists in her chair trying to drape it over the back. "I'm sorry," she keeps muttering.

"No worries," Polly assures her, tucking the jacket over the chair-back so it won't fall.

The meeting begins with a round of introductions, even though all of us, except the new woman, know one another. Her name is Minnie, she's newly divorced, and she's come today because last night she ate the entire dessert she'd prepared for her mother's Christmas dinner, and the mashed potatoes, she adds in a whisper.

She's so ashamed, she cries.

"I phoned my mother and told her I'm sick, I won't be coming, because I am sick! What's wrong with me?" She dissolves into a puddle of sobs.

"Minnie, you've come to the right place," says the woman sitting next to her.

We keep moving around the circle as a box of tissues is passed to Minnie, and when all the introductions and check-ins are finished, we begin to discuss today's topic: How to deal with family members who push food on us.

It's a lively discussion, a lot of stories and advice, a lot of laughter, and by the end of the hour, even Minnie has a soft smile on her face. Probably the group's honesty cracked her open. I know that's what happened to me the first time I came.

At the end, as members are gathering their coats and pressing their phone numbers into Minnie's hand, I go around with the box of roses. They're a big hit and I'm glad I brought them.

"What are you going to do with yourself tonight?" I ask Minnie.

She shrugs uncomfortably and looks away.

What is she going to eat, is the real question.

I ask, "Do you have anything to cook for dinner? You won't find much open for takeout tonight."

"Oh, I'll manage, I guess."

I remember my promise to Jane about not inviting any 'strangers' but poor Minnie! What's she going to do on Christmas night all by herself?

"Would you like to come to my house for dinner?" I find myself offering.

Jane's a big girl. She'll cope with me defying her. It's my house!

FIFTY-TWO

· ▾ · ▾ · ▾ · ▾ ·

In my newly cleared out closet hangs the peacock-colored, sequined tunic I'm wearing tonight and a brand-new pair of ridiculously expensive but adorable turquoise jeans, somehow already beaten up, fraying on the thighs, and well-worn.

My fat clothes are gone.

I'm not sure the women down at the homeless shelter wanted them, but Suzy Q assured me, whatever they don't use, gets donated to textile recycling, and that's a good thing.

It's New Year's Eve, and Hendrick is throwing a big bash with his new boyfriend, Steven.

To think, last year at this time, Xavier was walking out the door, leaving me at home alone in the condo, crying, and eating the entire feast of Chinese Food I'd ordered for the two of us. My tears and sobs mingling with chicken balls in goopy red sauce, grains of fried rice scattering everywhere, fortune cookies turning to glue in my mouth, tasting like sweet cardboard. I ate them *all,* reading, crumpling, and tossing aside each prophecy.

Love bad things from a good distance.

Follow your heart, see what shows up.

To thy own self be true.

Those messages felt painfully meaningless that night. I couldn't imagine what would transpire in the future. How far I'd travel from the pain of abandonment by Xavier, the man I'd set as my guiding star.

I pull on the jeans and peek at myself in the mirror over the dressing table. They fit like a bum-glove thanks to stretchy spandex woven in, but my butt still looks larger than I'd like. I have wide hips; when am I going to accept my body the way it is? Anyway, the tunic covers it. I've shrunk several sizes but I still look— *Ugh, just stop!*

The nasty belittling shrew in my head is never far off, waiting to fly into my brain and cause me to feel bad about myself.

"They look great!" Polly gushed when I bought the jeans at a Boxing Day sale with cash Mother had stuffed in my stocking.

"Holy crap, Trudy. You've lost a ton of weight!" Jane agreed, with her oh-so-tactful phrasing. "But not on 'the girls.'" She drew circles in the air in front of my breasts.

I laughed. She was right. My 'girls' are still an ample, but smaller, more manageable pair. I purchased the sequined top for 'the girls' because glitter is what we should all wear on New Year's Eve, isn't it? I think so. I'm also wearing a shimmery new eyeshadow tonight.

My wedding rings are gone, pawned at a store near Dr. Arnot's office, and Madison has my blue topaz, so tonight I slide on the silver filigree moonstone Polly gave me for Christmas. It glows dreamily against the cobalt and teal of my tunic, offset by periwinkle nail polish Debbie talked me into. I find some dangly earrings to complete the ensemble and look at myself in the mirror. Spectacular enough for New Year's Eve, I'd say.

When I head downstairs, I find Mother sitting at the dining room table, mindlessly eating jujubes from a crystal bowl. All the lights in the house are on, and she's got an open notebook in front of her. Wally rests on the table near her, his paws tucked under his chest, watching life in our house from half-slit eyes. He barely acknowledges my presence.

Mother looks at me, assesses what I'm wearing, giving me a foot-to-chin inspection. Instinctually, I brace myself.

She asks, "Aren't those jeans rather casual for a New Year's Eve party?"

Not the nasty comment I was expecting.

"It's just a bunch of friends at a house party. Nothing swanky. I don't think." A frizzle of doubt shoots through my mind. Did I misread Hendrick's invitation?

No, I don't think so.

Anyway, who cares if I did? I'm a new me this year. Nothing's going to sink me.

I ask, "What are you and Wally up to tonight?"

"I'm working on my Steps." She taps the end of her pen on the notebook. "And my sponsor is coming over."

"Wow, your sponsor is coming over?" I marvel. "Is that to make sure you don't drink tonight?"

"It doesn't work like that, Trudy," she scoffs, rolling her eyes at me. "He's not my *babysitter*. We're keeping *each other* sober."

I gawk at her. "Your sponsor is a *he*?"

She looks back at me with defiance, jutting out her chin. "Yes. What's wrong with that?"

"I dunno," I stammer. "I just thought you'd want a female sponsor."

I detect a faint coloring, high on her cheeks.

"John is very nice," she pronounces. "And *he* offered to sponsor *me*. Not the other way around."

I don't even know how to respond to this information. Mother's sponsorship arrangement might be entirely innocent, but something tells me she's cooking something up.

"I better go get dressed," she says, rising from the table, avoiding my eyes.

She's wearing her customary velour tracksuit, and if she goes upstairs to get spiffed up, perhaps change into the one with the rhinestones, I'll know it's for the benefit of this John character who's coming over.

"What's the matter with what you've got on?" I tease.

She stalks past me and starts up the stairs. "There's nothing wrong with dressing up a little on New Year's Eve."

"Ah ha!" I cry. "You are interested in this guy!"

Her face contorts in a coy smile as she continues up the stairs. "Maybe I am. Maybe I'm not."

She's incorrigible. She finally stopped boozing, and now she's romancing a man she met a few weeks ago. Curiously, I'm delighted for her.

It's about time she had some fun.

I just hope she stays off the liquor.

I pick up my phone and summon a car from an app. It's five minutes away so I hurry to zip up my new leather ankle boots and head out into the evening.

Polly lives in one of those ugly low-rises from the 1950's; not much charm or character, but I imagine the rent has been good for her. In a couple of months, she and I and Madison will be moving into a bungalow we found to rent not too far from here.

The front door of the apartment building opens and Polly appears, dressed all in white, grinning, waving, and ready to party.

"This is so exciting!" she squeals, climbing into the back seat. "I haven't been to a New Year's Eve party since high school!"

We drive out Lettuceville through the city streets toward the harbor where Hendrick resides in one of those tall glass condo buildings. All along the way, restaurant windows glow, and people swarm on the streets, enjoying the unseasonably warm last night of the year. Groups of teenagers gather on the street corners, heading for the beach to light bonfires and set off fireworks.

"You're okay without a date tonight?" I ask Polly.

She makes a dismissive puff sound with her lips.

"But I thought that was your goal," I probe. "A man by New Year's."

She laughs. "Not one of them had an offer that sounded better than Hendrick's party."

"It does sound like fun, doesn't it?"

She nods excitedly. "I have to tell you, Trudy, you've made such a difference in my life this year."

"Me? *You've* made a huge difference in mine!" I pat my stomach.

"Welcome to the Mutual Admiration Society," she laughs. "But I'm serious. Thank you for introducing me to your friends this year. I've never hung out with people who throw New Year's Eve parties."

"Me neither."

"What did and Xavier usually do?"

"Nothing much," I shrug. "Two decades with him. It feels as though our lives slowly and gradually shrunk. Do you know what I mean?"

"Sure."

"Oddly, as I grew bigger, our marriage got smaller, and at the end, we barely spent any time together or went out at all. On New Year's, we usually ordered pizza and watched TV. I don't remember even making it to midnight."

"Didn't you two have any couple friends?"

"Not really, and I don't know why I didn't notice. Or care. I guess I thought he should be everything I needed, which is bonkers, I realize now. And he was right, we didn't really have anything in common, except Madison."

"Thank goodness for your friends on Maple Street now. I really like Suzy and Jessica. You all seem so close."

"We *are*. Especially since Biz Buzz."

"Hendrick," Polly smiles. "He's a dynamo."

The car pulls up in the circular driveway of Hendrick's building and drops us off. Polly and I marvel at all the modern details of condo living as we enter through glass double doors, buzz Hendrick's apartment number, and wait for him to answer.

"Ahoy partier, who goes there?" he brays through the intercom. I can hear the party in full-swing behind him.

"It's Trudy and Polly," I shout into the metal grating I assume is the microphone.

Next to us, the door buzzes and we rush to push through to the elevators.

Polly says, "It sounds like everyone's already here."

"I know! I'm always way too early for these sorts of things. I can't believe I'm fashionably late!"

The door to Hendrick's condo is propped open, and we enter into a gaily lit space full of familiar people, some wearing sparkly black hats.

Catching sight of us, Jane rushes over wearing a glittering cardboard *Happy New Year!* tiara. "There you are! Finally!"

She ushers us into the living room where floor-to-ceiling windows overlook the harbor. Lights from sailboats along the shore twinkle, and across the way I can see into other condos: Christmas tree lights shining, candles flickering, a few windows curtained and dark.

Suzy and her husband, Mark, are here, as are Jessica and Debbie and their daughters. Sophisticated jazz plays in the background, and I feel like I've stepped into another world, a place I always sensed, but was never quite sure existed, or was meant for me. A realm of good cheer and camaraderie and hope.

Recruited by Hendrick, Madison, Laura, and Eve are circulating with trays of hors d'oeuvres. Hendrick appears at my side and pops the cork off a bottle of champagne, pouring tall flutes for all before sailing off to tend to his other guests.

Next to me, Madison offers a tray of nibbles: smoked salmon and cream cheese on rounds of dark pumpernickel.

"Happy New Year, Sweetie," I say to her.

She smiles and plants a kiss on my cheek.

"I've got something to tell you," she says, leaning in, holding her tray to the side so that anyone passing by can help themselves.

"Oh, yes? What is it?"

Polly and Jane turn aside, chatting with others, providing some privacy for our little mother-daughter tête à tête.

Madison tells me: "I'm not moving in with you and Polly. I'm moving out this weekend."

"You are?" I'm surprised. When did she decide this; I just saw her earlier today.

I expect she's about to tell me that she and Laura are getting an apartment. They've been inseparable since Laura returned from Croatia, and it's really no surprise that a girl her age would want to move in with a friend rather than her mom and her mom's friend. "Where are you going?" I ask.

"Mom, don't freak out," she says matter-of-factly. "I'm moving in with Dad."

I stare at her.

I couldn't be more shocked if she'd splashed ice-cold water in my face.

"What?"

Her clear gray eyes hold my gaze.

I stammer, "With *Zelda*? You're moving in with Dad and *Zelda*?"

I can't believe how much this idea hurts.

Bluntly, Madison answers, "She moved out."

Now, I almost drop my champagne.

Polly nudges my shoulder. "What's up?" she asks, as if sensing I'm over my head.

"Zelda moved out," Madison repeats.

I'm not sure which part is more shocking; that their marriage is over so quickly, *I told you so*, or that Madison wants to be with her dad more than me. I wish it didn't feel like I'm in a competition with him, or with Zelda, but it does.

"Dad says she's a shrew," Madison dishes.

Jane joins us, plucking a few smoked salmon rounds from Madison's tray. "Who's a shrew? Who are we talking about?" she asks, cramming her mouth full.

Madison informs her: "Zelda and Dad had a big fight, and she moved out."

"Oh, that," Jane dismisses.

Polly and I exchange wide eyed looks while Jane fusses with a napkin at a smear of cream cheese on her lips.

"How long have you been sitting on this information?" I huff. "When were you going to tell me?"

"She went back to her first husband," she answers, as though that sufficiently explains her neglect of our friendship.

A burst of Hendrick and Steven's friends crowd through the door and the volume in the party rises several notches.

Madison leans toward me again, making sure I hear her. "Mom, my moving in with him is nothing personal. I just think he needs me right now. You've got friends. He's got nobody. Don't worry, I still love you."

As she spins away with her tray of hors d'oeuvres, Jane smiles at me and shakes her head, as though Madison is the one whose judgement is questionable. Polly gives my arm a companionable rub. I'm in shock, but miraculously, I'm buoyant. I'll survive.

Jane waves her champagne glass. "So, peoples, any resolutions?"

"I don't believe in resolutions," Hendrick declares, busting into our little circle with the bottle of champagne, refilling to overflowing. "Besides, I've snagged my man, what more could I want?"

We all chuckle, clink glasses, and take big sips.

"What about you, Polly?" Jane asks. "You look like a girl with resolve."

Polly thinks for a moment before answering. "Once we move into our little house, I'm going to plant a garden. I've always wanted to grow my own vegetables." She animates, as she imagines a life in a house with a yard and a white picket fence like the one we're going to rent. "I've been cooped up too long. I'm going to buy a barbecue!"

"Sounds good to me!" I clink her glass with enthusiasm.

"I resolve to meet somebody new this year," Jane announces. "I'm over Lydia. It took a long time, but I'm finally past it all. Ready to move on."

I'm amazed to hear her say this. I raise my glass to her romantic aspirations. "Jane, I had no idea you were grieving Lydia all this time. You never let on. You always seem so strong."

"Yea, well, never mind about that. Will you help me set up an online dating profile?" she asks, her eyes meeting mine.

"Me?"

"Sure, why not?" she replies. "You're good with all this internet stuff."

"Me?" I repeat, and protest. "Polly is the queen of the dating sites."

"I'll show you both how to do it," Polly says. "It'll be fun."

She might be right. It might be time to put myself out there. It's been a year. I'm certainly not going back to Xavier. Am I ready to start dating?

"What about you, Trudy?" Hendrick asks. "You've already lost all the weight. What's your New Year's resolution?"

I need to think for a few moments. What *do* I want?

Even though these are my closest friends, I'm still a little shy about sharing the real me, and how I feel about her.

Bashful, but honest, I answer, "I think I'm just going to savour *me* for a while."

They all nod, as though I'm making perfect sense.

Suddenly from across the room, someone shouts, "Ten, nine, eight, seven..."

· ♥ · ♥ · ♥ · ♥ · ♥ ·

The End

Join Sandy's email list for a Free e-book

https://sandyday.ca/free-book/

Rate or Review
on Amazon.com

Aim your camera
at the QR Code

Rate or Review
on Amazon.ca

Aim your camera
at the QR Code

ACKNOWLEDGMENTS

I wish I could name everyone who contributed to the creation of this book but it would be pages and pages long. There is a gang of people I hang with on a regular basis, whose very presence in the world makes my life feel worthwhile. A special nod to our friend JoAnn for the expression, "Life gets life-y!" As always, I owe a debt of gratitude to my housemates, Sue and Shirley for putting up with the way I ignore them and the housework. More than anyone, I need to thank my writing coach, Kevin T. Johns. This book began as a spark of an idea in his Story Plan course, and then exploded from there. Kevin helped with every aspect of this book, so if you didn't like it, take it up with him. I've met a host of sensational writers through Kevin; they all helped, week by week, to bring this book to life. Thanks to all the beta readers who offered their astoundingly helpful suggestions for revisions. If you found this story satisfying, it's because of these generous and thoughtful people. On Sunday mornings, since God invented Zoom, I've been writing with Alana Barker, Maggie Head, and Nancy Day. Without their constant creative support and laughter, this book would not have been written. Finally, thanks to you, dear reader, for your keen interest and enthusiasm. You are so appreciated by me.

Sandy Day is a recovering chatterbox and writer of riveting slice-of-life poetry, memoir, and fiction. She has authored five books to date, with more in the works. A graduate of Glendon College, she studied creative writing under Michael Ondaatje and bp nichol. A lover of cheese, coffee shops, and illustrations, she lives on the shore of Lake Simcoe in Georgina, Ontario, Canada. You can find and follow her on Substack and sandyday.ca - it rhymes!